To: Smiddy
Best +

THE DEPUTY

The Deputy

Reaping the Whirlwind

by

Ted Snedeker

First Edition

Cover designed by Library Partners Press

Produced and Distributed By:

Library Partners Press
ZSR Library
Wake Forest University
1834 Wake Forest Road
Winston-Salem, North Carolina 27106

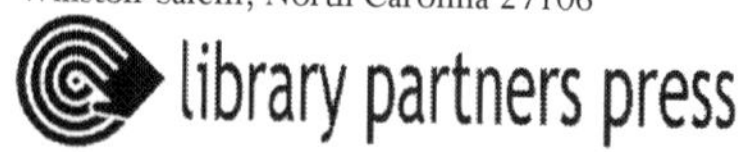

www.librarypartnerspress.org

Manufactured in the United States of America

This book is dedicated to the wonderful

LOLA KAY AMACHER,

a wonderful mother,

a tireless partner

and my best friend

for over fifty years.

ACKNOWLEDGMENTS

I am deeply indebted to Walt C. Snedeker for his years of encouragement and assistance. Without his patient and knowledgeable input, this book would never have been completed. Once completed, the several thousand changes he incorporated through months of patient editing made the book as much a product of his endeavors as the author.

Walt is a distant cousin, but a close friend, and is an accomplished author in his own right, having written dozens of humor articles for magazines, as well as an acclaimed historical novel, The Cadet – The Adventures of a New World Pioneer in the 17th Century; and lately an alternate history of WW2 based on two historical events, "The Bat and Balloon War."

Also, Ron Hewitt and Larry Reidy are due a debt of gratitude as well, for their never ending encouragement and assistance.

My daughter Lisa found time in her hectic schedule, raising two teenage boys, teaching Sunday School, writing for the HuffPo blog and working eighty hours a week, to read the MS and locate a publisher. Without her, it would still be a manuscript gather dust on my desk.

Finally, last but not least, my long suffering wife is overdue for praise. She went word for word through the edited final manuscript and cleaned up over a hundred punctuation oversights as well as pointing out clumsy wordings and vague descriptions.

PROLOGUE

It would have required a nation-state to have the resources to pull it off. It would have taken a nation-state controlled by a clique of religious fanatics to even conceive of the idea.

Unfortunately, for the world, there was such a state in the Middle East.

The plot was years in the making, months in planning, and millions of dollars in cost to execute.

The Mullahs of Iran had declared war on the Great Satan of the West in the 1970s and had been waging a clandestine "just-beneath-the-radar" war ever since. They were aided and abetted by the leadership of the United States, who inexplicably refused to recognize they were being warred against.

The resources to implement the plan were provided by an Administration ideologically committed to avoiding overt war and theologically indoctrinated in Islamic mythology.

This cabal, elected in large part by media manipulation, voter fraud, and an apathetic voter base, was allowed to stay in power by a toothless opposition party frightened of the leftist media that controlled information available to the people with an iron fist.

The massive infusion of cash available to the mullahs was already patriated in the U.S. when the sanctions were lifted. The funds were used by the fanatics to facilitate their plan. The mosques scattered throughout the country by the Saudis provided the operatives safe haven and storage for explosives, weapons, and supplies to implement their perfidy.

It was a brilliant plan. The first stage was to destroy a large chunk of strategic infrastructure across the country including bridges, refineries, and electrical generation facilities. But the first stage was simply a catalyst. The objective was to bring the entire leadership of the country together in one place at one time to excise the head of the snake.

It worked perfectly.

The simpering, whining, incompetent leadership gathered to discuss the unbelievable devastation spread across the country as if it were some natural disaster instead of a deliberate attack. That's when the mullahs struck their death blow.

A 1.5-megaton truck bomb was detonated three blocks from the Capitol where the president was giving a State of the Union address to Congress. It vaporized the leadership of the entire country in a 20-block-wide fireball.

CHAPTER ONE

My first thought was, "That's way too much gun." The old man stepped onto the porch and brought the S&W wheel gun to bear on the group gathered in his yard. The hole in the barrel resembled a stovepipe. ".44 mag," I thought, "at least, if not a .50 cal."

He was dressed like he meant business, or had been on his way to cut wood when he was interrupted by the clamor in front of the house. The pockets of the heavy, wool shirt he was wearing over a black turtleneck bulged with what I guessed were speed loaders, one in each. The Smith was a double action if he chose to go that route. In trained hands, 18 enormous slugs could be sent down range in less than 30 seconds. That was pretty slow by current standards when most would-be gunfighters carried Glocks, Brownings, Sigs, or, at the least, a 1911-type semi-auto.

I don't imagine it bothered the old man much. From the electronic red dot sight and the 8-inch barrel on the Smith, it was obvious he was a handgun hunter. Hunters tend to favor accuracy over volume and knock-down power over multiple hits. From my angle, I could see the dull, black reflection of the lead hollow points in the open cylinders beneath the massive barrel. The Smith & Wesson magnums were designed for a hunter to be able to take down any game on the North American continent, up to and including brown bear. What one of those slugs would do to a man was not going to be pretty.

No one saw him come out of the house but me because they were focused on the dog they had just shot. From the look on the old man's face, I was fairly sure that was going to prove to be a significant mistake. I saw him glance my way as he came through the sliding-glass door by the two-story stone chimney that took up most of the front of the house. His eyes stayed on me for a couple of seconds while he processed the situation. "No threat" he seemed to decide as he swung away from me to confront the five men standing in his driveway watching the life drain out of the beautiful German Shepherd at their feet.

One of the men was holding his arm where blood was oozing through his fingers giving evidence of the dog's displeasure. Their battered van was parked sideways in the circle drive, the sliding door still open where they had come piling out just moments before. I don't know what the old man thought of my being there, or if he even tried to make sense of it. Once he decided I was not an immediate threat, he dismissed me and turned to the business at hand.

Finally, he cleared his throat with a deep growl that seemed to come from an impossibly deep chasm somewhere beneath where he was standing. He didn't speak. He was studying the group of men trying to determine who their leader was. I had an idea since I had been there when they arrived and heard the bearded one giving orders.

They were all armed. The one with the bloody arm dropped an AR-type long gun when the dog attacked him. The other three had come out of the van pulling short-barreled semi autos out of various pockets and holsters. They experienced a bit of trouble getting to the dog since hitting their friend was a distinct possibility in the melee that had ensued.

I don't know what they had expected to find at the end of the quarter-mile lane leading up to the house. I am quite sure they had not expected to be attacked by a 125-pound, ex-police dog when they exited their vehicle, but from my vantage point, I was beginning to think their troubles had just started.

I really didn't think they would come down this lane since it was a dead end. I had been going house-to-house alerting the neighbors of the terror cell that had been activated in their area. I had been deputized by the local sheriff along with a half dozen other volunteers to bolster the security in this rural Southern Illinois county where our remoteness was supposed to be our shield against the Islamic terror that had been consuming so much of the world in the past decade. With the advent of the open border to the South and the flood of illegal aliens spreading throughout the country, nowhere was safe any longer.

We dodged a bullet in 2014. September 11 came and went with no significant strike on the U.S. mainland. For anyone who was paying attention, this was little comfort. ISIS had taken over a large chunk of Syria, Iraq, and threatened Jordan. The entire northern periphery of Africa was in a desperate war with the Islamists, who were killing Christians and Shia Muslims indiscriminately and without mercy.

The 600 A.D. demon was out of the bottle again.

Unfortunately, the voters in the U.S. saddled us with a Muslim sympathizer as the commander in chief. We elected a man to the highest office in the land who was unprepared, inexperienced and possessed a worldview totally unrelated to reality.

The Islamists were not rocket scientists. Some 1,500 years of marrying first cousins, education in little but the Koran, and a primitive hatred for anything modern or secular had pretty well stifled any creativity out of the Muslim culture. They did understand one thing. They knew power. They knew instinctively that the U.S. being led by a clueless introverted narcissist, was a weak horse. They knew if they were going to strike and make it stick without serious repercussions, it would have to happen while the presidency was held by a Muslim sympathizer.

For the third time in a generation, the Democrats had gotten their hands on the levers of power in Washington, and by the numbers, had again started hollowing out our military. The Democrats' real enemies were Republicans and conservative voters. Since the military was overwhelmingly Republican and conservative by nature, it was viewed as the enemy by the Democrats in Washington and dealt with accordingly.

A deserter was treated as a hero and an active duty Marine was left to rot in a Mexican jail. The Russians and Chinese saw the drawdown as an invitation to act out some of their long-suppressed goals to increase their power and advance the agendas of the oligarchs in authority in those two countries. The U.S. reacted with words of gentle rebuke and turned our back on allies and friends leaving whole countries to the tender mercies of the Communists.

Crimea was lost to Ukraine; Libya was turned into a failed state with no government but competing warlords. But for the military, Egypt would have been lost to the Muslim Brotherhood. The Saudi princes peddled their Wahhabi hatred around the world and right into the heartland of America with the aid and assistance of both parties in Washington.

All of the above was aided and abetted by the American press. Journalism schools in the U.S. had been turning out avid leftists for a generation. Mainstream media — both print and broadcast — covered up Democratic scandals, ignored danger signals, and partied their way through life hand in hand with the leftists and statists in Washington.

There were warnings. Many business leaders and economists were aghast at the ruinous debt the Federal government was racking up. The printing presses were spewing dollars, and the resulting inflation was ignored or lied about in official reports.

The only thing propping up the dollar was its status as the reserve currency for the world. The Chinese and the Russians dealt us the death blow when they engineered the switch to the Chinese Yuan. It was cleverly done. The Chinese dumped their trillions of dollars of U.S. bonds on the world market at discounted rates. In concert, the Russians refused to accept anything but Renminbi for oil and gas flowing to Europe. The dollar collapsed overnight, and the inflation rate in the U.S. soared to previously unheard of numbers. Government checks became almost worthless. Riots broke out in every major metropolitan area of the country outside of Texas.

In the midst of the chaos, the Islamists struck. This time, they were smart. They hit the infrastructure. They dropped six of the main bridges spanning the Mississippi, both highway and rail. They hit pipelines and electrical substations. They paralyzed what was left of the economy. When a joint session of Congress was called to hear a speech from the president to address the crisis, the Brotherhood detonated a suitcase nuke six blocks from the Capitol building effectively decapitating the Federal government.

This was where they outsmarted themselves.

I was not going to be much help to the old man. All I had in the way of a gun was a little snub-nosed .38 backup piece in an ankle holster. I was more of a shotgun guy as my primary armament, but my Benelli M4 was in the car where I left it when I came up to the house. I was on my way to what I thought was a routine conversation with a neighbor when the van surprised me coming up the lane.

I ducked into the tree line and was making my way back to the car when the excitement began. The terrorists were a good 25 yards away from my position making any likely hits a matter of luck. The best I could do if the shooting started was distract them a bit with a few surprise shots from an unexpected direction.

All five of the terrorists stopped dead when the old man cleared his throat and looked up at the porch where he was standing. He had assumed a stable shooting stance, both hands firmly around the large pistol grip, feet comfortably spaced with his right foot slightly behind, knees slightly flexed. He didn't look nervous. He looked pissed.

"Which one of you shot my dog?" he asked finally, slowly, enunciating each syllable between partially clenched teeth.

The men on the drive said nothing, but three of them glanced involuntarily at the guilty party then recovered almost instantly. It wasn't quick enough.

"Kaboom!" The magnum going off sounded like a cannon.

Fire shot out of the barrel in an 18-inch flame. He had not aimed for center mass. He went for the head shot. He was a hunter shooting at a stationary target less than 30 feet away, going for shock and awe. Shock and awe were what he accomplished. The man's head virtually exploded, covering the side of the van behind him in gore.

The other four reacted instantly. The wounded one with the bad arm dived through the open door into the dark interior of the van. The bearded one went left, while the two others went right, their pistols coming up to return fire.

"Click. Click. Kaboom!" Single-action aimed fire; I was not surprised. Hunters don't intend to miss. His second shot was not aimed at the bearded man moving right. It was aimed at where he was going to be when the bullet arrived. This one was aimed at center mass. The man was dead before he crashed to the ground with his spine blown completely out of the back of his body.

"Pop, pop, pop." My little .38 rattled into the echoes of the magnum. I missed, of course, but the terrorists were distracted, which ruined their aim as they returned fire, missing the old man with their first volley, but shattering the glass door behind him. He swiveled left, dropping the barrel a smidge.

"Click. Click. Kaboom!"

The third terrorist wasn't quite as fast as the old man anticipated, so he had led him a bit too much. The bullet impacted him right at the shoulder joint and spun him around making him almost a stationary target.

"Kaboom!" The second shot came double action, right on target, but a little high, catching the man in the throat just above center mass. The result was not as spectacular since there was little solid tissue to expand the bullet, but it did almost dislodge his head from his shoulders.

Five seconds — three down. The fourth man dived under the edge of the porch out of the line of fire. He was safe for the moment from fire from the deck but was concerned now about me. I was coming up quick, and he swiveled around on his back firing at me between his knees.

"Kaboom! Kaboom!" The magnum roared twice more, the old man firing right through the wooden deck and the thin cedar fascia the gunman was leaning against. Both rounds entered just below his shoulders along with a shower of splinters they carried with them. He never felt the splinters.

The van's engine came to life. The van started throwing gravel from its rear tires as the last desperate chewed-up gunman tried to make a break for it. I rolled over in the grass to a prone firing position to take a couple of shots at the van's windshield as it passed me.

"Kaboom! Kaboom! Kaboom!" The three quick shots from the deck sounded impossibly louder than the magnum. A glance over my shoulder showed the old man now with an AR long gun firing at the van. The barrel of the AR was large for an AR, bigger even than the magnum handgun he had been using; it had to be a Beowulf .50 cal.

The left rear window of the van exploded inward. The van came to the corner of the circle drive but never turned, just headed straight into a large oak tree on the other side of the lane. It remained smashed against the tree, its rear wheels spinning futilely in the gravel.

I stood up, brushed myself off, and met the old man about halfway to the van. He was carrying the Beowulf in his right hand with the stock balanced lightly against his belt watching the van warily.

"You must be a deputy," the old man stated simply. "Thanks for the help. They probably would have got me if you hadn't been here." He walked up to the back of the van and peeked in cautiously, then stood up and looked in for a long moment before he walked around to the driver's side out of my view. I heard the engine cut off. He reappeared a moment later. "The second round went clear through and into the engine compartment," he said with a certain amount of satisfaction. "One doesn't mess with the Beowulf."

As I turned around to survey the debris of the past few minutes, the old man swung his head around, his gaze settling on the fallen shepherd. All of the determination drained out of him as if he were an inflated doll punctured with a pin. He stumbled over to where the dog lay on the driveway, a pool of blood forming around his inert form. He stood for a minute looking down at the brown-and-black form then he collapsed to a sitting position beside the dead animal. He gently lifted his head and sat it in his lap.

"Oh, Zoro … Zoro, old friend, why did you have to do it? I was going to take care of…" His words trailed off into a broken sob. He looked up and asked plaintively, "Where are the Feds?"

What could I say? The States had stepped up after the Federal government had been effectively decapitated, filling in the gap. After a while, no one seemed to be interested in going back.

"Blowing in the wind," I replied. "Blowing in the radioactive wind."

CHAPTER TWO

"Daddy, why do your friends call you Roy Lee? Your name is Leroy," my daughter asked when she was little.

"My step-father started calling me that when he came to live with us. He said Leroy was a nigger's name."

"Daddy! You said the 'N' word!"

"I can't help it — that was the way he talked. It was a different era."

"You are going to be in a lot of trouble with mama if she hears you talking like that," my daughter exclaimed.

These days, folks call me a lot of things including "Deputy" or even "Asshole," depending on which side of the law they fall.

Both of my girls were always trying to raise me it seemed. They had as little success as my present boss.

Milo Baker is the county sheriff. Since I am a volunteer deputy, he has this strange idea that I should consider him a person to be obeyed. From time to time this attitude puts us at a slight disagreement.

Now, I have been known to take a drink. Milo, bless his heart, is a teetotaler. The good sheriff is a hard-shell Baptist and thinks my Lutheran faith in repentance and forgiveness is a license for sin. It doesn't matter, I love the old man like a second father.

"Bapaw, Auntie says it's time to eat," my grandson Chance called up the steps to my den. I was sitting at my desk staring at a blank screen trying to come up with some dialogue to pull together two disjointed thoughts in my manuscript. Writing is therapy for me. Since reality has become so dark, my rodeo stories let me escape to a happier time.

Riding rodeo was the one thing I was really good at. I miss it every day. I even miss working on the railroad. At the end, being an operator wasn't really work. I just sat in a tower and dispatched trains, passed communications, and supervised crossing guards, but I loved the folks I worked with and it gave my life purpose.

For 20 years the railroad *was* my life. I loved every bit of it. When I was on a line gang, I had been young and strong. I savored the hard work and the rough, raucous camaraderie of a line crew. It reminded me of my time in the Marine Corps, and the intense lifetime bonds formed out of the bloody chaos of battle. At least on the railroad, no one was shooting at us.

"Daddy. your dinner is getting cold!" Amanda's irritated voice coming up the stairs reminded me that I had been noodling off. Amanda is my youngest daughter. She had moved back home when my wife died to help me raise my grandson. She had been trying to raise *me* since she was five years old and, in her mind, still had not succeeded.

"Chance, will you *please* get your banjo off of your grandpa's chair and get me another pitcher of milk from the garage refrigerator," Amanda chided my grandson. She was standing by the open kitchen refrigerator door holding an empty glass pitcher with a bemused look on her face.

"I could swear this was full…"

"He is a growing boy," I laughed. I knew my grandson could drink an entire pitcher of raw milk in one sitting. He didn't get to be six foot four at 19 years of age on water.

"Well, he doesn't have to put an empty pitcher back in the fridge!"

"It still had milk in it," Chance defended himself as he disappeared out the door toward the garage. Amanda looked at the splash of white in the bottom of the clear pitcher and shook her head. She smiled in spite of herself. She was incapable of being angry with her nephew. She adored the boy.

Chance was her older sister's son and the product of a failed marriage. Melissa had come home eight months pregnant and Chance had been born in our front room. He was the son Genevieve and I never had. Melissa disappeared out of our lives shortly after the boy was born, heading off to the city to seek her fortune.

Chance called Genevieve "Nana." I called her "Gen." When she was killed, the hole she left in both of our lives was indescribable. I have no idea how we could have survived if Amanda had not come home immediately to take care of us.

I retrieved the banjo from my chair at the head of the kitchen table and carried it into the formal dining room. Just as I had suspected, the case was sitting open on the dining room table. Where the boy got the talent he had for stringed instruments was a mystery to me. I have been told I have a good singing voice and they are always after me at church to join the choir, but I am certainly all thumbs when it comes to stringed instruments.

As I closed the case, I noticed the disassembled AR10 spread across a thick white pad where Chance had been working on it. He had a bench at the back of the attached garage where he practiced his gunsmithing hobby, but from time to time he liked to bring his projects in the house so he could visit with Amanda while she was working in the kitchen.

"Do you think Delbert is going to be joining us?" Amanda asked as I came back into the kitchen. Chance was hovering behind his chair eyeing the tableful of food spread out before him. Gen had been insistent that no one sat until I did and no one left the table without permission until the man of the house stood at the end of a meal. Genevieve's rules still applied even though she had been gone for a long while. Her presence was still very much felt, especially in her kitchen.

"I don't think so," I said checking the ancient clock ticking away on its shelf on the back wall. "It's after six. He would have been here by now if he was coming." Delbert Jones was a friend, old enough and close enough to be thought of as a second father. He was fond of Amanda's cooking and was a frequent uninvited, but welcome, guest. He would always insist that he didn't come to eat, but Amanda thought it was darn funny he always showed up around meal time.

"Do you mean that we might actually have a meal with just the three of us?" Amanda exclaimed. "Are you sure the Rapture hasn't occurred and we have been left behind?"

We had a lot of company.

"If you weren't such a good cook, we wouldn't be near as popular."

"Mom started it. I am just carrying on the tradition."

It was true. The food that came out of Genevieve's kitchen was famous across the county as well as the notion that anyone was welcome at our table at any time. Gen had always prepared enough for at least three unexpected guests in addition to our nuclear family. It was a rare meal that saw us eat alone.

The dogs would eat well this evening. Our two German Shepherd cross breeds were lying on the porch with their heads resting on the ledge of the kitchen floor patiently awaiting any leftovers.

I pulled out my chair and looked over the table. Chance had moved the Crock-Pot to the center. It was full to the brim with round steak, onions, red and yellow peppers, and diced tomatoes. The house had been redolent with the wonderful aroma all afternoon.

Surrounding the main course, white bowls of mashed potatoes, peas, carrots, corn, and green beans looked like pawns guarding their king jealously. No vegetable was safe in Amanda's kitchen. If one appeared it would instantly be put in a pot to be stewed, boiled, or steamed. She thought "salad" was an old Indian word meaning "to be cooked."

Amanda came to the table carrying a large platter of biscuits.

"Biscuits are for breakfast," I complained.

"You get me some flour that will rise, and I will bake you some yeast rolls. Until then, if you want bread, biscuits are it."

"There are 300 acres of hard, red wheat ripening in the high meadow as we speak," I told her. "It should be ready in the next couple of weeks."

"You keep telling me that, but I can't bake bread from promises," she retorted.

"I like biscuits just fine, Auntie," Chance said, leaping to her defense. He knew where his meals came from and didn't want any hint of them being slowed down.

I returned thanks after everyone got settled and we passed the bowls around while Chance served meat and peppers from the large center pot. When everyone's plates were filled to the side boards, we dived in. There was silence for a while.

"Bapaw, we are almost out of oats for the horses," Chance informed me, taking a breath.

"Did you check the bins at Burdett's place? I think there might be some left in the drive-through behind the house."

"There may be a pickup load left there, but even if we grind it in with some corn, it won't last more than a week."

"A week should do it, son. The field over by the interstate should be dry enough to cut by then."

"I hope so, Bapaw. It's going to be cutting it close."

"I like the meat better since we stopped feeding the beef cattle corn," Amanda interjected. "I know you thought the meat would be tough feeding the shorthorns grass and hay alone, but I like it better without all that fat."

I did not reply since she had me on that one. I had lost the argument out of necessity. After the chaos, there just hadn't been enough corn to feed the herd of shorthorn beef cattle that was the main product of our farm. I hated to admit it, but she was right. The leaner cuts of beef did seem to be more flavorful. It was counter-intuitive and went against everything my step-father had taught me.

The "whooeo, whooeo" of a train whistle cut through the evening like a sharp knife. It was followed by the rumble of a westbound freight approaching the Spiketown crossing.

"It's good to hear the trains again," Amanda said smiling. It was a small return to normalcy. "Are you going back to work on the railroad now that they have started up again?"

"I doubt it. It's a new company and there is only one train a day so far. They won't need operators for a long time."

"Besides, he's a lawman now," Chance informed her. "The sheriff wouldn't know what to do without him." My grandson had an outsized opinion of my worth to Sheriff Baker.

"I think Milo is more interested in Amanda's fried chicken than anything I do for him," I ventured, explaining the reason for the sheriff's frequent presence at our farm.

"I don't know, Bapaw. He doesn't seem to want to do anything much without consulting with you first."

The boy had a point, but it wasn't so much that the sheriff needed my advice on law enforcement. I led a small militia during the worst of the chaos after the disappearance of the Federal apparatus. The militia was made up of my neighbors and friends. The sheriff depended on us to enhance his small staff, if and when anything serious came up. We were his SWAT team.

As a result, he kept a close eye on us and made sure we were up to date on what was happening around the county and that we kept current at the range. He provided us ammunition for practice and maintained a personal relationship with all of my guys.

"Bapaw, don't forget to ask the governor about my ranger application," Chance reminded me. I knew that was coming at the first mention of law enforcement. My grandson had a dream of being a Texas Ranger.

He had been after me to have our governor talk with the Texas governor to facilitate his ambition. I tried to ignore him. I wanted him to stay on the farm. Law enforcement had never been exactly safe. Since the chaos, it was downright dangerous on a daily basis. It was not a life I wanted for the light of my life.

"I need to run into town and talk to the sheriff," I told my family. "There was an incident at Mr. Sinclair's place today and there are some bodies out there that will need to be dealt with."

"Really Bapaw, what happened?" Chance exclaimed, suddenly forgetting his Ranger ambitions for the moment.

I told him and Amanda the story, minimizing my part in the affair.

"Wow Bapaw, it's a good thing you showed up!"

"I don't know; the old man seemed perfectly able to take care of himself. All I did was provide a distraction for a moment or two."

"Right Bapaw," Chance said dismissively.

He was convinced I had actually dealt with the situation single-handedly. I would like to buy myself for what I was worth and sell myself to someone for what the boy thought I was worth. I would be rich beyond imagination.

"If you're going to town, let me fix a container for you to drop off at the pastor's house," Amanda said as we all stood up. She kept a steady stream of food flowing into the parsonage.

I stopped by the courthouse where the sheriff has his office and let them know about the bodies at Mr. Sinclair's place. I dropped off the container of steak and vegetables at the parsonage, dodging the pastor, who was out on a call. I needed to move the cattle herd out of the north pasture this evening, so I headed back home. I was about halfway down the mile of gravel that leads to our farm from the paved road when I saw a white T-shirt bobbing down the road ahead of me. It was Chance coming back from his evening five-mile run.

He lifted his hand as I passed. I parked my Caddy under the big oak tree in front of the house and waited for the boy. He jogged up and gave me a smile. He wasn't even breathing hard.

"You need to run with me Bapaw, it will keep you young," he told me. This was almost a liturgy with him, I knew it by heart. "Come spot for me?"

I shuddered. He was headed out to the shop to work out with the free weights. My spotting always ended up with my competing with him on the bench press. Lately, I was coming up on the short end of the competition. It was embarrassing.

I flirted with the idea of making excuses and begging off, but in the end, I walked out to the shop with him. Spending time with my grandson was becoming a rare event and was not to be missed — no matter the pain.

I had just reached the door of the shop when the radio on my belt squawked at me.

"Leroy, what's your 20?" It was Milly, our dispatcher. She loved talking like she was on a 1950s cop show.

"I am at the farm, Milly. What's up?"

"That State boy, Roscoe, is looking for you. I told him I thought you would be at the farm. He'll probably be showing up shortly."

"Thank you, Milly … I think. Did he say what he had on his mind?"

"No, but he was in an all-fired tizzy to find you."

"Okay, thanks for the heads up."

"Chancy, I may have to take a rain check. It looks like I am going to have company."

"S'okay, Bapaw, no problem."

I could see the cloud of dust coming up the road when I started back out to the car. The cloud soon solidified itself into a brown-and-cream-colored cruiser of the Illinois State Police. He was driving much too fast for the gravel. I hoped he could get it stopped before he slammed into my Caddy.

In the end, he did neither.

He slammed on the brakes much too late and slid right on past our place to finally come to halt 25 yards down the road. He slammed it into reverse and spun gravel all the way back. He didn't even try to park. He just stopped in the middle of the road.

Roscoe Clemens stepped out of his car and looked back at the dust covered Chevy with some obvious distaste. It was clear the car had been immaculate before his little sojourn down our access road. He was a small prim man with a pencil mustache and a severe case of "Little-Man Complex."

"Leroy, when is the county going to get this road paved?"

"Probably never," I told him truthfully. "It wasn't paved before the trouble; I doubt it will ever be now."

"Well, why don't you move over by the lake?"

The state had built an enormous lake a few years before the collapse. The far end of it washed up on the backside of our farm. We could have built a house on or near the lake and had paved access from that direction.

"I like my privacy."

He shook his head in disgust and looked at my dust-encrusted Caddy with overt disdain. I was glad he couldn't see the two bushels of shelled corn in the back seat; he would probably have shit himself.

"Whatever. The governor is having a meeting on Friday with all the county sheriffs, and he wants you to be there."

"Roscoe, you know I'm not the sheriff. I'm just a deputy."

"Don't shoot the messenger," Clemens said holding up his hands as if surrendering. "I'm just telling you what I was told. But from what I understand, the Guv was pretty adamant about wanting you there."

"Okay Roscoe, consider your message delivered. I have an appointment with my grandson so he can make me look like an old man."

"Can I watch?"

I started to tell Clemens no way in hell, but then thought, why not?

"You'll need to get your car out of the road, there's one other place down there you know." I pointed on down to where my only neighbor's house was obscured by the brush and trees. "We'll be out in the shop."

I walked through the access door and left it open for Clemens. My grandson was standing on the big rubber mat practicing his katas. I stood and watched his graceful, practiced movements for a moment appreciating the beauty of the near dance. I wasn't fooled. It was a dance of death. Each of the kata movements was a blow or block, practiced until they became second nature in an actual confrontation.

He had studied Okinawan Karate since he was eight years old. His hero is Hohan Soken. Through his high school years, his room was plastered with charts of human anatomy outlining strike points and pressure sensitive areas with arrows delineating the direction of the strike to affect that particular area of the body to numb or disable.

In a dark alley fight, there is no one I would rather have at my back.

I walked over to a set of coat hooks and started to shed my "uniform." I always wore the same thing, differing only between winter and summer. Since it was late fall, I was still wearing my summer dress. It consisted of a black Stetson, a white short-sleeved shirt with a bolo tie, a black sports coat, blue jeans, and burgundy alligator Tony Lamas. Today, in deference to the boots, I wore a burgundy belt around my waist.

I went all the way down to my boxers before retrieving the one-piece jumpsuit from a hanger left there for this purpose. As I slipped into it, I noticed my daughter had freshly laundered it. That was nice. I sat down on the weight bench and pulled on a pair of light tennis shoes. I looked up to see Clemens come through the door and nod to my grandson. He leaned against the door jam.

"Spar or lift?" Chance asked.

"You're on the mat already, how about we spar for a bit?" He smiled and winked at the State policeman. He was getting cocky, my grandson was. We'd see.

I had been sparring with him since he was just a kid. We both knew each other's moves like they were our own. It was difficult for either one of us to come up with many surprises. Cagey old character that I was, I always kept a few moves in my pocket for emergencies. Today we had an audience. That qualified as a bonafide emergency in my book.

He dropped back into a defensive stance with his feet apart at shoulder width. His weight was forward on the balls of his feet ready to move quickly in any direction. His hands were up almost in front of his face, open with elbows tucked in close to his body. He was waiting for me to make the first move.

He would have a long wait. I wasn't about to step into that buzz saw.

I stepped in front of him just out of reach and took up a boxer's stance, fists lightly clenched leading with my left. He watched my eyes. He knew the left was the thing to watch. I had a mean jab and knew how to throw my entire body weight behind it. I would bounce the right around like it was a cobra drawing attention. The left would hang in the air, motionless as if only meant to be a blocking tool then BAM! recoil back and BAM! BAM! When I was younger, I had practiced on the heavy bag for hours until I could land three hard jabs in less than two seconds. It was usually a fight ender.

Chance was more than familiar with my shtick so I knew I could never touch him with the left. I danced around counter-clockwise circling him. He smiled and moved easily, conserving his energy, keeping me in front of him. I opened my left hand and signaled him to come to me.

He took a half-step forward, faked with his right hand, and snapped kicked with his left foot. It was one of his favorite moves. I expected it and turned my right hip in, deflecting the blow across my thigh. It still hurt. Damn, that boy was getting strong!

I made a grab for his extended leg, but he was too fast. The kick had been just a blur and even though I was expecting it, I could do nothing but avoid it. When I dropped my right to catch his leg, I left an opening. He snap-punched with a left knuckle, striking just below my right breast. Snap! Snap! In-out so quick I hardly recognized it except for the sharp jab of pain on top of my rib cage. He had pulled his punch. If he had been serious, I would have a cracked rib.

I was beginning to breathe hard. He wasn't even breaking a sweat. I was getting my ass kicked! Okay, time to end this. I rolled into him with my left shoulder high, brushing his hands up as I went. I dropped to one knee, grabbed his left leg behind the knee and lifted hard. It landed him flat on his back! It was a move from high school wrestling that in a real fight would have probably gotten me a knee in the face. But it surprised my grandson, who thought he knew all of my moves. I got away with it.

I bounced up and reached down, pulling him to his feet.

"That was new," my grandson said, laughing. "You knew I couldn't block it without severely hurting you. Don't you feel bad about that?"

"Absolutely not! I'll take any advantage I can. I'm an old man."

My grandson enfolded me in a big hug, then held me out at arms-length. "Not so old," he disagreed. He saw what he wanted to see.

"Okay, good show!" Clemens said from the door, feigning applause. "I have to go; you make sure you're at the governor's meeting. They'll have my ass if you aren't there," he said over his shoulder as he left the shop.

"The governor likes you," my daughter said appearing in the shop door. I turned around and almost couldn't breathe. The pain was so great, I thought it would bring me to my knees. She looked so much like her mother standing there with her dark brown hair up in a braid wrapped around her head. With the light behind her, looking at me with her mother's silver-gray eyes, it was uncanny.

The guilt and angst I felt over my wife's death wrapped itself around me like a huge python and squeezed. I gasped for air. I had not been a good husband. I drank too much and played harder. I had girlfriends. We had been married much too young, and I took her very much for granted. She had been a saint, who overlooked my indiscretions.

I only realized the treasure I possessed after it was taken from me. I have been faithful to her memory, for what it is worth. My daughter has taken untold delight in reminding me how I am a husband to a memory that I was not to the living lady. This causes my daughter no end of traumatic wonder. I can't help it. It is what it is.

"The governor likes me when he has a problem," I told her. "Otherwise, he doesn't know my name."

"Do you have any idea of what his problem might be this time?"

"No, I don't have a clue and I am not really looking forward to finding out."

"Will the sheriff be upset that the governor is asking for you personally?"

"No, he knows the governor and I go back a ways."

"Will you go to the meeting?"

"Probably. I don't want Roscoe to get his ass in a crack."

"I've got blackberry cobbler and ice cream when you two get done playing out here," she said, changing the subject. It sounded good to me. Perhaps I could skip the weights.

"It will be a while," Chance said. "We need to lift for a bit."

Groan…

***

Hulman Field – Terre Haute, Indiana

The C21 Lear that dropped out of the sunrise to land in Terre Haute had been repainted to cover the USAF markings but the paint used was not the quality of the original Lear factory baked-on enamel. The high-altitude sun exposure had faded the covering, and the Star and Bars of the Federal plane were bleeding through.

The airport was deserted. All that was left of the main terminal building was a burnt-out shell. Some of the adjoining hangars had large chunks blown away leaving blackened edges. There was litter and trash everywhere. It was evident that a battle had taken place on the grounds of the airport.

There were carcasses of planes scattered across the tarmac. Some were scorched frames; others had been stripped of fixtures and sat like forlorn skeletons on wheel-less stalks of landing-gear struts.

There were three black, GMC SUVs sitting in a line on the taxiway. The little Lear pulled up to the waiting vehicles, spooled down the Pratt engines, and the cabin door opened down forming a stairway. Four dark-suited men emerged.

The driver of the middle SUV hopped out and opened both rear doors and the front passenger door. Four armed men dismounted from the leading and trailing vehicles to stand beside their respective SUVs while surveying the area as if looking for potential threats.

The four men exiting the plane were a disparate group. All were late middle aged, but of different races. The leader was a Caucasian male, easily six feet in height with black hair and wire-rim glasses. He was dressed in a three-piece, wool worsted suit. The others were of Asian, African and Middle Eastern backgrounds. All wore expensive suits.

The white man climbed in next to the driver of the middle SUV while the other three piled into the back. The men in the other two vehicles mounted up as well, and the little column left the blackened and ruined airport at a high rate of speed.

The column turned east on a county road, then north. The vehicles rolled north as fast as the unmaintained surface of the road would allow. They turned west onto a gravel road and rolled along behind the lead vehicle leaving a large dust cloud. When the Wabash River blocked their path, they left the road and bounced through the ditches following a well-used path to a railroad embankment. The vehicles crossed the river using the railroad bridge, bouncing and jouncing along the ties.

On the west side of the river, their journey followed another path down from the right-of-way to a country road running west. It was a hard road in somewhat better shape than most Indiana county highways. Where it joined the old Illinois Route One, the column turned south.

The first vehicle came to a concrete lane bordered on both sides by dogwood trees. After a moment's hesitation, it turned west followed by the other SUVs. After an eighth of a mile, the column came to a large arch with a sturdy wooden gate blocking its path. The shotgun passenger of the lead vehicle jumped out and opened the obstruction. The little column passed quickly through, leaving the AR15 armed guard at the gate. He closed it as the vehicles disappeared and took up station in a little guard shack that had been unmanned prior to their arrival.

The column proceeded for another eighth of a mile passing the entrance to a private, 18-hole golf course. Looking eerily like a large snake, the vehicles forded a creek and drove up to a massive log house. A lone older gentleman stood waiting on the covered deck at the top of a flight of four steps. He was dressed casually in slacks and a collared pullover. His hair was white and the skin on his face was tight, as if he had cosmetic surgery. He was holding a cup of coffee, and his demeanor was serious in the extreme.

The armed men in the two escort vehicles dismounted and took up station around the deck. The driver of the middle SUV jumped out and started opening doors. The white passenger opened his own door and stepped out. He was closest to the stairway leading up to the deck. He nodded to the older gentleman waiting at the top. Neither smiled.

The host walked to the main entrance and opened the door. He stood holding it open while his guests filed up the steps and entered the main house. No one spoke; they simply made eye contact and passed out of sight inside of the house. Two of the guards took up position on either side of the door. Whether they were there to bar entry or exit was indeterminate.

***

Governor's Office – Springfield, Illinois

Springfield had come through the chaos unscathed. The governor's office was spacious and elegant. It would be easy to forget the trauma of the past couple of years sitting in one of the high-backed leather chairs in front of the chief executive's desk. I looked up at the massive painting behind the desk of Abe giving his Gettysburg Address. On either side of the picture were two stands. Both were displaying the flag of the State of Illinois. The one on the left appeared to be newer. I knew it replaced the Stars and Stripes that had hung there since the Capitol building had been built.

I was waiting for the governor. One of his aides collared me after his speech to the county sheriffs and asked me to accompany him to the governor's private office. He left me there with a cup of coffee and an assurance that the governor would be with me shortly. I finished my coffee and debated about what to do with the empty cup. I certainly wasn't going to set it on the immaculate desk in front of me.

To my left and right against either wall were long sofas with flanking end tables. I finally decided. Before I could stand, the governor walked in preceded by a young lady who walked over and relieved me of my burden with a smile before disappearing out the door from which they had entered. I stood and shook hands with the governor. He bid me regain my seat as he walked around to sit behind his desk.

Okay, I thought, it was going to be that kind of meeting.

If B. C. Braun thought I would be intimidated by the trappings of his office and the massive wooden desk, he was sadly mistaken. I didn't mind. We were lucky to have him behind that desk when the wheels came off the wagon. He was a self-made millionaire and a Republican, managing one of the bluest of blue states.

While the cities were burning and chaos was stalking the land, Governor Braun's quick actions saved the state. He had arrested a half-dozen, long-entrenched leaders of the Illinois Senate and laid down the law to a joint session. His speech had been short, brutal, and effective. The Legislature had given him the authority he needed to quell the riots and put the state back on the road to recovery.

I liked him personally and admired him immensely. He didn't need to try to intimidate me. I would do anything he asked me to do if it were in my power to do it.

The governor had an outsized view of my abilities. Through an amazing set of coincidences, I had been leading a militia force of volunteers during the worst of the riots when we confronted a convoy of gang bangers headed south and up to no good. They had a handful of white, teenage girls as hostages. One of those girls had been the governor's daughter, kidnapped from a summer camp as the gang had passed through the area.

It had been a closely run thing, as the Duke of Wellington described Waterloo. It ended much the same way for the gang bangers as the aforementioned battle had for the little Emperor. None of the girls were killed, a couple were banged up a bit, but miraculously, all survived. I don't know what kind of story the young lady had told her father, but after that, he thought I wore a big red S on my chest.

He had called me on two other occasions, and I had been able to accomplish his objectives. I had been lucky. As my old daddy used to say, "I'll take a lucky man with me anytime over a smart one." The riverboat adventure could have gone either way. I almost felt like I had experienced some divine intervention – but that is another story.

"El Dee, I appreciate you coming up. I hope it won't cause your boss any heartburn."

My middle name is Dwayne. The governor had this habit of affixing a pet nickname to his closest aides and confidants. I don't know if I actually am either of those, but I have my handle. He was just talking. I knew he didn't give a hoot or a holler about the sheriff's feelings one way or another.

"What can I do for you, Governor?" I said cutting through the BS. I crossed my legs and sat back. The movement caused the cuff of my razor pressed Wranglers to slip up a bit and expose the intricate thread work on the saddle-leather Tony Lamas I was wearing.

"Are you armed?"

He couldn't know because the aide had walked me around the security guards and the metal detector generally required for anyone gaining access to the State Office Building.

"I have a shoulder weapon and an ankle gun."

"What do you carry under your arm?"

"Well Governor, it depends. Today, since we were going to be in the city in close proximity to a lot of folks and in close quarters, I brought along a PMR 30."

The KelTek PMR 30 is a slick little .22 magnum, semi-automatic that fires a 45-grain, soft-tip bullet at 1400 fps. I use Hornady FTX Critical Defense rounds that will penetrate 15 inches of ballistic jell. It has a 30-round magazine with one in the pipe. The Hornady round is packed with flashless powder specially formulated for handguns.

Standard .22 mag ammo will yield a stream of muzzle fire brighter than a flash bulb. In a near-dark, or even a heavily shadowed hallway or room, the second shot can be problematic since the shooter is more than likely blinded by the fire of the first shot. The Hornady was like firing an air rifle. The compact bullet is perfect for a crowded room. It won't penetrate a wall or door. It will — nine times out of ten — remain within the body of the targeted bad guy.

"That is good El Dee. It's what I like about you. You are always thinking."

"Governor?" I inquired, trying to get him back on the subject of just exactly what was I doing here.

"Hmmm," the governor mumbled, evidently reluctant to get into the meat of the issue. "Have you heard of the Federalist Party?"

"Sure. They are a bunch of disgruntled, ex-government employees, welfare recipients, leftists, statists, and other assholes who want to drag us back into mother's lap."

"That pretty well states the case — somewhat crude, but accurate." The governor paused, still reluctant to admit his angst, but then he turned and looked me straight in the eye.

"The assholes, as you refer to them, are setting up big downstate. They are intent on stirring up trouble here and trying to win folks over to their way of thinking by making life under the Feds seem safe and sane."

"And this affects me how?"

"We think their headquarters and center of gravity are in your county."

"Oh shit!" I replied brilliantly.

CHAPTER THREE

"I want you to look into this group's activities, see what you can find out about who is involved, where their money is coming from and how much of a threat they are," the governor told me. The way he said it sounded like he was asking me to pick up a gallon of milk after work. It wasn't going to be anywhere near that simple.

"Governor, it seems to me this should be a job for the state police or even the National Guard. I am just one man; I have no resources to draw on for backup. I have..."

The governor held up his hand to cut off my objections.

"My administration is riddled with holdovers from the previous four Democrats who sat behind this desk. As you are well aware, two of the three are in jail on corruption charges, and the third is under indictment. Until I can get the dead wood cleaned out, I don't know who to trust. I am fairly certain the Federalists have some sympathizers at the highest level. My lieutenant governor may even be one of them."

I had no response to this little rant. I had heard it a couple of times before.

The governor reached over and pushed a button on the multi-function phone on his desk.

"Elaine, will you please ask Matt to come in?"

He had hardly released his finger from the button when one of the big double doors to his office swung open. A tall, handsome man in a three-piece suit strode purposefully into the room. Matthew P. Norman III, director of the Illinois State Police (ISP), had come to grace us with his esteemed presence. The only way he could be a bigger asshole, in my estimation, was if he gained weight. He gave me a dirty look and came to stand to my left by the governor's desk. He stood as if at attention, purposely ignoring me. "Fuck you too, Norman," I thought charitably.

"Matthew, you know Mr. White. He has assisted me on several occasions in the past. I have a task for him that will require some support from your organization."

The governor paused. His nibs, the director, glanced in my direction with an insincere smile. He nodded his reluctant acceptance of the governor's statement, but said nothing. His face turned a little red, and he seemed to be grinding his teeth. The governor continued.

"I will need Mr. White issued a badge and ID showing him to be a colonel in the investigation division of the ISP. His position, and the fact he is working directly for me, is to be known to no one else," he held his hand up as Mr. Tight-Ass looked as if he was going to say something. "I will give you a written authorization for the file; it will not leave this office. Further, any support Mr. White requires, you will provide. I want to reiterate, the fact he is working for me goes no further than this room." There was a long silence as the director looked in my direction. His expression might well have been reserved for a pile of dog poo on the wool carpet of the governor's office.

"Yes, Sir. I understand," he said finally.

"That will be all, Matthew. Thank you."

The ex-Marine captain spun on his heel in a perfect about-face and marched out the door with thunderclouds forming on his countenance. The man really, really did not like me.

"What is it between you two? I would think both of you being USMC," he spelled out the letters, "…would have hit it off."

I thought about a response — I could have gone on for some time. "You thought wrong," is all I said. With this, the governor shrugged.

"I trust him, and I need you two to work together. If there is anything you need that you don't think you are getting, you call me, and I'll make it happen."

I thought he was going to dismiss me with this, but he slid open the drawer to his right and retrieved a thick manila envelope. It had a string fastener that he unwound and spilled the contents onto his desktop. It was a badge and two ID cards. He slid them over to me. It was a carry permit and an ID card with my picture on it stating I was an investigator for the Indiana State Police. The badge said, "Colonel."

"You are scaring me, Governor," I told him truthfully. "I think you are getting me into something way over my pay grade," he ignored my comment. "I guess this merger with Indiana Law Enforcement is further along than is generally being published." Again the governor ignored my comment.

"The documentation in this file contains all of the information we have on the organization. There is a password and a link to our most secure database where you will be able to keep us up-to-date with your findings. It will also allow you access to any intelligence we come up with. I trust you will know what to publish and what to inform me of in confidence." With this, he stood and held out his hand, dismissing me.

I still had lots of questions, but I figured I had better study the file and peruse the database before I made myself look stupid. I was usually pretty good at that, and I don't mean studying and perusing.

I started for the door but paused just before opening it. I turned around.

"Just how far do you trust your director?"

The governor regarded me across the room. He hesitated as if trying to find the correct word.

"Implicitly," he said finally.

Whatever, I thought to myself and took my leave. *Well, Governor, you may trust the sonofabitch, but I don't. He left my platoon on the beach in Beirut with no fire support and I left two good men there, who never came home. Hizzoner looks after his own rear end, and everyone else is expendable.*

The area outside the governor's office is light and airy. The floor-to-ceiling glass doors at the far end complement the floor-to-ceiling windows spanning the entrance area, allowing the entire space to be filled with natural light. The governor's assistant, Elaine Martin, came up to me as I left his office.

She was strikingly beautiful with strawberry-blonde hair that fell in wavy locks around her face. Elaine had magnificent blue eyes with perfect whites as if they were bloodless. She had the creamy, white skin that some blondes and redheads are blessed, with just a hint of freckles sprinkled across her nose. She was wearing a silky one-piece dress, white with a floral pattern. It was open at the top, exposing an attractive cleavage, and ended just above her perfect knees. When she strode across the marble floor with her two-inch heels clicking on the marble, everything inside the dressed jiggled in all the right places.

"You look as if you have received news of a death in the family. Are you okay?" she asked me with a concerned smile. When she stopped in front of me, I caught the hint of White Diamonds perfume. I tried to keep my eyes off of the white bead necklace accenting the cleavage below but was not too successful. I worked up a smile. With Elaine standing there, it was easy.

"I am okay," I told her. "You are looking breathtakingly beautiful today, as always. Seeing you is the one bright spot in these little visits."

I then noticed something. She was holding a manila folder similar to the one the governor had extracted my Indiana State Police ID. She had it cradled in her left arm with her hand around the far edge. There was a white band on the third finger where a wedding ring had been. At my compliment, she seemed to color a bit but left it unremarked.

"The director left this for you, Rhett," she told me and handed me the folder. She always calls me Rhett, as in Rhett Butler, because I bear a striking resemblance to Clark Gable. I encourage that since I wear a little mustache exactly as he did. When our hands touched, I noticed something else. She kept contact for about two breaths longer than was necessary to affect the transfer. She was still smiling.

"Are you a real cowboy?" she teased as she reached up and took the ends of the string tie I was wearing in her hand.

"I rode rodeo, and I have 200 head of shorthorn cattle. I can sit a horse fairly well and hit what I am shooting at. I guess you could say I am a real cowboy."

She glanced around as if suddenly realizing we were on display and dropped the tie. She moved back a step to put some business-like distance between us. I didn't need to look in the folder. I knew there would be a .40 caliber Glock and my documentation within. I also knew the Glock would be empty. It would be the director's way of giving me the finger. I toyed with the idea of walking down to his office and giving him a double tap with the KelTek, but decided it would probably not be conducive to our working relationship.

As I started for the door, I noticed Elaine had fallen in beside me. She walked me to the glass doors. She stopped as I opened one. As I stepped through, she said softly, in almost a whisper, "I have always had a thing for cowboys."

That almost stopped me, but I walked on out with the hint of White Diamonds still wafting around my head. Wow, the governor's gal! Calm down cowboy! The two thoughts came one after the other as if they were train cars joined end to end. This thing the guv was getting me into was going to be dangerous enough.

I had almost made it to the exit door when I heard someone clear his throat behind me. I knew that sound. I stopped and turned around. The director stood glaring at me.

"Fuck you, Norman," I said seriously.

"Look, White, if you are going to work for me…"

"Stop right there!" I interrupted him and took a step in his direction as I shifted the folder to my right hand. "First and foremost, I don't work for you, Norman." I knew using his last name pissed him off. That is why I did it. "I work for the governor, and it is Mr. White to you." That statement took some gall since I had just called him by his last name, but I didn't care. I wanted him to be pissed off.

His face turned white, and I could see his fists were clenched on either side. "Yes, please take a swing at me, you sonofabitch," I thought evilly.

I am not a nice person.

I was looking with pleasure at the point on his jawline where my jabs would land. I felt an itch in my left hand. If I hit him hard enough, I could dislocate…

He took two steps back. Damn!

"You have to give it up, Leroy," he said, stumbling over my name. "Lebanon was a long time ago, and I was under orders. I had no choice."

What really ticked me off was I knew he was telling me the truth as he saw it. I knew he had been under orders and in his Annapolis-trained mind, he really thought he had no choice. It didn't matter. It was my grudge, and I was going to nurse it. Not everyone in those situations obeyed their orders to the letter. I know I damn sure didn't and wouldn't have been standing here if I had.

I felt the anger drain out of me as I realized what he said was true. I was about to go in harm's way, and I would need his help.

"All right Matthew, truce," I said, biting back the gall. He smiled a tight, little reluctant smile and held out his hand. I wanted to spit on it, but I shook it instead. I squeezed hard and considered giving him the treatment — I have a powerful grip. I milked cows through high school and keep a grip spring at my desk and in my car. It helps me work off frustrations. I could break a couple of the tiny bones in his hand with ease, but I backed off.

Sometimes I do the right thing, in spite of myself.

"Anything you need…" he said to my back as I walked down the steps in front of the building. This was going to be harder than I thought. I really hated that man.

I walked the six blocks to the barbecue place where I was to meet Sheriff Baker. It was his favorite spot in Springfield. They had some of the best brisket I had ever eaten, and I had spent a lot of time in Texas. The restaurant had a micro-brewery in the back and made a bock beer that I favored. Today, in deference to the sheriff's tee-totaling proclivities, I would be drinking sweet tea.

When I entered the establishment, I saw Sheriff Baker sharing a laugh and a four-top table with three other county sheriffs. They were chuckling at some sheriff joke, I supposed. When I walked up, the three other officers gave me wary looks. I was a civilian dressed like some drugstore cowboy in their eyes.

Sheriff Baker stood up and introduced me as one of his deputies. The wary looks relaxed a notch. I still was not in uniform. He explained that I did investigations and undercover work requiring my civilian attire. It was almost the truth and got some grudging acceptance from his peers. Sheriff Baker excused us, and we found an empty table near the back where we could talk privately.

I had my hands full with my hat and the folder. I put my burden in the third seat at our small table. The Marine Corps habit of not wearing a hat under any overhead (ceiling) still could not be denied. When I walked through a door, the hat came off.

"Did the governor elaborate on our merging forces with the other states?" the sheriff asked. The governor's speech to the sheriffs had been about plans afoot to merge the law enforcement assets of the neighboring states. The tentative plan would consolidate the management and deployment of state police departments of Illinois, Indiana, Wisconsin, Michigan, and Ohio. There were a lot of practical reasons where it made sense, but folks were leery of any hint of returning to any kind of Federal government. The governors would have their hands full trying to sell it to their respective constituents; starting with the sheriffs probably made sense.

"No, he has a project he wants me to look into."

"I thought as much," the sheriff said. He left it there. It was one of the things I admired about the man. If I wanted to tell him about my personal business with the governor, fine. If not — that would have been fine, too. Of course, I was going to tell him everything. I trusted no one in the world more than Milo Baker.

"Milo, I will fill you in on the way home. I don't want to talk about it here."

He nodded his acceptance. We were somewhat private at our table, but it was still a public space.

"Milo, I think I need a beer. Do you mind?"

He smiled and shook his head; he had given up on his deputy years ago.

***

Lyman Womack's Ranch

The four men who had arrived in the black SUVs were shown to a large living room built around a massive stone fireplace at one end of the room. The overhead lofted up two-and-a-half stories to a redwood ceiling that came down on either side to the eight-foot high log walls in a modified A-frame configuration. There were leather couches arranged on three sides facing the fireplace with a massive black table that looked as if it had been sliced out of a single, huge log centered between.

The men had paused at the bar just inside the entrance door and been served drinks before they took their places around the table. The Arab declined alcohol and sat with a glass of sparkling water.

The host stood in front of the fireplace and regarded his guests. No one spoke for some time. Then the host cleared his throat and began.

"This has not been easy for any of us," he said needlessly as everyone present knew exactly where he was going. "Almost all of my business had been with the Federal government. It is all gone now."

Lyman Womack was an arms merchant. He owned small factories across the country providing support material for every branch of the armed services. His specialty had been difficult-to-manufacture sub-assemblies for aircraft, missiles, and armored fighting vehicles. It had been a very lucrative business. His machine shops turned out titanium castings and carbon-steel machine parts. He built the six bolts that connected the wing of a Lear Jet to the fuselage. He sold those fasteners for $350 apiece. They cost him $12 to make.

The other four gentlemen were in similar situations. Their primary customer had disappeared from the face of the earth. The state governments that replaced it had no need of the products and services these gentlemen used to provide the military industrial complex that Eisenhower had warned of.

"The question is, what can we do about it?" The tall Caucasian wearing wire-rim glasses interjected.

"Illinois was able to come through the chaos primarily on the strength of its agriculture and its refineries. Since Illinois was self-sufficient in gas and diesel, the farmers were able to plant and harvest once things began to settle down a bit. If we can disrupt their supply of fuel, it will drastically affect their economy and quality of life."

"Haven't they increased security dramatically at the refineries?"

"From what we have been able to determine, the refineries in the north close to the city have put in some iron-clad security with full-time Illinois National Guard stationed there. The Occidental refinery in Carmi, however, has made do with a few more rent-a-cops. They are vulnerable."

"We can make it happen," said the Arab gentleman, who went by Abdul.

"It should be soon," the Asian man interjected. "Every day that goes by, the people become more accustomed to the status quo, and making any dramatic change will be more difficult."

"We will need explosives," Abdul stated shortly.

"We have all the C4 you will need," Womack informed him. "I have it right here. When your team is ready, send a truck."

"We'll need some money, gold preferably."

"I can take care of that," the Asian man offered. "Let me know how much and where to deliver."

Abdul nodded but didn't respond.

"Anything else gentlemen?" Womack asked. Getting nothing but negative physical responses, he extended his open hand in the direction of the hallway door effectively calling the meeting to a close.

***

Beirut, Lebanon 1984

The fire from the Amal-held areas east of the airport had slacked off the past couple of days. I guess they knew we were leaving and were anxious to occupy our fortified positions, so they didn't want to mess up what was going to be their own nest.

The whole situation made no sense to me.

The U.S. had spent a medium-sized fortune building fortified positions at the airport. The Seabees had brought in hundreds of steel Conex containers, buried them and capped them with reinforced concrete. The engineers then replaced the dirt, making the containers impervious to attack from even heavy artillery. For the first time since Marines had been stationed in this third-world sewer, we had quarters where we could sleep and be safe. The Marine engineers and Seabees had set up "dragon's teeth" around the periphery and filled in the gaps with wire, sandbags, and junk vehicles.

Just when we had almost completed building a relatively safe position, we were abandoning it and pulling out, leaving our Christian allies to the tender mercies of the Muslim militia. The political situation in Lebanon had finally become too much for the American public to fathom. The Washington bureaucrats, bending to popular opinion, were throwing up their hands and walking away.

I didn't particularly care one way or the other. My platoon had been involved in the fighting almost continually since we left Grenada. We had lost some good people, including a couple of good friends. I had seen enough blood and witnessed enough agony to last me for a lifetime.

For weeks, we had been taking intermittent fire from a four-story building east of the airport. The captain had finally had enough of it and had sent our platoon to deal with it so the last company could be extracted without harassing fire interfering with the exfiltration.

Our platoon was down to 15 men, basically a reinforced squad. Second Lieutenant Otto Permian, Annapolis graduate, class of 1983, commanded. Under him was staff sergeant Mick O'Malley. I had my fire team of five grunts and the other slick arm Sergeant Ralph "Gordy" Gorder had five soldiers in his team as well. The Navy Corpsman tagging along with us was the bravest sonofabitch I ever met. His name was Stan Owens.

For this little party, the captain had attached a sniper team from the weapons company to accompany us.

We were currently bunched up along a four-foot concrete wall an eighth of a mile east of the airport. The lieutenant was scoping the building with the sergeant at his elbow. The sniper's spotter was the last in line closest to the airport and he was looking at the same building through a spotting scope.

I was getting my breath back from the 50-yard dash across the open area behind us when the mortar round came in that killed the lieutenant. I heard the "thonk" of the mortar round leaving the tube and had enough time to think, "Oh shit, that is close!"

"WHOOMP!" The round exploded 15 yards ahead of where the lieutenant was crouched down looking through a gap in the wall. I felt the pressure wave and heat rush by me and squinted my eyes against the dust. "*Good, far enough away — we are okay. Then, this can't be happening!*"

My brain refused to acknowledge what my eyes were telling it. The lieutenant fell away from the wall grasping his throat. The sergeant had collapsed across the wall and wasn't moving. The platoon was frozen in place for a long moment. "*Shit. Shit. Shit. The Sarge is down; that means I am in command. No! I don't need this. Tomorrow we will be aboard ship and out of this shithole place.*"

"Sergeant, you are up!" Gorder yelled at me. I could barely make out his words as my ears were still ringing from the blast. There is one thing about Uncle Sam's green machine. There is never any doubt about the chain of command right down to the last two men alive. One of them will be senior and will be expected to take charge, and both of them know which one it is.

Before I could even get a grip, Owens was working over the lieutenant. He shook his head and turned to the sergeant. Moments later he turned and looked straight at me. He shook his head again. Both gone.

That mortar had been close, where…?

I heard the crack of the sniper's Remington behind me. I glanced over my shoulder. The spotter looked at me and nodded. The firer of the mortar was dealt with. I saw the sniper drawing another bead moving the muzzle slowly as if tracking a moving target.

"Crack!"

The spotter checked and turned to me with two fingers up. Both of the mortar team was down.

"Sergeant?" Gorder asked with the implied, "What now?"

"Indeed, what now?" I am just a slick-sleeve, three-stripe sergeant. I am not supposed to think. I just do what I am told, go where I am sent, and kill who I am told to kill. The Corps tells me I am not required to think until they sew a rocker under those three stripes. The first stage of grief is denial. I had about three seconds to get to the next phase.

One option would be to call off this entire clusterfuck and retreat back to the airport. The lieutenant and the staff sergeant were killed. The lieutenant had the mission, had the orders. What did I know?

Unfortunately, what I knew was the mission. The lieutenant had briefed the fire team leaders along with the sergeant. *"Hoo Rah! Semper Fi and all that shit!"*

I moved to the head of the column, signaling the spotter to come with me. Owens handed me the lieutenant's binoculars as I went past. Great minds, gutters, and everything associated.

Through the binoculars, the targeted building looked deserted. There were some big holes in the front where evidently it had been targeted by naval artillery. All the windows were blown out, and the top-floor windows were framed in black as if there had been a wicked fire inside. It certainly looked tame enough.

"Anything?" I asked the spotter over my shoulder never taking my eyes off the building.

"No movement that I can see."

It seemed like hours had flown by since the mortar round had impacted in front of the column, but less than a minute had actually passed.

"Gorder, lay the bodies against the wall so we can pick them up on our way out," I said optimistically. "And get their ammunition. We are on our own here."

There was one single-story building between us and the building we were supposed to clear. There was a single trash-strewn street between us and the relative cover of the next concrete structure.

"Mitchell," I called to one of my fire team. "Sprint over to that building, bob and weave, and keep as low as you can." I pointed out where I wanted him to go. He didn't hesitate. He was up and running before I even finished talking. It was less than 50 feet; he was up against the building in seconds. He received no fire. I signaled the next man in line. When he received no fire, I watched for a couple of moments while the two men at the next building took up firing positions to cover the rest of us.

"Let's go!" I shouted, and we all got up and ran for the building. Thankfully no one opposed our movement.

I had held the sniper and his spotter back with me until the rest of the squad was in place across the street. As we were sprinting across the open area, I saw a flash coming from our targeted building.

"WHOOSH! WHOOSH!" I heard the two rockets pass overhead an instant after I saw the flash.

"Crump, crump," the explosions echoed back from the airport as the rockets impacted there.

"Alpha team report," the lieutenant's radio squawked. Gorder handed it to me with a shrug and a smile.

"This is Alpha," I keyed the mike.

"Who is this?" the captain exclaimed sounding annoyed that the lieutenant had not responded to his inquiry.

"This is Sergeant White, the lieutenant and the platoon sergeant are both KIA." I spelled out the letters. Somehow it seemed to take the sting out of the bad news.

"Sergeant, we are taking rocket fire here," the captain informed me. I wanted so badly to respond with, "Really Sir? We are having a picnic over here. Why don't you come join us?" I said nothing as the captain went on. "You need to take out those rocket launchers, sergeant. The choppers are on their way in. We could have a disaster here."

"Aye Sir, understood. We are working on it," I responded. "Any chance we could get some naval fire on this target? We are in a good place to spot the incoming."

"No can do sergeant, those buildings are in an area now considered populated with civilians and are a 'no fire zone.'"

I thought that was somewhat unreasonable and wondered how we were supposed to deal with it since we were seriously short on Tasers and pepper spray, but I held my peace.

I handed the radio back to Gorder like it was a live grenade and edged over to the side of the building where I could get a better look at our target. It looked to be just out of range of one of our rifle grenades.

"ThonkThonkThonkThonk." I saw the flash coming from one of the top windows as the concrete from the edge of the building where I was standing exploded in a shower of shrapnel. The heavy machine gun sounded like a slow-speed, single-engine motorcycle motor.

Hmmm, not good, I thought.

"Shooosh" — three heartbeats, then "Crump." *I have to do something; we can't stay here!*

CHAPTER FOUR

Somebody was shaking my shoulder. *"I can't find my rifle! I have lost my rifle!"*

"Daddy wake up!" someone said. It was a woman's voice. *"There are no women here. What is going on?"*

"Daddy, please wake up! You are having a nightmare!"

It took me a long moment to come around. My room had suddenly become O'Hare International. My daughter was standing beside my bed shaking me, my grandson was leaning in the door with a concerned look on his face, and there were two brown-and-black faces at the foot of the bed staring at me, ears up and eyes wide.

"What are you two doing in here?" I growled.

The two dogs were not allowed in the house. They slept in the entryway and normally could not even be coaxed into the living quarters. The mother was a purebred German Shepherd; the male was a 125-pound puppy. He was a product of our neighbor's purebred Chow male hopping the fence at an opportune moment and passing his Chow genes to the single offspring of that mating. Tasha had been too young to mate. Very probably the old Chow male had caught her in her very first cycle.

The result was a one-pup litter and the smartest dog I had ever seen. I swore the animal spoke English. I could talk to him in long sentences, and he would react as if he understood every word.

Both animals dropped their heads and slinked out of the room as if they had been caught killing chickens.

"You shouldn't scold them, Daddy. They were just reacting to your screaming. They were coming to protect you."

"I was screaming?" I blinked my eyes, and the room swam into focus. My grandson turned away from the door and disappeared.

"You were screaming something about, 'we can't stay here,' over and over. Was it Lebanon again?"

I seemed to have been unable to take the good director's advice. I was not putting Lebanon behind me. At least, it seemed my subconscious was still mulling it over. Evidently being confronted with the captain's presence once more had awakened the demon I thought had been put to rest some time ago.

"It wasn't really a nightmare," I admitted. "I was just back on the line, reliving the moment. It was so real…"

"Are you okay now?"

I sat up and untangled myself from the single sheet that I had been having a life-and-death struggle with. I sat up and swung my legs over the edge of the bed. My daughter took a step toward me and hugged me for a long moment before kissing my forehead and turned for the door.

"You need to try to go back to sleep, Daddy. It's 4 a.m." she said, pulling the door softly closed behind her as she left.

"Fat chance, I am up now," I thought.

I knew there would be no going back to sleep with the dream still vivid in my conscious mind. I reached up to the bed post and retrieved the navy blue robe hanging there. I stood and pulled it on debating my next move. Coffee, strong, black and lots of it. I didn't know if I really wanted coffee or if it was just an ingrained habit since plugging in the percolator was the first thing on my morning agenda every day.

I knew Amanda would have the pot ready on the kitchen counter next to the sink. She always prepared the pot just before she went upstairs to bed. She and Chance had separate rooms and shared a full bath on the second floor of the house.

It was pitch-black dark, but there was enough light in the room from a small night light in my bathroom for me to make out the outline of the bedroom door. The submarine cells in the basement fed a 12-volt system throughout the house. The public power grid had been restored for more than a year, but I had never bothered to hook back into it. I was perfectly happy to stay off-grid.

I had been a "prepper" prior to the chaos, so we had come through the worst of the trauma much more comfortably than most folks. It was good news and bad. It was the rumor of our stash of food and other commodities that had attracted the terrorists who killed my wife. It had been a fluke and a terrible, impossible accident that caused her death. Not one of the despoilers had left the property. There had been 13 of them. Maybe they should have considered the unlucky portent of their headcount before coming, but they didn't.

My grandson and I had piled their bodies on a house-size brush pile, doused them with gasoline and burnt them to a crisp, but not before I butchered a hog and soaked their individual bodies in pig blood.

I can be a vindictive sonofabitch.

The percolator was making its "gurgle-gurgle" sound, and the bobwhites were competing with the whippoorwills at the edge of the woodlot behind the house. The tree frogs were adding to the cacophony of a rural Illinois morning. I knew it would not be long before the bullfrogs down by the lake would be adding to the din, soon to be joined by the single rooster, penned up now, safe in the hen house with his charges.

I was aware of the serenade outside the kitchen window, but it was just part of the environment I had grown up in, so I took no conscious note of it. The huge, white mug with the globe and anchor symbol on its side held four regular cups. I filled it without guilt. I knew my daughter would make a fresh pot for herself and Chance when she got up later.

The girl was an unmitigated blessing.

The dogs were standing in the entryway, tails up over their back, smiling and wiggling a welcoming greeting. They were both still harboring a little guilt for coming into the house and were anxious for an ear scratch and a word of forgiveness. Bo was the male and still an overgrown puppy.

He leaped up and put his paws on either shoulder, licking my face. If I hadn't been expecting it, I would have spilled my coffee. But it was a morning ritual, so I managed. I scratched his ears with my free hand and patted his mother's head after he stood down. I let both of them out for their morning adventure. They both sprinted off for the woods, side by side and messing with each other the way they always did.

It gave me joy to watch them. An outside observer seeing the dogs interact with their family would have thought them harmless puppies. This would have been an erroneous judgment. When the terrorists came, Tasha had killed one; Bo had managed to dispatch two. The attackers shot Bo, but he had recovered completely. Any strange man was now in serious, life-threatening danger approaching our house if one of us was not there to corral the dogs.

Bo was not forgiving, and he forgot nothing.

My den is over the attached garage. When I sat down at the laptop on my desk and switched it on, a Word document popped onto the screen. It was an unfinished book that I had been writing about a gentleman in our community. He had been a National Guard officer and when the chaos was at its worst, had been by my side in the militia. To say I admired him greatly would be understating the reality of my feelings for the gentleman.

A blank screen stared back at me. I seemed to be stuck. I pushed the up arrow and pages of the segment I had written about his experiences in Viet Nam flashed down one after the other. I reached the beginning and started to read from the top of the page.

> *"I see," Delbert replied. He had a lot of respect for Eddie but did not hold him in awe like Clarence did. He had always been an employee and wondered at Eddie's ability to wrest a living out of the economy on his own. Delbert worked for TRW for 30 years, had worked himself up to the No. 3 spot in their local factory. He had always played by the rules, from being an altar boy to Eagle Scout.*
>
> *If Delbert Jones told you something, you could believe it, he held the truth as a sacrament. He had joined the National Guard right out of high school, got his commission when he graduated from* Rose-Hulman *and was activated three times. Folks in town thought of Delbert as a quiet, dependable type, always willing to lend a hand, never missed church; friendly and respectful. All of this was true. What folks didn't know was:*
>
> *Delbert was a killer.*
>
> *Most National Guard units fill in support niches in the U.S. military. Those tend to be transportation, supply, logistics and support functions that the members can bring their civilian work skills to the table when needed. Delbert commanded a small detachment of communicators that were initially intended to work in the intelligence network two or three layers behind the front lines; consolidating, filtering and putting raw intelligence in perspective so that the Washington brass could understand what*

was going on in the field. That was all well and good until the first deployment.

Viet Nam 1969

"Sergeant, this is just crap!" Captain Delbert Jones said with disgust looking down at the stack of papers on his desk. The heat was oppressive, the smell of the burning barrels was nauseating, and the early morning rocket attack had knocked out the post generator. The office inside of the Quonset hut was as dark as the captain's mood. "I can do nothing with this, it is the same shit that we have been getting for weeks; body counts for Christ sakes! I need real actionable intelligence, enemy troop movements, NVA unit numbers and deployments, something, anything we can put together, build on and send up the line," he threw the papers down on his desk, walked over to the little library book-sized window and stared out for a moment, turned around and stormed out the door.

"Sergeant, I am going to the field."

I don't mind telling you "I was pissed." The lieutenant had called me into his hutch earlier in the morning and gave me the assignment.

"There is an intelligence captain coming in from MACV this morning," the lieutenant informed me in his usual no-nonsense manner. "He has some hair up his ass about the intel he has been getting from the field and is coming out here to look around," he was studying the telex in his hand as if it were a poisonous snake. "I want you to show him around, keep him out of trouble, and for the love of God, do not make us look bad," he looked up from the telex at me, eyes moving up and down as if I were at inspection. He half smiled, evidently not too disappointed in what he saw.

"Do you know why I picked you for this detail, White? He asked, still looking at me with that semi-approving gaze.

"No sir, and if you don't mind sir, I would like to volunteer to be excused." I took a chance that if he was somewhat happy with me, maybe I could skate on this one.

"No, dammit White!" the approval look disappeared to be replaced with what I took to be frustrated disappointment. "You are a smart guy, E5 Sergeant in less than a year, turned down OCS ...by the way, why did you?" He was now looking at me with some concern that maybe his first idea wasn't the greatest.

"My dad was at Omaha beach, el Tee." I jumped right in; I had this part memorized, the Army had been trying to drag me kicking and screaming into OCS since basic battery testing at boot camp. "He told me first and second lewies," I paused and inserted, "begging your pardon Sir," he nodded, and I continued, "had a life expectancy of minutes."

He didn't reply, so I went on with my spiel, "he said sergeants who lived through the first couple of days came home to raise families." That got zero response, so I guessed I needed to add the kicker. "Sir, I plan to go home and raise a family." That, by the way, was an out-and-out lie. Bill and I had figured out long ago; long by Nam standards, a couple months actually, that we were already dead; but I had recited my little soliloquy so many times it was hard to change in the field, on the fly.

"Look, Sergeant, I don't give a damn if your dad was at Gettysburg. Understand me Sergeant?" The approving look had long since departed to somewhere back in the world on R&R.

"Yes, Sir." I am a slow learner, but the Army is pretty persuasive and adept at teaching some things. This was one of those things. The lieutenant asks the sergeant if he understands. The sergeant replies, "Yes, Sir," even if he doesn't have the ghost of a notion of what the lieutenant is talking about. I know it seems counterintuitive, but that is how the Army works.

"White, I want you to meet this captain, keep him out of trouble, show him around and get him the hell out of here," he stopped, and I waited for the inevitable . . . sure enough, "Do you understand me, Sergeant?"

"Yes, Sir," I replied brilliantly.

An hour later, brushed, polished and pressed as I could get in a forward OP, I stood at parade rest as the chopper doors opened. The first thing I noticed, it was a General's personal bird. The little plate that held the stars was, of course, empty, since it was only bearing a captain and it was landing in Indian country. Even a General's pride plays second fiddle to his ass. I was expecting some sissy civilian looking dude with coke-bottle-bottom glasses to come sneaking out the door, looking everywhere for Charlie to come bounding down into the LZ, spooked at every noise.

Much to my surprise, John Wayne stepped down from the chopper. He was tall, probably six foot two, at least, solid black hair, cut close, Marine style. His field camos bore neither rank nor insignia. The tiny twin bars embroidered on his hat were the same color and barely distinguishable across the 12 feet separating us.

He turned and secured his gear from the chopper. He came out with a black rifle and some civilian ruck with an aluminum frame. It looked like he meant business. He bowed his head in deference to the rotor tips and walked up to me.

I saluted, expecting some Guard slouch in the general direction of his forehead, to my surprise, he snapped to attention and returned my salute as if on a West Point parade ground. I didn't know what to think. If I had known what kind of man Delbert Jones was, I would have turned and run right through the wire. It would have been safer.

After introductions were out of the way, I thought I should follow orders and get the good captain safely ensconced on a shelf somewhere. "Sir I will take you over to the officer's hooch and get you set. . ." That was as far as I got.

"Sergeant, I didn't come all the way out here to lounge around at a firebase," he said in a tone that brooked no argument. "I came out here to go to the field," he sat the fancy pack down on the tarmac, unzipped a pocket and retrieved a map. I had never seen a map like it. It looked to be imprinted on silk or something. He was studying the map and ignoring me. Later I learned that was a good thing, but like the dummy that I am, I couldn't let it go.

"Sir, the lieutenant said that it would probably be safer if you …" I stopped because the look that I received from under those bushy black eyebrows would have killed an entire Viet Cong squad in their sandals. "…or not," I whispered under my breath. "Sir, if you are bound and determined to go out beyond the wire, there will be a couple of patrols going out this eve…" I got the same look, more Cong died behind me out beyond the wire.

"Sergeant, I came out here to gather intelligence," he looked at me as if he were explaining something very simple to someone very stupid. "How much intelligence have you seen inside this wire?" He asked as he swept his arm around pointing to the periphery of the base. I had to admit, he had a point.

"When do you plan on going out, Captain?" I asked, though I knew it was a rhetorical question, he had picked up his ruck, slung that black rifle and was headed for the west gate in long strides. He ignored me and kept walking. I did get him slowed down enough for me to grab my ruck, my rifle and a few odds and ends that might make our camping trip in Indian country a bit more comfortable.

We had been humping all day toward the west. The captain didn't talk much beyond the wire. In fact, he hadn't said a damn word all day. He also didn't stop much. For some damn pansy guardsman, he was the savviest woodsman I had ever followed. He avoided the footpaths but seemed to have a sixth sense for finding game trails and natural breaks in the undergrowth. He had absolutely no compunctions about wading off into the paddies, and across streams, but never raised his head above the dikes like one would expect an FNG to do.

We followed that setting sun like it was leading us to nirvana somewhere. I was in the best shape of my life, but my legs were burning, my breath was coming in gasps, and I was about to request a halt when we came to the edge of a tree line. He held up his hand and stopped behind some dense undergrowth. The sun was setting over some low foothills just beyond. There was a river flowing right to left a mile or so to our west.

He stopped at the tree line and retrieved that fancy map. He studied it for a short time, got out his compass, took a shot at the horizon, looked around at our surroundings and spoke his first words on the hump.

"This should do for this evening, don't you think, Sergeant?" If I had ever heard a rhetorical question, that was it. Actually, it could have hardly been a better spot. It was on a slight rise above the surrounding terrain; there was a long hummock stretching away from a massive teak just to the north. We could tuck in behind the little ridge beneath the brush, set our claymores on both flanks, yep, it looked like home.

"Do you know what river that is, Sergeant?" He asked, softly, almost reverently.

"Yes, Sir, it is the Ia Drang," I whispered back.

"Damn, this is Indian country, isn't it Sergeant?" He said with a grin that chilled me to my core. He was lovin' this stuff! That is when I started to get really, really scared.

We were setting up our position; I had put out the claymores when the captain pulled out a tube from his pack. It looked like the base of a large flashlight. When he opened one end, it revealed a string of what looked like little bells of varying sizes stacked one on another. I looked at him quizzically.

"Captain?" I asked, looking at the contents in his hands.

"This is an idea I had," he said. "I removed the clappers from these bells so they would stack and not make any noise while they are being carried, but strung out in different quadrants the various sizes will give us a directional indication if anyone gets too close."

"Sir, I hate to rain on your parade, but the slightest little breeze in the night is going to ring those damn bells," I said skeptically. "What is wrong with mess tins?"

"Just how many mess tins do we have, Sergeant?" He asked as if talking to a four-year-old. He had a point, the foil coverings for the freeze dried LRP rations we were carrying would not be much of an alarm system.

"Look, if you string them like this ..." he explained as he slid them onto some fishing line from the pack, pre-knotted at intervals. "The wind blowing won't deflect them enough to ring, but when the string is distorted by being stepped on, or moved," he demonstrated as he tinkled a couple together. Unlike the lieutenant, he did not ask me if I understood but crawled out of our little nest into the growing darkness to start setting up his alarm system. I thought it was a bogus affectation, but if it made him happy, what the hell.

He returned some time later humming to himself, "silver bells, silver bells," he sang the lyrics softly as he came back into the little cave in the brush we had carved for our night time hide. "If those ring, it won't be sounding a lot like Christmas," he finished his little song as he crawled in and made a spot for himself where he could watch to the west, I was lying beside him where I could watch our back. We had eaten and finished our first canteen. It was going to be a long night.

"Captain," I whispered, "what are we doing?" I asked, knowing that I was not going to like the answer. Before he could say anything, I added. "You do know this is crazy, don't you sir?"

"No sergeant, this isn't crazy, but tomorrow you are going to meet crazy." His voice came softly out of the pitch black dark. I thought he was finished, but after a while, he went on.

"There is this major; he has been out here in the valley for almost six weeks, by himself, watching the NVA build-up. He has a prisoner. We are going to relieve him of said prisoner and bring him back for questioning," he said the last as if to say we were going to meet at the club for lunch. About 20 excellent questions immediately popped into my head following that revelation. Like, why us, why just two grunts, on foot, in hostile territory? Why not chopper him out? Why not ...?

I kept my peace.

To my surprise, the captain actually started to fill in some of the details. "This is one of the few operations of this type that has been successful. The Army has tried inserting teams behind enemy lines since this thing started in 1966. The casualty rate has been almost 100 percent. This major, I don't even know his name, lost his partner on another mission in Cambodia last year. He won't accept anyone else; goes out alone now," he said with awe in his voice. "He has been operating out here off and on since this thing started in '64," he paused a moment, then added, "that — sergeant, is crazy."

I thought about it for a bit, then opined, "Captain, this just isn't done, a major tooling around in the boonies by himself, you and me stumbling around in the NVA's back yard. . ." I left the thought unfinished; the incongruity of the whole thing was mind-boggling. He didn't reply for quite a long time; I thought perhaps he had gone to sleep. It was my watch, after all.

"The major is from another era; he was out here when our presence was limited to advisers. They did things a lot differently back then; besides, he's a green beanie mustang, got his commission in the field," he whispered softly then paused for another long period before continuing. "I'm 'Guard' on a voluntary deployment, no one much cares one way or the other what I do as long as I produce." After another rather long silence, he concluded. "I'm producing, Sergeant."

The night had passed uneventfully, and we had gathered in our accouterments from the bush. The captain, who had been hell-bent on getting out here yesterday, seemed in no hurry to go any further. He was lying prone scanning the river in the distance with a small set of binoculars.

"What now Captain?" I asked, my impatience showing.

"Now, we wait, Sergeant," he replied, his eyes still glued to the binoculars. A bit later he added. "I am reasonably sure; we are where we should be. The good major will come to us," he said, finally finished with his observations he slid back from the hummock, turned and sat back against the hill, hands on his knees with the binoculars held loosely in his left hand. How the major would ever find us was a mystery to me. The little cave we had wallowed out of the brush was almost perfect concealment. One could walk by close enough to reach out and touch and never see us.

"You know we are bailing out on this country, don't you Sergeant?" The captain asked after a while. He was gazing off

into the brush looking at a place somewhere in the future. He clearly did not like what he saw.

"Bailing out sir?" I asked, but I understood his meaning alright. I just didn't buy it. From what I could see, we had pretty well wiped out the Cong during Tet in '67 and were kicking the NVA's ass anytime they stood and fought. At Khe Sahn, we had sent a whole division of Uncle Ho's finest on to their final slant-eyed reward. From my point of view, the war was won, all we were doing now was mopping up.

"I came through Tokyo on my way in country," the captain replied with what seemed to be a non-sequitur and then continued. "I met with a contractor from my hometown; he is working there at Fuchu, fifth air force HQ. He is installing a worldwide direct dial system for the military," he paused for a second and then continued. "Garet told me that he had been assigned to come to Saigon later this year to install a modern telephone system for Saigon. That the equipment had been shipped and was sitting in a warehouse at one of the bases, waiting for his crew to come down and install it. Then, for no expressed reason, the project was canceled."

"I'm sorry sir, I don't get the connection."

"Good money after bad, someone has decided that we are not going to be around to use those telephones, so why expend the funds to install it."

"But sir, we are winning the war!" I exclaimed. This was insane, all the heartbreaking casualties, the mountains of dollars expended and we were just going to walk away! I didn't buy it. He might be a captain, but what he was saying just didn't make any sense.

The captain turned and looked at me for what seemed a long time. His expression indicated sympathy and understanding. "I know, Sergeant. It makes no sense in the real world.

Unfortunately, these things are not decided in the real world. This war, like most wars, will be decided finally, in the political world," he said sadly. "At home, the political winds have turned against this war. The lefties in the Congress are smelling blood. As soon as they can, they are going to turn off the money. When they do, it is all over."

I still didn't buy it, but his words left me with a sinking feeling. I was suddenly aware of a sense of foreboding that I hadn't experienced before. I would have liked to continue the conversation, but the captain was suddenly preoccupied with some movement at the edge of the forest 50 yards to our rear. I hadn't been looking in that direction, so I had missed it.

Following the captain's focus, I too saw the apparition moving toward us through the jungle. It looked like a scarecrow in ill-fitting, filthy camos wearing an Aussie bush hat, one side pinned up, pulled so far down on his forehead that his bearded face was barely visible beneath. He was carrying what appeared to be a pump-action shotgun with a sling hanging loosely beneath it. He wore crossed bandoliers of shotgun shells across his chest with a sling-supported shoulder holster under his left arm which revealed the butt of a 1911 held therein. He walked directly to the entrance of our little hideout and stopped.

"Doctor Watson, I presume," he said surprisingly. I would have bet my life, literally, that we were invisible in our little aerie.

"Good morning Major," the captain said as he exited out of the brush to the rear, stood and came to attention. I saw his right hand come up. "OMG he is going to salute," I thought to myself, remembering the West Point act from the base; but he didn't, he held out his hand. The major took his hand with a smile, and they shook as if old friends reunited after a long separation. "I am glad to see you, Captain," the major said.

"I am honored to see you, Major …?" The captain said with a question in his voice.

"Bill Wilson, Captain, I see your info was a bit sketchy, right?"

"Sketchy is not the word; I could have gotten more information on a ghost. In fact, that is what a lot of folks refer to you as, the 'Jungle Ghost.'"

The major chuckled a bit at that little tidbit of information, then inquired, "You wouldn't happen to have something to eat in there, would you?"

"Oh, of course, come on in," the captain pointed toward the entrance and waited for the major to enter. I was uncomfortable. I had never met a senior officer in the bush, wasn't quite sure of the protocol, knew a salute in the bush wasn't correct, so I held my position. "Major Wilson, Sergeant White," the captain made introductions. The major half way nodded in my direction, took off his hat and seemed to collapse into a seated position, his back against the berm at the rear of our makeshift cave. When his hat came off I was shocked, he looked like a refugee from a concentration camp. I had never seen such an emaciated, worn out, shadow of a man, the dark circles under his eyes were painful to look at.

We sat in silence and watched as the major polished off two of our "breakfast" LRPs. "I could eat two more of those, but I had better take it easy, I'll make myself sick," he said with a sigh as he sank back against the bank behind him. "Now, a brandy and a Monte Cristo, and I would be a happy camper," he related dreamily, "then three or four days' solid sleep." He let his eyes close for an instant and then snapped awake.

"Where is the prisoner, Major?" The captain asked gently as if inquiring as to where he had laid his car keys.

The major did not reply immediately staring at the captain as if he were seeing a vision or something beyond his understanding. Finally, he seemed to shake himself mentally and focused. "I had to shoot him," he said quietly. "It got to be too much, two of us moving through the bush." He didn't finish the thought seeming to run down like a wind-up train. He looked away from the captain, and his eyes appeared to light on me. The major looked at me for what seemed a long time. "How old are you son?" he asked softly.

"Nineteen, Sir," I replied with a smile. He reacted as if I had slapped him.

"Nineteen, Nineteen," he mumbled, "Nine fucking teen, Jesus, son what the fuck are you doing out here?" He exclaimed, suddenly seeming to be overcome with emotion. There didn't appear to be any pat answer, so I kept my silence. So did the captain. We were both looking at the major as if he were some display out of a crazy wax museum. The embarrassing silence was hanging in the air as if it wanted to choke us all. He finally shook himself again and looked over at the captain.

"I'm coming out Delbert; I'm at the end of my rope." As he said this, he seemed to deflate and shrink to even a smaller, thinner shadow of himself. "I've got it all here, in my journal," he said, tapping a lump in his vest beneath one of the bandoliers. "Unit numbers, troop counts, staging areas. I've got it all," he said flatly, and then began to weep, softly at first, then long anguished sobs. The captain looked as if he was going to go over and try to console him, but I caught his eye and shook my head slightly. I didn't know how I knew, but I knew it wasn't the right thing to do.

After a while, the sobs ran down and the major sat, his head in his hands, rocking back and forth. "I didn't want to shoot the sorry son of a bitch," he whispered between his fingers. "I really didn't," he looked up at us with a pleading expression as if seeking dispensation. "I actually lost it, this time, ...weeks without any human contact ...being hunted like an animal ...then that squirrelly little colonel falls into my lap ...taking a shit ...running again ...hiding ...both of us starving."

He lapsed into silence, remembering, hurting, and then continued. "He was a bright little bugger, went to school in Paris ...loved the ladies ...hated Ho, but loved this country ...and then he had to run... a crying shame, crying shame," he shook his head, then seemed to re-inflate, sat up straight, slipped his hat on, lifted his chin, slipped the drawstring beneath his chin and declared. "Well, gentlemen, shall we?"

We were on our way back to the world. Ready or not, we were coming back inside the wire.

The major and the captain had a short parlay on how to proceed. We had no communication with the outside world, so we were going to have to hoof it back. Unless we ran into a patrol or other U.S. unit, we were on our own.

The major had been communicating through drops where he would leave messages and reports at a particular point to be picked up and brought to the MACV intelligence unit that was running his operation. He never wanted a chopper landing closer than a day's march away giving up his location. That had been the key to his success for years. The downside was it was strictly one-way communication.

The captain's HQ was way the hell and gone to the South far out of reach of any hand-carried radio so the only radio he brought was the little line of sight box that the pilots took for communication with rescue birds. We might catch a stray with it, but the odds were not favorable. The two officers were taking inventory of our supply situation.

"What is that rifle you are carrying, Captain?" the major asked.

"It is an M14 carbine," the captain replied, turning it right side up where the action was visible and very obviously M14.

"I never heard of a carbine version of the M14," the major said skeptically.

"It is specially made for me by our armorer at the Guard unit in Paris," the captain explained. "The stock is a new material they have been experimenting with; carbon fiber. The barrel is stainless, shortened and fitted with a flash suppressor and muzzle brake," he handed the weapon to the major. "See, it is not much heavier than an AR15." The major took it and balanced it in his left hand, and then handing it back nodded his agreement.

"That is good, Captain, but how many rounds can you pack to the field?"

"Yes, I know, that is seen as a problem, but I've got 150 rounds of 7.62 on me." The captain acknowledged one of the shortcomings of the big rifle; the ammo was heavy. "But here is the thing, I know I can fire all 150 of 'em even after crawling through a paddy." The captain punted back, referring to the M16's propensity for deciding to malfunction at decidedly inopportune times versus the M14's legendary reliability.

"How many mags you got for the M16 Sergeant?" The major asked, now apparently taking command.

"Ten Sir, on my vest," I answered, reflecting that I actually had 330 rounds available. I noticed that the major did not add his shotgun rounds to the inventory. I also noticed that he would be traveling light, all he had was a couple of canteens and a little web pack that couldn't hold much more than some foul weather gear.

I was mentally psyching myself up for another hard slog back to the base. I shouldn't have bothered. Following the captain had been like trying to keep up with a long-distance runner in serious competition. Following the major was like attempting to follow a cloud. He led off into the jungle and disappeared. Where the captain had sniffed out game trails and natural breaks, the major merely melted into the jungle. It was an entirely different game.

Instead of steady head-down slogging, we would take a few steps, stop, reconnoiter, wait, look some more, then take a few quiet running steps across a planned route, pointed out with care by the major to the next concealment spot. It became apparent, what had taken us a full day at a forced march would take a week at this rate.

Every so often the major would call the captain up, point out something of interest, they would discuss, the captain would nod his head in acknowledgment and we would proceed. Sometimes we actually took established trails, the major seemed to know the routes that the NVA used and would not be mined or booby-trapped. We made good time on those legs.

At noon, we stopped in a small clearing under an old Banyan tree. Evidently the root limbs hanging down like long white stalactites in a circle around the main trunk made for adequate concealment that the major was comfortable with a short break.

"Sergeant, I owe you an apology," the captain said as he knelt down beside me while I was digging into one of my last LRPs. "I could have . . . no, should have, gotten us killed on that sprint out here."

"Luck's a Lady, sir." I appreciated the captain's new found knowledge of jungle craft, but I had spent enough time in the bush to know that the captain's self-flagellation was somewhat misplaced. He had done alright. We were living proof.

"Sir, if we don't pick up the pace we are going to run out of everything," I added needlessly to take some edge off of his beating himself up. We had brought one extra day rations when we left, which meant we had enough for the two of us for four days. Adding the major cut it down to a couple of days with one already gone.

I mean I really appreciated all of this "Heart of Darkness" stuff, but I was anxious to get back to the base, have a shower and a hot meal. I had enjoyed hanging out with a "Snake Eater" about as much as I could stand. Besides all that crying stuff had somewhat tempered my hero worship. That all changed when we came across an enemy platoon setting up to ambush a U.S. patrol.

It was getting close to sunset, and I was beginning to get a little antsy about getting us set for the night. In the jungle there isn't a lot of twilight, the sun goes down and boom, it is cold, black dark, like someone flipped a switch. I didn't want to be stumbling around in the dark, trying to find a place to shelter for the night.

The major had taken us off the main trail to a little game trail that ran somewhat parallel. He was on point about 15 yards ahead. He suddenly stopped cold, raised his hand and went to his knee. We followed suit instantly. The major rose slowly, looking left and right, then in a crouch ran back to where we were kneeling.

"There is an NVA ambush being set up just ahead on both sides of the main trail," the Major whispered. "I have been tracking this platoon for a week now; they are mean sons-a-bitches. They specialize in ambushes, fan out far from their primary units and carry a lot of heavy firepower," he said with a tight grin. That worried me; talk of ambushes and grinning didn't seem to mix.

"That is the bad news," he continued, "the good news is: when they get all that firepower set up to cover the ambush area their fields of fire are very limited to protect each other, and it is hard to get those heavy weapons up and turned around," he had been talking very low just above a whisper, our heads together so we could hear.

"Sergeant, have you been in a firefight?" He was still taking inventory.

"Yes, Sir." I had seen my share but didn't think he wanted any war stories.

"Well, gentlemen, to quote General Patton, 'this is where we grab 'em by the hair an' kick'em in the ass.'" There was that scary grin again; I was beginning to think I preferred the crying. "How many claymores ya got?"

"Three Sir."

"OK, gimme one," he ordered. "I am going to cross the main trail, move up to engage on the right. You two move around to the left, quiet like, and try to get your claymores positioned to take at least some of them in the rear, when you hear my claymore go off, kick 'em in the ass, understand?" This was not the lieutenant's "understand?" This was honest-to -God, your-life-may-depend-on-it understand. The captain and I looked at each other. I nodded.

"Yes, Sir," the captain replied for both of us.

The major dug around in his little pack and came up with a clapper, grinned and disappeared into the jungle without a sound. The captain and I circled slowly around through the undergrowth in the diminishing light.

The captain came to the edge of a little clearing, parted the grass carefully with his M14 barrel then, slowly let it close. He pointed to the small hump of dirt beneath where his barrel had been. I held up one finger, he shook his head, held up two. I handed him my claymore, he put his on top of the dirt pointing directly away from us and placed the one I had been carrying a couple feet to its left. He slid back a little way toward me trailing the electrical wires.

He motioned me back; we retreated about 35 feet where he hooked the wires to the clapper. He held up his hand and gave the signals, seven soldiers direct ahead five to seven meters. I signaled back a question: Should I flank right or left? He replied back, "No, follow me directly over the mines." The light was fading fast. I slipped the safety off my M16 and waited.

KaBOOM! The unmistakable explosion of the Claymore across the trail was followed closely by our two simultaneous KaBOOMs; the captain was already up, charging through the huge gaps in the brush cut by the Claymores.

"Bam, Bam, Bam!" From across the trail, the crash of the shotgun followed the Claymore explosion.

"Bulaap, Bulaap!" The distinct sound of the 7.62 on single fire came ringing back from where the captain had disappeared ahead. I jumped to my feet and started pounding toward the action. I almost ran into an NVA soldier who was struggling to get his heavy machine gun up and around to bear on me. Evidently the captain had run right over him. He had been so close to our position that the Claymore balls had sailed right over his head.

"Blap, Blap!" The M16 sounded like a cap gun compared to the M14 and the shotgun, but it did the job. The enemy soldier collapsed over the machine gun.

I looked up to a scene of complete carnage. The Claymores had torn the heart out of the half of platoon of soldiers on our side of the trail; there was blood, uniform parts, guns, and flesh in writhing piles at my feet. The captain seemed to be engaged in a firefight with a single soldier who had been flanked far left enough to have avoided the initial blast of the Claymores. The enemy soldier had taken cover behind a fallen tree and was spraying the area in our direction with automatic fire from his AK. Luckily, most of it was going well over our heads.

From the other side of the trail, the shotgun blasts had been replaced with AK fire and the occasional Whap, Whap of a 1911 .45. Soon the AK fire was silenced. The only fire was now coming from the enemy soldier ahead of us behind the log. I had gone prone after shooting the soldier now lying beside me and was considering how I could get close enough to toss him a grenade when I heard a single Whap! from his direction. The AK fire ceased abruptly. I looked up to see the major walking our way up the trail; that evil grin plastered all over his face.

It was getting seriously dark. We needed to get out of here while we still could. "Major?" I pointed at my watch. He said nothing, just nodded and gave the signal to follow him. We gathered up our rucks where we had dropped them behind us and followed him. We didn't go far. Within 300 yards, with the light barely sufficient to see his signal, he guided us off the trail, around a grove of teaks to a clearing between the trunks. It was a sweet spot, dry and elevated with the trees for cover. The captain indicated that he would take the first watch. I collapsed against the sweet smelling root of a teak and went immediately to sleep.

I stood one watch in the night, staring into the black dark and listening to the noises of the jungle, once in a while a faint shaft of white moonlight filtered through the canopy causing eerie shadows out beyond our position. The captain's little bells remained silent, so we stayed tucked in until I was shaken gently from a troubled dream filled sleep by the major and awoke to the soft light of a false dawn. We were moving shadows once again.

Our little adventure ended in an anticlimax; we came on the patrol that the ambush was set up to intercept. After a couple of tense moments, while recognition of all parties was established, we were back in radio contact with the world. A chopper was called in, and we were lifted out of the bush and back into the world.

I stared at the blank page thinking about my 19-year-old grandson and all that he had been witness to right here at home. The trauma he had experienced without leaving the county exceeded anything I could write about, even though Delbert swore every word of the narrative I had related was word-for-word fact.

I decided I needed to talk to Delbert about this latest mission the governor had saddled me with. I made up my mind to drive over to his place first thing this morning.

CHAPTER FIVE

I sat and stared at the blank screen for some time willing something to well up out of the cloudy corridors of my mind that would make sense out of the "Alice-through-the-looking-glass world" in which we were living.

I was trying to write a novel based on the supposition the Washington immolation never happened. I wanted my story to be full of hope reflecting the shining city on a hill that Ronald Reagan saw when he looked at the country using the particular prism through which he viewed his world. I kept running up against the dark stone wall of reality that stubbornly refused to crack open and allow an optimistic glimmer of light shine through.

The ugly truth was the country had been heading for a cliff like an old bus full of party revelers, drunk with success and filled with hubris. The country had been drifting leftward since Wilson dragged us into a European war on behalf of the banks that stood to take a bath if

Germany won. We were denied the inconclusive finish that would have left the old order still in place, battered and bloodied after four years of war, but in place to muddle along for another couple generations.

The U.S.'s involvement tipped the scales too radically in favor of the French and British, who then could not help themselves, and sought to dip deeply into Germany's already empty treasury, setting the stage for the next conflagration.

The next war resulted in the death of the idea of America as it was founded. Too much power accrued to the central government. There was an incomprehensible amount of money flowing to Washington attracting the worst lot of politicians ever foisted on a people.

The Democrats sent amoral and immoral folks to the Capitol with their only mandate being to rob the treasury and send the proceeds back to their constituencies. They were aided and abetted by a media populated with legions of j-school grads indoctrinated in statist theology.

When things got so bad under the mismanagement of the leftists that the people called for change, the Republicans were called on to straighten things out. When they arrived in Washington, all bright-eyed and bushy-tailed ready to clean house, they shortly became enamored of the power, glitz and money afforded the people's servants, and, for the most part, could not keep their own fingers out of the cookie jar.

The people became disillusioned and tuned out of the process. No good could come of it.

Try as I might, I could not imagine a good ending to the direction the country was going prior to the fall. If I could not imagine it, I could not put the pixels on the screen.

I finally gave up. My coffee was cold.

By the time I had come down to the attached garage and pulled on a one-piece cotton leisure suit, the sun was peeking up over the woods. It came up a menacing red. There was rain in the offing. The suit smelled of fabric softener. I gave my daughter a mental hug. She was priceless.

Both dogs came bounding back to join me when they heard the garage door open. They ran around me in a circle, wagging and smiling. The puppy had been named Bojangles because of his proclivity to dance. They were begging for a walk. In their world, there was only one thing better than going for a ride in the back of the pick-up and that was going for a morning walk.

I had two four-mile routes that took me around the periphery of the farm. One went down to the Mill Creek Lake; the other ran along the western edge of the place and the ridge overlooking Interstate 70. These runs accomplished a number of objectives. They exercised the dogs, kept my wind in shape, let me examine the fences and keep an eye on the different pastures so I would know when to move the cattle.

My grandson liked to tease me about running with him but experience told me those runs always turned into a competition, and the last year, the 36-year handicap was beginning to show. My grandson thought I leaped tall buildings, and I didn't want to disillusion him.

I called my morning sojourn with the dogs, "walks" but I pushed it. I always completed the four miles in less than an hour and usually in 40 minutes. It was more like a walking jog. Since some of the routes included hills and ran through areas of tall grass, it was a pretty good workout.

I had an old mechanical stopwatch that I used to time my journey but this morning I didn't start it immediately. I stopped at the concrete block outbuilding that set off 100 yards from the house in the direction of Mill Creek. The generator building was the size of a one-car garage and held two natural gas-fed generators.

The katunk, katunk of the single-cylinder engine could be heard faintly through the insulated steel when I came up to the door. I pushed in the combination above the latch and opened to a pitch black interior. The single 100-watt bulb revealed two identical motors when I finally found the switch. They were salvaged from the Martinsville oil fields where they had powered pumps there for years. The motors had massive flywheels and ran at some ridiculously low RPM. As a result, they ran for decades with little maintenance.

Once a week, I switched the motors powering the house, sheds, and barn. This allowed me to do any maintenance necessary on a cold motor and not lose power. Both engines were connected to a single shaft by belts wrapped around wheels on each engine's power shaft. I turned on the gas to the offline engine and engaged the belt tensioner to start the flywheel turning on the standby motor. The running engine bogged down a bit under the added strain, but soon both motors were thunking away powering, the old DC oil-field motor I had rewired, turning it into a gen set. It provided the farm with 20KW of power.

I locked up and muttered a prayer of thanksgiving for the natural gas well that kept our farm powered and fueled. The well had been drilled some time before the chaos, but the planned pipeline to bring it online for the company that had drilled it never happened. Part of the lease had been for them to hook up the house and generator shed to the operating gas well. Luckily, or providentially, depending on one's viewpoint, they had completed that portion of the contract.

Both of my tractors, my combine, baler and the one-ton pickup had been modified to run on natural gas as well. This allowed us to keep going even in the worst of the traumatic time. We had been able to salvage enough legacy seed from the old Harvestore silo my stepdad had installed after WW2 to put out a crop the first year.

That one crop provided seed for us and some of our neighbors to continue farming until the system started producing seed corn four years later. I don't know how many times I had thanked God for the broken auger which left more than a 100 bushels of corn trapped in the air-tight silo for years.

We ate a lot of cornbread that first year.

We kept enough seed to plant 80 acres. We didn't get the kind of yield from the old legacy seed the hybrids provided, but we were able to fill the 6,000-bushel silo at harvest.

The first couple of years had put a significant dent in my herd, but they were coming back. When my brother and his wife had been killed in a motorcycle accident, I had inherited his adjoining 600 acres. I had added his 80 head of Charolais to my short-horn purebreds and let my short-horn bull run with the combined herd. The tan calves that result from the cross-breeding are handsome and I felt the resulting herd was healthier.

This morning I decided to check what had been my brother's fields along the lake, so I jogged down to the bottom of the ravine to walk along the spring-fed creek at the bottom. Both dogs went on ahead of me running along on either side of the creek. It was more like a brook since we hadn't had rain for more than a week. Without runoff, the spring fed a steady stream about a foot wide in most places but widened out to pools three or four feet across where the running water had uncovered slabs of limestone more impervious to its nibbling away at the landscape.

I jog-walked along jumping from rock to rock, familiar with every step — I had run this route from childhood. The hollow stretched up on either side the height of a three-story building. It became darker as the woods on either side grew thicker. Nearer the lake, the timber hadn't been cut for 30 years, so some of the hickories and oaks were getting some size on them. I noticed one tree near the creek where the last heavy rain had caused the runoff to carve a large chunk of soil from beneath its root ball.

"It won't last long now; it needs to come down this fall for next year's firewood," I thought as the south-running creek made a hard turn to the east opening up onto a view down the length of the lake. Before the bad time, there had been pleasure boats and skiers on the lake. Today I saw one aluminum rowboat pulled up 50 yards away with an old man and

a little girl fishing. I had been enjoying my walk, remembering my childhood and enjoying my time with the dogs. The stark reality of the empty lake brought everything crashing back.

I hated that.

I turned left and looked at the footpath leading to the top of the north hill. I took a deep breath and attacked it at a run. By the time I topped the hill with both dogs right behind me I was panting, and my heart was racing. As I broke out of the woods, the wheat field in front of me stretched out almost to the horizon. It was 300 acres in one plot, the largest single field on the farm.

I clicked the stopwatch off and walked out into the blowing wheat, pulled off a head and rubbed it together between my palms to free the kernels. I popped a couple in my mouth and tasted the nutty goodness of the fully ripe grain. I knew it was ready from the darkening color, but the taste confirmed it. This field needed to be cut.

I walked out deeper into the field pulling the standing wheat aside in different spots to inspect the clover growing beneath. It was thick and green; it would shoot up as soon as we cut the grain and let the sun get to it. I was happy with what I saw. It took off some of the edge from my angst of seeing the empty lake.

"Preterup, preterup.." The distinctive sound of a BSA single-cylinder motorcycle interrupted my anticipation of the wheat harvest. I looked up to see my grandson flying down the edge of the wheat field in my direction standing up on the footpegs of the old motorcycle as it bounced and danced beneath him. I could see his grin across the eighth of a mile that separated us. He had been riding motorcycles since he was five and was as relaxed as if he were on an escalator.

He came bouncing up to me and slid the bike sideways stopping mere inches away. He was still grinning.

"Bapaw, Mr. Fraser stopped by on his way back from town when I was going down to milk," Chance informed me. "He said you should know: John Palmer is back in town."

Reality bites.

John Palmer was bad news. He hated me with a cold, hard intensity that was difficult to describe or to even understand. John Palmer was a bully, a bar fighter and next to a particular captain of Marines, the biggest asshole I ever met. His displeasure with yours truly began many years ago when my younger brother had put him in hospital after John had started a fight with him outside of the American Legion. John had started it; my brother Burdett had more than finished it.

I had experienced a couple of run-ins with him in my capacity as a peace officer. The last time I had apprehended him and a couple of his cohorts with two heifers belonging to someone else in the back of their truck. This altercation resulted in one of his partners lying dead in the road, with another seriously wounded by pellets from the same load of double-aught buck that killed the first one. Mr. Palmer himself would walk with a decided limp for the rest of his life caused by wounds incurred at knee level by the second discharge of my Benelli.

Some people will not listen to reason. Pulling handguns on a deputy who has the drop on you with a 12-gauge shotgun is just plain dumb.

Mr. Palmer had spent the past two years as a guest of the county at the county farm. The county lockup after the trouble was not a place one would want to spend much time as a guest. It was more like a concentration camp where no nonsense was tolerated; work was required, and the food was barely adequate to forestall starvation.

I had been informed that Mr. Palmer blamed me for his incarceration, his wounds and his general lack of good humor. It was rumored that upon release he had intended to find me and wreak some vengeance upon my graying head.

Chance informed me of the imminent arrival of trouble in the person of Mr. Palmer with an anticipatory smile.

"I almost feel sorry for him, Bapaw."

Chance has an outsized estimation of my capabilities. I wasn't exactly afraid of the man, but I certainly was wary of him. He was a back shooter and an evil SOB. Having him floating around in the background was not something I particularly relished or something I could afford to let slide. I would have to deal with it; more likely sooner, than later.

***

Indian Ocean – Day of attack on Washington, D.C.

The United States Ballistic Missile Submarine Maine was cruising at operating depth just north of Diego Garcia in the Indian Ocean when the word came that the National Capital had been obliterated from the face of the earth.

This message caused no small consternation among the senior officers present.

"This can't be happening!" the executive officer exclaimed in denial.

"It came in from Raven Rock, sir. It is the real McCoy," the communications chief told him.

The captain's expression was grim. His mind was moving at warp speed running through the multitude of different war plans and scenarios he had been trained to react to. This was not one of them.

"Was there any hint of who hit us?"

"No, Sir," the chief responded. "There was no radar warning. It looks like it must have been delivered by truck or heavy van to the blast site."

"Did we receive any orders from Pennsylvania?" the captain asked doubtfully. He knew that if there had been orders it would have been the first thing he was told. He was still acting from the first stage of grief, denial.

"Nothing sir, we are told to stand by."

"Who is running things?"

"Really sir, it sounds like no one is at the present moment. They are still trying to sort out who is left of the Cabinet to take charge. It looks like the entire Cabinet was in Washington for the president's address to the joint session of Congress."

"My God man, you mean to tell me the entire government of the USA has been destroyed?"

"One moment sir, there is an encrypted message coming in. It will take me a few minutes; this is the highest level of security. I will have to decrypt it by hand." It seemed to take hours for the message to track across the screen. The data rate for the low-frequency radio was uncommonly slow.

The gaggle of officers gathered outside the door to the radio room had grown to a half-dozen, effectively blocking the hallway. Two more were on their way coming up the hall to join the quorum.

"GQ gentlemen, the boat is at General Quarters, duty stations — please!" The captain said please, but it was clearly an order. The crowd broke up leaving the old man and the exec standing alone in the darkened hallway.

"My God sir, it is the combinations," the first-class communications tech looked up from his partially decrypted pad with an alarmed look on his face. "It has to be real ...the combinations!"

In order to make certain a rogue captain or even rogue group of officers could not fire their missiles without authorization, the launch codes were stored in two separate safes. Without the codes from both safes being inputted simultaneously, the missiles could not be launched.

Since the past few administrations were much more concerned about our military starting an accidental war than they were about our weapons actually be able to function, they had loaded safety upon safety to the point there was a question as to whether the systems could actually be made to work in an emergency at all.

Certain Admirals in the silent service took umbrage at this insane policy of sending men and officers into harm's way with no means of using the billion-dollars-plus weapon for which they were responsible.

"I already have the combinations, Sparks. What else does it say?" the captain told the senior petty officer using the nickname for radio man. Back in the day, a radioman was identified by four lightning bolts on his rating badge. When they combined the rate with the data technicians it changed to Information Technician, but the rating symbol remained lightning bolts.

The tech looked up at the captain in disbelief but turned back to his task, working feverishly. After a couple more moments, he looked up. "That is all Sir, the combinations, and the PAL codes. It says, 'Use at your discretion.'"

"Who signed the order?" the captain asked skeptically.

The communicator looked back at his screen and scrolled up to the unclassified part.

"It says, 'President Delseck sir.'"

"Omigawd, Ralph," the captain said to his exec. "We are going to start WW3 on the word of the Secretary of Agriculture!" He stared at the crumpled paper in his hand as if it might come to life and bite him at any second. "Get the Supply Officer and the Weapons Officer and meet me in my cabin in five."

***

In the public domain, it was never determined where the 15 nuclear weapons that detonated above Iran came from. In addition to the U.S. missile boat, there had been a British boomer and two Israeli submarines patrolling in the western Indian Ocean where the satellite observation platforms detected rockets surfacing, and then streaking off on pillars of flame toward the Middle East. When the warheads separated from their cocoons far above the atmosphere, 45 black packages of death streaked off to impact the Persian nation's principal cities and all of their nuclear installations.

When the dust settled, it seemed the Iranian mullahs had been granted their wish. The seventh century had indeed returned to Iran and its environs. The gift of technological regression was not limited to the mullahs of Iran. It seemed the Arabian Peninsula had been blessed with its own set of thermonuclear fireworks. Mecca was now a 100-acre black glass, self-lighting parking lot. Riyadh had joined Washington, D.C. blowing in the radioactive wind.

The calm crystal waters of the Chagos Archipelago quickly regained their crystal blue beauty soon after the missiles disappeared from sight. Within five minutes, there was no sign on the surface that the hand of man had ever visited their white coral vastness.

***

White Farm – Downstate Illinois

"Put the calves in with the cows this morning," I told Chance. "Ride over to Mister Easterday's place as well as the Jamisons' farm. Tell them the west field is ready to cut and I want to get it in before the rain." I was not happy with the layer of black forming on the western horizon. This time of year we could expect torrential rains, high winds, and even hail.

Planting the entire 300 acres to wheat had been a gamble. If we weren't able to get the crop in, we would lose the most productive part of the farm for this year. It was already too late to plant corn. Since I had already committed to clover and spent a prodigious amount on the rare clover seed, I wasn't about to plow it under and plant beans, so getting the wheat safely into the three storage bins at my brother's place had become a priority.

The amount of effort to get a crop in the ground and in the bin had become daunting in the half-barter economy that had sprung up after the chaos. Obtaining seed became difficult to impossible.

It had taken a trip to Kentucky in the ton truck, a significant percentage of my whiskey and laundry detergent stash and 700 pounds of ground corn to obtain enough red clover seed to plant 300 acres. I had used just over a ton of red clover mixed with timothy.

The hard, red winter wheat seed had been difficult to find. It had taken me two years. Most Illinois winter wheat is soft red but I wanted grain we could readily make into yeast-rise bread, and the soft red does not lend itself to being used that way. I had eaten enough biscuits to last me the rest of my life.

We had gotten word through the sheriff office's communication web of a couple bins discovered down on the river close to Metropolis. When my brother had been killed just prior to the chaos, he had left a significant insurance policy and a couple of CDs. As the beneficiary of the estate, those funds accrued to me. I took a big chunk of the $1 million windfall and bought gold. I stayed away from Krugerrands and one-ounce coins. I favored the Canadian twentieth of an ounce maple leaf and the tenth-ounce American Eagles.

In the long-term, buying gold was smart. In the short-term, the commodities I had purchased — whiskey, vodka, laundry detergent, fabric softener and freeze-dried food — was much more valuable. When the wheels come off the wagon, folks figure out very quickly one cannot eat gold. I used my new-found wealth and filled my basement and a big part of the haymow in the old barn with case after case of cheap whiskey in pint bottles and good vodka in half-gallon jugs. The cases of commodities in the old barn were covered carefully with moldy straw bales that looked as if they had not been moved in years.

By the time I went shopping for wheat seed, the economy had returned enough that I was able to pay for it with maple leaves. It took three full ounces of gold by the time the bargaining was complete plus a case of half-gallon vodka bottles to purchase the 300 bushels of wheat necessary to plant the big field. It was a ruinous exchange rate. I had paid more than $4,500 for those coins prior to the trouble. The economy wasn't that far recovered.

Since there was a rock quarry in the county, coming up with the lime had not been a problem, but the potash had been a challenge. All told the amount of effort, money and risk this one wheat field represented was prodigious. I wouldn't be ruined, by any means, if we didn't get it in the bins, but it would represent a serious hit to my grandson's future, and a severe watch-our-pennies winter, instead of a comfortable one.

I rode behind Chance on the little pillion seat. He took it easy on the old man and didn't frighten me — much. I had him drop me off at the old farm east of the main house where the rickety equipment sheds were sheltering our best equipment. I had stashed my brother's almost-new John Deere combine beneath an open, east-facing shed.

Chance and I had been all through it the previous week cleaning, greasing and getting the grain head installed. We had switched it over to natural gas before the trouble. It still used a small amount of diesel to start the engine and provide a drop of liquid injected on the compression stroke for ignition, but it meant the machine would run all day on 10 gallons of diesel instead of a couple 100 gallons.

By the time I got it started and rolled it out of the shop, my grandson had returned from the neighbors. When I pulled out into the barn lot and stopped, he climbed up onto the platform and opened the door.

"Do you want me to start, Bapaw?" I knew he would want to drive the combine. He loved working the farm machinery and had been doing it since he was able to reach the wheel and pedals.

"Sure, son, it is ready to go," I told him. "Just watch the head height. I don't want to lose any grain, but we need to keep the straw as high as possible," he knew that, but I couldn't help myself. I had been instructing him for more than 15 years and didn't know how to stop. He didn't mind, he just grinned and nodded.

I scooted over to the left side and let him slide under the wheel. I wanted to ride along on the first couple of passes to check the yield and the moisture of the grain. I was pretty sure we were well within the limits to store it without any further drying, but I wanted to make sure. We had three gates to open and shut before we got to the big field, so I would be there to help with the opening and making sure none of the cattle escaped during the evolution to the field.

"Squawk," the county radio beeped at me. I glanced down; Chance had it on his belt. He reached down and handed it to me. "I thought you might need it," he mouthed silently.

"Leroy, what is your 20?"

"I am in the field; we are cutting wheat today," I told the dispatcher.

"Milo wants to know if you are coming in."

"Tell him not today, I need to get 300 acres of wheat in the bins before the rain."

There was a two-minute silence.

"Leroy, this is Milo, we need to talk."

"If you want to speak with me today, Milo, it will be on a combine or in a truck. Come on out, we could use the help." This went unanswered for a couple of minutes.

"Okay, Leroy, I am on my way."

"Meet me at my brother's place in an hour. I will be offloading the trucks there, as soon as we get one loaded."

"Roger Wilco," the sheriff answered in his best WW2 Hollywood radio voice. The entire sheriff's office thought they were playing to a 50's audience.

I closed the last gate and climbed up to sit beside my grandson as we pulled into the field. He dropped the head and engaged the reel. It started turning looking like a wide paddle wheel on an old steam riverboat. The wheel had long bars with what looked like black straight wires protruding out from each bar.

The bars were called "bats" and the wires "tines." As the machine moved forward, the bats pulled the wheat back into the sickle bars, and the cut grain fell into augers moving it to the center of the header. The gently cut grain fell on a conveyer belt that pulled it back into the heart of the combine. There were whirring and soft thumping sounds, like someone beating a drum with a padded mallet, emanating from deep within the bowels of the machine under us. Soon a river of yellow grain started pouring into the hopper above and behind us. The aroma of fresh cut grain soon filled the cabin.

I loved harvest time.

I glanced up at the digital readout above the windshield on the driver's side. I was overjoyed at the numbers. The BPA readout (bushels per acre) was hovering around 30 bouncing up and down between 35 and 26. The moisture reading was fairly steady at 12 percent. It could hardly be better.

I looked at the numbers, checked the speedo and did a quick calculation: We were cutting close to 10 acres per hour. We would never finish before the storm hit.

"Are you going to work today in your jogging clothes?" Chance teased. I guess he was worried I would embarrass him when the neighbors showed up.

"It is better than swim trunks," I told him. When he had been a little tike, and farming had been a hobby, I had farmed all season in a pair of ragged black swim trunks. He shrugged as if to say I was hopeless. I had him drop me off in the corner of the field closest to the house. I got back in time to see my daughter walking to the house from the barn carrying two, five-gallon milk cans.

"You didn't have to milk; I told Chance just to let the calves in with the cows today," I told her.

"I don't mind, and the mothers get difficult to deal with if you let the calves in and then take them away."

It was like I didn't know anything.

Her argument would have had some merit when we milked by hand, but since we used machines now, it didn't matter. The cows were well restrained in full body stanchions and had little choice but to cooperate.

"You do enough around here without having to milk," I tried to reason with her. I knew I should save my breath, but again I couldn't help myself.

She sat the cans down on the porch and turned to look at me with her hands on her hips.

"Look, Daddy," she said, and I knew I was going to get a lecture. "It has nothing to do with what I do or don't do. You want me to hang around the house dressed all frilly and feminine like some pampered city girl. I am a farm girl. I get dirty and wear work clothes. You just have to get used to it."

This she told me standing there in a pair of designer jeans, wearing a pair of $400-Ariat Heritage boots, a white silk blouse with a sky blue scarf tucked carefully in the cleavage, soft makeup and hair carefully braided on top of her head without a single strand out of place. She looked like she was dressed to go on stage at a rodeo. What could I say?

"You have cow shit on your boot."

She looked down in alarm at her spotless boots and then looked back at me with a glower.

"Oh Daddy," she said and twirled around to walk into the kitchen letting the door slam behind her. We certainly knew how to push each other's buttons. The door popped back open almost instantly.

"Are you going to eat?"

"I don't have time. Chance will have the hopper full by the time I get the truck back to the field."

"I knew you would say that," she said handing me a brown paper sack. She was a treasure. "There are sausage-egg biscuits and potato cakes in there for you and Chance as well. Wait," she said ducking back into the kitchen to reappear moments later with a thermos.

"Are you changing to swim trunks?" My progeny seemed to be concerned with my personal appearance today for some reason. Perhaps they thought a fashion editor might be coming to the farm or something.

"No, my sweet, I will dress appropriately. The Sheriff is on his way."

"Your khakis are in the garage closet. They are clean and pressed."

"Thank you my sweet, for everything you do." I meant every word. She waved me off in the direction of the garage as if her fingers were a little broom sweeping some unwanted dirt off the back step. She knew how to press my buttons as well.

A short time later, appropriately clad in khaki wash pants, brown work boots, and a matching khaki short-sleeved shirt, I drove the 10-ton grain truck into the field. I was right. The hopper was starting to exhibit a mound of yellow kernels near the edges of its top. I pulled in alongside the combine driving in the cleared area. Chance didn't even slow down, he merely swung the auger head over the bed of the truck and started unloading the hopper.

We hadn't reached the other end of the field when the hopper was emptied enough to where he swung the discharge chute back to disgorge its treasure into the hopper once more. I turned the truck around in a big circle and saw two more combines lowering their heads and mowing into the grain along the windrow already started by Chance. I watched their progress.

Chance would have to slow down. The neighbor's combines weren't as new as my brother's rig and my grandson would have to slow his pace to keep everyone in synch. It was still much faster than us trying to go it alone.

I checked my watch and looked at the growing black cloud wall coming in from the west. We were still not going to make it.

The truck I was driving wasn't near full. It could haul 600 bushels, twice the capacity of the combine hopper, but I told the sheriff I would meet him in an hour, and it was fast approaching. As I drove down the gravel access road to my brother's house up on the blacktop, I passed two grain trucks being driven by my neighbor's sons headed for the field.

When I turned into the drive, I noticed the lawn at my brother's house needed mowing. There was so much to do and only a finite amount of time to do it all.

Sometimes I felt overwhelmed.

I ignored the grass and drove around back to where the grain bins were located beside the old red barn with a white roof that my sister-in-law and my wife's great-grandfather had built. It looked like it had been erected last week. I had it painted in the spring, and they had done a good job.

The sheriff's car was parked beside the grain bins. It looked like someone had mowed a half-acre area around the bins. It must have been one of the neighbors who were looking forward to helping me with the harvest.

I drove the truck over to the steel grate above the concrete pit where the grain would be dumped. There was an auger in the pit that would send the wheat up to one of three steel conveyors leading to each of the 6,000-bushel unpainted aluminum bins.

The sheriff had removed the steel plates over the grates and stood beside the opening giving me hand signals to center the dumper over the pit.

I left the motor running and hopped out to walk back to the control box for the dump bed at the driver's side rear. The sheriff had already slid the door up at the back, and grain was spilling out of the truck into the hole. The sheriff held his hand under the stream and came back with a fist full that he held beneath his nose for a long moment savoring the aroma. He dumped most of it into the pit but kept a few grains to pop in his mouth.

"I do love the smell of fresh cut wheat," he told me. The sheriff had been a farmer once himself. "Your brother's yard needs mowing," he further informed me. My daughter was not the only person in my life who knew how to push my buttons.

"Did you drive all the way out here to tell me that?"

Sheriff Baker smiled. He knew he had gotten under my skin. He enjoyed it.

I had to do a couple of things before I could dump the truck. I started over to the generator shed to get some power going for the augers conveyors and spreaders. The sheriff fell in beside me.

"John Palmer is back."

'Yes, I heard."

"I still think the bastich killed his wife," the sheriff exclaimed. Milo Baker was a gentleman who would not say shit if his mouth was full of it. The mangled substitute describing the progeny of an unwed consummation was as close to swearing as he would come.

Palmer's wife had disappeared before the chaos. She had gone missing under suspicious circumstances leaving her family's farm to Palmer as well as a significant cash settlement from a rather recently purchased life insurance policy.

There had never been evidence significant enough to bring charges, but it made the State's Attorney crazy at the time because the lady had come to him days before her disappearance distraught and frightened. She had told the prosecutor that her husband was going to kill her to get the farm.

The State boys had been brought in as well as the FBI. They had combed the farm and interviewed hundreds of folks, but no evidence sufficient to charge the seemingly distraught spouse had ever been unearthed.

The case was never closed and remained a burr under the sheriff's saddle.

After a sufficient time had passed the lady was declared legally dead and Palmer collected from the insurance company. It was a sizeable sum, and the insurance company had dispatched its own investigators who had dug around for several weeks but went home with their tails between their legs.

It looked like Palmer had gotten away with murder. I had my own ideas but kept them to myself. Now that the son-of-a-bitch was back (as you can see, I am not the gentleman the sheriff is) it might be an opportune time to look into some of my more esoteric theories. If I could nail him for his wife's murder, it would certainly get him off my back.

As the sheriff and I were standing at the back of the raised dump truck watching the last of the wheat flowing into the pit, another truck pulled up. Two young men jumped out.

They were the Jamison brothers.

"Hello sheriff," the older one said. "Mr. White, my brother can take your truck back if you want to stay here and load the bins." It was a thoughtful gesture since making sure the bins were filled correctly would become a full-time job as the trucks started rolling in. "Mr. Casemeyer brought his rig into the field after you left. Dad says he thinks we can finish before the rain hits," the young man continued.

That was good news. It was good to have helpful neighbors. We were close. We had all been militia together. Sharing danger and being under fire tends to weld folks together.

It took a while to get the second truck unloaded, and the boys headed back to the field, but the sheriff hung around. I knew he had something else on his mind.

"We got a call from Effingham today," he said. *Ah hah, here it comes.* "Somebody stole two trucks from the train yard," he stopped there, but I said nothing. I knew there had to be more. The sheriff didn't drive all the way out here to tell me about a couple of stolen trucks.

"What struck me about this particular heist was the trucks they stole are the type equipped with railroad wheels in addition to road tires."

Okay, I don't get it, Milo – where are you going with…

"I was thinking about the Federalists and them wanting to make trouble for us down here. Then I started thinking about railroad tracks and where I could take a truckload of explosives that would make a big enough dent in our economy to make folks want to rejoin the Union."

"What did you come up with?"

"The Occidental refinery in Carmi would be a perfect target."

Damn, Milo, I think the governor called the wrong guy. I immediately tried to discount the sheriff's idea and think of all the ways it could not be right. I could not think of one thing.

"Milo, I believe you may be onto something and that something is a damn scary thought. The Carmi refinery produces most, if not all, the diesel and gasoline for downstate. We would be in a world of hurt without that fuel."

Neither of us said anything for a while as I considered the implications of his idea. I didn't like any of them.

"Do you have any ideas about where we go next on this?" I hated having to ask him. I was supposed to be the hot-shot operator and investigator.

"I think we need to slip over in the dark of the moon and take a look at the Womack place."

This gave me some pause. Since the states became the final arbiter of the law, most of the finer points of search and seizure by law enforcement had been laid aside for the present. A county sheriff had almost unlimited power to drive into anyone's place and look around to his heart's content. The idea of slipping into the richest man in the county's place under cover of darkness was disconcerting, to say the least.

"You know Womack has a dozen or so armed guards out there, and they are not known to be overly concerned about the finer points of the law. Milo, what are you not telling me?"

"Nothing in particular, just that Mr. Womack was one of the folks named in the report the governor gave you. If he is involved, he is likely to be a major player, not someone sniffing around the edge."

"Say, do you think Palmer getting sprung from the farm …might …?"

"See Leroy that's why the governor picked you. You are right on the money. I think Palmer is in this up to his size 26 brogans."

CHAPTER SIX

The last truck rolled in just before 11 p.m. The storm hit just after midnight. It had been a closely run thing. Measuring the small gap remaining between the grain and the top of the two bins we had filled told me we had put just under 9,000 bushels into storage.

The younger Jamison boy had informed me the neighbor's combines were working on their last hopper, and Chance had left the field. The volunteer harvesters would take a couple hundred bushels each home with them as their payment for helping with the harvest.

Paying for the harvesting help with full hoppers was more than generous on my part. A couple hundred bushels of wheat equated to $2,400 in 2014 dollars. In addition, the volunteers would leave with full fuel tanks, supplied from our diesel tank at the main house. It was generous. But on the other hand, if they hadn't come to help, two-thirds of the crop would no doubt have been left on the field after the storm. It was a doozy.

The storm brought all the nasty assemblage of an early summer Midwest thunder bumper: 40 mph, straight-line winds with gusts to 60 mph. Lighting and hail came blowing in from the west and sat on us through the morning hours. When the welcome yellow sun, nestled in a clear blue sky, peeked up over the woods, it revealed a backyard littered in sticks from the stand of oaks keeping sentry there.

I had taken the route around the far west pasture along the ridge overlooking Interstate 70 on this particular morning. I was encouraged to see a few trucks were starting to ply their trade along the super slab once more. Through a herculean team effort between Missouri and Illinois, the Chain-of-Rocks Bridge had been rebuilt across the Mississippi. Interstate 70 was open once more to the west.

Back at the farm, I observed the west pasture needed to be mowed off. The horse weeds, morning glory vines, and cockleburs were coming back. It was a never-ending battle. The west field had been in pasture now for three years. It was time for it to be plowed under and planted to corn next year.

Sometimes I wonder about providence. I am under no illusions of my own fallen nature and my selfish inner being. I am, in the words of the liturgy, a poor miserable sinner. Thus, when grace appears, I am always surprised. I was standing in front of the house under an old oak thinking about all the work we had to do to get ready for winter when a dust cloud appeared coming from the west. I knew it was too early for my neighbor to be up and around, so more than likely, whoever it was, had our place as their destination.

I reached into my vest pocket and turned the .357 magnum derringer around to where it came to hand quickly. Both dogs went on alert. They didn't bark since I was standing there, But the hair on the back of Bo's neck stood up, and a menacing growl came up from what seemed to be a spot near his tail. I was glad he was on my side.

The truck slowed early and the cloud dissipated. The driver was evidently familiar with driving on gravel. I recognized the old, battered work truck of Harvey Jamison. When the truck pulled off the road and stopped next to my Caddy, the younger Jamison boy hopped out smiling.

"Good morning Mr. White," the young man said as he walked over with his hand extended. Both dogs were wagging and smiling. Robby had been in and out of our place their entire lives. "I hope it is not too early to stop by. I knew you would be out for your morning jog."

"Not at all Robby What's on your mind?"

The boy shuffled his feet and messed with the dogs, who were both acting like he was a long-lost owner. If the dogs liked him, it was a testament to his character. Dogs are smart like that.

I had begun to think he wasn't going to respond when he looked up and blurted out in a long string of uninterrupted words:

"Sir, I am getting married, and I don't want to live with my folks and your brother's place is sitting empty and needs to be kept up and I would treat it like it was my own and with those bins full of wheat someone should be there to keep an eye on them and I would work two days a week for you and…"

"Yes, Robby!" I cut his carefully planned speech off. "I will let you live in my brother's house for two days' work per week. It sounds fair enough."

Robby looked stunned. He apparently thought he was going to have to do a lot of convincing. I had been thinking about the place and had come to the point where I knew we needed to turn the page and move on. It had been six years.

Burdett's house was sitting there just as he had left it to go for a motorcycle ride with Charlotte the morning of the accident. Afterward, my wife Genevieve had gone to the house and cleaned out her older sister's kitchen, so there wasn't any food left to spoil and rot. I had made a pass through the house and brought all of my brother's guns back to my place. We had locked the master bedroom door on all of their clothes and personal effects and left it as it was.

I knew the place had turned into a type of shrine to my brother's and sister-in-law's memory. I also knew it was time to move on. There had been a couple of obstacles earlier that were no longer a factor.

The main one had been power. The geriatric diesel generator at the house was okay for backup and temporary powering of the sheds and bins, but it would not have been practical for full-time electricity. Since there was grid power in front of the house once more, lack of electricity was no longer an issue. Water was now available with electricity to power the pump, so this was no longer a barrier to someone living there full time.

"Oh thank you, Sir, you don't know what this will mean to Debbie and me," the boy blurted as he grabbed my hand in both of his and pumped as if he were trying to draw water from a very deep well. This caused Bo to jump up and put his paws on my shoulder, seeking assurance that everything was okay, and that he wasn't supposed to eat anyone. Any overt display of emotion triggered a protective instinct in his shepherd genes, a trait that had become enhanced by the unpleasantness that resulted in my wife's demise.

"I have a pretty good idea son…"

"Who can that be?" the boy said, noticing another dust cloud coming our way.

I checked my watch. It was a little before 6 a.m. An immaculate Ford pickup emerged out of the cloud to pull in beside the Jamison boy's vehicle. I didn't recognize the truck and the heavily tinted windows obscured the view through the driver's door. The glimpse I had of the driver through the windshield had revealed mostly hat, so I was on edge. Bo and Tasha stood on either side of me pressing tight against either leg, growling. I slipped my hand into the vest and got a grip on the derringer.

The driver's door swung open, and Delbert Jones stepped out. He was immediately mobbed by both dogs. Delbert was a dog person and had been around since they were puppies. They were obviously glad to see him.

My front yard was beginning to look like someone's family reunion, and I was still dressed in my jogging suit. I would catch flack about that from my kids, no doubt.

"It must be breakfast time," I remarked as Delbert walked over, still messing with the dogs, one on either side. He didn't reply. He just grinned. He loved my daughter's cooking and was not at all bashful about showing up at meal time. He knew I didn't mind. As far as I was concerned, he was welcome to share three meals a day with us.

I introduced Delbert to Robby, who took his leave with more words of appreciation and thanks. We watched the boy back out and drive off, waving and smiling. That was one happy young man.

"So you finally are going to do something with your brother's place," Delbert said with satisfaction. "It is high time." Delbert had been one of my stepdad's best friends. When we had lost dad to heat stroke, Delbert had stepped up and been a surrogate father to me. Sometimes it was a bit much, since Delbert could be a bit overbearing in carrying out his self-imposed duties. But he meant well, and I sincerely appreciated his counsel and advice.

"John Palmer is back," Delbert told me, revealing the actual reason for his presence. I knew the pickup would be well stocked with firearms. He was wearing a short-sleeved plaid shirt with the tails over the belt of starched and pressed khakis. I was pretty sure there would be a 9MM Glock tucked into a holster at the small of his back. Delbert Jones was not a man to be messed with.

"I know Delbert, and there is more to it than meets the eye," I informed him. "I need to shave, shower and get dressed. I'll get you a cup of coffee if you want to sit on the front porch. I want you to read what I have written about your Vietnam adventures."

I brought him the promised coffee and the laptop with the manuscript already up on the screen. I left him there to head into my bedroom through the front door. I could smell bacon frying coming from the kitchen, and I heard the back door bang as Chance headed out to the barn to milk. The White household was up and moving.

Breakfast was a big deal at our place. We ate a little after seven every morning, and we always ate together. The other two meals were hit and miss as Chance had interests away from the farm, and I could not always be there since my deputy duties kept me away for extended periods, but breakfast was a given.

I buzzed off my whiskers with the Braun, bounced in and out of the shower. and walked into my closet. There were six pairs of polished Tony Lamas sitting in a row with a matching belt for each pair hanging above on a belt rack. Black, it feels like a black day. There were two pairs of black boots. One was plain with a simple, subtle decoration running from the ankle to the toe. The other was more ornate with white thread woven into the pattern. I chose the less elaborate of the two and a matching belt.

I ran my hand across the dozen or so short-sleeved white shirts hanging in a line like a military company standing at attention. They were identical save the buttons. I selected one with pearl snaps in place of buttons and grabbed the string tie, which featured a mountain lion as the clasp. It was one of my favorites.

I surveyed myself in the mirror and was reasonably content with the reflection I saw there. My hair was still dark brown, almost black, with a splash of silver in front of each ear. I brushed the sides back and let a tumble of curls fall across my forehead. The hat was going to mess it up anyhow, so it didn't matter that much.

Before I stepped out into the hall, I walked over to the shoulder holster hanging on the bedpost at the head of the bed. I slipped the KelTek out of the holster, popped the mag out and jacked the live round from the chamber leaving the slide open. The top drawer of my dresser was full of guns. It had started with a black foam block that had then been carved into spots for six sidearms. There was a .41

magnum Smith with a seven-inch barrel, two 9MM Glocks, a spot for the KelTek and two 1911s. I slipped the KelTek into its spot and retrieved the .45 caliber service gun.

With the return of John Palmer to our neighborhood, a little heavier ordinance was called for. I slipped the Colt into the shoulder holster but left it hanging on the bedpost. I didn't think it necessary to go armed to breakfast in my own house.

Subsequent events would prove this to have been an erroneous assumption.

***

The tide of anger that had swept the country after the terrorist attacks and the nuclear detonation in Washington, D.C. was palpable. There were more than 300 million guns in the USA. Events of the past month had seriously pissed off the folks who owned the majority of the weapons.

The anger was not clearly focused on one group. There were three targets for this disparate discontent. The Muslim terrorists were on top of the list. Illegal aliens living among the citizenry committing crimes out of proportion to their numbers were also reviled among the working, law-abiding majority.

Surprisingly the most intense anger and wrath fell upon the Federal Government and the inane and utterly stupid policies that had precipitated the violence wreaked upon the homeland. The law of conservation of energy states that for every action there is an opposite and equal reaction. With all deference to Sir Isaac Newton, the response to the attacks on the homeland was perhaps not proportionally equal.

There was no national leader standing up after the attacks cautioning about over reaction. There were no voices babbling inanely about "Islam is a religion of peace." What there was manifested itself almost instantaneously into deadly action. Mosques were attacked and burned across the country. Women wearing headscarves were attacked and their scarves torn from their heads to be burned on the spot. Muslim clerics who had preached hate were hanged over the ashes of their charred buildings and left as a message.

Dark-skinned individuals without proper identification were rounded up, loaded into trucks and shipped south to be dropped in the desert to find their own way home. It was thought they had been able to find their way north when they sneaked in the country; they could certainly find their way home.

Speaking unaccented English became a necessary life-saving skill. Soon self-deportation became much more than a political phrase. It became a matter of life and death.

The militias that formed across the country were made up of men who had been marginalized and ignored for a generation. They were not amused. The Gadsden flag became the unofficial calling card of the militia nationwide.

The cities became charnel houses.

Statist policies had produced three generations of dependent people. They had no skills, no useful education and were unable to participate in a working society. They had only appetites. When those desires were not satisfied, they lashed out. They rioted and burned their own houses down around themselves, then sat in the ashes with stupefied looks of incomprehension as starvation and disease stalked through their ranks, leaving dead and dying in staggering numbers.

When they tried to flee the cities they themselves had destroyed, the escapees ran into roadblocks manned by hard men, armed and merciless.

It was not pretty, but it was necessary. The gods of the copybook headings had come back in a pitiless reminder that reality will not be mocked for long.

When voices were raised in an attempt to guilt the producers into working against their own interests, they were dragged off stage and summarily dealt with. Soon those voices were silenced.

What had taken 100 years to pollute and prostitute was set right in six months of cathartic fire.

When the dust settled, one thing became clear. None of the producers had any interest in going back. "Union" had become a four-letter word second only to "media" as words not used in polite company.

During the worst of the chaos, the Church stood tall. The only areas of sanity in the burning cities were pools of sanctuary centered on the inner-city churches, missions, and clinics. The members formed their own militias supplied with arms and supplies smuggled in by fellow believers.

The churches in the hinterland experienced a revival of unimagined proportion as folks came back seeking a point of sanity and assurance in the world gone mad.

The economy crashed then rebounded as a cash and barter society. For the first couple of years, money talked. Even though there was no Federal Government backing the fiat currency, it was all that existed, so people accepted it just as they had when Saddam Hussein's government collapsed but his government's money was taken in trade for goods and services for years after the issuing authority disappeared.

Where cash talked, commodities screamed. If one had food, fuel or alcohol to trade, there was an unending line of potential customers. It seemed overnight 1930 had returned to America.

With banks disappearing across the country, possession being nine-tenths of the law soon became the entire law. Since the Feds had ended up holding most of the mortgages in the country those mortgages disappeared with the disappearance of Fannie Mae and Freddy Mac.

In many cases, those windfalls were offset by the demise of Social Security checks, military retirement pay and the disappearance of millions of Federal make-work jobs. Power devolved down to the most fundamental unit of government. The counties again became the centers of local power and authority. The county sheriff became the principal law enforcement officer in communities large and small across the length and breadth of what had been a large, united nation. Sheriffs were elected, so they were trusted. Appointed police – not so much.

With the reinstatement of a cash economy, counterfeiting became a problem almost immediately. It was the rearing of the head of this demon threatening to kill the nascent reemerging demand economy that saved the states.

A consensus formed around the idea that the counties just weren't large enough communities to do all that was necessary for a modern society to preserve the welfare of the people. Since the states were there, formed and had the machinery necessary to reassume a modicum of control, it was reluctantly permitted.

New elections were held replacing career politicians with citizens. State Constitutions were revisited with protections for individual rights re-examined and strengthened where necessary. Texas was the first state government given a vote of confidence of its people. Oklahoma and Missouri followed.

Surprisingly Illinois came next, despite once being one of the bluest of blue states. This confidence in Springfield was based primarily on the outstanding performance of her sitting governor navigating the worst of the chaos. The Legislature was swept clean in the special election as the career politicians were replaced by working citizens.

Cook County was not allowed a vote in the gubernatorial and state legislative election that followed. The new Illinois Constitution denied the vote to anyone receiving state assistance and only tax-paying citizens were allowed the franchise.

The Republic had returned to the heartland.

***

"You make me out to be a hero. I was just doing my job," Delbert said as he handed me back the laptop. We were walking down the hall toward the kitchen. I did not reply to his denial of hero status. He was a hero in my book, and it was my book, after all.

The aromas floating down the hall from the kitchen were enticing. Amanda sometimes took a slapdash approach to lunch or dinner, but she never slacked off on breakfast. When I came into the kitchen, I noticed six steel baking pans sitting on the counter with white cheesecloth over them.

She had bread rising made from the flour Chance had brought in from the mill in the shop yesterday evening. Everyone was anxious to experience some fresh, yeast bread for a change. My mouth watered in anticipation. I knew the house would be filled with the aroma of bread baking later this morning.

As Delbert refilled his cup from the ancient steel percolator, as comfortable as if he were at home, I looked around the kitchen and savored the scene. Amanda was standing in front of the range finishing up the eggs. The table was set with a large, steaming tureen of sausage gravy sitting next to a platter of biscuits and cornbread piled high in the center of the table. Next to the bread sat a glass pitcher of fresh milk. There was a bowl of fried potatoes, another of sliced fresh tomatoes from the garden and a bowl of cooked apples. The meat platter was loaded down with thick, sliced bacon and pork-venison sausage.

Chance was already at the table working his way through a large white cup of coffee. It was one of a set I had acquired back in the day. The globe and anchor adorned one side of the mug. The opposite side was decorated with the ribbons I was authorized to wear; among them was a purple heart and a bronze star. There had been a time when I was quite proud of those decorations. It seemed now to have been a long time ago.

I felt a pang of remorse, guilt, and sadness that Genevieve was not here to see the fine young man her grandson had grown into and the selfless, mature lady her daughter had become. I looked around the clean, bright kitchen and realized something: I was happy. I had a good friend and my family around me; I needed nothing else.

Trailing this thought was a stab of fear. Anytime I had ever felt this way in my life something had always come along to upset the apple cart. Perhaps, this time will be different. I tried to force the sudden foreboding feeling away, but it lingered to taint the perfect moment.

"No bass today," Delbert remarked as he looked over the groaning table. The last time he came we had bass and eggs from Chance's efforts at the lake the evening before.

"I guess we'll just have to make do," I told him. He smiled and shook his head in appreciation of the feast laid out on the table. In this era of want and deprivation, it seemed like a small miracle.

Amanda brought the huge skillet to the table and served the eggs on to each of the empty plates. How she managed to get some eggs fully cooked and others over-easy out of the same skillet I could never fathom, but she knew exactly how everyone liked their eggs done, and they always came out perfectly.

As soon as she sat down, we joined hands, and I returned thanks. I thanked the Lord for his endless mercy and grace, for all the things He provided for us and asked His protective hand to remain in our lives. I got hearty amens around the table when I finished up.

As we were eating, I glanced over at the back door. The back porch was one step down to a stone floor. At one time, it had been a back porch, but when we remodeled the house, it was weathered in. It now functioned as a mud room and the home for our two shepherds. They were lying on the stone floor with their chins resting on the top step patiently waiting for their portion of the bounty that they knew would come their way after we finished.

What had drawn my attention was movement in that direction. Both dogs had stood up and were looking toward the front of the house, ears perked up and eyes wide. Bo started growling deep in his chest. This was not a good sign.

***

Springfield, Illinois

Elaine Martin stepped out of the shower and wrapped a big, white, terry-cloth towel around her after she removed the shower cap that kept her long tresses dry. She wiped her feet on the white mat in front of the shower and let the big fluffy towel wick the remainder of water from her body. She shook her head and let her hair cascade down around both sides of her face. It was naturally blonde, but her hairdresser had teased streaks of auburn through it. She stopped in front of the full-length mirror and let the towel fall away. She examined her reflection studiously and was pleased with her inspection.

She had just turned 30, but she knew women seven or eight years her junior who would have killed for the body she retained. She worked at it. Sometimes she wondered if her breasts may have been too large for her slender frame, but secretly she was proud of them. Unlike some women blessed with large breasts who had almost no nipples, hers stood up like little haystacks with pencil eraser-sized tips.

Her glance moved down across her flat stomach to the tiny wisp of blonde pubic hair, then down to survey her long, slender legs. She stood on tiptoe and turned to look over her shoulder at her round rump and perfectly formed calves and thighs.

What she was thinking of when she looked at her own buttocks was Roy Lee White's hands moving up and down across them.

The man had been on her mind constantly since he had left the governor's office two days before. Since she had been a city girl born and raised, she had little contact with the kind of man the deputy obviously was. She could imagine him astride a bucking horse arm waving and wearing that maddening grin as he bent the horse's will to his own.

What was even more enticing about the man, was he seemed to ignore her completely. Oh, he would compliment her on her beauty and flirt with her briefly, but she sensed it was an automatic response from him. He treated all the ladies the same. It was part of his cowboy chivalry. When she had dropped a less-than-subtle hint of her interest in perhaps pursuing a more personal relationship, he had acted as if he hadn't even heard.

She dropped the towel on the bed and padded naked to the dresser. The top drawer contained her frilly personals. She dressed on the outside as a professional lady favoring full or knee-length, one-piece dresses, but beneath she dressed like a hooker. Since her divorce, she had spent a big chunk of her meager earnings working for the governor at Victoria's Secret.

Her marriage had been unsatisfying and dull. She suspected her ex had been secretly gay. From what she read in Cosmo, there had to be more than the brief, uninspired sessions she had experienced in her married life. She had decided she wanted a real man, and Roy Lee White seemed to be the most authentic man she had ever met.

He still wore a wedding ring, but she had discovered from surreptitiously reading his file in the office that his wife had been killed years ago. There were notes that led one to believe that since her death there had been no other women in his life, not even a single, short-term liaison. The investigator who had written the report had been fairly certain of this information since the governor had requested an in-depth analysis of Mr. White's character.

There had been some anecdotal information about Mr. White's younger days gleaned from interviews with friends and neighbors. It seemed that when the gentleman had ridden rodeo he had been quite a different person than the one Elaine had come to know.

It was this part of him that excited her. Roy Lee White rodeo star was the man she wanted in her bed.

When she had pulled on her hose and dressed in her underwear, she stepped in front of the mirror once more. The thigh-top hose were held up by a shocking red garter belt, and the lace bra and panties revealed more than they covered. She grinned wickedly. I am a $1,000-a-night lay — if not more.

She pulled on a light, nylon hip-length slip to mask the outrageous underwear then slid a knee-cut, white-and-blue floral dress over the slip. She stepped into black, three-inch heels that were barely more than straps.

At her final inspection, she was pleased the way the dress flowed smoothly down across the top of her hips and jiggled ever so slightly when she walked. She was ready to face the world. Elaine selected a small, black purse to match the belt and heels. Just before leaving she picked up the model 42 Glock .380 from her bed stand and slipped it into her bag.

Her apartment was on the third floor. When she got to the elevator, it was not working. Again! "Is anything ever going to work right in this world?" she thought to herself as she tread carefully down the concrete steps in the slim heels she had selected. By the time she had reached the ground floor, she was regretting the choice.

When she stepped out into the early morning light, she looked over at her little red Miata. There were two rough-looking men standing beside the car staring in her direction. When the larger one saw her, he grinned. She did not like the look of that smile. She opened her purse and slid her hand around the handle of the little Glock. She thought to herself, "I may look like a defenseless lady, mister – but looks can be deceiving."

CHAPTER SEVEN

Beirut, Lebanon 1984

I suddenly felt a calm, resolute wave flow through me as time seemed to slow down. The impacting rounds in the wall seemed to take moments between strikes and the clouds of dust generated by the fire I could see as individual puffs, billowing out slowly as if someone had decided to sit down by the wall and enjoy a cigar.

I felt a presence near me that only I was aware of. It spoke to me. I decided it was an angel. The angel talked to me for what seemed to be an extended period of time, but it could not have been longer than a single heartbeat. She told me not to worry. It was not in God's plan that I should perish on this field on this day. She said I needed to go home and take care of my family and my community. She told me to do what I had to do, protect the men that were with me.

I will show you, she said in an audible voice.

The chaos, noise, smoke, and dirt became a stage set, upon which I was to act out a well-rehearsed scene. The reality and danger seemed insubstantial and ephemeral. The entire tactical scene laid itself out in front and below me as if I had suddenly been transported out of the action and was viewing the scene from a helicopter hovering overhead.

From this vantage point, it became apparent that moving directly toward the target building had been a mistake and had placed my shrunken platoon in an exposed and dangerous position. The only way forward was back the way we had come.

A spotlight appeared over the scene and focused on the mortar tube where the two fallen terrorists lay sprawled in their final positions.

One lay over the tube, the other was a few yards away where he had been trying to escape the deadly fire of our sniper.

I hate mortars.

The whole idea of a mortar, in my view, is an ill-conceived, stop-gap, Rube-Goldberg solution to a difficult problem. The initial concept was to put artillery-like power in the hands of the infantry. When it works, it can be a useful tool, but all too often it doesn't work. I often wondered if there had been a way to amass the actual statistical numbers of just how many deaths had been inflicted on the operators of mortars, if the numbers would not exceed the intended targets of the infernal devices.

This contraption was designed by Murphy. There were, at least, six different chemicals that had to dissolve, burn, ignite or explode in sequence at the exact right time for it to work as designed. Any number of things could cause Murphy to rear his ugly head. If the chemical composition of any of the components had deteriorated in the heat, humidity and handling during their indeterminate life enough to change their chemical structure, the results would differ from the spec.

If, in the manufacturing process, the quality control was lax and allowed a bit more of chemical A than chemical B then… well, you get the picture. Dozens of things had to go right, and stay right, for the little bomb to go boom-BOOM as it was engineered to do. When it went BOOM-boom or shooosh – pause BOOM, it was not good.

Oh, I got it all right. From the instant the light shined on the Soviet 82MM mortar and the dozen rounds stacked next to it, I understood the implications and the plan.

I was kicking against the traces.

From the first time I fired a mortar in training, and the round I dropped in the tube turned out to be a misfire, which then belatedly decided to ignite when we extracted it from the barrel; I wanted no part of the damned things.

I had witnessed a hang-late-fire on a heavy, truck-mounted mortar. The propellant charge did not ignite fully. It just pushed the flaming projectile out of the end of the tube into the air about three feet where it fell burning into the truck bed. The two operators had bailed out before the business-end exploded, but the driver was killed.

My third encounter with the infernal device was an observation of a Hezbollah mortar team. I was watching from one of the observation towers at the airport Marine complex. The rag-heads were set up next to a school so we couldn't bring indirect fire on them.

They were firing on Druze positions up the mountain, so we didn't engage them. In the end, it turned out we didn't need to. As I was watching, the mortarman launched three successful rounds. The fourth one's warhead exploded in the tube. Extremely short-range cannon, I thought uncharitably. When the position was again visible, there was little left but pieces of bodies and wreckage.

The mortar the Arabian knights were using on that day was identical to the Soviet manufactured 82MM POS that was sitting idle about 50 yards away. If precision-made American mortars worried me, the Russian tubes scared me to death. It was impossible to tell when the rounds were manufactured. If they were built on Saturday afternoon, most of the men would be half-drunk getting ready for the weekend. Monday morning built rockets were even worse because of the terrible hangovers visited upon the workers by the cheap vodka that was so readily available.

Mitchell, on the other hand, loved mortars. I swear he had an orgasm every time he heard the "thonk" of a bomb leaving the tube, thinking of the nearly 10 pounds of "whup-ass" he was bringing down on some bad guys head down range.

"Mitchell, can you get to that Russian POS and bring some fire onto our objective?" I asked, pointing toward the position where the two Hezbollah fighters had recently departed to claim their 70 virgins.

"Sure Sarge," Mitchell smiled in anticipation. "Should I take Vinny?" He wanted to take his buddy to help him load.

"Yes, go now!" I told him. I leaned back and looked at the top of the structure we were huddled next to. It looked like the mortar position should be in fire shadow from the 12.7MM gun firing on us from the enemy-held building, but I decided not to risk it.

"Gorder, have one of your guys take a couple LAWs around the other side of the building. See if they can get an angle on the window from where the heavy gun is firing."

Gorder just nodded in the direction of two men furthest from the front, each of whom was carrying an LAW across his back. They disappeared around the edge of the building while Mitchell and Vinny were working their way through the rubble to where the mortar tube awaited their tender ministrations.

I needed to backtrack my team to the wall where the lieutenant and the staff sergeant were stashed, but we couldn't move as long as that machine gun had us pinned.

"Swoosh!" Pause. "Crump!" Another rocket left the roof and impacted somewhere in the airport area. "Thonk-Thonk-Thonk!" The MG continued to chew away at our cover.

"Sergeant White report!" squawked the radio, right by the numbers. It was like one of Pavlov's dogs. I ignored it. We were doing everything we could. I watched Mitchell and Vinny slither over a broken wall and cross over into the courtyard where the mortar was set up partially hidden by a mound of sandbags. So far they weren't taking any fire.

Mitchell turned the tube's base around to redirect the fire in the direction of the building. Vinny was digging around in the pile of mortar shells evidently trying to identify the type. When he was satisfied, he handed one to Mitchell, who held it over the tube and looked at me. I gave him thumbs up and gritted my teeth. He dropped the shell into the tube, and I held my breath.

"Thonk!" The shell left the tube as designed and arced up over us. I was watching the building carefully. The shell exploded just in front of the target sending up a cloud of dust and smoke.

I turned to Mitch, pointed toward the sky and held up two fingers. He messed with the tripod and held out his hand for another shell.

"Thonk!" This one arced up and came down directly on the roof of the building. Mitch was a pure D genius with a damn mortar. I looked at him and pumped my arm up and down. Mitch gave me an evil grin and started pumping bombs into the tube as fast as Vinny could get'em to him.

The rooftop of the building took three more hits before the secondaries kicked in. It was Fourth of July all over again. The entire building was shaken as rockets exploded, and engines were ignited sending them screaming off in all directions. A complete balcony on the fourth floor crashed to the street. The entire structure was enveloped in dust and smoke.

I gave Mitch a thumbs up and then a finger across the throat to cease fire. He and Vinny were huddled down taking cover from the storm of rockets zipping off in all directions and exploding all over the area.

As the dust began to clear, the building started to discharge black and white-scarved fighters as if an ant hill had been kicked over. They were spreading out and headed in our direction. There must have been 50 of them.

Oh, shit!

***

Springfield, Illinois

Elaine had been drilled by a small-arms instructor who had immigrated to the U,S. from Israel. Moshe Aaron had been an instructor for Mossad in the same discipline. He was a no-nonsense type of guy who took his job seriously.

The fact she was a woman made no difference to Moshe. As the result of the mandatory conscription of women in the Israeli Defense Forces, some of his best students through the years had been female.

He had drilled her mercilessly until she lost all fear of the weapon. It became just another tool, like a word processor or copy machine.

As she walked confidently across the parking lot, she remembered clearly two things Moshe had told her over and over again. Never expose your weapon unless you are going to fire. When you fire, shoot twice. Those two things were a mantra to Moshe and came immediately to the forefront of her mind as she wrapped her hand around the handle of the little .380.

In today's world, the "full body mass" mantra had evolved into "over or under the vest." All too many threats were armored in the current era.

The man who had grinned at her walked over to her car and opened the driver's door, motioning her to take her seat in the little car. She stopped five paces away but said nothing.

"Miss Martin, we just want to have a short chat with you," he said smoothly. "You are in no danger." He had a Middle Eastern accent and rolled his "t"s, or eliminated them entirely. This short statement revealed the man knew all too much about her. It meant he was knowledgeable about her divorce and that she had reverted to her maiden name. This was not public information.

"We just want to have a short chat with you about a certain Deputy White," he said still wearing that scary, insincere grin. The alarm bells raised the level of intensity. There were fewer than six people in the entire administration aware of the deputy's involvement with the governor. There was a leak at the highest level. Her hands became sweaty, and her breath started coming faster.

She remembered her training: "Relax, take a breath, hold it. Calm down and take charge!"

"I am armed," she told them. "And I will defend myself." In spite of her training, she just could not shoot someone, anyone without warning.

"Now, now miss, no need to get upset," the talker said and took a step in her direction. She dropped the purse to the ground. Both men's eyes followed the bag. When they looked up, she had a gun in her right hand, had moved her left hand to beneath the handle of the little Glock and had assumed the stance.

Instinctively both men grabbed for their weapons. This proved to be a fatal mistake.

"BAP! BAP!" The little .380 was not overly loud on the open tarmac of the parking lot. In spite of her training, this was her first real action, and she had jerked the muzzle just a bit. Her point of aim directly over the nose of the nearest assailant was deflected by the involuntary movement one-quarter-of-an-inch left and an eighth-of-an-inch down. Two red spots appeared just beneath the man's right eye. The first round shattered the bone below the eye and deflected the bullet to the target's left. It impacted his spine just above his neck, severing the nerves carrying motor movement information to his lower extremities.

The second round following 500 milliseconds later found no meaningful obstruction. It traveled through the man's face, exiting his neck and severing his carotid artery. He stood with a startled look on his face, frozen erect for a couple of heartbeats before toppling forward, spurting blood from his neck like a beheaded chicken.

Elaine took one step to her left to avoid the falling man and shifted her aim toward the second adversary. Abdul dumbass was having difficulty getting his pistol free from his shirttail where his weapon was now tangled near the small of his back.

"Leave it alone!" Elaine told him. "If you pull the gun, I will have to shoot you!"

Abdul was a radical-believing Muslim. Women were lesser beings, who had a particular place in life. Telling a man what to do was not part of the scheme of things in Allah's creation. Here was this woman, dressed shamelessly, and made up with Western cosmetics, as alluring as she was unavailable.

He hated her for who she was and what she represented. He would not be humiliated and shamed in front of this hussy! His gun came free, and he smiled. He was still smiling when the double tap caught him just beneath his chin. The impact knocked him straight back against the car. He slid down to a sitting position with his legs stuck out in front of him.

He was unable to lift the gun. When he tried to breathe, blood ran down into his lungs. He looked at the blood running down his shirt and wondered whose it was. He was still wondering when everything went black.

***

White Farm – Downstate Illinois

I heard wheels on the gravel in front of the house and the dogs went nuts. Tasha turned to her left and leaped up to the window sill where she could see around toward the front of the house. Bo came straight across the kitchen and streaked down the hall. Moments later he returned, backing down the hall and barking furiously. That meant one thing. There were men with guns.

Bo understood guns.

Chance was up instantly moving toward the back door where there was an old Winchester model 97 exposed hammer shotgun over the entrance to the porch. The gun had belonged to my maternal grandfather, but Chance kept it oiled, cleaned and in perfect working order.

Delbert was up with his gun in hand standing beside the stairway door looking down the hall toward the front door. There was a drill; everyone knew what to do. Amanda jumped up and headed for the basement steps with me right behind her. The arsenal was in the cellar. As I went through the door, I saw Chance sliding the chest freezer away from the wall to take up a firing position behind it.

"I want you to go into the safe room!" I ordered Amanda. The basement was divided into two sections. The part beneath the house contained what most basements do, which is a heating A/C plant, water heater, water treatment, shelves of canned goods, and miscellaneous junk.

The other half, which was dug out north of the house in a 50-by-50-foot section, was a combination storeroom, root cellar, and tornado shelter. It was windowless with a ceiling 6-feet below grade. There was one door to access it. This door had formerly been a vault door from a bank in town acquired after it had moved to a new building and torn the old one down.

It was not the bank's main vault door, 10-feet high and 6-feet thick. It had been the door to the administrative and record vault. It was 4-feet wide, 8-feet high and 14-inches thick. It was plenty sturdy enough. When it was closed into the steel jam, itself poured into the concrete wall, four bolts an inch in diameter and 6-inches long secured it.

Unless one had several pounds of C4, once it was closed, it would stay closed, until someone on the other side wanted it open.

"Don't be silly," Amanda told me. "Hand me the ranch gun." She favored the little Ruger carbine chambered in .357 magnum. I handed her the rifle. She had opened the door to the weapon safe before I had even reached the basement floor. The safe's lock was biometric, opened with a thumbprint of any of the three of us.

I had been thinking of which gun to bring back upstairs from the time I left my seat. I settled finally on the Benelli even though it limited me to five rounds between loads. We were likely to be outnumbered and in close quarters. I liked to have a weapon where if the threat was east, I shot east.

I pressed the release and slid the pump back to check if there was a round in the chamber. There was. I grabbed a belt from the back of the safe that was preloaded with 12-gauge rounds. I looped it around the shotgun and picked up an AR15 Grendel. Amanda had been stuffing her pockets with clips for the ranch gun. When she saw me select the Grendel, she grabbed four mags of 6.5MM and turned for the stairs.

I had been listening intently, but other than the dogs barking, I could hear nothing overt coming from above.

***

Springfield, Illinois

Director Norman was used to the cell on his belt buzzing at all hours, so he was not surprised. He was a little shocked, however, when the caller ID told him it was Elaine Martin. This was a first. He was nonplussed. He really couldn't imagine…

"This is Matt."

"Matthew, you need to come over to my condo right away. I have just killed two men in the parking lot." She sounded a little put out, as if she had come downstairs and discovered a flat tire on her Miata.

"Are you all right?"

"I am better than these two sorry bastards, that's for sure." Norman was more than shocked. He had never heard the least vulgar phrase slip from Elaine Martin's stunning lips, let alone a profanity.

"I'm on my way. Should be there in seven or eight minutes. Talk to no one until I get there. Do you understand?"

"Okay, Matthew. But you might want to hurry. There seems to be a crowd gathering."

He ran for his car. He had come down from his apartment near the capitol and was in the basement parking lot when the call came in. He was soon zipping up the ramp with the blue light flashing above where he had fastened its magnetic base just over his head on the driver's side. The 1989 BMW M6 was not the fastest car on the road today, but it was quick enough for him and handled like one put it on like a garment.

He made it to Elaine's condo in six minutes flat. He arrived simultaneously with two ISP patrol cars. The four uniformed officers recognized him and saluted. They allowed him to walk ahead to the scene. Elaine was talking to a security guard from the condo. There was a crowd of 20 or so milling about, but the security guard evidently had been on his game. He had secured the site with yellow crime scene tape wound around four vehicles strategically placed to keep the curiosity seekers at bay.

"Disburse the crowd," Norman told the uniformed officers, who nodded and strode off to do his bidding.

"Have you called the governor?" Norman asked Elaine as he walked up.

"You told me to talk to no one else," she said reasonably. "Jason, this is Matthew Norman, he is director of ISP. Matthew, this is Jason Purdue. Jason is in charge of security for the compound here." The two men nodded acknowledgment of each other's presence, but neither offered to shake hands.

"This is clearly self-defense," Purdue said. "Both assailants were armed with their weapons in their hands when I came on the scene. I was the first one here. We have a video of the entire incident in the office."

"Thank you, Mr. Purdue," Norman said frostily, apparently not desirous of any advice from a civilian security guard. "We'll take it from here. I am sure you have other duties." Purdue colored a bit at the blatant insult but said nothing. He looked at Elaine, who nodded as if to tell him it was okay for him to leave the scene. He turned on his heel and walked away.

"Matthew, did you take lessons on being an asshole, or does it just come naturally to you?" she asked him bitingly. "Mr. Purdue is a gentleman and was only trying to help. He acted professionally and quickly as you can see." She pointed out the taped-off scene.

"Well, I …" Norman stuttered. He had a serious thing for Elaine Martin and was embarrassed and hurt that she had seen his behavior toward the security guard as insulting. He had not meant it to be. There were procedures to be followed. She had to be protected, and the fewer people involved, the better for her. Now she was standing there looking at him as if he was something she had stepped in and was stuck to her shoe.

"Never mind," she said. "What do we do now?"

CHAPTER EIGHT

White Farm — Downstate Illinois

I stopped Amanda at the bottom step and called up to Chance.

"Chancy, 'Plan B.' "

I didn't know what we were up against, but from the racket the dogs were making, it was serious business. They were genuinely frightened, and they don't scare easily.

I walked quickly to the rear basement wall and pulled a shelf of canned goods out revealing a 4-foot, 6-inch diameter tunnel. It wasn't comfortable walking, but it was large enough that crawling wasn't necessary. After the experience with the 13 terrorists, I was determined never to be trapped in the house again.

I had borrowed a backhoe so Chance and I could dig a long, deep ditch out to the generator shed. We then installed steel culverts to make an escape tunnel. This was the first time we had needed it, but I was extremely glad we had invested the time, effort, and not inconsiderable expense to build it.

Chance and Delbert came clopping down the stairs after Chance closed and locked the steel Pease door at the top. "Plan B" called for securing the dogs on the back porch where they would be relatively safe and out of the line of fire but were still making a racket leading anyone outside to believe we were still in the house.

It also called for us to get out of Dodge post haste.

"Chancy, grab Delbert a Grendel and a couple of mags from the safe, and get another belt of shotgun shells for yourself," I said. "And lock the safe behind you." I pulled a flashlight out of its charger on the bench after slinging the two guns I was carrying over my left shoulder and handed it to Amanda. I took the second light and shined it down the tunnel. The white diode beam revealed 12-inch wide planks running along the bottom, disappearing into the darkness beyond.

Chance thinks for himself. As he and Delbert filed by me into the tunnel, I noticed he had traded the shotgun for the .50 cal. It was heavy, clumsy, and awkward to carry and maneuver. I had to admit, however, if we needed it…

He is a good boy.

The cabinet that hid the tunnel entrance was hinged and mounted on crazy wheels. When I slid the bolt home, locking it from the inside, there was no indication it was anything but a storage shelf for canned goods.

Chance was first up the ladder leading to the generator building. There was a heavy manhole cover to be lifted at the top to gain access to the little blockhouse, but he had little problem with it. Since the tunnel sloped slightly downward, by the time it reached the generator shed, it was 8-feet below grade. From the end of the tunnel to the ravine beyond, a 6-inch pipe carried any water that might accumulate away to be discharged into the brook.

We would have been safe enough in the generator shed. It was was constructed of steel-reinforced concrete; proof against anything up to a .50 cal. There were no windows, but there were two firing slits in each of the four walls. Rooting us out of the shed would have been a painful, bloody process, but I had no intention of being trapped anywhere.

Chance was looking out of the slot nearest the house when I came out of the tunnel. By the time, I slid the manhole cover back in place, the generator "chunk-chunked" to a stop. "Plan B" called for cutting power to the house. Chance had shut the gas off as soon as he had emerged into the building.

A further plan was beginning to form since I noticed Chance bringing the Barrett. "Plan B" was complete once we exited the generator shed. It was designed to get us out of the house and the dogs locked into the relative safety of the back porch. I would rather have had them with me, but their ingrained inhibition of coming into the main house, and the difficulties of the vertical access into the shed, precluded bringing them in any emergency egress from the house.

Amanda had her eye glued to the little peephole glass in the door when I stood up. Chance turned in my direction and shook his head indicating he could see no assailants on our side of the house. Amanda unlatched the door and let it swing open. It was on the backside of the building facing away from the house and revealed a 10-yard open span of mowed grass between us and the heavily wooded edge of the ravine beyond. The building would provide cover from anyone looking our direction from the house.

There was an off-prem extension phone on the wall. I lifted the receiver and heard the welcome sound of dial tone. Evidently our potential assailants had not cut the phone line. Apparently they were either self-confident bordering on arrogant or had no idea what they were up against. Perhaps a bit of both, I thought as I dialed the four-digit code that would ring a 26-port conference call to the militia.

"This is Roy Lee," I said as soon as the ring back tone cut-off indicating someone had picked up. I would let them pass the word. "We are under assault at the home farm by an unknown number of armed assailants. We are free of the house and will engage on our own. Close the access road and send what help you can, but approach with caution because indications are the bad guys are armed with long guns."

Whoever was in front of and flanking our house was suddenly in a world of hurt. Very soon, 20 to 30 armed, experienced fighting men would be converging on their position with blood in their eye.

One could almost feel sorry for them; the operative word being "almost."

"Be advised," I added. "The barn will be our point of presence. Friendlies are Chance, Amanda, Delbert Jones, and myself. Chance and Delbert will be deployed on the ridge south of the house." My militia all knew Delbert. We had combined forces with his larger group on occasion during the chaos. "And someone call Milo to let him know the situation. We had to bail before I could call him." I doubted the sheriff would even react. With the militia being activated, any help he could send would be redundant. We were who he called when he was in trouble.

"You aren't going to wait for the militia are you daddy?" Amanda asked resignedly. Her natural female caution would have had us holed up in the generator shed, waiting for reinforcements. It was a tempting option. If we had been able to extricate the dogs, I would have considered it, but the shepherds were still in danger, and they were family.

We paused at the top of the hill as soon as we had entered the cover of the brushy woods. It was decision time. The hollow ran off to our left to the lake. It was the route of my morning walk in that direction. To our right, it sloped easily up to level off just behind the barn. The fields on the other side of the road drained down this hollow through a square 6-foot culvert just beyond the barn.

"Chance, I want you to take the Barrett and go through the culvert and make your way to the top of the ridge where you can cover the front of the house. Delbert, I would like you to go with him and watch his back." I phrased my statement to Delbert as a request since I would never attempt to order Delbert Jones to do anything. There were two reasons for this. First, I respected him like a surrogate father. Second, he might just have a better idea. Unfortunately today, he did not. He just nodded his agreement and we set off for the barn.

***

Capitol Building – Springfield, Illinois

Moshe Aaron had just walked into the Capitol building when he was stopped in the hall by a uniformed State Trooper and informed of the events earlier in the morning involving the governor's aide. The story was spreading through the building like wildfire.

Moshe turned on his heel and went straight to the governor's office. Moshe was responsible for the governor's personal security. In the former Federal government, he would have been the head of the Secret Service. In the present administration, he was part of the ISP, but reported directly to the governor with a dotted line to the director. One of his collateral duties was training ISP officers and staff in the use of handguns.

The staff was milling around in little groups talking when he came into the large, open, well-lit office. When he asked the whereabouts of

Miss Martin, he was pointed toward the closed door of the governor's office. He knocked twice softly then admitted himself.

Miss Martin was sitting on the sofa to the left of the governor's desk. Director Norman had pulled one of the chairs that typically sat in front of the desk to face the couch. He was writing on a yellow legal pad, balanced on his right knee. The pad was mounted on a clipboard. He looked like a census taker interviewing a citizen.

Miss Martin looked relaxed and calm, but her face was ashen. When she saw Moshe, her eyes grew wide, and she stood suddenly.

"Matthew, please. Could you excuse us for just a moment?" she asked, never taking her eyes off of the Israeli.

Norman was non-plussed at this request, but he reacted quickly. He was still a little embarrassed at the lady's reaction to his comments to the security guard and was anxious to please. He said nothing, but nodded his agreement and exited the room quickly, softly closing the door behind him.

"Oh Moshe," Elaine gasped and stumbled into his arms. She started sobbing uncontrollably.

"There, that is better," Moshe told her softly. "Let it come out, it's normal and expected." He silently thanked the God of Abraham that he had been close when the breakdown occurred. He had a deep affection for this lady. He was extremely glad he could help her through the crisis and avoid her being embarrassed in front of any of the other staff.

"You are a good person," Moshe whispered into her ear where Elaine's head was still buried in his chest. "You were forced into doing something that no one should ever have to do, but it was necessary. You are here now, and you are alive. Nothing else is even relevant."

When the trembling ceased, she stood up and stepped back as if surprised to find herself in his arms. There was a box of Kleenex on the side table beside the sofa. She took the two steps to reach them and dabbed at her eyes. When she looked up, color had returned to her face.

"Do you have a pastor?" Moshe asked her softly.

"Pastor?" Elaine looked confused as if his question made no sense to her. Since Moshe did not respond, she thought about his question for a long moment.

"I am not a religious person," she told him. "No, I don't have a pastor."

This surprised Moshe. In his experience, almost all citizens in Middle America had, at the least, a nodding acquaintance and nominal affiliation with some church. Since the traumatic times following the breakdown of national authority, a religious revival had swept the land.

"My parents did not go to church and I just never …" she let the thought trail off as if uncertain where to go with it.

"I can introduce you to my Rabbi," Moshe told her. "It's important you have someone to call."

Suddenly Elaine knew the little dark man was correct. There was something missing from her life. There was an aching void that called out for something clean and pure to fill. She couldn't put the feeling into words, but it was as real as if one of her limbs was suddenly missing.

"Thank you, Moshe, you are a good friend." This caused the little man to smile. Elaine realized she had never seen him smile before. She discovered she liked his smile. She liked it a lot. She walked over and kissed him on his receding hairline. He blushed.

"Will you be okay for now?" Moshe asked.

"Would you mind staying while I give Matthew my statement?" she answered his question with a question. That told Moshe all he needed to know. She was still not doing so well.

"Of course. Should I ask him to come back in?"

Elaine did not reply but nodded her affirmative answer and regained the seat where she had been when Moshe entered the room.

As Elaine regained her seat, an image formed in her mind. It featured a cowboy with a black hat, and she was enfolded in his arms. She felt safe there and determined as soon as she could, she was going to call that cowboy and tell him her feelings for good or ill. This morning's events had given her a strength of will she didn't realize she had.

The entire country had experienced an attitude adjustment after the disastrous attacks on the homeland. There was no cadre of bleeding-heart journalists waiting in the wings now to jump on any story about a white person defending themselves with deadly force. Prior to the chaos, Elaine would have been portrayed as some lunatic "pistol-packin' mama" who had gunned down two innocent bystanders, who had only been trying to help her get into her car. There would have been interviews with friends and neighbors of the "victims," who would have been portrayed as quiet, devout family men who loved puppies and orphans.

That genre of journalism blew away in the same radioactive wind that destroyed the Capitol.

However, given the nature of Elaine's position as a trusted aide to the sitting governor, the story would have legs. It was essential that every detail be recorded and reported accurately and framed in a manner that would not bring discredit to the chief executive's office. Luckily for Elaine, the perpetrators had been quickly identified as illegal aliens from Syria with contacts to a notorious Russian mob. Their tattoos had told the story as plainly as if someone had pinned a note to their lapels.

What was of paramount interest to Matthew Norman was the assailants' interest in Roy Lee White. It was this thread he began to tug on when Elaine's questioning resumed.

"So they told you they wanted to talk to you about Mr. White?" Norman said reading from his notes. "Did they say anything else?"

"They knew of my divorce, my position with the governor and that I had retained my maiden name. Matthew, none of that is public knowledge," she told him.

"Yes, I have that," he said trying to pull her back to the White angle. "But I am concerned about why they would be interested in Mr. White's connection to the governor. It makes no sense. White is just an intelligence resource for the governor, one of many, and not even official. I don't get it."

"I am afraid I can't help you there, I have no idea."

"I know, I was thinking out loud," Norman replied, studying his notes as if there was something there he was missing.

"Did they make any overt moves that you felt were threatening?"

"They were between me and my car. One even opened the door and was standing by it. I would have had to put myself in an indefensible position to get into it. It was a position I had been trained to never allow myself to be put in." She looked directly at Moshe, who nodded his encouragement and approval. She had done well.

"So nothing else about White?" he asked routinely. They had been over it from every angle.

Elaine shook her head, but she was clearly thinking.

"Matthew, there has to be a leak at the highest level. How could anyone even know that Leroy was working for the governor again? And, he hasn't done anything that we know of. He has only had this new assignment for a couple of days. Even I don't know what he is working on. Do you?"

Norman was reluctant to admit he didn't know specifically what White and the governor were up to. As head of the ISP, he should be intimately familiar with anything in his jurisdiction. But the governor had turned the cowboy loose on a particular vague threat that so far had not materialized into anything concrete.

Leroy White was an uncomfortable burr under the director's saddle. The man had been a rather famous militia commander during the chaos and reformation. As a professional law officer, Norman had a jaundiced view of the militia. To him, they represented vigilante tendencies and were a law unto themselves. During the period of anarchy, they may have been necessary, but now they posed a threat to establishment law and order.

The other consideration was: he *had* left the man on the beach. It was a fact of which he was not particularly proud, but he had been under orders. He had protested those orders stringently to the point where he was threatened with loss of his command. In the end, he had done what he was told. It had been a miracle that White and his platoon had survived. Command had been convinced they were all dead and was unwilling to risk more lives to claim their bodies. The politicians running the military had become quite casualty-averse by that time.

***

Beirut, Lebanon 1984

Little puffs of dirt in front of his position got Mitch's attention. He was under fire. A couple of the advancing foot soldiers of Allah on the far right had seen his position and were firing at him with their AKs.

He looked up at me and gave me a two-hands open, "What now?" signal. I pointed to the ground and held up three fingers, "lower arc three degrees." I pointed to the right of where he was taking fire and held up one finger. I pointed over the top of the building and held up two. Lastly, I pointed to my left and held up one. He bent over the tube and five seconds later a little 10-pound can of destruction dropped on the two men firing at him. A few hundred milliseconds later they ceased fire. Actually, they ceased all activity of any kind, including breathing.

Unsurprisingly having mortar shells dropping among them slowed the enemy advance dramatically. In fact, it stopped them cold. They were pretty well evenly split in their activity. One-half was diving for cover; the other half was busy dying.

We finally had the break I had been waiting for and I pulled the remainder of my little group back to the wall from whence my sortie into military command had commenced.

For the very short moment, I was reasonably happy. We had accomplished our mission and dealt with the rockets impacting the airport. I had not lost any more men. We had used almost none of our limited supply of ammunition. Now, if the lieutenant would just wake up and re-take command my day would be perfect.

I checked. Nope, he was still dead.

"Sergeant White, report!" the captain seemed to have his panties in a bunch. Now that I had a short respite, I decided I could spare him a moment.

"This is White; the rockets have been dealt with." I gave him the short version.

"Sergeant White, this is Captain Norman, do you read?"

I checked my radio; it looked okay. I thought maybe it had taken a hit, or been damaged in the crashing and banging moving between positions. As far as I could see it was undamaged. I tried again.

"This is White, I read you five by five," I replied in my best aviation lingo.

"Sergeant if you read this transmitter, I have to tell you, you cannot return to the airport the way you egressed. There is an entire company of Hezbollah filling the gap outside the wall in that direction. You will have to circle around and come in from the north. It is the only way back."

Well, isn't that just precious?

A row of buildings a half block to our rear had gotten my attention when I had experienced my helicopter view of the tactical situation. Firstly, they seemed undamaged. That seemed odd when everything else in the area had been beaten up pretty bad. Secondly, I had seen a little white face peering out of a darkened doorway just above street level. Either the child was lying down, which didn't seem likely from his posture, or he was standing in a stairwell.

I knew there was a warren of connecting cellars and underground passages beneath this ancient city, some of which dated back to the Crusades. I had a feeling that it might offer us a way out of this mess.

Mitch and Vinny came pounding up from behind us where they had taken a different route back to the wall. Mitch was smiling. He was pretty proud of himself.

"What now Sarge?"

"Ya done good dog face," I told him. "Did you destroy the tube?"

"Yeah, Vinny dropped a grenade into it as we were leaving," he replied sadly, as if reporting on the death of a friend. Did I mention? Mitch loved mortars. I shook my head. Human behavior is sometimes inexplicable.

I did a quick head count and took inventory of our weapons and capabilities. I had 11 grunts and myself, two snipers, and a medic. We had three LAWs since the guys hadn't been able to get a shot off in the direction of the machine gun. We had one M60 machine gun, 10 M16s, a shotgun, and the sniper rifle. The sniper's spotter carried an M1 carbine. Each of the line Marines carried 300 rounds of 5.56 except the two assistant gunners with the M60. Since they were burdened with close to a thousand rounds each of 7.62 machine gun ammo, they would only have a spare mag or two for their M16s.

Each of the grunt Marines had half-dozen grenades, plus Gordo and I had M203 grenade launchers attached to our rifles. These wicked little 40MM tubes launched grenades of twice the power of an ordinary hand-thrown item and could be lobbed down range over 100 yards.

The sailor carried a 1911 side arm and was not at all reluctant to use it. I had taken the lieutenant's 1911 but with only two spare mags, I wondered if hauling around the extra weight was worth it.

That sounded like a lot of ammo, but even with what the two assistant gunners were carrying, the M60 could burn through what we had in less than five minutes of continuous fire.

So, we were in pretty good shape for ammunition and for a small unit, were heavily armed. The only fly in the ointment was, we had little food and a one-way radio. It was supposed to be an in-and-out mission back in a couple of hours, so the lieutenant had loaded us down with ammo. If we got stuck out beyond the wire for any length of time, we were going to get hungry and stay that way.

Now that the mission was accomplished, getting back inside the wire and on a bird out of this third-world sewer was our next to top priority. No. 1 was staying alive to get back inside the wire in the first place.

"Has anyone got a flashlight?" I asked generally. I saw the question being sent up the line. Soon the word came back. We had three little penlights between us, and the sniper's spotter had an issue flashlight with fresh batteries. That would give us a couple hours of being able to see in the warrens. I would just have to hope that would be enough.

***

Womack Ranch — Downstate Illinois

Lyman Womack was not happy. From his perspective, his life had been shattered. Even though he was living in a mansion surrounded by his family, servants and sycophants with food and every comfort modern life could offer prior to the crisis, it was not the same.

He was struggling to keep everything together. He was not accustomed to struggling, and he hated it. Before the chaos, he had been rich. He had not been wealthy like a Rockefeller or Walton heir, he had been wealthy like a small country. Some individuals had a Lear jet or other corporate plane. He had a fleet of those plus his own personal DC10 that he flew his race cars around the world to compete in the International Gran Prix.

He was personal friends with Edwardo Slim, purportedly the richest man in the world. He and Slim owned a race track in Mexico together and shared a passion for open-wheel racing. He was on first name basis with the King of Saudi Arabia and had spent many nights at the palace. He was used to spending his time moving from one world capital to the next on a daily basis. Prior to the bottom falling out of his world, he would seldom spend a week when he was not on at least three continents in the same seven-day period.

Now he was trapped here on his farm in the country. He had been here for months and was becoming restive. While the income from his operations dried up almost overnight, the expenses had not. He had been burning through a prodigious amount of money daily, but as long as it came in faster than he spent it, he had no worries.

The world banking system had crashed. There were debts everywhere. There were national debts incurred by every country in the world. There were corporate debts and private company notes, bonds and obligations. It was all paper. It was ton after ton of red ink on paper.

When the primary engine of the world's economy stuttered and stopped, the whole rickety structure came crashing down. A great deal of Mr. Womack's wealth had been stored in the ones and zeros of the world banking system's computers.

As bank after bank owners threw up their hands and locked their doors, the Womack fortune dissipated like the cloud of ash blowing across the country from the general direction of Maryland.

In the end, like thousands of others, he was forced to flee to his family's farm in the country. It was a velvet-lined prison since he had made provision for disaster. He had stored gold, cash, food, and commodities in the bins and buildings on the 25,000-acre farm built around his family's homestead place, so he was surviving in luxury, but for him, it was bare survival. He wanted his life back.

Even his farming operation had suffered. He had farmed on an industrial scale. As a result, he was at the mercy of the seed, fertilizer, and fuel providers. When those commodities disappeared, his farm operation ground to a halt. Trying to keep his employees working became a drain on the large stocks of food and supplies he had stored. While significant, they certainly had not been infinite. He had been forced to shut down all but the small part of the agriculture operation providing direct food and fiber for the household.

He could hardly stand to walk out on the deck and look across the rolling acres growing up in useless weeds. It was infuriating.

He was sitting in his office staring at the phone on his desk debating on whether to answer it. It seemed there was nothing but bad news these days. The blinking light would not give him peace so finally he pushed the button.

"Mr. Womack, it's Mr. Rollins in Springfield. He says it's urgent," his secretary told him. Of course, it is urgent, everything these days is critical, Womack thought.

"Okay, put him through," he told her resignedly.

"Mr. Womack, this is Ed Rollins," the man told him. Womack could tell from the tinny mechanical sound of the man's voice he was on the secure satellite link. It had better be important! That link cost him $200 a minute! "Ivan is dead, sir."

"What the hell happened?!!"

"The lady they were interviewing shot them," the man's disquiet somehow made its way through the mechanical security filters. He sounded genuinely terrified. Womack's initial reaction of fury became tempered quickly with his own sense of fear.

"Can they be tied to us?" he asked the man in Springfield.

"It is highly unlikely," Rollins replied. Womack considered this for a couple of minutes. It was imperative they find out what was going on between the governor and this militia leader. The man was dangerous, unpredictable, and he was here, almost in their face. If he was going to be an obstacle to their plans, he would have to be dealt with. If not, he was a local law officer and any action against him could cause its own set of problems.

"Do you have an alternate plan?" Womack asked.

"Yes, Sir, we do. We are setting it up now; we should have results before the end of the week."

"Make it happen, the sooner, the better," Womack growled and slammed the button down with his thumb breaking the connection.

CHAPTER NINE

White Farm – Downstate Illinois

I watched Chance disappear under the road lugging the massive Barrett semi-auto .50 cal as easily as if it were a Browning .22 and had a moment of unreality. For a long breath, my brain would not accept what my eyes were telling it. He should be the little boy I carried around the farm on my shoulders and rode down the road on the gas tank of my motorcycle, laughing in joy with the wind in our faces.

I felt rage. A cold fury welled up in my breast at the monumental stupidity, greed, and selfishness that led to this. My grandson, who should be carrying his books to class or a football down a homecoming field to cheers and adulation of his peers, was instead carrying a combat rifle. He was moving to a fighting hole on our own farm!

My anger wasn't directed toward whomever the threat in front of our house turned out to be. It was immaterial. They were a faceless evil that must be dealt with. In a way, it wasn't even their fault. They were doing what they felt they had to do. I was their enemy. The bitter bile in my throat was raised by the generations of men who went to

Washington, raised their hands and took an oath to protect the Constitution and then sold out.

I so wished it were those traitors waiting in front of my house instead of some poor slob who was there because someone paid him to be there, or because some insane mullah had filled his head with gibberish, or even some criminal who saw me standing in the way of his business. At least, there was honesty in their hostility. It made sense.

What had happened to the country my ancestors carved out of the wilderness, made none.

I gritted my teeth and slipped into the barn. Amanda went up the haymow ladder ahead of me. She went over to the double doors facing the house and peered through the crack. While she was opening the doors, I was setting up bales of hay and carrying 50-pound feed sacks to build a firing position.

Both doors were open giving us a clear view of the front of the house when I dropped into the firing position behind the feed sacks three paces back from the door. This left us in the dark to anyone looking in from outside.

I settled in behind the feed sacks and rested the forearm of the Grendel across them as if I were on a bench rest at the range. I twisted the adjustable scope back to its lowest magnification which gave me a clear view of the front porch and the yard leading out to the white picket fence. The fence ran across the yard to the garden beyond separating the lawn from the parking area next to the road. At this magnification, the white pickets were visible to my left as well as the grill and headlights of the van the visitors had arrived in.

Amanda climbed up the bales to where a three-foot wide ventilation window with angled wooden shutters was located just below the roof line. Out of the corner of my eye, I saw her slip the muzzle of the ranch rifle through the lowest slat and sight down the barrel. I knew from her vantage point she was covering the porch where the dogs were sequestered. They were still raising Cain.

From my vantage point, it seemed there was some disagreement among the members of the visiting team. There were two men standing midway between the fence and the front porch. They appeared to be keeping an eye on the dormers at the front of the house. That would make sense. If someone was going to be defending the house from the interior, an upper window would make a sensible defensive position.

There were three men on the porch. One was standing in front of the door with the other two backed up on either side of the opening with their backs against the front of the house. The sixth man in my view was standing with his back to me facing the porch from a position on the ground where he could look along the south side of the house. He seemed to be urging the men on the porch to do something they were unwilling to do.

He seemed to be upset. He was waving his arms and gesticulating toward the house. He was yammering away in Spanish. Colombians! Aha, it makes sense now. It has nothing to do with the Federalists; it is the damn Colombians coming back on me for the riverboat incident. I had killed Julius Esteban Escobar a little over a year ago. His father was a big-time, drug-dealing warlord in Columbia who evidently still bore me some ill will.

"Señor White! You must come out now, or we will burn your house!" the man facing the door shouted. I wondered if he was bluffing or was there something going on out of my view. I looked up at Amanda; she turned and looked at me shaking her head. There was nothing happening from her viewpoint. Just when I made up my mind they were bluffing, a seventh man appeared into my sight from the fence's gate. He was carrying a bottle of some liquid. It had a cloth stuck into its top. He seemed to be struggling with a lighter.

I let him light it before I shot him.

***

Springfield, Illinois

The Rabbi had been listening to the young lady's life story for more than an hour. She was obviously intelligent and quick witted. She would have to be endowed with some exceptional managerial qualities to have obtained to the position she currently held at the governor's office. On the other hand, she was so blissfully ignorant of anything pertaining to spiritual matters she appeared a blank slate.

When he asked her how the earth and the surrounding cosmos came to be, she mouthed the platitudes of big bang and evolution. When he asked her about her understanding of natural law, she mumbled something about survival of the fittest. He was about to write her off as a hopeless case of liberal brainwashing when she asked him a question.

"Rabbi, I know I should feel no guilt because it was self-defense, and those men would have done terrible things to me if I had not defended myself. But I still feel horrible, almost sick. Why is that?"

Aha! Now we can talk, he thought.

"Miss Martin," the Rabbi began, but the young lady interrupted him.

"Please call me Elaine. Using the 'Miss' title seems so formal."

"All right, Elaine," the Rabbi agreed reluctantly. Keeping a bit of formality was probably best, but he didn't want to give the least offense. The young lady was obviously hurting and was as vulnerable as a cracked egg shell.

"First, let me assure you, one of our faith's fundamental tenets is the right of self-preservation. You did what you had to do, and that is the end of it," he told her unequivocally.

The look of relief and gratitude she gave him with the attendant color returning to her face touched the Rabbi. His heart went out to the lady.

"Secondly, the fact you are experiencing emotional trauma in the aftermath reflects well on you and your essential humanity," he said and smiled reassuringly. "We believe that a Creator God wrote the law of right and wrong into the heart of every individual. Some of his creatures are more attuned to this message than others. You seem to possess a soul very much attuned to His inner voice."

The Rabbi watched the comfort of his words wash over the young lady and was gratified to see her visibly relax and actually smile for the first time.

"My grandmother told me on her deathbed that I had been baptized as an infant," she said as she looked up at the stained-glass window above his desk. "Do you know what that means?"

"Uh-oh, I may be in trouble here," the Rabbi thought to himself.

"Elaine, do you know what faith your grandmother practiced?"

"They went to a Lutheran church; would that mean they were Lutheran?" she asked him after a long pause. It was as if she had been struggling to remember something from a far past.

"It would mean they were Christian of the Lutheran denomination."

"My parents always laughed at my grandparents for going to church and believing, what my parents said, were fairy tales and dark-age superstition."

"Elaine, I know a Lutheran pastor. Would you like for me to introduce you? If you are at all interested in exploring the faith of your grandparents, I believe that would be the place to start."

"But don't you believe in the same God?"

"Oh boy, this is was what I was afraid of" he thought. It was the Rabbi's turn to stare over his desk at the stained-glass window from the armchair next to the lady where he had sat down. He wished now that he had the reassuring and formal presence of his desk between them.

"*Hear O Israel, the Lord our God is One.*" The words of the Shema echoed through his mind and seemed to be written in fire across the stained glass. The Christian heresy of a Trinitarian God filled his mind with misgiving, but he was not about to give voice to his unease.

"We start from the same place, share the same roots," he told her carefully. "Two thousand years ago, we took different paths."

He got up and went to his desk, flipped open his card case and turned a few pages. Finding what he was seeking, he stared at the card for a long moment.

"Elaine, this is a Lutheran pastor with whom I have worked on the Food Bank committee. He is a sweet, gentle man, and I would like for you to meet him. May I?"

"Yes, I would like that."

He picked up the phone. A church secretary answered. A few minutes later the pastor himself came on the line.

"George, this is Eli Blumstein. I have a young lady here with me I would like for you to meet. Would it be okay for me to bring her to your office?"

***

Beirut, Lebanon 1984

"Colonel, I will not leave my men behind! I have an entire platoon still out beyond the wire. We cannot leave them!" Captain Matthew Norman was addressing the battalion commander of 22 MAU, 2nd of the 6th. The good colonel was less than happy with the company commander currently on the beach-end of the radio connection.

"Captain you lost contact with that platoon after the building they were assaulting exploded," the colonel told him needlessly. Captain Norman was well aware of the situation.

"Colonel, we don't know the platoon was *in* the building when it went up!"

"Captain I am giving you a direct order. When those birds go wheels up, you have the last of your command aboard and leave the area. We have an agreement with the Amal to occupy those positions at 3 p.m. and I intend to honor that commitment. You secure the colors as of right now. The birds are on their way in."

"Sir, I…"

"Not one word, Captain or I will have you relieved and court-martialed for direct disobedience of an order."

"Aye, Aye, Sir!" the captain replied bitterly and broke the connection.

***

"Sergeant White, you should take a look at this," the spotter told me quietly. He was standing on a four-foot wall looking back toward the airport through a set of powerful binoculars. I was huddled down just below him face to face with a young boy who could not have been a day older than 12. He was armed and had the eyes of an old man.

What I was discussing with the boy was a life-and-death matter. Had it been anyone else, I would have put the spotter off, but the sniper team was professional and as competent as any pair of combat soldiers I had ever met. If he thought I needed to look, I needed to look.

What I saw through the binocs made my blood run cold. They were taking down the colors at the airport! That meant the last train out of Dodge would be leaving shortly. It was pretty apparent to Mrs. White's favorite son that he and his accomplices would not be on it.

The spotter looked at me with a questioning gaze.

"Embassy," I told him.

"It's a long way, with a lot of Hezbollah between us and them."

"If you have a better idea, I am all ears."

"Tat, tat, tat! Tat, tat tat!" The M60 being fired in short bursts interrupted our conversation.

"We need to move Sergeant," Gorder told me. We had taken up a position in the doorway of the building where I had seen the young boy peering from the stairwell. There were two burnt-out cars sitting at the curb, one of which the MG team was using as a base for the M60.

I looked down the streets in all four directions from where we were huddled behind the cars and walls of the building. Moving in any direction seemed to be a daunting task. The streets were littered with debris, downed telephone and power lines, wrecked and burned-out vehicles and trash of every description. It reminded me of some of the pictures from World War II Germany where the cities had been bombed into rubble.

It was a damn shame. Beirut had been the Paris of the Middle East, cosmopolitan and wealthy. And poor Lebanon. It had been caught in the vortex of world politics with the West lining up on the side of the Christians and Israelis, and the Soviets supporting the Druze and Syrians. Into this confusing mix, the Iranians could not stay out of the fray, so they sent their own revolutionary guards to back the local Shia.

The Lebanese people suffered and died.

There was one unifying theme by 1984; all sides hated the U.S. We had entered this powder keg of violence, hatred, and animosity thinking our good intentions would protect us. This naiveté had left my little contingent stranded in the middle of a nasty civil war where we were legitimate targets of all sides. The one-third of the country that was Christian and had been our nominal allies felt betrayed and abandoned. The other two-thirds saw us as natural enemies, as the Great Satan and supporters of the Lesser Satan, Israel.

"I can take you to the French," the boy said. He was tugging on my arm, trying to get my attention. "There are tunnels."

He was pointing toward the darkened stairwell from where he had emerged. It was the direction the angel had given me. Angel, intuition, subconscious linking of various bits of seemingly unrelated information; call it what you will. From the instant I saw the little white face peering out of the rubble, I knew this was where we needed to go.

"Do you trust him, Sergeant?" the spotter whispered. "What if he is Druze or Hezbollah?" Despite the whisper, the boy had overheard.

"I am Christian – Phalanges," the boy said looking directly at me as if his concentration could somehow convince me of his sincerity. When he saw me hesitate, he went on. "I believe in God the Father Almighty, creator of Heaven and Earth, and in his only Son, our Lord Jesus Christ, who…" He started reciting the Apostles Creed.

"I believe you," I told him as I held up my hand to cut off his recitation. It seemed odd and out of place here in the midst of so much bloodshed, hatred, and violence.

"You two go with him and scope it out. I'll give you five minutes. If you don't come back, I'll follow with the rest of the platoon."

The spotter didn't reply immediately. He looked at the boy skeptically but then seemed to make up his mind. He nodded and stepped away to get his partner. They reappeared shortly from around the edge of the doorway and disappeared down the steps. I checked my watch.

"Tat, tat, tat – pause – tat, tat, tat." The MG team was keeping the bad guys down with short bursts. Occasionally a single or double tap from one of the riflemen's M16s would be added to the din. So far they were doing a good job of keeping our assailants at bay. I knew it couldn't last. Allah's faithful soldiers would be bringing up some heavy stuff anytime.

Right by the numbers, I saw two rag-heads step into opposite sides of the street about 50 yards away holding RPGs and aiming them in our direction!

"Tatta, tatta, tat – thonk!" The M60 team had spotted them as well and fired off a long burst at the one on the left. Gordo had handed his blooker to Mitch. It was a little mortar after all. The grenade caught the enemy soldier right in the chest just as he triggered the RPG. It did two things. Most importantly it caused him to jerk the launcher up at the critical moment deflecting the rocket to sail off over our heads to explode above in the second story. It showered us with dust and concrete, but no one was hurt. The second result was that it blew the man in two.

I checked my watch. It wasn't quite five minutes, but we had to get out of here.

"Okay, Gordo take your team and follow the snipers," I told my fellow sergeant. "Vinny, trade me pieces," I instructed Mitch's partner and handed him my own blooker. "You and Mitch are rear guard." They nodded their understanding and took up positions on either side of the doorway as I handed him the belt of 40MM grenades I was carrying. The rest of my team followed Gordo's guys down the steps. I ran out to the MG team behind the nearest vehicle.

"Jimmy, give me your C4," I told one of the ammo bearers. I knew he and his fellow team member were carrying a couple bricks each. "I need to close the door behind us."

CHAPTER TEN

White Farm – Downstate Illinois

"AARGH! MAMA! MAMA!" The Columbian screamed in agony as he rolled around on the sidewalk wrapped in flames. It was a ridiculously easy shot. At 75 yards, I could put an entire magazine through the same hole with a 6.5 Hornady Amax bullet. The bottle in his hand exploded when the little 240-grain boattail smashed through it, covering the now screaming soldier in burning gasoline.

I shifted my aim to the apparent leader standing by the house. He was frozen in place watching his charge rolling around on the ground screaming in the middle of a huge yellow-and-orange fireball.

I brought the cross hairs to rest just below his hairline and squeezed the trigger.

"Crack!" He fell as if he had been pole-axed.

As I was bringing the crosshairs back to the gangster on the deck, I felt the cold press of metal beneath my left ear.

"Stan away frum da gun, señor..."

Oh, shit! One had come up the ladder behind us! The question was: How close behind us? And how many were there?

"KABOOM!" The shock of the explosion sent a puff of superheated air through the haymow door, distracting my assailant for the briefest instant. Evidently Chance had brought .50 cal incendiary fire onto the van.

"Crack! Crack!" Amanda's little ranch gun barked twice. The double tap from the .357 knocked my antagonist onto his face. The full-body mass shots impacted on the side of his vest beneath his right arm, knocking him back against the hay bales to my right, spinning him around clockwise, and leaving him face down in the bales.

I took one step and delivered a long kick between his splayed legs driving his gonads somewhere north of his kidneys. I heard a coughing sound come from the hay as he curled up in a fetal position.

I retrieved the AK and drove the butt into the joint between the back of his head and his collar. He spasmed then lay still.

I pointed to the ladder hole, and Amanda slid down the bales to take up a watch position at the entrance to the haymow.

Better late than never.

I returned to my firing position and gazed out on utter chaos. My fence was on fire. Other than that it was quiet. Once the shooting started, the dogs dove for cover. Now they were silent. A greasy, black smoke from the burning van drifted up to the haymow door. It had the distinct aroma of roasting meat.

From my vantage point, I could see a dust cloud coming our way. The cavalry was arriving. They were just a tad late. My front lawn was covered in bodies, some still smoldering and giving off a black, sick-smelling smoke. Others lay sprawled where Delbert had dropped them.

One lay over the fence missing his head. Evidently Chance drilled him with the .50 cal. It is rather messy when aimed at a single individual.

It was a fine mess and would take a long time to clean up. I shook my head. This is no way to live.

My anger toward the former leaders of my country came boiling up again. I shook my head and tried to tamp it down. It was pointless now.

"Do you always wear a tie to a gunfight?" Amanda asked as I walked to the haymow entrance. She brushed a couple of stray strands of hay from my jeans and smiled. "And you came out without your hat. You are out of uniform."

I shook my head. What could I say? I knew she was being flippant to cover her anxiety.

"Cover me as I go down. I think it's over, but there might be one or two left in the barn."

I looked as far as the four-foot hole would allow me but I didn't see anything or anyone. I dropped to my stomach, stuck my head through the hole for a quick survey, then jerked it back up. I didn't detect anyone, but the barn was relatively dark.

I changed my mind.

I walked back to the haymow door. I heard numerous wheels on the gravel crunch to a stop in front of the house. When I looked out, the yard was filled with armed men, who were spreading out around the house. Two were coming in our direction. It was the Jamison brothers.

"Robby, it's Roy Lee. I am in the haymow, coming to the door now." The boys would be jumpy. Friendly fire is just as deadly as any.

"Okay, Mr. White."

"Be careful, there might be one or two in the barn. One came up the ladder and surprised me a bit ago."

They nodded their understanding and split up to enter the barn through two separate doors. I heard them come in and sprint for cover. Pause – sprint. Robby's head popped up at the top of the ladder.

"All clear, Mr. White. Where's your hat?"

It seems there are fashion consultants without number out here in the country.

Who knew?

***

Springfield, Illinois

"How's this thing is going to play out?" Director Norman asked the governor. They were sitting in the chief executive's office. The governor was behind his desk; the director was sitting in an armchair with his ever-present iPad on his knee. They were discussing the proposed merging of the five-state law enforcement plan.

"Eventually, I think we will see four or five separate nations where the United States used to be. We were just too big with too many disparate interests to be successfully governed as a single country. Texas and four bordering states have already formed a confederation. I have been talking to neighboring governors about emulating what Texas is doing. This thing with merging law enforcement efforts is the first step."

Norman asked, "Do you think the states be willing to give up their power now that they have it back?"

"Oh, I don't believe that we'll ever see a central government with the kind of power that evolved in Washington. We've learned that lesson. I think we *will* see a number of federation-of-states forming around geographic and economic interests. Real power over people's everyday lives isn't going to be allowed to get far beyond the counties."

Norman continued his query. "What about the cities? The overwhelming dependent democratic majorities in the metropolitan areas are what knocked the wheels off the old Union."

The governor replied, "I think everyone recognizes that now. Perhaps we'll have a few city-states like Singapore. For sure the folks in the hinterland aren't going to let the cities dictate the way the folks in the country live their lives or spend their hard-earned money."

Changing the subject, the director asked, "Governor, what are we going to do about these militias?"

"We aren't going to do anything about them. They are the people. Thanks to the militias, there is law and order across the state." It was clear, the governor was a great fan of militias. The director, however, was not.

"But Governor, they are a law unto themselves, vigilantes in some cases, and little more than armed mobs."

The governor regarded his director of police for a long moment, studying him as if he were trying to determine who he was talking to.

"Matthew, where were you during the chaos?" The governor knew exactly where his director had been during the upheaval. It was a rhetorical question to set the premise of the governor's argument.

"I was aboard the ship with my unit." When Washington disappeared, the director was a major of Marines aboard the USS Guam. They had been deployed in the Mediterranean at the time, ready to react to any repeat of the trauma of Benghazi.

Without what he considered legitimate orders, the admiral in charge of the task force under which the MAU was deployed merely brought his fleet back to the States, discharged the entire body on his own authority, and sent everyone home.

"During the worst of the trauma, the militia was the only thing that held the country together," the governor said definitively, effectively cutting off any further discussion.

Director Norman knew when to say "Aye, Aye, sir," and shut up. He changed the subject once more.

"Are the Federalists a serious threat?" He was itching to query the governor about the activity of one ex-rodeo cowboy but didn't want to approach the subject directly.

The governor didn't reply immediately. He thought about the question for some time. When he finally reacted, he didn't answer directly. He reached over and pushed a button on the phone.

"Elaine, is Moshe in the building?"

"Yes, sir, he is attending a briefing in conference room A."

"Is he presenting?"

"No sir, he is attending."

"Please send someone to get him. I need to see him."

"Of course sir, right away," Elaine's voice came over the intercom.

"Ahem..." the director cleared his throat as if to speak, but the governor held up one finger cutting him off. Evidently their conversation was on hold until the chief of security arrived.

Moments later the door opened, and Moshe entered the room. He was dressed in a two-piece, silk-wool worsted suit, the creases of which looked like they could slice raw steak. When he walked across the room, he seemed to bounce off the balls of his feet as if they were spring loaded. He looked like an unsprung steel trap.

I am glad he's on our side was the unbidden thought that appeared in the director's mind. That is one dangerous little man.

"You wanted to see me, Governor?"

"The director just asked me if the Federalists are a serious problem. What say you, sir?" The governor asked without preamble.

Moshe's eyebrows wrinkled slightly, and he started pacing in a circle at the end of the governor's desk with his left hand near his face, fingers tugging at his upper lip. He was like a shark that had to keep moving to breathe. He seemed to be considering a lot of various data points, trying to summarize.

"They have a lot of resources," he said finally. He stopped in mid-stride and seemed to study the portrait of Lincoln behind the governor's desk, but it was apparent he didn't see Gettysburg.

"This is my opinion, strictly based on guess-work and bits of data we have been able to gather. There are a lot of chiefs and few Indians. I think this is a weakness. I honestly believe they aren't nearly as strong or as much of a threat as they perceive themselves to be."

"Moshe, Mr. White is coming in shortly with his report. I want you to be here."

"Yes, I saw him talking to your aide when I came in."

"Oh, he is here?" the governor asked surprised. Elaine was supposed to notify him when the deputy arrived.

Moshe didn't reply, but he nodded in the affirmative.

The deputy had been on board for some time, but he had been intercepted by the governor's aide. The pair was in deep conversation when the intercom on her desk interrupted them.

"Elaine, would you please have the deputy come in?" She looked at the intercom with frustration. She wasn't finished. She was determined to let Roy Lee White know the depth of her feelings for him. She had only begun her confession when the governor's order halted her in mid-sentence.

Elaine knew the deputy was coming this morning. In fact, she talked to him briefly when he called in and asked to see the governor. She had spent extra time getting dressed and made up to look her best for his arrival.

When he appeared at the glass door of the governor's office, dressed in his usual black sports coat, jeans and cowboy boots carrying that black cowboy hat, she felt a thrill she had never experienced before. It almost took her breath away.

When he strode over to her desk, she stood up wanting to rush to him and fold him in an embrace, but she knew she could not. He cocked his head to the left slightly looking at her curiously.

"What?" he asked quizzically. Somehow her body language had betrayed her feelings. Elaine found herself tongue-tied. She didn't know where to start. Then Moshe walked by, and she had to tell him to go on in. When she turned back, she finally was able to come up with something to say.

"I am so glad to see you, Roy. I heard about the home invasion. I was terrified that you might have been…" The intercom interrupted her spiel.

The deputy started to walk to the door but hesitated. When he turned back to face her, he said one word. That one word made her day.

"Lunch?"

She couldn't even respond verbally, she just smiled and nodded. She hoped her smile was not a stupid adolescent girl's grin.

He was waiting for her when she came out of the glass doors. He was standing three steps down with his butt against the iron railing. He was wearing his hat and sunglasses. When he saw her, he grinned.

"My God, the man is handsome," she thought involuntarily. She wanted to throw herself into his arms, but contented herself to take his offered arm, and they walked down the steps together. She sensed the faintest hint of the cologne he always wore. It smelled of limes and peppermint. She liked it. A lot.

Later she couldn't remember what they talked about as they walked to the restaurant he favored. It didn't seem to matter. He was so easy to speak with she discovered, she laughed and relaxed in his presence. She discovered she hadn't been able to be truly comfortable in a long time.

They ordered lunch, and he ordered a dark, brown beer. Though she seldom drank, and never at lunch time, today she ordered a single glass of white wine in celebration of finally getting Roy Lee White to herself.

Roy Lee took a sip of the brown liquid. He sat the mug down and reached across the table to take her hand in his own. She felt a tingle run up her arm when they touched. It was magical. He looked startled. She felt another thrill pulse through her when she realized that he had felt it too!

"You are truly beautiful," he said. "I know, I say that a lot being polite and I am a notorious flirt. But in your case, I am being strictly honest. Just seeing you gives me a thrill that I thought I would never experience again."

She may have forgotten what they talked about coming to the restaurant, but those words were burnt into her memory as if placed there with a branding iron. She glanced around the restaurant. It was still early, and there were few other patrons. Everyone was ignoring them.

"Will you kiss me, Roy Lee White? Right now, and please hurry." She could say no more because his mouth was covering hers. It seemed he had the same idea.

When he regained his seat, she was trembling, and her breath was coming in accelerated gasps.

"Do you have a room?" she whispered.

"What about lunch?"

"We can eat anytime," she said softly, squeezing his hand as if frightened he might drift away.

***

Womack Ranch — Downstate Illinois

"Mr. Womack, there is a John Palmer out here to see you," said Womack's secretary, who sounded frightened. He couldn't remember her ever sounding like that.

"It is okay, Julie, send him in."

The clop of boots coming down the long hall sounded like a herd of horses was approaching. The big double doors exploded inward to bang against the stops and a giant entered the room.

Palmer was a mountain of a man, 6 foot 5 inches and 375 pounds. He would have made a great NFL lineman or linebacker. Certainly there wouldn't have been anyone bigger facing him on a given Sunday.

Womack felt a stab of fear run up his back. The man had a reputation. It was conventional wisdom throughout the county that the man murdered his wife for her property and got away with it.

Palmer had been in dozens of fights and had put a good number in the hospital; crippling some permanently. Until he crossed Roy White's brother, he had never lost a fight. The one fight he did lose put Palmer in intensive care for more than a week. One crossed a White brother at one's own peril.

Palmer took three steps across the large office and stood in front of Womack's desk. He walked with a decided limp. Palmer was wearing khakis and an untucked, short-sleeved shirt that hung over his expansive waist, its irregular tails flopping. His biceps strained his shirt sleeves. Womack observed Palmer's arms were larger than Womack's thighs. He shuddered.

Palmer's face was rugged and scarred. His nose looked like it had been broken a couple of times and set incorrectly on at least one occasion, leaving it skewed slightly to one side. He was wearing an International Union of Operating Engineers hat. His dirty blonde hair stuck out the sides and back. He needed a haircut a couple weeks.

"*You are one ugly bugger!*" Lyman thought to himself then clamped his mouth shut, suddenly afraid he might have spoken out loud.

Palmer was wearing leather, lace-up boots that could be ton trucks if you added wheels.

"Mr. Palmer, please come in and have a seat."

Palmer stopped in front of Womack's desk and looked at the expensive leather chairs with disdain.

"I'll just stand, if you don't mind. I won't be here long," he growled.

"I guess I owe you for getting me out of the slam, though I can't figure out why you would do that," he said, squinting his eyes as he regarded Womack behind the desk. "Why *did* you do that?"

There was no doubt now; there was menace in that statement.

"We have a common…" Lyman hesitated on how to describe their mutual interest in a particular deputy. "Problem," he said finally. "There is a certain deputy sheriff who has recently been causing me some, let's say, sleepless nights?"

Palmer was not a stupid man. In fact, he could be quite clever on occasion. He knew precisely to whom the older man behind the desk was referring, but Palmer wanted his benefactor to present his case in detail.

"Am I to understand it would be considered a service to you if this deputy were to disappear?" This rhetorical statement was accompanied by an evil grin, which exposed numerous crooked, yellow teeth.

Put in those terms, it caused a second wave of fear to run up Womack's back. He wasn't used to dealing with life-and-death issues, at least, ones that might include actual bloodletting.

"Well, disappear might be a bit…final," Lyman mumbled. "If someone was incapacitated for some time, it might be adequate."

"Well, Lyman," Palmer mocked him. "Let us call a spade a long, slender shovel, shall we? You want Leroy himself White out of the picture for a spell. Is that not what we are talking about here?"

As he was speaking, Palmer placed his hands, which resembled dinner plates, over the back of the white leather chair in front of him. His quarter-sized nails were broken and dirty, Womack had never seen hands the size that were gripping the top of the chair. The man squeezed, digging his fingers deep into the expensive leather.

Womack fully expected to see it rip beneath the giant's grip.

A long silence filled the room.

"BANG!" Palmer lifted up the chair and slammed it down. "Well? Yes? Or no?" The room seemed to shake, whether from the mistreatment of the furniture, or Palmer's bellow, Womack wasn't sure.

"Yes, yes, for a while. Yes," he mumbled quickly, almost inaudibly. "That would be good."

Palmer released his grip on the chair leaving deep, black marks on the white leather. He turned and clomped toward the door, favoring his left leg. He turned at the open doors and looked directly at Womack, causing another twinge of fear to run up Womack's spine.

"Then we are square, right?" he asked ominously.

Womack wanted mightily just to nod and get the man out of the room, but he sensed it would not be enough.

"Yes, if the deputy is 'out of action,' for a month or more, we would be square, as you say," Womack told him.

The giant nodded and clomped out of the room and down the hall, shaking the walls as he went.

***

Beirut, Lebanon 1984

I had decided to use all four sticks of the C4 on the doorway. I wanted to bring the entire wall down into the stairwell. It wouldn't do us much good to escape into a tunnel and bring a company of rag-heads with us.

I was molding the last stick onto the door jamb and inserting a blasting cap when Gordo came clomping up the stairs behind me.

"Sarge, you will not believe the tunnels down there," he said, panting from running up the stairs. "They go on for miles, and they are deserted."

"Deserted. Are you sure?"

"According to your little Phalanges friend, the Palestine Liberation Organization built them. When they split for Africa, they sealed the entrances and bugged out. The Christian Militia discovered them somehow. They have been using them for their own ends."

"Why didn't they seal this entrance?"

"According to the boy, this stairway leads to a basement that the Christians opened up into the tunnel complex after the PLO split. Anyway, I just wanted to tell you; we got the lieutenant and the Sarge into the basement. We are ready to move as soon as you close the door." He had to shout to be heard over the clatter of gunfire our last two rear guard guys were bringing to bear on our tormentors.

I inserted the last wire into a blasting cap and pushed it into the little gray block of putty-like composition I had molded to the door. I handed Gordo the spool. He started backing down the stairwell, stringing the wire behind him as he went.

I bent over, keeping my head down, and stepped out into the little alcove where the last two Marines were crouched behind the improvised fighting position we had built by throwing together rubble and big chunks of concrete.

Mitch and Vinny were keeping up a good rate of fire, interspersed with an occasional 40MM present. They were burning through ammunition at a prodigious rate. It couldn't be helped; the incoming fire was building. It was only a matter of time until we were the recipient of an RPG. So far the cars at the curb were shielding us from a direct line of fire, but that wouldn't last.

I slid up behind Vinny and shouted into his ear, "Give 'em a couple rounds of blooker and let's go." I told Mitch the same thing and scooted back into the relative shelter of the darkened doorway. Four 'thonks' later the pair came scooting my direction.

"Watch the wires," I warned them as they slid past me and started down the stairs. I placed my last claymore facing the street in the middle of the doorway and covered it with a black-and-white checkered scarf Gordo had thoughtfully brought up from the basement.

I chuckled as I wrapped the scarf around the mine mimicking the way the rag-head warriors wore theirs. I left a little space where the mouth would be facing away from the door. I stepped back, admired my handiwork, and sprinted down the stairs trailing the wires as I went.

CHAPTER ELEVEN

"That's the last time I come to your place for breakfast," Delbert told me. "It's just too damn intense around here." He and I were standing in front of the barn watching a couple of the militia volunteers helping Milo's deputies get remains stuffed into body bags.

Chance had sprinted off to the generator shed to retrace our steps and unlock the canned-goods door as well as replace the Barrett in the safe. Delbert and I hung onto our long guns. With the monumental debris from the attack still evident, it felt premature to be storing our armament.

"I am slipping, Delbert," I admitted. "One of them got the drop on me in the barn. I may be getting too old for this. I was just lucky the silly bugger didn't shoot me."

Delbert took a half step back and looked at me for a long moment as if studying my posture. He shook his head, then said earnestly, "Just like the sergeant in the book you are writing told me, 'luck's a lady' and had little to do with it. You had a backup and your backup dealt with the problem. That is planning, not luck."

I wasn't going to argue with him, but the Colombian could just as well have shot me from the haymow ladder. Only the fact that Escobar probably wanted me kept alive, and delivered to him, accounted for my still breathing with my God-given equipment, and not wheezing through some holes in my back.

***

Springfield, Illinois — Two days later

The events of the day before yesterday were still very much on my mind as well as the meeting I had just left with the governor and his two hot-shot security guys. I still had no use for Norman, but I was impressed with the little Israeli. He was a no-nonsense, intelligence professional and definitely knew what he was doing.

I was intrigued by the classy lady the governor had picked as his primary aide. She was smart as a whip and strikingly beautiful. And she quite obviously could have any man in Springfield she chose, but for some reason, she seemed to be attracted to me.

When I was younger and riding rodeo, I used to attract a particular type of girl that followed the circuit. These young ladies were drawn to the winners and top performers just as rock stars, singers and entertainers drew their own groupies, who wanted to bask in the reflected light of fame and wealth.

I soon became immune to their advances. They were so predictable, and since I was married, they were trouble with a capital "T." But that had been a lot of years and many thousands of miles ago, in a different world, and this lady was as far removed from the air-headed circuit followers as could be imagined.

What this professional lady at the very top of the social ladder saw in a broken-down deputy from the hinterland, I could hardly imagine, but I was interested to find out.

I took up a position leaning my butt against the rail, extending my legs out to admire my favorite pair of burgundy alligator boots. They were the pair I wore when I really wanted to dress up.

I saw Elaine walking toward the glass doors. She was wearing a professional silk one-piece dress cut at the elbows and just below her knees. She was carrying a medium-sized purse slung across her right shoulder that matched the black, high-heeled shoes and belt she was wearing. Her wavy strawberry blonde hair cascaded around her shoulders and swung in synch with her stride.

I had to admire the subtle, understated sexuality she exuded. Everything about her wardrobe said, "I am a professional, unavailable and unapproachable." Yet, beneath the soft silk dress, everything was very subtly unrestrained. When she walked, all of the curves had a very soft jiggle, almost undetectable, but very much present. She either spent an inordinate amount of time perfecting her appearance or she was gifted with a natural allure that most movie stars would kill for.

I decided as I watched her walk down the steps in high heels perfectly balanced and as comfortable as if she was wearing tennis shoes, it was the latter. Her ex-husband had to be some kind of dufus to let Elaine Martin go.

When she came up to me, she was smiling, and I caught the most nebulous hint of Opium perfume. I was shocked. Genevieve had worn Opium. I wondered if my senses had betrayed me, but I could hardly go sniffing around her to find out. I took a deep breath but could sense nothing further.

I stood up and offered her my arm. It was a few blocks to the barbecue restaurant and we set off at a leisurely pace. It was good to have a woman on my arm again. I realized it had been quite a long time.

Elaine did most of the talking, telling me about a Jewish Rabbi she had met and a Lutheran pastor. She told me about her grandmother, her infant baptism, and some of the discoveries in her meetings with the pastor.

I knew she was just making conversation, but the spiritual life she had been denied growing up was naturally now intriguing to her. I was quite taken with her naiveté since the things she was discovering I had known since I could remember. Hearing her talk about Christ, faith and forgiveness as if it were something new gave me a renewed appreciation for my parents and my upbringing.

After we were seated, I reached over and took her hand. I actually felt an electric shock streak up my arm! I had never experienced anything like it, and I had been with dozens of ladies.

Then she asked me to kiss her. It was as if she was reading my mind. I had been thinking of doing just that.

It was three blocks to the Hilton. We didn't say a word to each other until we walked into the room; we just walked arm-in-arm perfectly in synch as if we were dancing down the street.

As I shut the door and hung the "Do Not Disturb" sign on the outside knob, she set her purse on the dresser and gave me a soft half-smile. I was suddenly nervous and ill at ease, uncertain about what to do next.

Elaine stepped over, took the hat from my hand and carefully slid it onto the top shelf of the closet. She then reached up with both hands and slipped my sunglasses off. She took a step back, placing them beside her purse on the dresser. While she was doing this, I slipped out of my jacket and tossed it over a chair.

Elaine reached up and kissed me gently, tenderly on the lips. I followed her lead and returned the softest pressure reveling in the velvety fullness of her lips. She trembled and moved a half step back, slipping the clasp off my string tie and placing it beside my sunglasses. One button at a time she undid the fasteners on my shirt. When she reached the bottom, she pulled the tails out and slipped the garment back off my shoulders letting it fall to the floor.

Beneath the short-sleeved summer shirt, I was wearing a sleeveless T. She pulled it out of my pants and slipped it over my head, adding it to the growing pile on the floor behind me.

Elaine then turned around and pointed over her shoulder to the zipper running down the back of her dress. I very slowly moved the zipper to where it ended just above her hips. My hand kept moving, sliding down over the top of her hips to gently caress her buttocks before pulling away. She shrugged out of the dress, and it fell to the floor. She was wearing a nearly transparent slip beneath.

When she turned back around she gasped at the long, jagged scar that ran from my left shoulder to my navel. She ran the tip of her finger down the scar looking at me with a question.

"It was a rogue bull in El Paso..." At the mention of the beast, something that had been restraining her snapped, and she grabbed me, pulled my face down to hers, and started kissing me hungrily.

After that, things happened in a hurry. I had never made love with my boots on before.

***

Ed Rollins hated his job. He hated his employer, and he loathed the business he found himself in. He had been a high administrator in the Environmental Protection Agency. He was a true believer in the sanctity of Mother Earth and an avowed enemy of the despoilers of the planet, including the evil oil companies.

Pure desperation had forced him to take any job he could find. Working for Occidental Oil Company was the only thing that came his way. He had lied on his resume, lied through his teeth at the interview and thanked Mother Earth for the disappearance of government records that let him get away with it.

His job was renewing oil leases throughout Southern Illinois, where the technology of horizontal fracking had opened up old fields to new production. Illinois had, at one time, been the largest producer of crude oil in the nation. The facile production of the mammoth reserves of the shallow Robinson Sand had fueled the planes and ships of World War II and provided a significant amount of the cheap fuel feeding the prosperity of the early 50s across the whole country.

With the new technology, the Robinson Sand was back, and Occidental was snapping up expired leases and renewing existing ones across the entire state.

Environmentalism was a discredited political force.

After the dust settled, and the new economy was struggling to put food on tables and clothes on people's backs, there was little appetite for restrictions and regulations on the businesses attempting to pull the country up by its own bootstraps.

Rollins had been shocked at the depth of animosity and disgust toward the regulators. He counted himself lucky to have not been strung up on a light post with a "Federal" sign around his neck by some roving militia group.

EPA and OSHA were two of the most reviled agencies, and a lot of his fellow bureaucrats met untimely ends when they tried to exert their authority immediately after the chaos.

His present job paid less than a quarter of what he had made working for the government. He was forced to leave his expensive home on the lake and move in with his wife's parents. This was the ultimate degrading embarrassment and fueled his animosity toward the new establishment.

When he was approached by some of his old colleagues to join the Federalist Party, he jumped at the chance to put the world he used to know back together again.

It was not easy being a Federalist. They were looked down on with fear and loathing by most of the populace around them. Their situation was roughly equivalent to being a Unionist in the South or a Copperhead in the North during the Civil War.

There were some perks, however. The amount of money flowing into the coffers of the party was fantastic. There were a lot of interests whose rice bowls were broken at the disappearance of the Federal Government.

His current little side job — monitoring the intelligence apparatus of the Illinois governor — paid him more in a month than Occidental paid in a year. Unfortunately, he needed the Occidental job to maintain his cover, so he was being stretched.

He didn't understand the paranoia in the upper levels of the party with this little podunk deputy sheriff from downstate. From what Rollins could ascertain, he was an ex-rodeo rider and small-time farmer. This White character wasn't even a paid LEO.

The State of Illinois had absorbed large chunks of the FBI and Secret Service's resources in the restructuring after the chaos. It seemed to Rollins the party's efforts could be more efficiently directed than chasing after a hick farmer, but he had his orders and was complying.

He had been watching the aide for some weeks. It had been his idea to question her to try to ascertain exactly what the governor had tasked the deputy with. Since the wheels had come rather dramatically off that wagon; he had decided to double down.

Rollins was going to kidnap the head of the governor's security.

To his way of thinking, it would be a twofer. The man should be an intelligence trove, and his elimination would be a blow to the governor and his administration.

For a bureaucrat, Rollins thought big thoughts and had big plans.

On this day, he had been watching the front of the State House trying to determine if the little security chief had a pattern that could be used to facilitate his capture. To Rollins' surprise, he saw the deputy come out of the building and take up station on the steps. Very soon thereafter, the governor's aide came out, and they walked off arm in arm.

Sensing an opportunity and not wanting to pass up low-hanging fruit, he had followed them to the restaurant. They had not remained inside nearly long enough to have eaten. When they exited, he followed them closely. It was easy; they had eyes for no one but each other.

They went into the Hilton. Rollins smiled to himself. This opened up a whole new approach. He immediately put the idea of abducting the little security chief on the back burner.

Miss Elaine Martin had suddenly become target No. 1.

***

Beirut, Lebanon 1984

I counted the steps; there were 26. It was a deep basement. It was dark at the bottom, but I saw some light coming through a door to my left. When I arrived, Gordo was waiting just inside the door, peering around the corner at the rectangle of light at the top of the steps.

The basement light was coming from a torch the Christian boy was holding just over Gordo's back. "That's good," I thought. "We'll not be limited by the flashlight batteries."

Gordo already had the clackers hooked up. One was connected to the Claymore, the other to the C4 detonators.

I took Gordo's place at the edge of the door and watched the light at the top of the steps. He handed me a clacker. "Claymore," he whispered. I nodded and waited.

It seemed like a long time, but I knew it could only have been minutes before the doorway was filled with shadows, then a head peering over the edge of the top step. He had an RPG. He pointed it down the steps, and I double tapped the clacker.

KABOOM! The little rag-wrapped package filled the doorway with fire and projectiles. The light dimmed appreciably as the foyer above filled with smoke. When it cleared, there was no sign of the RPG.

"Get back," I told Gordo and the young man. I retreated back as far as the wires would let me and double tapped the second clacker. For a split second, I thought something had gone wrong.

"KAAABOOOOM!" The explosion rocked the entire room, and a massive cloud of concrete dust whooshed in from the stairwell. It was followed shortly by the crashing and banging of the stairwell being filled with broken cement.

"You are a man of faith," Gordo told me. I got it. I had just shut the door on the only known way out.

***

Sheriff Milo Baker's Office — Downstate Illinois

"Sheriff, you wanted to know if John Palmer came to town," said one of his deputies, who was standing in the doorway to his office. "He and that sidekick of his, Ken Coward, just went into the VFW."

"Okay, Ralph, draw a pump gun from the armory and meet me downstairs. Make sure it's loaded with buckshot and slide one into the pipe."

The sheriff waited inside the glass doors of the courthouse until his deputy came down the stairs to join him.

It was just two blocks to the VFW, and the sheriff knew that Palmer wouldn't be there long. They had voted in a new commander while Palmer was in the slam. His name was Eric Sinclair, and he was a no-nonsense leader. He served in Nam and had been in the thick of some of the bloodiest battles in the Ia Drang valley.

Sinclair told the sheriff Palmer was not allowed in the VFW after he started a fight in there a year or so before he went up the river. The previous commander didn't have the balls to back up the prohibition, but the sheriff knew Sinclair was not cut from the same cloth.

The sheriff knew Sinclair was in today because he saw his pickup parked outside. Baker timed his arrival to the party well The front door slammed open, and Coward backed out onto the street followed closely by Palmer, who was swearing and stomping his giant feet.

"You miserable son of a bitch, I'll get you. You watch your back. I'll get you some dark night, and you'll not know what hit you," Palmer growled at the man standing in the door.

Sinclair was holding a .44 mag Smith in both hands pointed down at the pavement in front of him. His face was red, and he looked like it was all he could do to restrain himself from shooting Palmer on the spot.

"Anytime, Palmer, make it easy on yourself. And next time, I'm going to shoot first. You've been warned." Sinclair nodded to the sheriff and let the door slam shut.

"John, I need to have a word," the sheriff said, cutting off any rebuttal. "First, if you come back over here making trouble and the commander shoots your sorry ass, there won't even be an inquiry. We'll just throw your body in the Wabash and let the catfish clean up the mess."

Palmer turned and gave the sheriff a long up-and-down look. He glanced at the armed deputy, who had the shotgun leveled and pointed directly at Palmer's stomach. In this post-apocalyptic world, one didn't mess with county sheriffs. They were a law unto themselves.

"Okay, I get the message, Sheriff, Anything else?"

"Yes. I understand you have a crow to pick with one of my deputies. I just want you to know that if anything happens to Deputy White, I will come looking for you. I don't care what it is: car wreck, farm accident, or his hair gets messed up riding his motorcycle. You are the man," the sheriff told him forcefully. "John, I will come *gunning* for you, not *looking*. Are we clear?"

"I have no idea what you're talking about Sheriff," Palmer replied. "I let bygones be bygones."

"Just so we are straight."

"Oh, we're straight Sheriff, we're straight. Can I go now?"

"Yes, just keep in mind what I told you."

Palmer and his buddy turned and walked across the parking lot where they got into an old, dusty Ford pickup. They drove slowly out to the main street and turned in the direction of Terre Haute.

"We haven't seen the last of him," the deputy said with foreboding. "Maybe it would've been better if Eric had just shot him on sight."

The way the sheriff looked at him, the deputy thought he might be upbraided. Instead, the sheriff just nodded.

"There's a certain amount of truth in that statement," the sheriff said as he turned and started back for the courthouse.

***

Escobar Ranch — Mexico

"They went to his house in the daytime?" Juan Edwardo Escobar exclaimed. "That is so stupid. I told them to hit him at night when they were sleeping."

"It was early in the morning, very early. I imagine they thought he *would* still be sleeping."

"They are farmers! You idiotoso!" Escobar shouted in disgust. "They get up in the dark!"

Escobar was angry and frustrated. The mission to capture the killer of his son had been prohibitively expensive, and now it had failed. It was so difficult to operate north of the border now.

Even private citizens had no compunctions about stopping a brown man and demanding ID. Finding operatives who spoke perfect English and were light-skinned enough to pass for gringos was becoming more and more difficult.

It wasn't like he didn't have money. He had warehouses full of stacks of U.S. dollars, but there was no new money coming in. The drug business that had made him an incredibly rich man had disappeared with the cities and the government money that sustained the ghettos.

With the rampant inflation that had settled in, his stash of cash was being depleted at an alarming rate. With no new money coming in, the end was in sight. For the first time in many years, Escobar was worried.

His personal vendetta with a particular Illinois deputy would have to wait. He had to come up with something to start the flow of cash once more. His most senior partner in the U.S. seemed to think this Federalist Party was the answer. He certainly hoped so. The way they were burning through his money, something better happen quickly.

"Señor, we received a long message from Illinois today. Our operative in Springfield has a plan to kidnap the governor's aide. He wants to bring her here."

"What's the upside for us?"

"The Federalists have a big operation planned for downstate soon. They need to find out if the authorities are on to their plan. This aide to the governor knows everything he knows."

"Who is this man?"

"It's not a man; it's a woman. I have pictures." His assistant walked over carrying a file. He took out a couple of snapshots. One was of a lady standing next to a cowboy on the Capitol steps. The other was a close-up. She was extraordinarily attractive.

Escobar thought about having this lady here and at his mercy. He smiled for the first time in days.

"We can make that happen," he said, smiling in anticipation. "Let's do it right away."

CHAPTER TWELVE

Hilton Hotel – Springfield, Illinois

"Elaine, where is this going?" We were sitting on the couch finishing up two monster burgers room service had delivered. I was wearing my navy blue, cotton robe; she was wearing one of my white shirts. I had to admit, it looked better on her. It was early evening. We had spent the entire afternoon in bed. We made love, talked, laughed, and made love again.

It was an extraordinarily pleasant way to spend an afternoon.

She scooted back against the arm of the sofa and tucked her long slender legs beneath her like a teenager. She studied me for a long moment, then she smiled a conspiratorial smile.

"You're going to ask me to marry you, and I'm going to say yes."

I was way beyond being shocked by anything this lady said. But when I realized she was telling the exact truth, it gave me pause. I was indeed going to ask her to marry me.

It was patently insane, even for me.

We had really only just met. Oh, we had been communicating on state business for more than a year, but it had been superficial banalities. I checked my watch: we just had a six-hour anniversary. This might set a record for short courtships.

"There are complications. You live in Springfield and have a job with…"

"I'll go with you," she interrupted my objections. "I'll live where you live, I will share your life. My life here was over the moment I realized you were my future."

"Was that right after your second orgasm?" I teased. It didn't even get a rise out of her.

"Sometime before."

"When?"

"I think when I saw the scar," she replied seriously. Her smile had disappeared, and she looked like she had been searching deep inside herself for the answer.

"You realize you may need psychiatric assistance, do you not?"

"No," she said emphatically as she slid her legs off the couch and scooted over next to me. She reached up and caressed my face with both hands then kissed me softly, gently. When she pulled away, her beautiful face inches from my own, she looked straight into my eyes.

"This is the sanest thing I've done in my entire life."

There was only one thing I could say to that.

"Will you marry me?"

***

White Farm – Downstate Illinois

"Auntie, are you ever going to get married again?" Chance asked Amanda. He was sitting at the kitchen table dipping into a blackberry cobbler covered with a pint of homemade, vanilla ice cream. The entire house was suffused with the pleasant competing aromas of fresh-baked cobbler and bread.

There were a dozen loaves of whole-wheat bread fresh from the oven cooling on the counter. The oven door was open and held the oven-sized pan from which a healthy chunk had been cut to fill the bowl Chance was attacking at the moment.

The ice-cream freezer sat in the sink with the metal canister surrounded with melting ice. The amount of work it had taken to put an afternoon snack together for her nephew had been prodigious, but Amanda didn't give it a second thought. It was what she did.

Chance had asked her the same question before, but she had never answered it. She turned and looked at her sister's boy for a long moment. Her heart glowed at the sight. He had turned into an almost perfect young man. When her mother had been killed, she had come home to help take care of Chance and her father.

She had felt it an imposition and a burden at the time, but now she felt like it had been an unasked-for gift. The relationship she had developed with her father surprised her. He was such an extraordinary man. He was gone much of the time when she was growing up and she hardly knew him.

They had become inseparable during the past four years, however. She relished the work on the farm. It took little conscious thought; she had been trained so extensively by her mother that it all was second nature. It was rewarding work watching the raw material from the garden, fields, and barns turn into food for the table and products to sell. Not having to think was a bonus. The security of being home again while the rest of the world was going crazy was more than a gift. It was pure grace.

She was still very much in love with her ex-husband. Other than her father, he was the most handsome man she had ever met. He was gentle, loving, and as faithful as an old collie dog. Unfortunately, he was also a pothead.

She had come to realize sometime after their wedding that a lot of the mellowness she admired about him was chemically induced. It also led to his being physically present but mentally absent much of the time.

She loved him deeply but just could not stay married to the man. It was frustrating in the extreme. Burying herself in farm work allowed her to not think about the insoluble problem.

"Who would take care of you and my father?" she finally replied to Chance's question. It was a deflection, but it was the best she could do at the moment.

"We could all live here," Chance replied reasonably. "It's a big house, and we could use another pair of hands on the farm. There's always so much work."

"Where am I going to meet this mythical Sir Galahad?"

Chance had to admit she had a point. She seldom left the farm.

"I could go to town and round up a few for you to choose from," he laughed. She threw the hot pad at him she had been holding. She did love that boy.

"What about Jim?" Chance asked, suddenly serious. Jim was a neighbor boy Amanda had gone to school with. Jim had been in love with her since high school. Chance really liked the man since they had a shared interest in firearms and powerful motors.

"I love Jim, I really do, Chancy, but I am not 'in love' with him. It will never work," she said with such finality that Chance knew she was telling him the truth.

It made him sad.

***

River Town – Downstate Illinois

"This is going to complicate things," Ken Coward said.

He pronounced his name "Koh'word." He had been teased relentlessly in school by the other kids calling him "Coward, Cow ward!" There had been dozens of fights. His name and the problems it caused him were a big reason he had developed a relationship with John Palmer. Once it became known that Palmer was his friend, no one dared taunt him.

"That sheriff was not bluffing, John," Coward continued. "He'll activate the militia and come after you if anything happens to White. They'll string you up like a hog for butchering."

They were sitting at a table next to the jukebox in a dive bar adjacent to the Wabash River in a little slum town known as

"Snakebit." It was actually an unincorporated assemblage of shacks built around the bar, but it was known far and wide by its rather uncomplimentary nickname.

The bar had served as Palmer's center of operation for years. Before the catastrophe swept the nation, the "Blue Moon" had been infamous for its fights and drugs.

Alcohol was only a sidebar to its primary business of providing recreational pharmaceuticals to half the surrounding two-state region. The Blue Moon was a hot spot for young ladies of the night to make their assignations as well. "The Moon," as it was known, was a full-service cornucopia of illicit activity. It fit John Palmer to a "T."

Palmer was disappointed to discover "The Moon" had cleaned up its act. The Wabash County sheriff had made a few perfectly timed raids, hauling off a dozen bad actors, who were now being housed, fed and entertained at the expense of the county. It was a different era.

One could still buy a quart jar of clear "lightning in a bottle," but moonshine distribution was the extent of the "Moon's" illegal activities these days. It was depressing, Palmer thought to himself.

"It does make things a bit stickier," he admitted reluctantly. Ken Coward was the only man in the world Palmer would allow to tell him things he didn't want to hear. In fact, Coward was the only person alive that Palmer actually considered a friend.

"The answer is obvious," Coward said. "The sheriff will have to be dealt with at the same time, or even before."

Palmer nodded and bunched up his eyebrows, thinking through the validity of Coward's statement and putting the details of the logistics together in his mind. They ordered a pitcher of beer and a jar of 'shine.

Palmer poured two fingers of the clear liquid in the bottom of his mug then filled it to the top with beer. He then drank the entire concoction in one long gulp. He settled in for an afternoon of getting pie-eyed.

He did some of his best thinking when he was stone-cold drunk.

***

Beirut, Lebanon 1984

"Gosh Sarge, you look like the Pillsbury Dough Boy," Vinny said as the three of us stumbled into the next basement room. There were three separate basements that had been joined by holes cut in the walls to be traversed before we could enter the tunnel complex itself. I looked down at myself and then at Gordo and the boy. We were all covered in white concrete dust.

The fact there were separate basements gave me some angst for a moment until the boy explained their entrances had been sealed off sometime before.

All of my troops, with the exception of the sniper team, were assembled in the last basement room that led the tunnels. The sniper pair had gone on ahead to reconnoiter. They had been led by two Phalanges girls. It made me wonder about our allies. *If young kids are all they have left, no wonder they're getting their asses handed to them!* I thought.

I decided to wait on the snipers for a bit and see what they turned up. Gordo and I tried to brush ourselves off the best we could, but we still looked as if we had been in a flour fight.

This would've been a good time to take a break and get a bite to eat, but since we didn't have any food, we settled for a little water from our canteens. I had started getting a bit concerned about the snipers when one of the two grunts guarding the tunnel side of the door stuck his head in and announced the scouts were on their way in.

The spotter soon appeared through the hole.

"What happened to you?" he exclaimed.

"We brought the wall down the stairwell. When we did, we ended up wearing a good portion of it," I explained. He nodded his understanding.

"Sergeant, you're not going to believe it. Those tunnels run on for miles. But that's not the interesting thing. They are packed with armaments, AKs, RPGs, primacord and C4. Tons of the stuff. That's the bad news. The good news is there is case after case of LRPs and Cs. If we have to bed down in the tunnels tonight, we won't be doing it on empty stomachs."

"Really? That is good news."

"And Sarge, wait until you get an eyeful of this chick who is leading us around. She is drop-dead gorgeous."

"Ahem," the boy holding the torch cleared his throat, getting our attention. "Sir, that's my sister."

"Oh, sorry son, in any case, you have an attractive sister," the spotter smiled. "No disrespect meant, young man."

" It's okay, no offense taken. I just wanted you to know."

"Sergeant, it's going to be rough going hauling the bodies. Some of the passages are wide with eight-foot ceilings, but others are barely adequate to slither through."

"Okay, get your sniper. Gordo, let's have a little meeting in the room next door."

I went back to the room we had just vacated with Gordo trailing right behind me. A couple minutes later we were joined by the sniper team. I was in command by the virtue of my senior position in the platoon, but the sniper and his spotter were both E5 sergeants as well as Gorder. If we were going to have to make a decision about the lieutenant's and staff sergeant's bodies, I wanted a consensus.

"I know we have this motto about leaving no one behind. But from what the scouts tell me, taking the bodies any further is problematical. What say you?"

There was no comment for a long moment, then the sniper spoke up. He was a bit older than me, and I assumed him to be a couple years senior.

"I don't think my spotter or I should comment or have a say. This is your show Sergeant; it is your platoon. We are just TAD assigned for support," he spoke for both of them, but I noticed the spotter was nodding his agreement.

"I hate leaving them, Roy," Gordo said, "but if we get in a tight in one of those tunnels and are attacked…we could lose some more folks." So it came right back to me. It was my decision. It is lonely at the top.

"Sir," the boy had come in to join us carrying the torch. "On the other side of the next room, the tunnels are catacombs. There are hundreds of dead buried there. You could lay them together on a shelf."

It sounded weird, but in the end, that is what we did. We made a map the best we could to turn over to the graves registration folks. We took off their boots and stood them at the end of where they were laid.

The medic said a few words and we all said the Lord's Prayer. I felt terrible about it, but I thought it best at the time. That's what command is, making tough decisions with inadequate information.

The spotter was right. The girl was strikingly beautiful.

The first time I saw her, she was dressed in green khakis and had her hair rolled up on top of her head stuffed into a green beret. The uniform was unadorned save a cedar tree emblem on her left sleeve. He face was dirty and her uniform unkempt, but she exuded a subtle femininity in spite of her outward appearance. She was carrying an AK, while wearing a bandoleer of magazines across her chest.

She was accompanied by another girl, younger and much plainer. The contrast between the two was marked. Both girls stood to one side and watched our little burial ceremony. When we finished, they crossed themselves and led off.

They were young, fit and knew where they were going. It was tough keeping up. The first mile was toughest. These tunnels had not been built by the PLO. These tunnels were ancient catacombs, dating back to the Crusades. There were a lot of bodies.

It was dusty. Each footstep stirred up a little puff, the last man in the line walked through a cloud. Soon Gordo and I were not the only ones covered in silt and concrete dust.

It took us a couple of hours to break out into the actual PLO tunnel complex. Everything here changed. There were electric lights and shelf after shelf of munitions, medical supplies, and food.

We took a break and set up guards at some distance in either direction from where we stopped. We refilled our canteens from the jugs of bottled water, broke into some cases of LRPs and had lunch. If we hadn't all been covered in eleventh-century grime, we might have been having a picnic.

I took the girl aside ostensibly to gather information, but mostly I just wanted to talk with her. Her name was Nour Lahoud. She was a Greek Orthodox Christian, which made her a minority within the larger Christian minority. Her family had lived in the Levant since the Crusades. She spoke fluent English and French as well as Lebanese. The Lebanese language was a derivative of Aramaic spoken throughout the Middle East at the time of Christ.

Lahoud was fascinated with America. She had relatives that had emigrated to the U.S. in the 50s, and she had grown up reading the letters and books they had sent back to Lebanon.

When the Marines had landed, she had been confident that peace would follow immediately because she was convinced the Americans could do anything. She was shocked and disappointed when the United States' politicians had given up on her country's indecipherable politics and abandoned them.

But like a lot of true believers, she had not lost faith. When she found out about the small contingent of men being left behind, she had immediately taken action to assist them. The Phalanges militia monitored the Marine radio band, so they were aware of the platoon's plight before its own commander was. They knew the Hezbollah strength the Marines were walking into and were aware the platoon was going to be in trouble before the platoon itself was aware of it.

"Then you are a real cowboy?" Nour asked in amazement. I told her about my rodeo riding in high school and how I intended to return to rodeo as soon as I returned to the States. Of all the things I could have claimed, it seems that being a cowboy was the most impressive thing an American could be in her eyes.

"I would love to come to America," she said wistfully. "And I would love to watch you ride your horse in the rodeo." She was only vaguely familiar with the genre. When she thought of rodeo, it was more along the lines of a Wild Bill Hickok western show.

I was concentrating on the conversation with this lovely young girl, so I missed the activity ahead. The lookout had come pounding back. Vinny came up and got my attention.

"Sarge, I hate to break up your little love nest," Vinny lied through his teeth. "We have company, Sarge. It looks like not all the PLO are gone. There are a dozen or so rag-heads coming our way."

I looked up the tunnel in the direction of the reported threat. What I saw was rack after rack and box after box of high explosives and ammunition. It was not the best place in the world to engage in a firefight.

CHAPTER THIRTEEN

Governor's Office — Springfield, Illinois

"Moshe, I think I'm going to take that bastard's picture down," the governor told his chief of security. He had turned around in his chair and was regarding the massive painting of Lincoln at Gettysburg. "If he had just let the South go their separate way, we would never have suffered what we did."

"What about the slavery thing? Wasn't that tearing at the fabric of the Union?"

"Slavery had proven itself economically nonviable by the time of the war. There had been half-dozen bills introduced in Southern legislatures to free the slaves and pay the owners indemnity for the loss of their property prior to 1861. Within 50 years, possibly even sooner, it would have faded away on its own."

"Who would you put up there in his place?" Moshe asked as he pictured the huge blank wall that would remain when the picture came down. "Robert E. Lee?"

"No, Bobby Lee blew the entire war at Gettysburg. If he had listened to Longstreet and let his top general attack Mead's right flank, the Union position would have been rolled up like a rug, and Lee could have taken Washington. That would have handed the South their independence. No, I was thinking Washington or Jefferson or maybe Franklin or a composite picture of the signers of the Constitution. It was their idea of a nation we should have followed."

Moshe just nodded. When the governor started venting his angst over the current fate of his country, Moshe just let him talk. There was little he could add since he was a recent immigrant and had little appreciation for the historical roots of the current situation. In his mind, it mattered little. He was a pragmatist and tried to play with the cards he was dealt.

Moshe knew one other thing. The governor was going to make no decision without consulting his aide. Elaine Martin was the brains behind the governor's administration. She had been the chief of staff of his campaign and the moving force behind the decision to arrest the gang of thugs running the Illinois Legislature. Until Elaine Martin had her say, the picture behind the desk would remain exactly where it was.

Martin's actual position was known only to a select few within the governor's inner circle. *Very possibly, the lady is unaware of it herself.* This thought sprung fully formed into Moshe's conscious mind followed closely by its obvious corollary, *maybe the governor, himself is unaware of it.*

The implications of that thought stopped Moshe in his tracks. He ceased pacing and stared at the governor as if seeing him for the first time.

***

Airborne between Springfield and White Farm

"*What have I got myself into*?" I was buzzing along at 5,000 feet at the controls of my Super Katmai aircraft. I loved the little plane. It is a custom version of a Cessna 182 built by a mechanical genius in Kansas.

The man's name is Todd Peterson. He created the STOL plane in the years after the Vietnam War. The roots of the design had been a plane built for the U.S. military called the Wren. It was a high-performance plane made to be used for low-altitude spotting and observation.

Where the Wren's performance went beyond the military's specs, it was supplanted quickly in its intended role by the twin-engine Cessna 337 because of the added reliability of the second motor. The performance edge offered by the Wren through aerodynamic genius was equaled by the sheer power of the second engine on the 337.

The Katmai is a backcountry version of the up-engined 260SE that Peterson had built for private aviators who liked the stability, reliability and load-carrying ability of the Cessna 182, but wanted more airspeed and short field capabilities.

My Super Katmai has a 300-horse engine, three-bladed prop and massive balloon tires that could land on almost any surface devoid of large stumps or boulders. The small canard wing mounted on the forward cowling de-loads the tail. This allows the airplane to climb aggressively while maintaining a level attitude and fly slow enough under control to land at less than 40 miles an hour.

Once I was clear of Springfield tower's area of control, I was on my own. With the demise of the FAA and their nationwide system of air traffic control, commercial aviation as it had been known, well, crashed.

The skies I was flying through were remarkably clear and uncluttered of other air traffic. Private aviation was all that survived, and it was 100 percent VFR. If a pilot could not see where he was going, he stayed on the ground.

It was a short 15-minute flight back to the farm where I kept a strip of grass mowed next to the equipment sheds on the "old" homestead.

Obtaining fuel for the plane had been a problem after the chaos. The 100-octane, low-lead fuel the FAA mandated had quickly disappeared and was no longer produced by any refinery. I stumbled onto a truckload of 130-octane racing fuel that had been originally bound for the Indianapolis Motor Speedway. The truck had been sidetracked and parked during some of the most gruesome aftermaths of the Washington immolation.

That same truck was now parked in one of my equipment sheds and provided a finite amount of fuel for my freedom machine. Since I couldn't be assured of fuel for a return trip, it limited my range to a 400-mile radius, but so far it hadn't been a problem. I could only hope the five gallons of fuel stabilizer I had poured into the truck's massive tank would keep the fuel fresh for as long as I would be dependent on it.

I was having some very significant second thoughts concerning Elaine Martin. I had allowed myself to be in the moment. The years of living a celibate existence had caught up with me. I was ashamed of myself now after letting my body and my old nature take control.

"*I am a poor miserable sinner...*" The words of the liturgy came up and haunted me. "*I thought all of that was behind me, but here I am, just like rodeo days, jumping into the sack with the first circuit follower who flashes her breasts at me. Crap!"*

I flew along for a while beating myself up and finally tired of it. *On the other hand, Elaine Martin is no camp follower. She is a sophisticated, intelligent lady. Apparently the governor values her input and what she does for him and she wants to get married. How is that going to work? She's a city girl. What's Amanda going to think about having another woman in the house?*

The lake appeared on the horizon, and I started my descent. I pulled the power back a smidge, dialed in a bit of nose down trim and let the rate of descent stabilize on 200 feet per minute.

I pulled the cowl flaps up a notch to keep the engine from over cooling in the descent and watched the airspeed indicator slip up toward 160kts. The big wheels added significant drag and would keep us well below the "never exceed" speed.

I flew over the wheat field and noticed the clover had sprung up into a solid mass of green. From where I sat, I could see no evidence of wheat stalks. We had cut the straw and baled it as soon as the field had dried after the rain storm. There was going to be a lot of hay coming off that field very soon.

I leveled off at 1,000 feet indicated, which put me about 400 feet above ground level. I flew a long, slow circle over the lake, again feeling sad at the absence of boats. I set up a final approach back across the wheat field, pulled the power back to idle and added 20 degrees of flaps. As the flaps came down, the nose wanted to elevate a bit, so I dialed in some more forward trim to maintain position on the glideslope.

The stall warning buzzer started its complaining as the speed dropped off to where the original plane would have been in trouble. I always wondered why the buzzer hadn't been adjusted for the modified plane's slower approach speed, but I never got a satisfactory answer. It was what it was, and I just had to listen to it.

I came across the last fence 30 feet AGL, pulled in full flaps and sat down on the grass at 35 mph. I pulled the wheel back into my gut and allowed the fat tires and the grass to pull me to a stop with just a hint of pressure on the brakes, a good 100 feet from the far end.

Chance was waiting at the hangar with the handle in his hand to attach to the nose wheel so we could push the aircraft back under cover. I saw the old BSA one lung'er sitting beside the hanger and knew I was in for a frightening trip back to the house.

"Let's run over to the lake," I told Chance. He was sitting on the putting motorcycle. We had put the plane up, and he was waiting for me to hop on to the pillion. I wanted to visit Genevieve's grave. I didn't have to elaborate, Chance and I communicated on a level beyond mere words. He knew exactly where I wanted to go when I mentioned the lake.

We had buried his grandmother on a high ridge overlooking the lake beneath an old growth oak that was eight feet across at the base and kept the gravesite in the shade all summer. It was a family plot where my mother's folks were buried going back four generations.

Chance stopped the bike outside the three-foot-high white picket fence that bordered the graveyard. The gate was on the north side bordered by two ancient red cedars that sheltered the plot from the winter storms. When we walked into the graveyard, the grass was mowed, and there were fresh flowers on Amanda's mother's stone.

We had purchased and set the stone well before the chaos. It was red marble, five feet across at the base and four feet high. It had a Lutheran Rose carved prominently on the front above a cross lettered with the date of our marriage. Over Genevieve's name was a bronze medallion of the DAR. She had been a member and officer of her local chapter for almost her entire life.

The back of the stone featured our two daughters' and our grandson's names as well as carvings of my airplane and one of my favorite motorcycles. There was a large bare spot where my USMC bronze plaque was to have gone. It looked like it would remain barren.

We sat down on the bench I had built after her death. It was a huge slab of limestone from the local quarry cut and polished by a local stone mason. The piece was 5 feet wide and 6 inches thick and sat on two round concrete posts I had poured by hand. The view over Genevieve's stone was the full length of the lake. It was a lovely spot. It seemed there was always a breeze here. The oak leaves sighed above us as if welcoming us back.

I sat down and looked out across the lake and shifted my eyes back to the stone where the date of my wife's death seemed to stand out from the rest of the carvings. All of the emotion of the past few days from the gun battle with the Colombians, Elaine Martin's dramatic appearance into my life, and the guilt and angst of our liaison suddenly erupted to the surface.

I put my face in my hands, and I wept. I cried until I felt an absolute peace flow into my spirit and calm my tears. I felt Chance's arm fall gently across my shoulders. When I looked up, I noticed his cheeks were wet as well.

"It's okay Bapaw, I miss her, too." The unconditional love in his eyes almost triggered another bout of tears, but I fought it back. We sat there for some time looking at the stone with his arm around my shoulders. He left it there until I started to get up.

"I met a lady in Springfield," I told him. We were standing looking over her stone at the lake. He didn't respond. "I asked her to marry me." I was telling Genevieve as well as Chance. Chance knew that.

I risked a glance in his direction. I had no idea what his response would be. He idolized his Nana, and I didn't know if he would feel my remarrying might be a form of betrayal.

He was smiling.

"That would be good, Bapaw. Nana wouldn't want you to be alone."

I do love that boy.

When he threw his leg over the motorcycle, he had hesitated before he kicked it to life. He was thinking. He looked at me as if the thought that had come to him was not pleasant.

"Auntie will not be happy," he said. "She'll probably leave."

That was a thought that had not occurred to me. I considered his statement for a long moment, and a depressing feeling came over me. He was undoubtedly correct.

Life is not fair. The little quip I used to tell my daughters when they complained about something came drifting back to haunt me.

Indeed, it is not.

***

Beirut, Lebanon 1984

"What are we going to do, Sergeant?" Gordo exclaimed.

I had come to hate and detest those seven words. I wanted to reach up and strip those three stripes from my sleeve and throw them as far away as I could. I didn't know what to do. There were no real options. It hardly seemed possible that we could fight our way out of this spot with sure and active death lining the walls clear to the ceiling.

We were Marines; we certainly weren't going to give up. It seemed to be an insoluble problem.

"There is a side tunnel, follow me," Nour whispered to me.

I decided I loved her.

"There is a side tunnel," I told Gordo. "Follow the girl." I knew it was a big gamble, but this whole diving under the city had been a gamble from the get-go. It had kept us alive so far. I hoped it wasn't the same "so far" as a guy falling from a t20-story building passing the sixth floor.

Nour took us back about 20 feet from where we had been sitting and started pulling down boxes from the side of the tunnel. A couple of the guys jumped over to help her. In a few seconds, they had uncovered a five-foot high by three-foot wide door into another passage.

Nour passed into the tunnel and Gordo started to follow her.

"Wait," I told him. "Stack the boxes inside, so we can replace them from the other side once we are in there." He didn't reply but smacked his head with an "I could have had a V8" gesture.

I waited, hardly daring to breathe until the last of my little troop had entered the tunnel. I still didn't see any activity ahead. I stepped up to the door and set three boxes across the entrance. I leaned over the boxes and brushed the dust with my sleeve trying my best to disguise the entrance to any passerby.

I reached back, and another box was pressed into my hand. I stacked two more, then turned and slid by Vinny, who was standing there holding a box. He immediately started stacking boxes behind me. When the last one slipped into place it got really dark, really quick.

The limits of our refuge became evident quickly when the spotter turned on his flashlight. Evidently there had been a plan for this tunnel to extend to thc surface because it slanted up at a relatively steep angle directly away from the main hall behind us. When he shined the light up the tunnel, his flashlight revealed a blank wall about 25 yards away.

I heard voices from the other side of the box. I signaled for the flashlight to be turned off. I felt a soft hand slip into mine. I was pretty sure none of my fellow Marines was into hand holding. I then felt the soft presence of a woman's body all along the length of my arm. I felt a little thrill run up my arm.

This is stupid, Roy Lee White. What are you doing? The little voice in my head chastised me. I did my best to ignore it.

The voices outside the tunnel seemed to be relaxed and oblivious to any threat. They were laughing at intervals as if they were telling each other story. Soon the voices trailed off the way we had come. I waited for another five minutes, savoring the soft presence against my arm.

Then we had to move. Vinny slid the top box off the stack and pulled it into the tunnel with us. The dim light of the tunnel appeared in the opening. No other sound followed. He quickly had enough boxes removed to slip his head out and look both ways. He turned back to me with thumbs up and a questioning look.

I pointed out into the main shaft. He nodded and crawled over the bottom box to disappear to our left. I reluctantly untangled myself from the girl's warm embrace and started clearing boxes. As soon as I had a clear path I looked out onto the deserted tunnel and came out myself. The sniper was right behind me. I sent him off ahead to scout our intended route.

"Nour, how far until we reach the French positions?"

"I am not sure," she whispered back. "I think about two or two-and-half clicks. I will know when we get there." I could understand this. Once one was in the tunnels, everything looked the same. It was hard to determine exactly where you were in the maze at a given moment. How she had known the location of the side shaft was a mystery.

"I want you to go with this man," I told Nour indicating the spotter who was waiting for orders. "Go ahead of the column," I told him. "Your sniper is on point. Catch him up and let the girl lead you. We have a couple of clicks to go to reach the first French position at the end of the Green Line."

"I want to stay with you," Nour objected. I didn't disagree. I wanted her to stay with me as well, but I needed to be with the bulk of our little force near the middle, where I could react to emergencies from either end of the column. She needed to be at the front to locate our exit.

"I know sweetheart," I risked an endearment. "I want to be near you as well, but for now, we need to do it this way." I really didn't have time to elaborate, and luckily she bowed her head to the inevitable and moved on ahead with the spotter.

We exited the tunnels as we had entered, through a basement. The building's stairwell door was about 30 yards from the sandbagged emplacement of a French Foreign Legion's guard post.

Nour went ahead to hail the guards in French to advise them of our presence and ask permission to join their party. She soon returned all smiles and told us we could join the French. She said they requested we come in pairs with our arms slinged. They had been bitten before by supposedly "friendly" troops.

I remained in the doorway with Nour until the last of our troops made the evolution. She and I walked hand in hand across the littered street. The French sent a column of armed vehicles to pick us up and take us to the embassy annex on the East side of the Green line.

Nour went with us to the embassy. Before she left me, she slipped a card into my hand with her address. She kissed me on the cheek as I turned away to walk through the gate back into the USA.

I thought I would never see her again. Thankfully, I was wrong.

***

Lyman Womack's Ranch - Downstate Illinois

"I hope we're not cutting off our nose to spite our face," Natty Ingraham remarked. He and two of Womack's heavies were studying the archived version of the Google Earth picture of the Occidental refinery near Carmi. "We need fuel too. If we blow this place, where is our fuel going to come from?" It was a rhetorical question since neither of his fellow guards was any more privy to their employer's plans than he was.

They had been busy all day stacking sack after sack of ammonium nitrate into the stolen railroad trucks. They were joined by an Arab-looking gentleman who said little but worked alongside them placing charges of C4 at strategic locations in the stack of sacks.

He carefully ran wires from each brick where the primers were inserted up to a common box on the cab of each truck. He then wired them into a radio device. Once his work was done, he disappeared without a word. Ingraham wasn't sure if he even spoke English. If not, he wouldn't last long outside the bounds of Mr. Womack's holdings. The militia was still very active in this part of the state.

Ingraham had a lot of respect for and not a small amount of fear of the militia. He suspected the activities he had become engaged in had every chance of drawing the attention of one of the militia groups. They would take a dim view of this activity, and they were very much a "shoot-first-and-ask-questions-later" bunch.

How Mr. Womack planned to get these stolen vehicles through the country more than 100 miles south without drawing attention to them was a mystery to Ingraham. Every farm, every house, every passing car could hold a citizen with ties to and contact with a militia contingent.

Ingraham knew one call could place a roadblock in their path with as many as 50 armed men. If the roadblock was manned by organized militia associated with a county sheriff, they would have more than hunting rifles. They would have LAWs and heavy machine guns. It was a frightening prospect.

Ingraham suspected there would be a couple of the associates of the man who installed the triggers in the fertilizer bombs driving the trucks. It would take some religious nut to take the kind of risk driving those trucks would entail. Certainly none of *his* fellow hired guns would do it. They were in it strictly for the money. There wasn't enough money, even in Womack's deep pockets, to pay for taking that kind of risk.

"The railroad tracks run right up next to the hydrogen storage tanks. If they can get the trucks onto the tracks, it will be clear sailing, no doubt." They zoomed the picture out and started moving the cursor to follow the tracks out of the refinery. They ran east for several miles then crossed a north-south line of tracks.

"There, follow that one," Ingraham ordered. The moving picture started north. The tracks ran for many miles before the northern leg ended in an east-west junction.

"Zoom out," Ingraham ordered again. When the picture expanded to the edge of town, Ingraham held a pencil up to the screen, marked a spot with his thumb, then moved it to the scale.

"Fifty miles," he said.

"They will have to stay on the roads for 50 miles before they can move to the tracks. That will be the dangerous part. Once they can get on the tracks, the right of way is mostly concealed by trees and brush. There are few houses and farms along the right of way. They will be okay once they reach the tracks," he concluded.

His two partners nodded their agreement.

"That's going to be a very dangerous 50 miles. I'm glad I won't be driving that truck."

"Natty, do you really think they are going to go through with this?" Johnnie Mueller asked. "I mean there are a lot of folks who know about this operation. It strikes me..."

"You're right," Ingraham said thoughtfully. "One of two things: either this is a clever ruse and a cover for another actual operation, or...," he let the "or" hang in the air ominously.

"Or ...?"

"Or, we are in deep shit, friends. If this goes down, anyone who knows about it, well, their life is in danger."

"How will we know?"

"If they move the trucks, we need to split."

The two other men nodded their heads in agreement. They were suddenly very frightened.

They had every reason to be.

What they were involved in was terrorism. Since the attack on the nation's capital, terrorism was handled very differently in the U.S. There were no constitutional protections for non-citizens. Simply being Muslim and a non-citizen was strong evidence of guilt. It wasn't fair, but there it was. Enough young Muslim men were executed that an exodus out of the country ensued. Soon there were few — if any — left.

There were special courts set up for citizens suspected of terrorist activity. These courts were made up of three-judge panels. Their word was final. They would look at the evidence, let the accused offer any plea or counter evidence, and make their determination. If the judges' ruling was guilty, the accused was marched out of the courtroom, led down to a wall behind the courthouse and summarily shot, period, the end.

It was not a system overly concerned with protecting the innocent. It was not perfect, and no doubt some innocents had been snared up in its deadly net, but it did what it was designed to do. It stopped terrorism cold in the heartland.

CHAPTER FOURTEEN

USS Guam, Eastern Mediterranean, 1984

"You may stand at ease, Staff Sergeant," Captain Norman told me. I was standing in front of his desk, cleaned up and dressed in starched fatigues. The Corps, in its infinite wisdom, had added a rocker under the three stripes on my arm. It was a battlefield promotion; nominal and not permanent until I successfully completed NCO leadership school, where the green machine would ostensibly teach me how to think.

"I am putting you in for a star," the captain informed me. He was recommending me for a bronze star for bringing the platoon home. I wasn't impressed. We shouldn't have been left out there in the first place. "You showed initiative, bravery and combat savvy above and beyond the call, Staff Sergeant. The Corps is proud of you."

"I left two of our platoon on the beach, Captain. I am surprised I wasn't court-martialed," I thought, but kept my stony silence. I would be damned if I was going to talk to this sorry excuse for an officer who would pull out and leave a platoon surrounded and under fire.

The captain looked at me as if he expected a response. When I said nothing but continued to stare at the wall over his head, he shook his head and looked down at the papers on his desk.

"You're volunteering to join the embassy guard?" The MAU* was reinforcing the guard at the Embassy Annex in East Beirut and had asked for volunteers. I was the only one.

"It's right there on the paper, numbnuts! Are you illiterate as well as cowardly?" I thought uncharitably. There was another long silence.

"Yes, Sir," I said finally still staring at the wall.

**MAU – Marine Amphibious Unit – denotes the command afloat off the coast.*

"White, are you nuts? You just got out of that mess by the skin of your teeth, and you want to go back in. Do you have a death wish?"

I said nothing, but I was surprised. The captain had admitted to me what we all suspected. The Marines on the ground were targets and expendable. The politicians were sticking it to the Corps again.

There was a long silence. I stared at the wall. The captain thumped a pencil eraser on his desk in nervous frustration.

"Look, Staff Sergeant, I know you blame me for pulling out and leaving your platoon on the beach. I protested that decision to the point where I thought I was going to be relieved. It was a decision reached a level above the Commandant himself. We have civilian bosses, and they ordered us off the beach."*I would have told them to go fuck themselves,"* I thought, but I was surprised the captain admitted the truth to me. He must have been extremely embarrassed to dump on the politicos. I still said nothing.

"White, if you don't tell me a good reason for wanting to go back into that shit-storm, I am going to disapprove this request."

I thought seriously about giving him some bullshit about God, Country, and the Corps, but finally, I decided to tell him the truth.

"I met a girl."

That stopped the drumming of the pencil eraser. I was staring at the wall over his head, but I could see his eyes widen and a shocked look come over his countenance.

"White, you amaze me. You are shooting, bombing, and blowing up half the city on your way out of town and in the midst of all that, you meet a girl?"

What could I say? When he put it like that, it did sound unlikely.

"She is Christian, drop-dead gorgeous, trilingual, and she has a thing for cowboys. I think I'm in love with her." I admitted defeat and talked to the bastard. I had no choice. He had the power to grant or deny my request, and I wanted to see Nour again in the worst way.

The captain looked at me as if I had just grown another head. I know he was trying to picture, *How in the world…?* In his button-downed world, one met girls at the Academy dance or in a college classroom, but on a battlefield? He was struggling, but finally, he gave up.

"I really shouldn't do this. As your commanding officer, I should protect you from yourself. But I owe you White; once they came under your command, you brought the entire platoon back. Okay, it's against my better judgment, but I will approve your request."

I said nothing more. I was damned if I would thank him. I was nursing my anger and animosity, and his letting me return to Beirut wouldn't change it. A part of me knew it was irrational, but I needed to hang onto this grudge to give me the strength to go back in. My feelings were at war with one another. One part of me wanted desperately to see Nour again, but the part of my self-preservation package buried deep in there somewhere was screaming its head off.

When I said nothing more, the captain finally shook his head in resignation, signed the sheet, and glared at me.

"You are an arrogant son of a bitch, White. Get out of my sight."

I spun on my heel in a perfect about-face maneuver and marched out of his office smiling a grim, self-satisfied smile. He was right. I was quite arrogant. At the moment, I was rather proud of it, but I was going to come to regret it.

***

Governor's Office —Springfield, Illinois

"I agree with you, Sir, the country would have been better off to have let the South pursue its own destiny, but it is too soon to take down the picture. People are desperate for continuity and stability. There is enough radical change in everyone's daily life now. Let's leave Abe up there for a while."

Elaine was standing in front of the governor's desk, and they were both looking at the Gettysburg painting.

The governor turned his chair around and looked at his aide. He had to admit, she was right. She was always right when it came to politics. She had an inherent natural instinct for picking the exact correct move out of a plethora of options. This instinct had served the governor well, and he knew it.

Elaine had come to his attention through a Northwestern classmate. The governor was an alumnus of the fabled university, proud of his alma mater, and active on the alumni board. The young woman was a poly-sci major, active in campus political life, and had been elected president of the campus Young Republicans.

The governor had hired her as an intern in his construction company. She had amazed everyone with her quick intellect as well as her knack for spotting waste and inefficiency. Where she had really shone was in facilitating state contracts. The governor's company was bidding on road work, bridges, and power-plant excavation. There was a labyrinth of political hurdles and legal minefields in those days because all state government work was rife with corruption.

Elaine had a talent for cutting through the red tape, identifying the roadblocks, and subverting the politicians with their hands out. She got the work, paid off no one and kept the company's skirts clean.

When the governor decided to run for office, he put her on his campaign staff. Within months, she was running it. It was largely through her efforts, ideas, and cunning political instinct that the governor was sitting in his chair, and he knew it. Moshe was correct in his assumption that Elaine Martin was unaware of the critical position she held within the governor's administration, but he was wrong about the governor. He was fully aware of how essential the lady was to him.

"The most critical thing facing us, Governor, in my estimation, is the timing of switching to Texas dollars to pay the state's employees."

Up to now the state had been paying in U.S. currency. It had been difficult. The state's revenues had all but dried up during the worst of the chaos when the economy crashed. The bulk of the state taxes were derived from sales tax. When economic activity at the retail level almost stopped, the only revenue accruing to the state was its share of the county real estate tax.

The first year the state government had almost ceased to exist. Finally, the counties realized they needed a more centralized power structure and reluctantly began to fund the state's activities.

Now, four years in, the sales tax revenue was starting to flow once more. Now the problem was a lack of physical money to continue to fund the growth. Since the Fed ceased to exist, all the cash in the economy was residual from before the crash. It wasn't enough.

Some of the states had attempted printing their own currency, but the plethora of scrip devalued the state issue almost as quickly as it was printed. Elaine had encouraged the governor to use Texas dollars. The Texans had seen the inevitable coming and had repatriated the state's gold. They had started a gold bank even before the crash. After the crash, they began issuing gold-backed dollars.

The Illinois governor had flown down to Austin to cut a deal with the Republican governor there. He had floated a multi-billion-dollar loan collateralized with Illinois's share of the Fort Knox gold, agriculture products, and finished petrochemicals from Illinois refineries. Texas had lots of oil, but their refineries had been hit hard by the terrorists.

The gold in Fort Knox had been inventoried and allocated to each state based on population. Since census data from before the chaos was all they had to go on, Illinois got a large share. The gold in Fort Knox was still protected by an armored division, but it now flew the flag of the state of Kentucky's National Guard. It was a reverse Federalization of the troops.

Some of the states had started issuing currency based on their share of the Federal gold. Unfortunately, the perception was that the state could not actually deliver on the promise, so the specie was not readily accepted.

Texas, on the other hand, had sufficient reserves within its state borders to make good on the paper promises, so it was soon accepted as legitimate currency nationwide. The problem was timing. There just wasn't enough Texas-issued money to fund a national economy. In the interim, the old Federal money would have to be used. It was a delicate balancing act.

The iron law of monetary economics said, "Good money drives out bad." This ugly truth was already pushing the inflation rate for old U.S. dollars through the roof. Illinois was having a terrible time keeping up so that its employees would have sufficient purchasing power to survive.

The governor could fix the short-term problem by paying them with Texas dollars. The issue was that he had a finite pool to draw from. Until there was enough Texas money introduced into the Illinois economy for tax dollars to start flowing back in using that currency, he could be putting the state on a road leading over a cliff.

"We have enough cash on hand to make the next payroll and add a 20 percent bonus. We can pay the Springfield employees in Canadian dollars. We have plenty left from the sale of the F16s to make at least three Springfield payrolls."

The Canadian government had been beefing up its military in a big way. There had been a lot of concern north of the border when the U.S. military establishment simply melted away. The Canadians had purchased six F16s that the Illinois Air National Guard had assumed from the Feds. They paid in cash; the Canadian dollar was viewed as gold.

"There is quite a bit of Texas money flowing into the state now. Occidental is paying its employees in Texas scrip statewide. The grain shipments Archer Daniels Midland has been sending south have been paid for lately in Texas dollars as well. As soon as we can start getting reports from all the small banks that have sprung up across the state on their Texas dollar deposits, we can launch a preference program for taxes. If the taxes are remitted in Texas currency, we can discount the amount owed." Elaine's speech was as much thinking out loud as it was for the governor's edification.

"That sounds good to me," the governor replied. "I'll tell the comptroller to do as you suggested. I like the idea of paying the locals in Canadian dollars. We might want to think about accepting CDs in tax payments as well."

"Governor, we need to start thinking about what we are going to do about Chicago."

At this, the governor frowned. He didn't want to think about that festering sore on the lake. There were no appealing options. The city had been mismanaged and sucked dry by 50 years of Democratic control, liberal policies, and rampant corruption. A good part of the south side had been burnt out and was now a charred wilderness.

Initially, the governor had simply cordoned off the city and froze residents out of state politics. He arbitrarily and unconstitutionally deprived Cook County residents of the franchise and let them twist in the wind. There had been a lot of deaths. It was estimated less than half of the 8 million people living there before the crisis survived.

Those casualties haunted his sleep, but it had been necessary. Had the governor not done what he did, the entire state would have perished in a wave of plunder and violence. Maryland, Pennsylvania, and New York were cautionary tales of what happened when a state tried to deal with an urban mess without sufficient resources. Those states would be basket cases for generations. The fact Illinois was approaching a time when there could be something done about the city was a testament to the correctness of his decision.

"Keeping the Guard deployed around the city is costing us a significant portion of the state's income," Elaine reminded him of the ongoing drain on the treasury. "Perhaps it's time to have a meeting with the city fathers."

"I would rather arrest them."

"I think the time for that has passed," Elaine said thoughtfully. "You're going to need them now. The survivors are the ones the people have picked. They might not be that bad."

At this, the governor snorted and shook his head. "Not that bad" and Cook County in the same sentence was an oxymoron in the governor's view.

"There is one other thing I need to tell you, Governor. I'm getting married, and you'll have to start looking for my replacement."

"Oh my God!" the governor exclaimed. The color drained out of his face. He hadn't even considered trying to run this office without his aide. Now that she had raised the subject, he couldn't imagine how he could.

***

White Farm — Downstate Illinois

"Daddy, do you want to fix some steaks on the grill?" Amanda asked as Chance and I walked in the kitchen door. "I have all the sides ready."

The aroma of fresh bread hung in the air as it had steadily since the wheat harvest. Amanda had both ovens going constantly. A steady stream of cars pulled up out front full of folks wanting to buy a dozen loaves at a time. Amanda was becoming a profit center in her own right.

I spotted the huge New York strips thawing in the sink.

"Sure, sweetheart, I'll fire up the grill." I walked over to the sink where she was cleaning bread pans and gave her a big hug and a kiss on the cheek. "Did I ever tell you how glad I am you came home?"

At this, she turned and looked over her left shoulder at me. "Not yet today," she teased. I told her that a lot. "And, you haven't told me you love me, for what? Ten hours or so?"

"An oversight on my part that I profusely apologize for," I teased back. We were so comfortable with each other that I could hardly imagine anything changing. Chance's observation that if Elaine Martin moved in, my daughter would more than likely move out, had brought the reality much too close to home.

I was headed out to the porch with the steaks when the phone rang. It was not the "Brrrp!" of the militia conference, so I let Amanda answer it. I had just gotten the gas burners going on the grill when she called out to me that the sheriff was on the line.

"Hello, Milo. What's up?"

"We have a break in the Federalist matter, but I don't want to talk about it on the phone."

"Look, Milo, I am about to put some steaks on the grill. How about coming to join us?"

"Will it just be us, or have you invited some Colombians as well?"

I don't know why folks are so nervous about joining us to eat. We have entire weeks go by between home invasions.

"No Colombians Milo, just us folks," I told him reassuringly. "And we have bread fresh from the oven this afternoon."

"Okay, that does it! I'm on my way." Amanda's bread was famous across the county.

By the time the sheriff pulled up out front, the steaks were showing 145 degrees on the meat thermometer. That's the perfect temperature for our grass-fed beef. We had grown to prefer the leaner cuts the grass diet yielded, over the marbled fat-loaded ribeye's that came from the cows being fed corn.

Chance met the sheriff at the front door and calmed the dogs down. They had become hyper after the latest invasion attempt. When I brought the steaks in, Amanda had the table set with bounty from our prodigious garden: new red potatoes and onions, arugula and kale salads, snow peas, and pickled beets. There was a massive plate piled high with her fresh Parker House rolls centering the table. Emperors of Ancient Rome didn't eat as well.

Chance had been down to the wine cellar and brought up a magnum bottle of Argentinian cabernet. He had then filled a glass at each place setting, with the exception of the sheriff's.

"Well, I see that we are going to have to make do with gruel again," he said approvingly.

I carefully slid a steak onto each plate, and then we stood and held hands while asking God's blessing and offering thanksgiving for our family and for the provision flowing from his hand into our lives.

We had a pleasant meal and visited about county things, crops, weather, different folks' plans, and foibles. It was as if the crisis had never happened.

After we had finished up with blackberry cobbler and ice cream, the sheriff and I adjourned to the front porch while Chance helped his aunt with cleanup duties. I went up to my office and retrieved a couple of Dominican panatelas from the humidor on my desk before I joined the lawman. We had cleaned up the mess in the front yard, but had not replaced the fence. The empty lawn looked naked in its absence. I couldn't remember when there hadn't been a fence there.

We had gotten the cigars going well when the sheriff finally launched into his spiel.

"We got a visit from one of Womack's tough guys. Evidently, he got scared and decided to come clean."

"What was on his mind?"

"It seems he thinks Womack is dabbling in something out there that could be considered terrorism and this worthy did not want to be caught up facing a three-judge panel."

"I don't blame him. What is the conviction rate for our county, 80 percent or so?"

"Closer to 90. Our judges are bloodthirsty bastards."

"No wonder he is scared. What is our next move?"

"I wanted to talk to you first. We could call out the militia and raid the place."

"Hmm, yes we could, but obviously, you have another idea or you would have just done it."

"I am thinking since we know where the trucks are..."

"Whoa! Trucks? You mean the ones that were stolen from the railyard?"

"Yes, that's what the informer wanted us to know. The trucks are out in one of the equipment sheds where Womack stores his race cars.

According to this joker, they are loaded with C4 and fertilizer. They are packed with 5-7 tons of explosives."

"Oh, no, Milo! That's what we feared!"

"Yes, and the target is the refinery at Carmi."

"Are we going to raid the place?"

"I don't think so," the sheriff said watching the smoke trail away as he exhaled a large puff. I was savoring the cool smoke of the Dominican and feeling the after effects of a perfect meal. It seemed incongruous to be discussing stolen rail trucks and explosives.

The front door opened, and Chance walked out onto the porch. "Bapaw, do you want some brandy or some of that Kentucky bourbon to go with your cigar?" Chance knows me so well. I looked over at the sheriff who mouthed, "Bourbon."

"Thank you, son, a couple glasses of Angel's Envy would be good."

He reappeared a few moments later carrying two fist-sized glasses with two fingers of amber liquid in each. Angel's Envy is magic in a bottle. It is 12-year-old bourbon aged in casks that had originally contained an excellent port. It is smooth as silk and kicks like a 10-gauge goose gun; in short, wonderful stuff.

The sheriff sampled his, then took a big puff from the panatela. He then kicked back in his deck chair and closed his eyes. "Okay Lord, you can take me now. After this evening, everything going forward is downhill."

Chance chuckled at the sheriff's comment and disappeared back into the house. The boy will drink a half glass of wine from time to time, but doesn't care for the hard stuff. I have determined his grandmother's genes predominate.

Neither of us spoke for a while, just sat there enjoying the smoke and after-dinner drink. When the sheriff spoke again, it was as if he had forgotten the potential terrorism subject.

"I know why you like it out here Leroy. I feel like nothing has changed. I keep expecting your stepdad to come out onto the porch and join us."

"Yes, and he would look at you with that glass of bourbon and remind me that you always take two Baptists with you on a fishing trip."

"Why would that be, Leroy?" the sheriff asked, walking into the punchline like a city boy.

"Because if you take one, he'll drink all your beer!"

The sheriff looked at me with a non-plussed expression until the implications of the joke struck him. "Bah,hah," he guffawed. "Well, you got me on that one, for sure." He thought about it for a minute and continued on a more serious note. "I guess I come down with you Lutherans on that score. There's nothing wrong with a social drink from time to time. Wasting one's time hanging out in taverns and roadhouses, getting drunk, and spending a working man's family's sustenance on booze is a whole different issue."

"That was my stepdad's opinion, as well."

"He was a good man, Leroy. I miss him a lot."

"He was good to my mom and my brother and I. We would have starved if he hadn't come along to help us." We both sipped at our individual glasses and burned the cigars down to stubs.

The sun was setting, and the tree frogs were starting up their chorus. There were a few lighting bugs beginning to illuminate the field on the other side of the road. A pair of bats was zinging down through the trees by the lane chasing bugs.

A whippoorwill behind the barn called out and was answered far off down by the lake. As if challenged, a bobwhite sang his two-note call over on the ridge and was answered to our right by a bird very close to the garden.

The sheriff was right, it would be easy to forget the recent past and imagine one was sitting here years ago.

I did love the farm.

I wondered briefly what a city girl would think of it. There were no fancy restaurants within 40 miles, no stage shows, no neighborhood bars. There would be no piano recitals or string quartets performing at the neighborhood theater. There were few people, other than the folks in the house; there was one neighbor within a comfortable walking distance.

I suddenly had a sense of foreboding. What I was feeling sitting here was the familiarity of home. Since Elaine would not have my set of memories or foundation, would she just be bored with the quiet of the farm? I had a premonition that would certainly be the case.

"Now that we have an informant in place, and we know where the trucks are, I think we let the game play out," the sheriff returned to the subject of his visit. "What say you, governor's man?"

"I say it's just too pat."

The sheriff stopped rocking in his chair and looked at me as if I had just slapped him. He was thinking, remembering, and putting pieces together.

"Shiiit Leroy, you're right! It is too easy, too …pat, as you say. I was trying to remember how I came up with the idea of the refinery. The more I think about it, I think it was a hint dropped in the office, by …by. Damn, I can't remember exactly, but I am fairly certain I didn't come up with it on my own."

"The question is, if the refinery isn't the target, what is?"

"And what if the whole thing is a ruse? They don't intend to use the railroad trucks at all. The entire thing is built to keep us occupied while the Federalists pull something entirely different."

"Wheels within wheels Milo," I observed. "If that's the case, someone is planning to drop a ton of shit on Lyman Womack."

***

Lakefront — Downtown Chicago

Living in the city had become like living in a Mad Max movie. Nothing worked. The power was only on intermittently, trash did not get picked up, and it was worth one's life to wander away from home out onto the street. The ghettos had become burnt-out, charnel houses of death. The gang wars had started immediately after the fires that consumed over a third of the city burned themselves out, thousands were killed. Many hundreds of innocent bystanders were shot, wounded, and killed as well.

It became difficult to impossible even to flee. The militias had set up cordons around the city with roadblocks on every street leaving Cook County. Unless one had a relative outside the city that would take a person in, you would be turned back. It became difficult to verify relatives when the cell service crashed after grid power went down.

The militias were cold-hearted and simply turned everyone back. Once they were replaced by National Guard, camps were set up where people with legitimate-sounding stories were allowed to wait while their families were contacted.

Once word went out through the countryside on what was happening, many families sent representatives to the cities looking for their relatives. Within a year, less than 2 million people remained where more than 8 million souls had resided before the chaos. Sadly, half of the 8 million were buried and burnt within the confines of the county line.

The mayor and his family had not suffered inordinately. The man who was ultimately responsible for dealing with the crisis visited upon the citizens of his fair city had failed miserably. If one were to ask Hizhonor one would find the mayor was not at fault in the least. All of the tragedy that had been visited upon Carl Sandburg's 'City of Broad shoulders' had been the responsibility of external forces over which the mayor had no control.

The fact the mayor and his party had effectively disarmed the tax paying citizens of the city, leaving them at the mercy of the predators, was conveniently overlooked. The surreptitious alliance between the ruling families and the drug gangs which perpetrated hundreds of casualties weekly upon the young men of the city, even before the crisis, left no mark on the mayor.

The mayor and his immediate political family had ridden high on the hog living in their penthouses and mansions overlooking Lakeshore Drive while the ghettos suffered and died. For decades, the money flowed from Washington to support the indigent and wastrels of the inner city.

The teachers' unions shipped millions to their political protectors, and the system made sure the teachers were unaccountable to parents or students, so generations of uneducated dependents were released on society.

It was an entire sick interdependent system of bribes, payoffs, and corruption. The seeds were sewn for three generations. When the reaping whirlwind came, the price was prodigious. Unfortunately, tragically, the price was paid by the victims. Those responsible for the tragedy lived above the mess in isolated, elegant luxury.

The center and soul of the Federalist Party lived in the heart of the city of Chicago. Here in the shining penthouses and condos of the Miracle Mile, the plutocrats plotted their return to greatness.

The mayor was standing on the deck of his elegant condo on the 35th floor looking out over the lake. It was after 2 p.m. so Hizhonor was imbibing. He had a massive bourbon glass half filled with a single-malt scotch. He liked his whiskey neat and warm. He savored the peaty aroma and enjoyed the warmth that suffused his body after the second or third swallow.

One of his councilman friends, a tall, portly black man, was holding forth on his favorite subject.

"It is obvious, your honor. The way to deal with these statists is the way the rag-heads dealt with Washington; we need to cut the head off the snake."

The mayor didn't disagree, but the devil was in the details. Springfield had become an armed camp. The governor's supporters were competent, determined, and ruthless men. Getting to the governor was not going to be easy.

The mayor no longer had even a sliver of the resources at his disposal that he had once commanded. His revenue basc had shriveled and died. He was at the mercy of drug dealers and disgruntled captains of industry to have even enough money to pay his bodyguards and maintain his living quarters.

The mayor was under no illusions that he retained even a vestige of power. That had slipped away in the chaos to be replaced by a gang of ruthless men bent on the restoration of the gravy train now long departed from the rails.

The mayor was not looking forward to the meeting. The dark-suited men had been filtering into his large living room for the past five minutes. Finally, he could stall no longer. He went in and started working his way through the room.

They all treated him like he was some errand-boy. He hated that.

When Escobar came into the room with his two rough-looking lackeys, everyone stood to attention. The real power had just entered the room.

"Gentlemen, shall we begin?" Escobar phrased it as a question, but it was an order. He nodded to his bodyguards. They walked through the rest of the apartment, sweeping with handheld radio detection devices. When they were satisfied, they left the room, locking the big double doors to the elevator lobby behind them. They had escorted the councilman out with them when they left.

"Gentlemen, the six of us in this room are the only people on earth who know of 'The Plan.' Let me assure each of you other five of one thing. If this doesn't succeed because of even a hint that word of it leaked out, I will hunt every one of you down and personally cut off your balls and stick them in your mouth *before* I shoot you. Am I quite clear?"

A spasm of fear ran down the mayor's back. He took another healthy slug of whiskey. How he wished he had never become involved with these people, but it was fanciful thinking. He was in it now – in for a penny, in for a pound.

"The first part of the plan is being played out. The fake threat to blow up the Occidental refinery is in place. Law enforcement from the local level clear to the top is obsessed with those trucks now. While they are looking there, like a magician, we will strike elsewhere," Escobar said with a malevolent grin, then continued.

"We have a ready-mix concrete truck packed with explosive waiting in Decatur. It's hiding in plain sight among a line of actual cement trucks at a plant on the west side. When the time is right. we will move the mixer to Springfield and decapitate the state government just like the Muslims did in D.C."

"You're leaving Lyman Womack swinging in the wind," the mayor voiced the thought that was foremost in his mind and then was terrified that he had let it slip out.

"Mr. Womack is expendable. His wealth has almost entirely disappeared. He is sitting down there with his massive farm around him and can do very little with it. His usefulness to us as a decoy far outweighs any actual value he might bring to the party."

The mayor shuddered. The cold-hearted way Escobar treated everyone around him frightened the mayor to his core. He wondered if he were next.

"We're six or seven weeks away from the governor's speech to the combined Legislature," Escobar continued. "On that day, we will strike. In the meantime, I'm going to invite his aide to a little party and see what we can find out about the governor's preparations that may disrupt our attack."

The mayor wondered if this invitation would be received in the same manner Escobar's last one to the lady had been.

The mayor was still wondering about this when his chief of staff came into the room. The mayor experienced a twinge of fear. The man was under strict orders to not interrupt the meeting. It must be urgent. When the chief of staff told him the governor was on the line, he almost shit his pants.

CHAPTER FIFTEEN

East Beirut, Lebanon 1984

"Welcome aboard Staff Sergeant." Lieutenant Etterman was smiling. He seemed sincerely pleased to see me. "You appear to be the hero of the hour. I understand they're putting you in for a star. You know if you had been wounded it would have been silver instead of bronze. Perhaps you should have had one of your guys shoot you." The lieutenant chuckled, evidently quite impressed with his own sick humor.

Serving as a target for a few months tends to do that to a person.

"Your CO told me you met a girl during your little adventure. Can that possibly be true?"

"It's true, El Tee," I told him. I needed his cooperation, so I was going to be as forthcoming as possible. "She's a Phalanges, who led us through the PLO tunnels to the Foreign Legion outpost on the 'Line.' We owe her our lives; I don't see how we could have gotten out without her."

"Do you know why I agreed to let you join us here, Romeo?"

"No sir, I guess I don't."

"You're lucky, White; extremely lucky. In this bollixed up assignment, we need all the luck we can get. The Iranians are going to try to hit the embassy here, sooner or later. It's our job to stop them. We are undermanned, underequipped, and a target for every disgruntled rag-headed follower of the Prophet who finds himself wandering around in this hell hole. We're going to need every bit of luck we can get."

This was quite a speech, but I was glad the lieutenant leveled with me.

"Here's the schedule," the lieutenant continued. "We are six-on, six-off around the clock. You're not going to have much time to pursue your fair maiden, but given your recent service to the Corps, I'm going to give you a couple days off before I work you into the rotation. You're relieving another staff sergeant, but he isn't shipping out until Wednesday, so we are good on the roster until then."

"Gosh, El Tee, that's great! I appreciate it!"

"Here's the deal, White. We're not authorized liberty in town. We're supposed to be locked down, so officially you are not here. You did not report in. I never saw you. You are officially in limbo for 72 hours."

"Understood Sir," I told him. I was surprised. I had yet to meet an officer who was not at least partly an asshole. Etterman seemed to be an exception.

"You got money, White?"

"Yes, Sir, I drew down before I came ashore."

"What about civvies?" the officer asked. He knew I was going to need some civilian clothes if I was going to be out and about in beautiful, romantic East Beirut, Lebanon.

"Yes, Sir, I have one change until I can get into a hotel and find a tailor."

"I don't know how long we're going to be here, White. There are rumors we will be pulled out and security turned over to Phalanges Militia. So if you're going to win the heart of the fair maiden, you might have to hurry."

"I understand Sir," I replied. I was not surprised, that rumor was floating all through the MAU. "Where can I change, Sir?" We were in a cramped little office the lieutenant was sharing with the OIC of internal security Marines. They were a separate group from the MAU Marines. The internal security guard was assigned to the State Department and answered to the Ambassador.

"I'll have someone take you to the guard Marine's area. Good luck, White."

Less than an hour later I made my way out of the complex dressed in wranglers and a short-sleeved white shirt. I would be fooling no one of course; my regulation USMC haircut and issue dress brogans identified me for who I was as readily as if I were wearing dress blues.

I weaved my way through the dragon's teeth to the two-lane street in front of the embassy carrying a briefcase-sized satchel the lieutenant had loaned me. It contained a shaving kit and a couple pairs of skivvies. I didn't want to be seen wandering around carrying a seabag.

Outside the dragon's tooth barricades, there were two sandbag strongpoints manned by jarheads, beside which, were parked a pair of AAV 7s.

"Can I borrow your militiaman to hail me a cab, Sergeant?" I asked the staff sergeant manning the nearest strong point. There were four grunts and a Phalanges militiaman manning the post. They had a single M60 and their shoulder weapons. I noticed they had no LAWs. How they were going to stop trucks and suicide bomb-equipped cars was an open question.

"You must be White," the sergeant said. "Where do you think you're going? We're in lockdown."

"The lieutenant gave me a couple days. I am not here yet, Sergeant. I know you think you see me, but you do not."

"You're going out into this third-world sewer by yourself?" the staff sergeant asked in amazement.

"Sarge, will you loan me your militiaman, or not?"

"Okay, okay. Try not to get your ass shot off, White."

The little brown man in a blue helmet squeezed out of the strong point and walked with me to the corner of the two-lane road. There wasn't a lot of traffic. We waited 10 minutes or so and then a small, white cab pulled up at the militiaman's waving signal.

"Tell him to take me to the nearest hotel in the neighborhood of this address," I told the soldier, handing him the card with Nour's home address. He and the cab driver looked at the card and got into an extended discussion. After a while, the militiaman turned to me.

"The cabby says there is a hotel closer, but it's not too nice. There's a small suites hotel a few blocks farther away, but it's very nice. He thinks it's more to the taste of an American. He did say it was expensive."

"Okay, thanks. Tell him to take me to the nicer one." I had drawn down a $1,000. I hadn't drawn any pay for more than three months and was flush for the moment. I had a nice nest egg from my rodeo winnings, but I hadn't had to touch a nickel of it since I had been in the Corps. The green machine hadn't let me out of its sight long enough to spend any.

The cabby was right. The hotel was beautiful, intimate, and expensive. I paid up front for three nights. It took half of my stash. Before I went to my room, I walked over to the little gift shop and bought a postcard with the hotel picture on it. I then went to the concierge desk, showed the young lady Nour's address, and since half of it was in Arabic script, had the lady transcribe it to the postcard. I then wrote on the message portion:

Nour,

I have 72 hours. I am at this hotel. Come and see me as soon as you can. I am anxious to see you again.

Your American cowboy,

Roy Lee

I gave the cute little concierge a $10 bill for the cabby. I tried to give her a tip, but she refused. She seemed intrigued by thc entire romantic nature of the message and its portent. She laughed and stroked my arm as she departed for the front door with her message. I could only hope the cab driver would actually deliver it and not just take the tenner and throw the card away. It was worth a shot. If it didn't work, I would get a cab and find her apartment later.

I went up to the room. It was beautiful.

Evidently this hotel had been a refuge for the French nationals when they ran the country in the 1940s. Everything was in French — the room service menu, the stationary — every printed document in the desk was French.

I didn't care. After months of living aboard ship crammed in with several hundred other grunts, sleeping in the dirt, and shipping containers at the airport, this unimagined luxury was as welcome as it was unsettling.

I picked up the phone and asked the operator for the concierge. After a couple of beep-beeps, the same girl who had helped me downstairs answered. I asked if there might be a tailor who could be contacted to come to my room. She told me it would be no problem at all. There was a tailor shop in the basement of the hotel. She would send him right up.

Before I let her go, I told her I needed someone to come up and pick up my laundry. I needed my shirt and jeans washed and pressed.

They had spent almost four months buried in the bottom of my sea bag and were somewhat wrinkled and forlorn.

By the time the tailor arrived, I had taken a shower, dispatched my entire wardrobe to be laundered, and had donned the fluffy white robe provided by the hotel. I called room service and had a couple of icy cold Heinekens delivered. I was sitting on the veranda sipping on the second one, feeling like a pasha when the door chime announced the arrival of the tailor.

The lieutenant said I was lucky. He must have been right. The tailor spoke some English. He was not fluent by any means, but he understood enough relating to his trade for us to communicate.

There was one other item in my little satchel. It was an old bedraggled copy of American Horseman. The cover featured a cowboy on a cutting horse pulling a calf out of the herd. The calf had just made a dodge to the left, and the horse was reacting, twisting around under the rider. The rider looked relaxed and comfortable as the horse moved beneath him.

It was me; I was the rider.

This issue of American Horseman was my 15 minutes of fame. It was a great action shot, and the magazine was doing a feature on Morgan horses. My stepfather raised Morgans, the mount I was aboard when the picture was taken.

They had done an interview and taken a number of other photos to illustrate the article. I showed the tailor what I wanted to be done. There were a number of advertisements for boots, jackets, shirts, and other cowboy paraphernalia throughout the magazine. We soon worked up an order.

I asked him how much. He asked me with what currency I would be paying. I told him Uncle Sam's greenbacks. He smiled. One hundred dollars would take me all the way. Wow! I had finally found a bargain in this Mideast nightmare of a place.

With the departure of the tailor, I was somewhat at loose ends. When in doubt, order beer; it was kind of an 11th commandment of the Corps. So that's exactly what I did. I ordered four more bottles of Heineken, a bucket of ice, and started hot water pouring into the huge tub.

I spent close to an hour soaking in the luxury of hot water, scented soap, and drinking beer. It was heaven. I then crawled into the king-size bed among a pile of pillows and crashed like a steam-liner driven full speed into a pier.

It was dark when I woke up. There was an insistent knock at my door. It took me a full minute to recognize my surroundings to determine where I was. I pulled on my robe and stumbled to the door. It was a bellman with my laundry. I tipped him a fiver that got me a wide-eyed smile as he bowed his way out of the room.

They did a great job on my clothes. The Wranglers looked like the creases could cut soft steel.

Now if I just had some boots…

The second knock on the door revealed the tailor with one arm full of clothes and a pair of black cowboy boots polished to a mirror finish in his other hand. I pinched myself to make sure I hadn't passed on to the next world.

I tipped the tailor $20 after he insisted I try the jacket on. It fit perfectly. Evidently he had simply tailored an already made jacket because there was no way he could have sewn up a coat from scratch in five hours. He had embroidered some fancy scroll work down the lapels giving it a western flair. I was more than happy with it.

He had found a silver cross that the jeweler next door to his shop had fashioned into a tie clasp and had even made a couple of little silver thimble-like ends for the string tie. The Levis were Russian knock-offs, but the tailor's helpers had cut and sewn them until they fit me perfectly when I stepped into them.

The mother-of-pearl buttons on the shirt were great. The boots fit as if they were custom made. I tipped the tailor another $20

I slipped out of my new jacket and shirt and shaved standing there in my knockoff jeans and new boots. Gosh, it felt great! I could almost imagine that I was home.

I was adjusting my tie and thinking some serious thoughts about the lounge when the phone rang. It was my little concierge lady.

Nour was waiting for me in the lobby.

I decided pinch or not, I had died and gone to heaven. I didn't care; I was just going to enjoy it.

When I saw her standing by the concierge lady, I almost didn't recognize her. She had come dressed for the evening in an open-shoulder, black dress with a thin-strapped back. The dress was hemmed just above her knees and revealed a pair of perfectly formed calves. The black-strapped, high-heeled shoes matched the patent leather purse and belt that accented her outfit.

She was wearing a thin, silver necklace from which hung a large cross that fell to the bottom of her impressive cleavage. I had forgotten how full her lips were. She had brushed out her coal black hair, and it flowed down either side of her face and across her shoulders.

She was laughing at something the concierge had said. When they saw me, they looked at each other in a conspiratorial fashion. I guessed I had been the topic of their conversation.

***

Miracle Mile – Chicago

"You have some nerve calling me, Governor, after not taking my calls for almost four years. Leaving the city to die…"

"Shut up Ron," the governor ordered. "You listen to me and hear me well. I'm considering calling an air strike on that little castle of yours and nipping anything you and that gang of criminals you're meeting with in the bud."

The mayor felt a stab of cold fear run up his spine. This governor did not bluff. The man had arrested the entire leadership of the Legislature, and those worthies were still locked up at some undisclosed location. The mayor imagined he could hear the distant roar of jet engines. The governor paused as if waiting for a reply.

"I am listening, Governor."

"Let me tell you what I know. I know that you're meeting with Juan Edwardo Escobar. Tell Mr. Escobar I'm aware of the attempt he made on one of my operatives last week and that all of his soldiers from that operation are dead and buried. Also, I know that Mr. Escobar brought a number of high-level Federalists in his plane from Monterey into Midway in the early morning hours before dawn."

The mayor's hand was shaking, and he felt a hollow vacancy near his stomach.

"Those are some of the things I know. Now I will tell you a couple things I suspect. I suspect you and your fellow conspirators are planning some covert attack on me and mine. I suspect you think if you can get me and a couple of other governors out of the way, the skids will be greased for a return to a national government."

"No, Governor…"

"Ron, do I hear you talking? Do you hear the distinct sound of F16s out your window."

"I am listening Governor," Ron said, his voice quavering.

Then a wave of panic hit him. He did hear jet engines! It built and built, and then the entire building was shaken by the blast of two F16s zooming over the structure on full afterburner mere feet above the top floor.

The mayor squinted his eyes shut and held his breath waiting for the explosion that would end his life. It was some moments before he realized the bombs weren't coming.

"Ron, now listen carefully. Can you hand the phone to Mr. Escobar or will he need to come to where it is?"

"I can hand it to him, it's wireless."

"Do that now, Ron. Give Mr. Escobar the phone."

The mayor's hands were shaking, and his face was the color of chalk. He walked across the room and handed the phone to Escobar.

"The governor of the State of Illinois, for you," as if telling the man it was his wife wanting to know if he was going to make it home for dinner.

"Hello," Escobar spoke into the phone with a look of confusion replacing the smug confidence of moments before. His eyes got wide as he listened, and the color drained from his face. The sound of approaching jet engines again filled the room. Just as they passed overhead again, Escobar exclaimed.

"Fifty million dollars!! You can't mean $50 million? It will clean me out." He mumbled into the phone. "All right, all right. I understand," he said, handing the phone to the mayor then stumbling over to a couch where he collapsed with his face in his hands.

After a few minutes, he looked up. Everyone's attention was focused on him.

"The bastard wants $50 million in cash to let me leave the city. If I don't have it to him in 48 hours, he's going to call in a strike on my plane and lock me in here." The thought of being stuck here with the mayor did not seem to be appealing to the Colombian drug lord.

"Let's get out of here, right now while we can!" exclaimed one of the men who had accompanied Escobar when they came into Midway.

"The governor said he has a sniper with a .50 caliber Barrett covering the airplane. Anyone trying to board will be summarily shot. We are trapped here!"

"What are you going to do?"

"I am going to pay the bastard. I have no other choice," Escobar said. "Unless we can accelerate the attack and take him out first."

***

Governor's Office –Springfield, Illinois

"Elaine, that was a stroke of genius. Escobar is going to pay up."

"I'm not so sure," Moshe disagreed. "He will agree to pay up, you have him by the short hair right now, but keep in mind, the man is a gangster. He'll be sitting there trying to come up with any way possible to renege. I'm afraid he'll try to strike first, Governor. I'm convinced we need to get you out of here and into a safe location."

"Where would be safe? The Federalists have agents everywhere," the governor asked.

"How about Leroy White's farm?" Elaine suggested. "After the events that transpired out there a couple of weeks ago, I would think it would be the last place anyone would look."

The governor and Elaine looked at Moshe. The man was thinking, weighing different angles and options.

"I like it," he said at last. "No phone calls. I'll contact the sheriff on the secure satellite link and get White to fly up here tonight after dark and pick you up. No one aside from the sheriff and us three will know, other than White himself. It should be safe for now."

"I'll be incommunicado." The governor was having second thoughts.

"No, we'll send a couple of secure satellite phones; you should be good to go."

"Okay," the governor said after he considered it for another few minutes. "Let's make it happen."

***

White Farm — Downstate Illinois

The dogs and I were just coming back from our morning walk when a dust cloud announced the arrival of another car. My access road was having more traffic recently than I-70 on the other side of the ridge.

A county car pulled up in front, and Ralph Warren stepped out.

"Milo sent me out. He wrote you a note." The deputy handed me a sealed envelope. I opened it, and there was a note in the sheriff's handwriting.

> *Leroy,*
>
> *The governor is in danger. He is requesting you fly in tonight and pick him up at his farm east of town. He wants to stay at your place until the danger has passed.*
>
> *Can you do that?*
>
> *Thanks,*
>
> *Milo*

"Ralph, tell the sheriff to consider it done."

I started back for the house and crossed paths with Chance, who was headed to the house with milk cans.

"As soon as we finish breakfast, we need to fuel the plane. I need to go to Springfield again. We're going to have company for a while," I told Chance. "You want to get a couple of hours of night flying in?"

"Sure Bapaw, you know I love to fly."

"And we will need to move the Foretravel out of the shop. We'll have guests for an extended period of time."

There was a 45-foot Foretravel motorhome stored in the four-bay detached shop building. The bay was configured so we could pull the front half of the motorhome out onto the concrete so anyone using it had a nice view and didn't feel like they were staying in a garage, but it was still fully hooked up with power, sewer, and water.

If the governor was going to be with us for an extended period of time, the coach was like a separate apartment.

The sunset was a glorious red, promising fine weather for the following day. There was a faint band of clouds to the west on the horizon where the sun was setting, but the sky was deep blue above. Venus was up a few degrees over the horizon, bright in this season, putting in her brief appearance as the evening star, before following the sun in an hour or so, to disappear just as the rest of the stars came out.

Since all I had to go on was the sheriff's cryptic note, I had no idea how many folks the governor might want to accompany him. I could bring two more in comfort or three rather crowded in the back. I was giving up a seat to have Chance accompany me, but flying at night after the demise of Air Traffic Control was dicey. Eyeball contact was all there was to avoid other traffic, and an extra pair of eyes might mean the difference between an uneventful flight and coming to earth in the middle of a fireball.

Chance and I had put out 10 lights on each side of the grass runway right after we fueled the plane this morning. They were solar-powered lights originally meant as garden and lawn ornaments, but they made excellent runway markers. All we needed was the outline and border of the track to give us a visual orientation of the runway's location. By the time we came back it, would be pitch black out here in the country. As it happened, it was the dark of the moon.

The governor had an excellent runway at his ranch east of town. He had a couple of twin-engine prop planes and a small business jet at his disposal, but none of his planes could land on my little grass strip behind the barn.

I had no idea of what was coming down, but I knew it had to be serious to warrant all of this clandestine activity.

I put Chance in the left seat for the outbound leg to let him get some night flying practice. He had quite a bit of VFR daytime flying but had little instrument time. IFR flying had all but disappeared. I knew smugglers, drug and gun runners still did it and took their chances with other traffic, but it was a scary, dangerous activity.

We lined up headed west on the grass strip. He ran the engine up, checked both magnetos, cycled the prop and we were ready. He held the brakes, coaxed all 300 horses to life and held us stopped until the fully braked wheels started to slide forward on the grass. He released the brakes, and we shot forward.

The plane bounced twice, and I felt it beginning to respond to the controls. When the airspeed indicator crossed 45 knots, Chance applied a bit of back pressure, and we were flying. We hadn't used more than a third of the short strip. As we passed through 1,000 feet indicated, he eased the power back a notch but kept climbing. The boy was a natural with the plane; it responded to his gentle touch as if they were connected at some subliminal level.

We turned to a west/northwest heading and leveled out at 5,000 feet. Before the crisis, flying across the Midwest at night could be disorienting. The plethora of white yard lights blended with the stars, making identification of the horizon difficult.

That was no longer the case. Grid power was returning, but it was still so expensive, yard lights were a luxury most folks were doing without. The farms and fields below us were dark, causing the horizon where the stars ended to be clearly delineated.

The governor had set up an ADF transmitter at his airstrip and hangar. I dialed in the frequency, but we were still too far out to pick it up. It was a pretty weak transmitter. We flew the compass and the Springfield VOR. I dialed in the radial that lay across the governor's ranch and watched the needle bury itself to the right of the display. It would start to center when we approached the correct heading. The route I planned brought us well east of the governor's place on a north heading. We would intercept the VOR and let it take us directly to his airstrip.

As the needle started to move back to the center, the ADF picked up the signal and pointed off to the left of the nose. As Chance brought the prop around to line up on the VOR, the ADF needle obediently came around and pointed straight ahead.

When I thought we were about five miles out, I dialed 112.0 into one of the comm radios and pressed the transmit bip-bip. Out of the black in front of us, the runway lights came up dead ahead.

"We are way high for a straight in approach," I told Chance unnecessarily. He could see it as easy as I could. We could either set up for a complete circle to a downwind approach or… Chance reached down, closed the cowl flaps, pulled the power clear off, cranked in left aileron and stood on the right rudder putting the plane into a steep slip. The left wing dropped down as the airspeed dropped below 80 and he started feeding in flaps. We were bleeding off altitude at a prodigious rate. I dialed the prop in for a deep bite if we needed to go around.

The airspeed settled in about 50 as the airport lights took on a more favorable attitude. About then, two white lights appeared to the left of the near-end of the runway. The governor actually had VASI lights. The acronym stood for Vertical Attitude Situation Indicator. The lights let an approaching pilot know if he was on the glideslope, too low or too high.

If there appeared a red light over a white light, the plane was exactly on the glide slope. Two white lights indicated the plane was too high and two red indicated the danger of being too low.

I heard Chance mumble, "White on white, too much height." It was a jingle that helped a pilot remember, the rest of it went: "red on white, you are all right; red on red, you're dead." As we settled toward the runway, the top white light started to turn red.

Chance let the plane recover from the slip, leveled the wings and pulled in the last notch of flaps. The burble of air caused by the slip returned to a smooth hiss. He reached down and turned on the landing and taxi lights. It illuminated the strip ahead showing us 50 feet above the grass.

"Beautiful job son, just like a pro!" I complimented him. Like a lot of other things, I was beginning to think he might just be a bit better plane handler than his grandpa. I salved my feelings with the realization he still couldn't fly instruments. At least, I still had that up on him.

He greased the plane onto the grass just barely beyond the end. We rolled to a stop using less than a quarter of the runway. I double blipped the runway lights off, and the entire field faded to black. Only the grass ahead illuminated by our taxi light was visible.

"I'll take it," I told him. He hadn't been here before, so I would taxi around to the pickup area. As I turned to the darkened hangar, I had a sinking premonition.

"Son, did you bring a gun?" I asked. Chance didn't respond verbally, but he unbuckled his belt, turned and dug into the leather flight case behind my seat. The Ruger SR45 he came up with answered the question.

"You, Bapaw?"

I nodded toward my left shoulder covered by the light jacket I was wearing.

"KelTek," I told him.

He shook his head. He thought a nine millimeter was a girl's gun. My favoring the .22 mag was incomprehensible to him; different strokes for different folks.

"There is a Benelli under the back seat," I said.

When things got truly ugly, I reached for a shotgun. He ran his seat all the way back and leaned clear up out of it to reach back at an impossible angle to retrieve the 12 gauge. It hurt me to even watch him do that.

He sat the shotgun down between us with the muzzle pointed at the ceiling, I noticed he reached over and slid the slide back to check if there was a round chambered.

Silly boy, it was my shotgun, of course, there was a round chambered. An empty gun does no one good.

I taxied around the two T-hangars to the pick-up area. There was no activity, no cars, and everything was dark. I looked up toward the house. The place looked abandoned.

I really began to get worried. I thought about it for a moment, added power and taxied back around behind the hangars putting the buildings between us and the house.

I shut off the taxi lights and let my eyes get adjusted to the dark before I shut down the engine.

When I stepped out of the plane, it was quiet. It was also dark. Even as my eyes adjusted, I could hardly see the aircraft beside me.

"Bapaw, put these on." Chance was rattling something against the passenger seat. I reached down and felt what he was trying to hand me. It was a pair of goggles.

I put them on and could see again. They were infrareds, and Chance had a powerful infrared flashlight he was shining toward the hangar. That boy has the neatest toys!

I noticed the wind had come up a bit. I could see the weeds moving causing shadows to slide across the side of the hangar.

I reached in and slid the Benelli out, pushed the safety off, closed my door and started for the building.

"That will be far enough Pilgrim. Stop right there!"

I heard the unmistakable chick-chick of a 12-gauge pump jacking a round into the chamber.

This isn't good, I thought as Chance shut the light off, and the world was plunged once more into darkness.

CHAPTER SIXTEEN

Estahl Nunnaker's Home – Downstate Illinois

"You can't do this on your own John, we need to bring in some muscle from Gary," Estahl Nunnaker told John Palmer. They were sitting in Nunnaker's dining room looking at each other over morning coffee. The relationship between the two men was complicated. Nunnaker was retired from his union job with the UAW and had come back to his hometown to spend his golden years.

Nunnaker had been an organizer and enforcer back in the day. When he had been in need of some out-of-town muscle in the mill towns of northern Indiana, Palmer had filled the slot nicely. Nunnaker considered Palmer a friend. Palmer looked at Nunnaker as a convenient acquaintance but didn't trust the man.

After Nunnaker had come back to Johnstown he had started to spend a lot of time with Palmer. He enjoyed being in the company of such an intimidating individual and liked the way people treated him with what he thought was respect, once his affiliation with Palmer became public knowledge. It was not respect; it was fear and disdain, but from where Nunnaker was coming from, it sufficed.

Nunnaker was the only person in the world other than Palmer himself who knew what happened to Vivian because Nunnaker had taken her body to Gary to dispose of it. It had been a big risk, but Palmer figured he had so much dirt on Nunnaker from their union days, he was safe.

Now that all of the union's power had dissipated with the demise of the Federal government's protection, coupled with the disappearance of the Federal court system, Palmer's leverage over his associate had all but disappeared. Nunnaker was unaware of it, but he was looking more and more to Palmer as a loose end and a liability.

Palmer didn't like to admit it to himself, but the sheriff's warning had severely limited his options. Any overt move on the sheriff, however tenuously linking him, would bring out the militia. Palmer feared very little in this world, but the militia scared him.

They were competent, determined men, armed to the teeth. They took no prisoners and gave no quarter. They would kill him and throw his body into the river just as the sheriff promised. If the militia thought he had anything to do with killing the sheriff; they might take some time arranging Palmer's meeting with his maker. It would neither be a quick nor a pleasant death.

"I cannot be linked to the sheriff's death. It either has to be a convincing accident or has to be laid on someone else," Palmer said thoughtfully. "We cannot go at this like a bull elephant charging a lion."

Palmer then smiled a little, admiring the image he had just described.

"I agree. I have been thinking about this," Nunnaker said. "I believe that we could lay it on the Colombians that attacked the deputy's farm."

"Hmm, that would be good," Palmer agreed. His eyes brightened. He liked that thought. "Any ideas?"

"We need a couple of bodies to seed the scene with," Nunnaker replied. Evidently he had been giving it some thought. "My big picture plan would entail snatching a couple of the Mexicans working for Womack; plant some Colombian IDs on 'em. You know, tattoos or some such, then set up a scene that looked like they ambushed the sheriff and were killed in the melee."

"I don't know," Palmer said skeptically. "That sounds terribly complex and brings in a lot of players. Anything we do needs to be kept within the bounds of you, me and Ken." Now that Nunnaker had introduced the idea, Palmer's thoughts were running more to hanging the sheriff's demise on Nunnaker and killing two birds with the same stone.

If Nunnaker had known what John was smiling about he would have peed in his pants. As a wise man once observed, "Be careful when you lie down with dogs, it is highly likely you will get up with fleas."

***

Beirut, Lebanon 1984

"I told you he was a cowboy!" Nour said to the concierge with apparent satisfaction. They were watching me walk across the lobby in their direction. They were smiling and holding hands, having formed an instantaneous bond, it seemed.

"Sir, shall I have the lady's luggage sent up to your room?" The concierge asked still smiling broadly as if she had been brought into the conspiracy. I looked down at the bag sitting by Nour's feet. I hadn't noticed it before. *Whiskey, Tango, Foxtrot! What is happening?*

The shocked look on my face must have been readily apparent because the girls' smiles quickly disappeared, replaced by similar looks of concern. I recovered quickly.

"Sure," I said and fished out a fiver for the bellman. "This is for the boy," I told the concierge and handed her the bill. Both girls looked relieved. I would think about this later. Now, I needed a drink.

The open-air lounge was on the roof, covered by a tent-like structure paneled in bamboo. There were various South Seas paintings and decorations as if someone thought to move Tahiti to the Eastern Med. There was a view of the Mediterranean out past the skyline. If one sat far enough back in the bar where the buildings were not visible, the illusion could be maintained.

I found a table on the open patio tucked under some palm leaves and an umbrella. It created our own private little nook. The tiny table was large enough for four glasses and not much else. When we sat down, Nour took my hand and laid it on the table palm up cradled in both of hers.

"My grandmother said a person's life is written in their hands," she said as she studied the lines, scratches and scars in my palm. Riding rodeo and growing up on a farm is rough on a person's hands.

"What is this?" she asked pointing to a black spot in the middle of my palm.

"It's a pencil lead from the third grade. I broke it off while trying to shove a sharp pencil into my desk." I often wondered why my body had not rejected the foreign object but had merely healed over it, leaving the distinct black mark there for life.

"And this?" she stroked the end of my middle finger where it had been broken at the first joint and healed crooked.

"A bronc in Abilene," I told her. It had caught in the rein when the horse threw me off and snapped like a stepped-on twig.

Her examination of my hand was interrupted by the waiter. She asked for white wine; I stuck with Heineken. When the waiter stepped away, she reached for my hand, but I slipped it out of her grasp and reached up to stroke her face.

"You are so beautiful," I said softly. "Thank you for saving my life."

She blushed a bit and smiled demurely. Her face was warm in my hand. I slid my index finger softly across her lips; they were her most prominent feature. Her eyes were a dark hazel green, solid without a trace of the brown that most people with hazel eyes have. I thought they were the most attractive eyes I had ever seen.

"You brought a bag," I said into the silence that had come between us. It was a statement and a question. I desperately wanted to know where she thought this was going.

Before she could answer, the waiter returned with our drinks. He poured my beer into a chilled glass. I thought it was a nice touch. I had little experience with world-class hotel service. The cheap hotels and bars I frequented on the rodeo circuit were a far cry.

"To life," she offered a toast as she raised her glass for me to tink against.

"Indeed, and thanks again for saving mine."

We sampled our drinks, and I waited for the response to my question. She seemed to be studying me and didn't respond for a few moments. When she did, both of our glasses were half empty.

"We don't have time to waste on preliminaries or protocol. Life in this city can be short and brutal. I have learned to grasp the moment and live it for all it's worth," Nour told me with the seriousness of a confessional and the wisdom of a lady of twice her years. After her little speech, she emptied her glass. She had barely set it back on the table when the waiter reappeared, as if by magic, with two more drinks.

I decided I liked world-class service.

"Tell me about Nour Lahoud," I asked softly. At this moment, there was no subject in the world about which I was more interested.

She told me her story and my heart went out to her. It was tragic and heartbreaking. She had lost her parents and older brother in the fighting three years ago. She had taken up her brother's rifle and joined the Phalanges fighters.

She and her little brother were living with an uncle and his wife in her parent's apartment. Her uncle's place had been destroyed in an Israeli air strike. It went on and on in the same vein. Friends, relatives, neighbors, and schoolmates killed, maimed, and wounded. It was a litany of horror. The boy to whom she had been betrothed had been killed in the same battle that claimed her brother.

What was amazing to me was her lack of bitterness and hate. It was as if the war were some phenomenon of nature like a storm or tidal wave that had swept through her life, leaving broken pieces lying around with no one to blame. I could hardly understand how anyone could have a soul so devoid of hate, given what she had been through.

I began to get the picture when she started talking about her church and her faith. She had let love and forgiveness flow into the void caused by the losses she had sustained. It was an amazing example of how someone should live, but almost no one does. By the time we finished dinner, I had come to realize what a treasure this girl was. We were having coffee and brandy when she turned the light back on me.

"What are you going to do when you return to the States?"

"I'm going to ride rodeo."

"That's it? Your entire plan for the rest of your life is to ride rodeo?"

When she put it like that, it seemed rather simplistic. But I hadn't had much thought beyond getting out of the Corps and going back to doing what I loved. I was raised to be patriotic and love my country. When the Ayatollahs attacked our embassy in Iran and kidnapped the staff, it made me angry. When Ronald Reagan won the presidency, I felt he would need people in the military to back him up. So in a fit of patriotic fervor, I joined the Corps.

The Lebanese exercise in geopolitics opened my eyes to a few realities. I decided when my hitch was up I would have done my part, and I was going to go back and live my life. That was contingent, of course, upon my living long enough to turn in my globe and anchor.

"When you're too old to ride rodeo, what are you going to do? Where are you going to live?"

"I'm going back to the farm and live with my mother. Someone needs to take care of her. And as far as when I am too old…" I had to admit, I really hadn't thought that far ahead. The fact that I might actually live long enough to be too old to ride never occurred to me.

"I never thought I would live long enough to be too old," I told her truthfully. It made me uncomfortable thinking about it, so I decided to defer any planning beyond rodeo to see if it would even be necessary.

"Are we going to the room?" Nour asked. I was stalling, lingering over my drink.

"I guess going for a stroll along the beach is out of the question, right?"

"We could go for a drive in the mountains," she said, paused, then added, "If your Marine Corps will loan us a tank."

That didn't seem likely, so we went to the room.

A bottle of champagne, sitting in a bucket of ice on the coffee table, welcomed us home when we came in. A hand-written note attached to the bottle informed us that it was a gift from the hotel.

I hung up my jacket and started working on getting the cork out of the bottle. Nour took her suitcase and disappeared into the bedroom. I got the little wires untwisted and began working the cork up carefully until it was almost out, then I covered it with my palm to let the cork finally come free with a little "pop."

I had never cared for champagne. After I had sampled what was in the bottle, I decided I had never had champagne. It was delicious. I took off my tie and laid it across the back of my jacket hanging over the desk chair. I pulled my boots off and returned to the couch.

It seemed like Nour was gone for some time. I was about to ask if she was okay when she came back into the room wearing one of the fluffy white robes the hotel provided. She had let the front come open practically to her waist. The cross was gone. I could tell at a glance she wore nothing beneath the robe. The cleavage now was more than interesting. Her nipples were covered by the edges of the robe, but barely. She hadn't taken off her high-heeled shoes and the robe ended well above her knees. She was mesmerizing walking across the room toward me. She was smiling shyly.

I stood to meet her. She stopped in front of me and reached up with both hands to cradle my face. She stepped closer and kissed me softly, then not so softly. Her body pressed against mine and I could feel the softness, telling me I had been correct in thinking she was naked beneath the robe.

After a long moment, I broke the embrace and pulled back.

"Are you sure about this?" I asked her breathlessly. I was suddenly and inexplicably shy. It was like I was being held back and inhibited by an invisible hand. I wanted her in the worst way. I wanted to strip off the robe and lose myself in the warm softness of her body, but for the first time in my life, I was afraid to go furthcr.

This wasn't my first time. I had not dated until my senior year. It seemed like I was slow to pick up on the girl thing. I was busy with my life working on the farm, riding motorcycles, and tending horses. I just didn't have time for girls.

Then a neighbor girl came into my life. She was a senior when I was a freshman. We had been friends and rode the bus together. I thought she was the most beautiful girl in the entire school.

Since she was three years older, a senior after all, I didn't even consider she would be interested in a mere freshman. She went off to college for two years and came home the summer between my junior and senior year.

I had been riding rodeo at the county fair and had just come in from the cutting-horse competition. I won of course; I had little competition in the county since I had ridden circuit. I was walking my Morgan back to the stables when I felt someone take my hand. She had come up behind me. It was Carla Redinger.

Two years at college had matured and changed her. She went from beautiful to stunning. She was a dead ringer for Raquel Welch. I thought she made Raquel look plain. I was stunned.

"What happened to you?" I blurted out and then felt stupid. Why did I always feel stupid around this girl?

"Happened?" she asked quizzically.

"You have changed, you look like a woman, not a girl," I stammered.

"You also have; you look like a man and not a little boy."

We dated the rest of the summer. She came to all my rides; we were hardly apart for the next three months. We made love for the first time in the haymow of our barn. I was in love and knew I would spend the rest of my life with her.

The summer sped by like a flash. It was the last week in August, and she was going back to school the next day. We were sitting in her father's Buick looking out across the lake south of town. The night was clear and the moon was reflected on the surface of the calm water.

I had made up my mind; I was going to ask her to marry me tonight. We had been kissing and fondling each other. I sat up and looked at her seriously.

"Carla, I…"

She held up her hand, scooted back, and pulled her blouse closed.

"It's time to go, Roy Lee," she told me earnestly as if I had said something to offend her. She said nothing all the way back to my house. I pulled up in front and started to turn off the motor. She put her hand over mine and shook her head. She motioned me to get out of the car. I was confused, hurt, and mystified. I got out and closed the door as she slid into the driver's seat.

"Don't fall in love with me, Roy Lee," she said through the open driver's door window. She put the car in reverse, backed out, and then drove off leaving me standing there. Like a big dummy, I had said nothing. A million times through the years I had beat myself up. Why? Oh, why, did I not tell her the simple truth? *It is way too late for that; I have loved you since the first day you sat down next to me on the bus.*

It was the last thing she ever told me. We never spoke again.

Life is strange.

Now here I was, almost all the way around the world, years older with much more experience, with a young lady in my arms willing, no more than willing, to climb into bed with me and I couldn't do it. What was wrong with me?

***

Governor's Ranch near Springfield, Illinois

I heard Chance moving softly in the direction of the tail of the plane. The big question was: Could our challenger see any better than we could? Did he have night-vision goggles, or was he working under the same handicap? The other question was: Friend or foe? I guess the order may have been inverted, but that was how my mind worked. When someone had a shotgun leveled at me, certain things became a priority over others.

"Are you Deputy White?" the voice asked. I got some direction from the sound. Whoever it was, he was standing next to the hangar about even with the tail of our parked plane. I couldn't hear Chance's movement any longer, but I knew he was going in that direction. I began to worry. That boy was wired to shoot first and ask questions later.

"I am White, who are you?"

"Who is the second person? Moshe said there was only supposed to be a pilot."

Aha, friend!

"Stand down Chance!" I ordered my grandson. We didn't want any friendly casualties.

"It's my grandson and an extra set of eyes for flying at night."

The lights along the roof line of the hangar came on suddenly. The shotgun-bearing individual was hidden in the dark of an open hangar door. I could see his shadow as my eyes became accustomed to the sudden light. Chance had worked his way completely around the tail and was in stance aiming the Ruger with both hands at the threat.

"I would like to see some ID," the man said.

I could see the shotgun was pointed in my direction. "If that shotgun moves in any direction other than pointed toward the ground, my grandson will shoot you where you stand." It was a statement containing two messages: one a warning, and the other an order. "You come out into the light, and I'll show you my ID."

There was a moment's hesitation before the shotgun moved down as the man stepped out into the light. He was wearing a suit and looked both buttoned-down and competent. There was little doubt he was one of Moshe's operatives.

I slowly reached into my inside pocket and retrieved my badge and ID. I met the enforcer about halfway with my credentials held out for his inspection. He glanced at the picture then the badge.

"Colonel, huh! You're coming up in the world, Deputy," the man smiled. "You're early; we weren't expecting you until around midnight. The governor isn't here yet. There was a convoy that pulled out headed west to throw off anyone watching the Capitol. They're bringing the governor out in the trunk of some beater. He should be here shortly."

"Now, if you don't mind, I would like to see some ID as well," I told him. The man looked up and glanced over at Chance, who was still in the stance with a sight picture of the man's chest over the sights of the Ruger.

"Okay sure," he said. He sat the shotgun down on its butt held loosely in his left hand; he slowly reached into a jacket pocket and came out with a leather folder. It revealed he was a captain in the secret service. His name was Cedrick Johansson

I nodded to Chance, and he stood down, reluctantly as if he had rather just shot him. The boy liked to keep things simple — black and white.

"Moshe said to be careful with you," Cedrick said.

"The boy would have nailed me for sure; I didn't hear him coming around," he said with a tone of self-criticism.

"I wouldn't be too hard on myself," I reassured him. "Chance hunts deer with a bow. You have to learn to move quietly to have any success at it." The man nodded his acceptance of the obvious.

"Are you alone out here?" I asked him.

"There are two more agents near the house."

"Well, perhaps you should let them know we are among friends. I don't want them popping up and bringing us under fire."

"Yes, you're right," he said as if it hadn't entered his mind. I began to wonder about the level of competence within Moshe's cadre. Cedrick spun on his heel and disappeared around the hangar in the direction of the house.

After the man left, I instructed Chance to turn off the lights when we re-donned the infrared goggles. There was no sense lighting ourselves up as a target in a shooting gallery. We settled down in the plane to wait. It was a good two hours before the governor showed up.

A single car came up the long lane and drove around the corral and race track up to the house. Chance and I got out of the plane and walked around to the edge of the hangar where we could watch. We could see shadows moving around the car and heard the trunk pop open. There were some subdued voices and soon a couple of flashlights were visible moving our direction.

Soon the three guards, Moshe, and the governor walked up to the front side of the hangars. Chance and I walked around to meet them. We took off our goggles and walked over, guided by the illumination of the flashlights.

"Good evening, El Dee," the governor said with a smile. He was evidently more than happy to see me. "Cedrick told me you were here already. Are you ready to go?"

"We're ready if you are, Governor," I responded. "What about your wife? Is she coming?"

"She's visiting her mother in Wisconsin," he replied. "She will be joining me later in the week."

"I don't like it, Governor," I said critically. "If she's vulnerable, you are vulnerable."

"Sheesh, El Dee, you sound like Moshe!"

"You're right, Mr. White," Moshe spoke up. "I've been telling him the same thing since he dropped the hammer on the drug lord."

"I'll send a plane to pick her up."

"No Sir!" I interrupted him. "It's imperative no one else knows where you are going. It's bad enough…" I pointed to the three guards. I held up my hand to squelch Moshe's objections. I knew he trusted his people, but no matter how trustworthy a single individual might be, the more folks who knew the more chance for a slip-up. "I'll drop you off and go get her myself."

"I agree," Moshe said emphatically.

"Whatever," the governor groused, admitting the point.

We hustled the governor and Moshe into the plane then shortly left the field for the farm. When we leveled off, Moshe leaned over from the back seat and started filling me in, talking softly, barely audible over the roar of the 300 horses straining ahead of the firewall.

"None of the guards at the ranch know where we are taking the governor. All they know is you were picking him up and taking him to a secure location."

"It's not exactly rocket science," I responded.

It wouldn't take a superb guesser to deduce I might be taking the governor to our farm.

"All three of them have been with me since I came to this country," he added. "I trust them with my life."

"It's done now. There's no use crying over spilled milk."

"We'll be fine," Moshe said, scooting back in his seat. He didn't want to admit he might have screwed the pooch. I wasn't worried about an overt betrayal. I was concerned about some inadvertent slip at an unguarded moment. No one was more aware of what the Colombians were capable of than I was. I wasn't exactly afraid of them, but I was certainly leery of the bastards.

I set up the radial that intercepted our little strip on the Terre Haute VOR. I flew well east of the place until I caught the radial and flew down it until we crossed the lake. The ground was black, but the water of the lake was a darker shade that let me orient myself to exactly where the field was. I decided I needed to install an ILS or, at least, an ADF if I was going to do much night flying. I was thankful tonight for the radar altimeter that Todd had insisted on.

The GPS satellites had been going dark one after the other. It was no longer safe to try to fly an instrument approach using the GPS. There just weren't sufficient birds left up there to determine accurately the plane's altitude enough to land blind.

I flew over the strip, picked up the lights and turned right to fly a clockwise approach and turned a right base and final. I had done it many times when there had been moonlight, but tonight had been a first for a total blackout approach.

I came across the fence at 30 feet indicated on the radar, flipped on the landing light to see the grass inches from the wheels. The stall warning buzzer was screaming like it always did. I guess I should have warned my passengers. They were probably peeing their pants. I felt the wheels touch, dumped the flaps and pulled the wheel into my stomach. We bounced once and were down.

"Nice landing – both of them," Chance teased. It wasn't bad considering, and he knew it, but he would never let a chance go by to needle me on my flying. I had been so hard on him, demanding perfection while he was learning, that he wouldn't let me forget it now.

CHAPTER SEVENTEEN

U.S. Embassy — Beirut, Lebanon 1984

I had the cab stop outside the dragon tooth maze. Nour was with me as I got out carrying my new suitcase packed with my freshly tailored wardrobe. I had run out of time and money almost simultaneously. I had three dollars left when I tipped the cabby. As we walked by the Marine outpost, I received a few appreciative whistles and comments.

"Welcome back cowboy. Who's the girl? She gotta sister?" The remarks were friendly and respectful. I appreciated it; grunts in a combat zone can get rather crude. What I didn't realize was that I had become a larger-than-life hero among my fellows. With this bunch, I was competing with Chesty Puller for USMC honors.

I had formed an idea during our fortnight together. Nour wanted to come to the States. I could certainly appreciate her desire to get out of this snake pit, but there was little I could do other than marry her and I wasn't quite ready to leap off that particular cliff.

What I could do was get the application for asylum started. She certainly qualified as an Orthodox Christian in a Muslim-dominated society.

I had one other idea.

I got her past the guards with my ID and to the head of the line at the visa application desk. I left her with a clerk filling out paperwork and went looking for my lieutenant.

Both officers were sitting in the shared office behind their respective desks when I arrived. The door was open, so I knocked on the casing and stood to attention.

"You're out of uniform, Staff Sergeant," Lieutenant Etterman said, but he was smiling when he said it. He was pulling my chain. The word had traveled fast about my return and the girl I brought back with me.

"I'm not here, Sir, remember?"

"What's the story on the girl?" The lieutenant asked, cutting to the chase.

"She's applying for asylum, sir. But I had an idea of introducing her to the Station Chief. She is super smart, speaks French and Lebanese as well as English and Arabic, is a Phalanges fighter, and I know the CIA is always looking."

"You're right, White; the Agency might be interested," the other officer spoke up.

Lieutenant Etterman apologized and introduced me to the guard officer. Then he dropped the bomb on me.

"You need to get into uniform, Staff Sergeant; you're rotating back to the Guam. The Corps, in its infinite wisdom, is reducing protective unit staffing and turning security for the embassy over to the Phalanges."

"You mean I'm going back before I even got here. Is that even possible?" I was referring to the paperwork. It was going to be a mess.

"I talked to your CO. The easiest way to handle this is to shit-can the paperwork. Your little foray into embassy security just never happened," the lieutenant explained. "There will be a chopper leaving in a little over an hour. You have a few minutes to say goodbye to your sweetheart, but don't miss your ride."

"We'll look after your girl," Lieutenant Brookman told me. "I think the Agency will have a job for her. If they pick her up, it will expedite her visa application, but either way, you can have her contact me if she runs into any snags."

"Gosh Lieutenant, that's big of you. I appreciate it."

"It's the least we can do for our resident hero," the lieutenant teased. "Now get out of here White, you don't want to miss your bus."

With this, he stood up and handed me his card. Both officers were smiling as I took my leave. I was going to have to reconsider my default position on officers. There were exceptions to the asshole rule.

I went back down to the reception area where Nour was still involved with the clerk. Someone had gotten her a red badge, so she was good to stay in the embassy until she was finished with the application process. I gave her the lieutenant's card and informed her of my imminent departure.

I had expected some water works, but she just nodded and gave me that old-beyond-her-years look. I felt part of me die inside. I would have rather dealt with the tears. My leaving was just another tragedy that Nour Lahoud had to deal with.

I bent down and kissed her one last time, turned around and went off to find my seabag. I had a bus to catch.

***

Nour Lahoud

Nour felt as if she had been caught up in a tornado, whirled around, and dropped into an entirely different world. The tornado had a name: Leroy White. She had never met anyone even remotely like him. In her eyes, he was larger than life, a hero of a romantic novel dropped directly into her world. She knew she would never love another man as long as she lived. No other man could ever compare to her cowboy.

When he turned around and walked away, she knew he was walking out of her life. He had little idea he was taking her heart with him. It was a tragedy, but Nour was no stranger to tragedy. It was as big a part of her life as breathing, eating, sleeping, or defecating.

The Marine Corps had a rough description of dealing with untenable situations the way she did. The Corps called it "embracing the suck." Nour thought of it as carrying her cross. Why she had been given such a heavy burden, she did not question. It was not her nature. Nour was a strange blend of naiveté and hard-won experience. She had been a virgin when she met Leroy White, and she still was.

She had shared his bed for three nights, and they had held each other, kissed, and shared intimacies, but Leroy had never touched her private parts. It was as if he was constrained by some force beyond either of their understanding.

His restraint had lifted him to godlike status in her eyes.

She saw the way the embassy staff treated him as if he were really special. She knew he wasn't even an officer, but it didn't seem to matter. Everyone appeared to know him and defer to his wishes. She wasn't surprised; gods were supposed to be offered respect.

She also wasn't surprised when the Marine officer came down and chatted with the clerk helping her with the visa and amnesty application. He patiently waited until she was finished, took her to the reception desk, and got her a yellow badge to replace the red one she was wearing.

He then took her behind the glass wall separating the large reception area and down a hall to a small conference room, got her seated at a six-chaired table, and brought her fresh coffee. Shortly after her coffee arrived, three other folks came into the room. The lieutenant gave her one of his cards and asked her to write her address on the back. As the other folks filed into the room, he stood by the door and studied her for a long time before leaving.

The three interviewers included a middle-aged man dressed in a wrinkled suit. His tie was loose around his neck, and he looked like he hadn't slept in days. There were large black circles under his eyes. He was accompanied by two well turned-out ladies.

The taller, older woman immediately started talking to her in French. She asked questions about Nour's family, how long she had lived in the country, etc. It was all strictly routine chit-chat, much like two strangers feeling each other out at a chance airport meeting. The woman then smiled and looked at the man.

"Her French is perfect, Chief. She has a bit of a Lebanese accent, but she is as fluent as a native speaker." The man nodded and the lady smiled at Nour and took her leave. The other woman started speaking Lebanese switching back and forth between her native language and Arabic. It was as easy for Nour to follow as if she was having a conversation with her family.

After a while, the lady handed Nour a sheet of paper with two sets of text written in Arabic. One was Lebanese, the other Arabic.

"Will you please read these aloud, first in the language in which it was written and then the English translation?" the woman instructed Nour.

Reading the passage in its mother tongue was easy; translating it proved to be more difficult. Some of it was technical, and Nour was unsure of the English words pertaining to the described hardware. Some was theological, and bridging the cultural gap was challenging .

Nour did her best, but was certain she had failed.

"She is better than good, Chief," Nour was surprised to hear the woman report. "We've got folks who do this for a living who could not have done better." The lady stood and held out her hand. When Nour took it, the woman gave her a soft squeeze and a conspiratorial wink. For some reason, the lady seemed to like her.

The man at the head of the table had been making notes on a yellow pad. He nodded as the woman left the room. She was met at the door by a grizzled Marine master sergeant.

"Take her to the range, Gunny," the man told the sergeant. "When you're finished, bring her back to my office."

"Are you sure, Sir?" the noncom looked at the slight, feminine lady sitting at the table with some apparent misgivings.

"Can you fire a handgun?" the tired-looking man asked her directly.

"I can," Nour answered the simple, direct question with a simple, direct answer.

Forty-five minutes later the gunny was standing in the door to the station chief's office with three sheets of thin cardboard in his hand. He stood aside and let Nour walk into the room. He had an amazed look on his face.

The station chief indicated a chair in front of his desk. The sergeant walked across and laid the three targets on the chief's desk.

"She shot marksman with the AK, a 1911 and the Browning." The sergeant was looking at Nour as if she might suddenly disappear in front of his eyes. "I have Marines on the line that can't do that cold."

"Thank you Gunny," the station chief said, dismissing the senior noncom.

"Young lady, if you are interested, I'd like to offer you a job."

***

Governor's mother-in-law's house – Wisconsin

"Oh shit Moshe, I think we're too late!" I was circling the house where the governor's wife was supposed to be waiting.

It was a burnt-out shell.

"Didn't you have security with her?"

"Two of my best people are with her," Moshe said defensively.

I noticed he used the present tense; he wasn't giving up quite yet. He was looking across my chest as I circled with the left wing low. Chance was staring out the left rear window studying the ground for details.

"We can come in across the lake and land in the yard Bapaw," the boy was looking ahead like he always did, trying to get a jump on the situation.

We had left the governor with Delbert and the Jamison boys at the house. The militia had closed my access road with a 10-ton truck filled with limestone boulders. The roadblock was manned by three militiamen in full battle rattle, 24-7 while the governor was staying at my place. It was as secure as I knew how to make it.

Milo was on board, but I cautioned him to only tell his deputies that we were on extra alert because of a threat to my person from the cartel.

The activated militia was on special status, officially deputized by the governor. They would be paid from the state treasury and would be considered legal LEO for the duration.

I flew over the charred rubble of the house, made a climbing right turn and re-approached the site from the north. I dove down as soon as we cleared the trees and made a low-level, full-power pass across the yard where it sloped off to the lake on our left. If there was an adversarial presence at the site, I didn't want to give them an easy target. Combining the shallow dive and full power we came across the yard at close to 200 miles an hour.

"Any threats?" I asked both my passengers. They both replied in the negative, so I repeated the maneuver at a much slower speed but further from the house. I flew along the lake shore 30 feet above the breakwater with full flaps, hanging on the prop barely 10 knots above stall. All three of us were looking for any obstacles to landing in the yard. None of us saw any. As usual, the stall warning buzzer was complaining all the way.

"You need to get that adjusted," Chance said. "It's annoying, and besides, you won't know when you really are on the edge of a stall." He had a point, but the Cessna would complain through the yoke shaking before she broke, and the stall warning buzzer did take on a different, harsher more frantic note just before the break. Chance knew this but getting the buzzer adjusted was a pet peeve of his. I reached down and pushed the little pencil eraser-sized breaker and let it pop up. The clamor cut off abruptly.

I turned left out across the lake and approached the shore with the house directly ahead of us high up on the steep hill that constituted its front yard. I pulled in full flaps and pushed the throttle against the firewall. The plane was laboring along on the edge of a stall at 35 miles an hour. We crossed the seawall, and I dumped the flaps, dropping us into the grass. We rumbled toward the hill. The house was coming up fast, but the hill slowed us down in a hurry.

I spun the plane around at the top of the hill and kept the engine running as we looked around. There was no movement. The entire site seemed deserted. There was no sign that the fire had been fought. It was as if someone had set fire to the house and let it burn to the ground. The three-car detached garage looked unmolested.

I felt a tap on my shoulder. Chance was handing me an AR Grendel. I was glad I had put long guns in the baggage area. We were all armed with the 6.5MM ARs when we stepped out of the plane.

"Moshe, how many folks knew the governor's wife was visiting her mother?"

"A few. It wasn't considered a state secret."

We spread out and kept a couple car lengths distance between us as we approached the blackened rubble.

I stopped about 10 paces back from where the house had been. Chance went around to the right, Moshe to the left.

"Hey Bapaw, you need to take a look at this," Chance called from behind the house. Almost simultaneously I heard the rumble of an electric garage door opener. The middle door to the detached garage was on its way up!

"Moshe, Bo'ged!" A man's voice shouted from the garage followed almost instantly by two closely spaced gunshots. It was a Hebrew word that sounded like "Bow-gead" to me. I would find out later it meant *betrayer.*

***

Parker County Rodeo 1989 – Weathorford, Texas

"You know, if you were to kidnap me and take me back to your hotel room, I wouldn't resist," Debbie Lee told me. She was sitting on the top rail of the corral with a friend of hers, and they were watching me gather my gear and pack my trailer.

"I wouldn't fight you either Roy Lee," the other girl laughed. "You could have a twofer."

The two girls were rodeo groupies. They showed up at most of the rodeos and hung out with the riders in the bars after the events. They were party girls and made no bones about it. Debbie Lee was a cute, petite blonde, 18 or 19 and dressed like a cowgirl. Her dark Hispanic friend wore jeans and a print shirt, but today had sandals on her feet instead of boots.

Debbie Lee had made getting into my pants a season project. Up to now she had been unsuccessful. With the finals coming up next week, she was getting desperate.

"I have already checked out, sorry," I told them not letting the banter interrupt my preparations for leaving.

"You know that 7.4 would have won last year," Debbie Lee said changing the subject.

"Sweetheart, I'm aware of that. I won last year with a 7.6."

"Oh, I guess that's right. I forgot."

"Debbie Lee, you are cute as a bug, but you are an airhead, do you know that?" She laughed, not taking any offense; we had known each other for a long time.

"Well, you won the cutting, and you're on top of the points for the championship." She was keeping a sharp eye on the competition. I was in the best position to win the championship since I had come home from Beirut. She was sure I was going to win, and she was bound and determined to put the champion's notch on her bedpost.

My horse had won the calf-cutting competition. I had been sitting up there while he did it and took all the credit, but of course, he did all the work. Once I picked out the calf, and we cut him from the herd, I gave Diablo his head, and he kept the calf away.

All I had to do was sit up there, keep my shoulders square, keep an eye on the calf's movements to anticipate what Diablo was going to do, and let him do his thing. He and I had been together since he was a colt and could read each other's mind.

I took second in roping with 7.4 seconds. Last year it would have given me a first, but this year there was a new rider, a black cowboy by the name of Cooper and his 7.2 pushed me out of thc top spot. It worried me a bit because I had done everything right. Diablo had performed perfectly nailing the calf to the ground; I had got a perfect grip for the throw, and his legs came together exactly right. I just didn't see how I was going to improve on 7.4 seconds.

It occurred to me that perhaps I was getting a bit long in the tooth for this game. It was a frightening thought. Rodeo was all I knew how to do. Beyond that, it was the only thing I wanted to do. Since my stepdad passed away, I had to train the horses myself, but I enjoyed that as well, and it kept me busy in the offseason.

The railroad was beginning to pressure me to come off of part time and get serious if I was going to continue in their employ. They had been more than patient, but I knew if I didn't step up and take a full-time position by the end of the year, they were going to send me on down the road.

My mom was on my case to grow up and go to work. She was always afraid I was going to get hurt and was the main reason I had left the bulls and broncs for roping and cutting. The cutting-horse competition was starting to pay some fat purses, but it was getting more and more competitive as the big money ranches started pouring their significant resources into breeding and training the horses.

"You know you could improve your time if you had a roping horse," Debbie taunted me. I was the only rider who used the same horse in both competitions. It just wasn't done. It was thought the two skill sets were so different, no one horse could master both. Diablo was the exception to that rule.

"It wasn't Diablo's fault. He did everything right. I was a full half-second slow sprinting to the calf. It was all on me. The bottom line is Cooper is faster than me."

I was in a black mood as I led Diablo toward the trailer, watching the two girls skip off hand in hand to harass another rider, I supposed.

"Hello, Cowboy." A vaguely familiar voice with an enticing accent brought me up short. She was standing by the trailer dressed in a business, silk-wool suit. Her green eyes were accentuated by the slightly lighter shade of the green blouse peeking out from under the jacket.

Nour had matured into a strikingly beautiful woman. I felt a catch in my throat, and an electric charge ran down my back. Diablo reared and whinnied; so attuned was the horse to my emotions, my reaction to the lady's presence had frightened him.

"My God, Nour how…?" Diablo was prancing around, eyes wide and white, certain now the woman was a threat somehow. "Nour, give me a minute, let me get him in the trailer." I calmed the horse down, and was able to get him loaded and secured. He was still not happy, but he wasn't going to attack anybody now.

He was as bad as a German shepherd about being protective. I loved that animal with a depth of emotion that was probably beyond what a person should allow himself to feel for an animal, but there it was. I patted him down, gave him a cup of oats and an apple, and the tension drained out of him. Once the routine of loading took over, his fear of an imagined potential threat dissipated.

He had a short attention span. It was a trait that we shared and it was endearing.

I knew I was stalling. I took a deep breath and walked down the ramp.

She was still there.

There were people around loading their animals and clearing out the stables. It was a busy time as the rodeo was packing up, preparing to move to Reno for the finals. Until today, I had been leading in points in both categories in which I competed. Cooper's win today had turned roping into a dead heat going into Reno.

All of the people, all of the movement and action, the dust and noise, seemed to disappear as my entire concentration focused on the lady in front of me. I gasped as I realized I had stopped breathing. My brain refused to accept the reality my eyes were telling me was there.

I was completely at a loss on how to proceed. I must have looked like an idiot standing there at the bottom of the ramp staring at her as if she were a ghost. She didn't seem to mind. She smiled and walked toward me, taking my hand. She looked up at me where I was a good 18 inches higher still standing on the ramp.

"I have never loved anyone else other than you," she told me. Her sad, tragic eyes broke my heart. I really didn't know whether to laugh or cry. Instead, I did neither. I took two steps down to her level, folded her in my arms and kissed her hungrily, frantically, as if she might disappear from my grasp. She pulled me to her with surprising arm strength. When we came up for air, we had attracted an audience.

I heard applause and whistles. We had acquired an approving audience. It was well known on the circuit that I had obtained a celibate existence on the road since my return from the Corps. Everyone knew me; a lot of my friends were concerned about the state of my mental health. They all saw this performance as a positive sign. There were relieved smiles and not a few thumbs up gestures.

I gave a half-bow to acknowledge the applause, and the group broke up, leaving us a modicum of privacy.

I looked around for a spot where we could talk, and my eye fell on the empty bleachers. I took her hand and led her over to a deserted section. I led her up a couple of rows, and we sat down.

"Nour, how did you find me?"

"I'm with the agency. We can find anyone."

I wasn't really surprised. When I had climbed on the chopper in East Beirut, I knew the odds were pretty good the agency would grab her up. With her talent and experience, they would have had to be blind and stupid to have let her go. The Agency had a reputation in some quarters for possessing a significant level of blind and stupid, but the group in Lebanon was an exception.

Lebanon had a way of tempering a person or an organization with fire and blood.

"The agency expedited my citizenship and brought me back to Langley for training. I have full status as a field agent. They changed my life, and I have you to thank."

"But, Nour, five years and not a word. I wrote letters…"

"The Agency put me incommunicado for the first two years. It was part of my contract and what I agreed to in return for my citizenship and security clearances." At this, she paused as if unwilling to complete the story she had been telling. "And I married Lieutenant Brookman."

I glanced down at her hands folded in her lap. There was no wedding ring. She saw the direction of my glance.

"He was killed in Afghanistan, supporting the Mujahedeen."

"Nour, I am sorry," I said honestly. It seemed if it weren't for tragedy, the lady would have nothing.

"He was a good man. We have a son. He is my life now." At this announcement, some of the darkness in her eyes seemed to dissipate for a moment.

"I really have to go now. I just wanted to thank you, let you know I made it out, and tell you I will never love anyone else but you." With this, she stood. She was looking out at the empty stadium ground as if seeing something I could not.

Then I heard the rotor blades.

The small, black helicopter circled the stadium, then landed softly in the middle of the field. Nour kissed me on the cheek, smiled, and walked out across the dusty field. When she reached the chopper, a side door opened. She stepped up on the skid, and a hand came down to help her inside. The door closed, and the helicopter lifted up, out and was gone.

I sat there with the little white card in my hand, looking for a long time at the empty sky where the helicopter had disappeared.

CHAPTER EIGHTEEN

Lyman Womack's Ranch – Downstate Illinois

"Lyman, are you insane?" Victor Karman exclaimed. He had coming storming into Womack's office unannounced and visibly upset. He was the only man in the world who dared to talk to the wealthy industrialist like he did. He was comptroller of all of Womack's disparate interests.

"Your father will be rolling over in his grave!" Karman had been comptroller for Raymond Womack, the founder, and patriarch of the family fortune. As a result, Karman was not impressed with the present occupant of the chair behind the old man's desk. In fact, he was barely tolerant of him.

Womack was more afraid of Karman than John Palmer. The old man knew where all the family skeletons were buried and was not impressed with Womack's handling of the estate. He made no bones about his feelings.

"Don't you realize how things have changed? You cannot just do whatever pops into your head. We no longer control judges and officials. That has all disappeared with the advent of true citizen government."

"Victor, will you calm down. Tell me, what has you so upset?" Womack asked, using the most comforting tone he could muster.

"Lyman, you idiot," he spluttered. "You're risking everything with those stolen trucks!"

Karman's face was beet red, and he was shaking. He was shaking his finger across the desk at Womack as if he were a 12-year-old caught smoking behind the barn.

"If the sheriff finds those trucks, they will put you in front of a three-judge panel. Fifteen minutes later they will march you down to the courthouse yard and put a bullet through that pea brain of yours!"

"They can't do that! We have lawyers!" Lyman exclaimed in shock at the idea.

"You incompetent boob! All the lawyers in the world won't keep your ass out of a Terror Court. That's what I am trying to tell you!"

Womack had stood to confront the comptroller but at those words he collapsed into his chair. "But the Federalists…" his voice trailed off.

"That bunch of goofy has-beens and dreamers," Karman grunted in disgust. "They stumble around hatching these great and glorious plots thinking they can turn the clock back. My God Lyman! That train has left the station. There's no going back, ever!"

"How did you…?"

"How did I? How did I? It was easy, Lyman. Fertilizer! Ammonium Nitrate! Do you know how difficult it is now to get the quantities of fertilizer you purchased? I was just going over the books, and it jumped out at me as if it were written in fire! Don't you think the State boys will be all over it? I am shocked and surprised they haven't raided the place before now."

"I didn't think…"

"You sure the hell did not! I came down here, asked a couple of questions and BANG! One of your heavies takes me out and shows me the trucks! My God Lyman," Karman stuttered. "Everyone and his brother around here knows what you are up to. You must have lost your mind!"

"What are we going to do?" Womack asked with a sinking feeling of panic. He suddenly had a very clear image of himself being hauled into the courthouse courtyard by two burly guards with a firing squad standing ready. Every member of the firing squad had Leroy White's face. They were grinning at him. He shuddered and felt tears welling up in his throat.

"I don't know exactly," Karman said more calmly now that they were planning some coherent, rational action. "Let's get those trucks unloaded and that fertilizer spread on some field, any field, as soon as possible. I mean, like yesterday afternoon would not be fast enough. Then we will have to figure out how to un-steal those trucks."

***

Governor's mother-in-law's house — Wisconsin

Out of the corner of my eye, I saw Chance sprinting across the yard headed for the back of the garage. At the sound of the gunshots, I had spun around and taken a prone position with my rifle aimed toward the opening garage door waiting for Moshe to come around. This was his show.

I was beginning to feel as if events were making me superfluous. The governor had brought me on board to address the Federalist threat downstate, and I hadn't done a thing but be pulled along like a rubber raft in a fast-flowing stream. Even worse, I had hopped into bed with his aide, who now wanted to jump ship, marry me and leave his employ.

I didn't appreciate feeling like an unfaithful servant, and I hated more the sense of being out of control and at the mercy of events. I experienced a feeling of déjà vu and realized I was reliving the moment in the rubble of Beirut when my lieutenant had been killed in front of my eyes.

Once again, I was responsible and didn't have a clue about what to do next.

Events then took control, and it appeared as though the rubber raft was headed for a massive waterfall. A woman's scream came from the garage cut off by the "bap bap" of another double tap! Moshe pounded by me zig-zagging toward the garage.

My first inclination was to jump up and follow him, but I decided providing cover was more important. I kept the red dot sight focused on the open door of the garage. The SUV that came backing out, engine screaming and tires burning, looked huge in the little scope.

At that instant, I wished I had a Beowulf.

I flicked the lever to full auto with my thumb and brought the sight to bear on the right rear tire. I came within a fraction of a second of cutting Moshe's legs from beneath him as his pounding feet filled my sight.

I was not having a very productive day.

"Give it up Emil!" Moshe shouted as he stopped dead, exactly between me and the SUV, completely blocking my line of fire! *Drat*!

I rolled to my right and came up to a kneeling position when the windshield in front of the driver exploded. Chance was standing beside the garage using the corner to steady his aim and provide a bit of a cover. I heard the "BRRUPT" of a Grendel on full auto accompany the sight of the exploding windshield.

Shoot first, ask questions later. That's my grandson.

The engine's roar shut down suddenly as if the driver's foot had come off the accelerator. The vehicle swerved sharply in my direction, and continued to roll backward across the drive, and onto the sloping yard.

My first terrified thought was it would continue right into the lake, but there was a planter bed surrounded by an 18-inch brick wall that stopped the vehicle.

For a long moment, the entire tableau was frozen. Then a woman's sobs could be heard coming from the SUV. Moshe sprinted toward the car. I got up and ran toward the garage. Chance was standing beside the open door with his back against the wall waiting for me to come up.

I pulled up beside him and leaned my long gun against the garage. I reached up and slid the KelTek out of its shoulder holster. Chance nodded and followed my example by retrieving a 1911 from his waist holster. We were going into a building where the range would be measured in feet and the ability to acquire a target quickly took precedence over firepower.

There was a walk-through door to my right. A glance told me it swung into the garage. The knob was on my side. I held up a finger to slow Chance down. I shoved the door, quickly drawing my hand back. The door slammed open, but nothing else happened. I nodded and spun to my right. We both crashed into the garage at the same instant.

Other than a Chrysler 300 and the two bodies lying trussed up on the floor, it was empty.

"There are three more bodies around the back of the house," Chance said. "They look like rag-heads or Mexicans."

I began to feel as if I was in a bad dream and couldn't wake up. I was supposed to be the great genius crime fighter, and I was totally at sea. I had no idea what any of this meant or how it fit into a larger picture.

Chance was looking at me expectantly to explain all of this. I didn't want to disappoint him, so I said nothing. I went over and checked the bodies. One was the agent who had called out to Moshe. The other was a much older lady. I guessed it was the mother-in-law. They were both very dead.

"Let's take a look at the other bodies," I said in my best Sherlock Holmes imitation. I had no idea what to look for but decided action was preferable to standing around with my finger in my nose.

Moshe was helping a lady out of the back of the SUV. It looked like her hands were still trussed up. I assumed it was the governor's wife. She was no longer crying. That was a good sign.

"Bapaw, there are three little brown men laid out side by side. They have all been shot, full body mass double taps. Shouldn't we just get out of here?"

That stopped me in my tracks. He was absolutely right. My examining the corpses would tell us little beyond what he had observed. We had no idea when more bad guys could show up. I was suddenly very anxious to put this place below and behind us.

***

Three blocks from the Capitol – Springfield, Illinois

One of the great ironies of the Federalist Party was the alliance of groups that had been former enemies of the state of which they were now trying to restore. It was a disparate group made up of Muslims, drug dealers, arms merchants, and bureaucrats. By far the greatest number was disaffected, former Federal employees.

The most pampered and rewarded class of people created by the welfare state was not, by any stretch of the imagination, the folks the system was designed for and advertised to serve. The poor, indigent population of the inner cities received a trickle of the river of Federal dollars poured into the system.

Most was siphoned off by the army of bureaucrats employed to distribute the money. It was those worthies who were now desperately trying to recreate the leviathan that had been their source of sustenance and power.

Elaine Martin didn't notice the cargo van that pulled up beside and slightly behind her as she was coming back from shopping. She had purchased a couple pairs of jeans to wear on the farm. She was anxious to join the governor. Having an opportunity to live and work on Roy Lee's home place was a dream come true.

As she came to the street corner, the cargo van pulled up going the wrong way and blocked her path. Simultaneously two men jumped out of the side door, came up behind her and slipped a bag over her head, pinned her arms, and hustled her into the van. The thick bag muffled her screams.

Her purse and the bag containing the new jeans were left where they had fallen on the sidewalk. It was a side street; there were no witnesses. It was more than an hour before a thoughtful citizen turned her purse and the bag in at the nearest precinct. It was approximately 20 minutes later the phone rang on the desk of the director of Illinois State Police.

"Yes Sophie, what is it?" he asked his secretary.

"There is an SPD sergeant on the phone for you. He sounds upset."

"Okay put him through."

"This is Director Norman, what can I do for you, Sergeant?"

"Sir, a citizen came by the precinct a few minutes ago and turned in a purse and shopping bag found lying in the street. The ID indicates she works for the governor. The bag belongs to an Elaine Martin. We're hoping she has just lost them somehow, and there isn't foul play. Do you know her sir?"

A feeling of panic gripped the director, and he felt nauseous. He got a grip on himself and his mind kicked into high gear.

"Did the citizen identify where he found the items?"

"Yes, Sir, and we dispatched a team to investigate the site, but there was no evidence of foul play. It is a little side street very close to the governor's office."

"Please give me the address."

Norman jotted down what the sergeant told him.

"Did you get the citizen's name and contact information?"

"We did sir, and we questioned him at length, but I don't think he knows anything else. We checked him out; he seems to be innocuous enough. He owns a couple of ABC stores, has a wife and a couple of kids. He appears to be a solid citizen."

"Thank you, Sergeant," Norman said. "Will you please have the lady's personal effects sent to my office?"

"Certainly sir, we'll send a car right away."

Norman broke the connection and pushed a speed-dial button on his phone. It rang six times. Norman began to think the chief of security was not going to respond. Then Moshe's voice broke the ring back tone. There was a loud buzzing noise in the background.

"Hello, Matthew," Moshe said. Evidently the caller ID on the satellite phone was working today.

"Moshe, Elaine Martin is missing and thought most likely abducted."

"Oh, no!" Moshe exclaimed. "I was afraid of that."

***

USMC Depot, Quantico, Virginia — November 1984

I was sitting at a little table in Harry O's in Quantico. Across from me was a grizzled old sergeant with stripes running down his arm that seemed to extend to his elbow. The worthy gentleman was the Master Sergeant of the Marine Corps himself, Robert R. Cleary.

The senior enlisted man of the entire USMC had come to Quantico to say a few words to a group of NCO's recently returned from our exciting, fun-filled holiday gamboling about on the sunny beaches of western Lebanon.

The sergeant had singled me out of the group after his talk. He asked if I might run him to the Amtrak station where he was going to catch the train back to D.C. later this afternoon. I thought this highly unusual since the Corps would undoubtedly have provided the top sergeant a car, but since I had taken a couple weeks leave and brought my '56 Buick back to Virginia, I was happy to oblige.

On the way to the station, the sergeant had suggested we stop at a bakery. It was midafternoon. The senior NCO stated he had missed lunch and wanted a bowl of Harry O's mushroom soup. He maintained it was the best in the world, and he seldom came to Quantico without stopping by the place.

I was sitting there trying not to stare at the assemblage of ribbons on the Master Gunnery Sergeant's dress green uniform. Prominent above the ribbons was a silver star. It put my own bronze to shame. I had few ribbons, but there were no "I was there" decorations on my jacket. I had a combat infantry man's badge, a purple heart, and a bronze star. Additionally, for a slick sleeve grunt, the rocker beneath the three stripes was almost unheard of.

"I have read over your jacket, Staff Sergeant. I was impressed. Your test scores are off the chart, your combat record is exemplary, and you have jumped ahead of your peers by at least four years, maybe six." I had a pretty good idea where this was going. The green machine had sicced the top enlisted man in the Corps on me to sweet talk me into signing on for another six years.

"I got lucky, Top."

"It was more than luck, Staff Sergeant. I read the entire after-action report filed by your CO after you extricated a platoon of Marines from an untenable position. That was not luck; it took skill, initiative, and a lot of courage. They should have given you silver."

"I came out clean, Top; the Heart is for a flesh wound in Grenada."

"Ah, I see," the NCO replied. He had assumed I had been injured in the fighting in Beirut. He hadn't studied my jacket all that closely.

"Staff Sergeant, you have made E6 in less than four years. Your next assignment will be the leadership school. When you graduate, your rocker will become permanent. With your record, including combat experience behind you, the sky is the limit. In fact, I believe OCS is more than possible, I would say it was inevitable."

"Top, becoming an officer in the Marine Corps is the last thing on my wish list right now; I have to be honest with you."

"What are you going to do, son?"

"I am going home to the farm and ride rodeo."

The illustrious sergeant didn't reply to this until he had finished his bread and soup. He shoved the sparkling clean bowl aside and gave me a long serious look.

"Staff Sergeant, rodeo is for kids. It's playing at life. The Corps is serious business, adult activity worthy of a man's time and effort. You're a good Marine. I hate to see you go out and waste your time playing with horses."

Some folks would have taken offense. I did not. I knew this warrior was telling me the truth as he saw it. He loved the Corps. The green machine was his life, and he had little use for those who didn't give it the respect he thought it deserved.

"Top, I don't want you to take this the wrong way. I admire you and what you have done for our country. I know you froze your ass off on the Chosin, crawled through the mud in the Nam, been shot up a dozen times, and fought America's enemies in third-world sewers all around the world. I respect your service, and I admire the Corps. I will be a Marine for the rest of my life." It wasn't just a speech, I meant every word.

"But Top, the truth is, I don't love the Corps like you do. I am sorry. The only thing I know is rodeo. It's all I want to do, and I am going to do it."

I didn't tell the senior NCO of the Corps the rest of the reason. I had seen what the politicians and civilians that ran things in Washington honestly thought of the fighting men they sent into harm's way. I was finished with answering to people who thought of me as expendable.

The sergeant studied me for a long time. He nodded sadly; I was certainly not the first young man he had tried unsuccessfully to convince to stick around.

He shook hands with me at the station, called me Roy, and strode off razor sharp and ramrod straight. He was truly an excellent example of a U.S. Marine. I wished him well and prepared to go home.

***

Airborne en route to the White Farm, present day

Moshe's mind was churning, trying to fit all the pieces of the fragmented puzzle confronting him together into some kind of a coherent picture. How his agent had been turned was still a mystery. How the Federalists had known the governor's wife was in Wisconsin at her mother's place was also an unanswered question.

He was afraid the entire bailing-wire-and-chewing-gum-constructed government of the State of Illinois was about to become unglued and come crashing down around him. For the first time since he had left Israel, he was truly apprehensive.

Getting off the ground with Virginia had been neither pretty nor easy. The lady was adamant about not leaving her mother's body, but there was no way they could bring the old lady's remains. The short distance to the water, even assisted by the downslope of the hill, would be marginal for takeoff, carrying the four living passengers.

To make matters worse, Virginia had been wearing a short bathrobe when she was rescued and nothing else. She had been stripped by her captors and was in the process of being raped when Moshe's operatives had interrupted the activities of her Arab captors. Other than some rough handling, coupled with the terror and degradation of being tied naked to a bed, she had suffered no actual sexual attack.

The fire Moshe's agents had set as a diversion had evidently gotten out of control. But it had flushed the perps out of the house where they could be dealt with allowing Virginia and her mother to be been pulled from the flames, singed but unhurt. Unfortunately, all of the governor's wife's clothes were consumed in the fire.

Virginia was now sitting in the back of the plane with Chance. She had refused to sit with Moshe. In her eyes, everything was his fault. She was wearing her mother's dress with blood stains running down the back, a result of where the rogue agent had shot her in the back of the head to silence her screams.

Virginia sat back there and stared holes in the back of Moshe's head. He knew she was planning the speech she would deliver to the governor which would mean the end of Moshe's career in the Prairie state.

Roy Lee had the plane trimmed and power applied for best speed. They were streaking across the sky at 5,000 feet altitude covering the ground below at better than 200 miles an hour. They were burning fuel at a prodigious rate, but Moshe was in a hurry.

"Elaine tells me you immigrated from Israel," Roy Lee said after he had the aircraft trimmed and set up for level flight. There was little to do now until they came into the pattern at the governor's ranch. "Why did you leave? It seems like the Israelis have everything going their way over there now."

Moshe was always amazed at the American's propensity to ask extremely personal questions of practical strangers as if they were asking about the weather. He was initially put off by the question since it interrupted his concentration on the problems at hand.

After he had considered it for a few moments, he decided he was in a closed loop, accomplishing nothing in his problem solving. Without some additional hard data, he was stumped.

He admired the deputy. Moshe alone among the governor's staff knew the level of trust the governor had in the LEO from downstate.

He knew the deputy was a volunteer. He wondered if the state was even buying the gas for the man's plane.

'I was in Israeli intelligence," he began. "After the extreme right-wing government came to power, subsequent to the attack on the U.S. things in Tel Aviv changed dramatically. The Prime Minister finally had the mandate to solve the Palestinian problem. The government marched into Gaza and the West Bank and just stripped both areas of the Arab population there. They shipped them off to Libya, Tunisia, Lebanon, and Jordon.

"Before they did, they drove their tanks into Lebanon and literally slaughtered the Hezbollah party in their trenches, tunnels, and hideouts. It was a bloody, but definitive action, and left Lebanon with the population mix of the early '70s.

"Before the government set off on this program, they cleaned their own house.

"I am a Samaritan," he told Roy Lee. "As such, when the government started purging their own ranks of possible dissenters, I was considered a risk. They pulled my clearance and forced me out of the service."

"You mean like the good Samaritan in the Bible story?"

"Exactly, as well as the lady Jesus met at the well. She was a Samaritan as well. At the time of Christ, there were more than a million Samaritans living in the Levant."

"What is a Samaritan? I mean, how are you different from the Jews? I thought you were all the same people," Roy Lee said.

As he made an adjustment in the autopilot setting, the needles came to life on the Omnis.

"Do you know who Joseph was?" Moshe had no idea if Roy Lee had any historical appreciation of the Old Testament.

"Sure, Joseph was Jacob's son who became a powerful man in Egypt and answered to the Pharaoh himself."

"Yes. Well, Joseph had two sons, Ephraim, and Manasseh. Our people trace our ancestry back to those two sons. When the Israelites settled in the land of Canaan, my people settled in the area around Mount Gerizim. My family has been there in that land since the original Mosaic Exodus from Egypt."

"What happened that your folks and the rest of the Jews got crosswise?"

"While the tribe of Judah was in Babylon, they let a lot of apostasies creep into their theology. When they came back, they built a temple in Jerusalem. My people already had a temple on Mount Gerizim and that is where God said he was to be worshiped."

"So basically, your people split over where the temple should be?"

"There were a few other issues, but mostly that is it."

"So now the Jews don't think you are pure enough to serve in the Mossad?"

"They were going for purity," Moshe told him. "I did not measure up."

"Well, I am glad you are here," Roy Lee told him with a smile and reached over to clasp Moshe's arm in a sign of acceptance and brotherhood. Moshe appreciated it.

"How many of your people remain in Israel?" Roy Lee asked after considering what Moshe had told him.

"Less than 800."

"Eight hundred! You mean like eight and two zeros? Eight hundred?!! What happened to the million that were there at the time of Christ?"

"The Byzantine Christians and the Muslims happened to my people. Most were merely slaughtered."

"Gosh, Moshe, I am sorry. That is a terrible story."

"It used to seem tragic to me. In the light of what has happened in our recent lifetimes, it seems rather inconsequential, does it not?"

Roy Lee had to think about Moshe's statement. After a while he replied.

"I'm afraid you are right, Moshe. I fear you are right."

CHAPTER NINETEEN

White Farm – Downstate Illinois

"Delbert, politics has become a contact sport in this generation!" the governor told Delbert Jones. "Elaine Martin has been abducted, my wife's mother has been killed, and her family home burnt to the ground." He was staring at the satellite phone in his hand as if it might be a bomb ready to explode.

They were on a John Deere side-by-side, four-wheel ATV. Jones had driven the governor over to the east side of the farm where they could sit on a ridge and look up the lake toward the headwater. The dam was off to their right.

At this end, there was nothing but trees, water, and grass. The recreational housing that had been planned had never come this far south. The marina and houses were still clustered around the little village at the near end, close to paved roads and utilities.

"That is awful Governor," Jones replied. "The Martin lady is your aide?" Jones asked, not sure of the relationship.

"She is my right hand, truth to tell. I feel like I am stumbling around in the dark down here without her."

"Do your people know anything about where she might be?" Jones was just talking to give the governor a chance to vent. He doubted there could be any news this quickly.

"My chief of security had people watching her, but she gave them a slip, turning into a street she never used before. They could not get to her in time to intervene in her abduction, but they followed the van. They know exactly where she is."

"That's great!" Jones exclaimed. "Are they getting her out?"

"Moshe and Leroy are on their way in. They should be there within the hour. Moshe has ordered his people to stand down until he gets there to lead the rescue effort. Elaine is like family to him."

"I would think the sooner…"

"It's Moshe's call," the governor interrupted, as much to convince himself that experience and technique were preferable to speed. "He is betting on the fact there are nothing but low-level operatives at the site where she is being held. He doesn't think she is in mortal danger until someone high in the organization shows up."

Jones didn't reply, but he thought it was easy for the chief of security to take that position. It wasn't his ass in the sling.

"Leroy has a beautiful place here," the governor said, changing the subject. "I had no idea."

"His ancestors homesteaded here in the 1830s. It's the only home he has ever known, other than the Marine Corps, I guess," Jones added.

"It must give a person a sense of permanence," the governor observed. "Perhaps that's why he seems to be impervious to all the chaos; he just appears to get up every day and go about his business, like nothing ever changed."

Jones knew this was far from true, but he didn't comment. If that's what the governor chose to think about his friend, it was okay with Jones.

"Would you like to see the graveyard? Leroy's folks are buried there dating clear back before the Civil War."

"Yes," the governor said. "I would like that."

***

Miracle Mile – Chicago

"I am surrounded by incompetence and stupidity," Juan Escobar said. He was sitting alone on the sofa in the mayor's living room. He had his face in his hands shaking his head in disgust. "Whose idea was it to have our agent reveal himself?"

"We've got the girl!" The mayor ignored the question and attempted to change the subject. He was hoping the news of the successful capture of the governor's top aide would mollify the drug lord.

"You idiot!" Escobar screamed at the mayor. "The entire situation has changed! What good is the girl to us now that the governor has me trapped here in the city! If one hair on her head is harmed, he'll vaporize this building and everyone in it."

"He wouldn't… the civilians…" the mayor mumbled.

"He could care less about the civilians. They are city people. They can't vote and are nothing but a burden and liability to this governor. Given any excuse, he'll take this building out without a second thought." Escobar was measuring the governor's corn beside his own half bushel. Nothing could have been further from the truth. Escobar was merely saying what he would do in the governor's shoes.

"As long as we have her he wouldn't …" the mayor trailed off weakly, letting the thought complete itself unsaid.

"Perhaps not," Escobar admitted. "But with our agent currently incommunicado, we are flying blind, and we still have not identified the governor's plant in our organization. Gentlemen, we are very vulnerable here."

***

Airborne bound for Springfield, Illinois

I was sick with fear and dread. The thought of Elaine in the hands of those thugs who had abducted the governor's wife and what they had done to her was eating at me and shutting down my mental processes. I talked to Moshe about his history and coming to the U.S. to let my mind travel down another path and get out of the worry loop it wanted to drift into.

We had formulated a plan on the fly and jumped into the plane to head for Springfield. Once Moshe stepped into the aircraft, his satellite phone was no longer functional. Cell service died after grid power went down and had not yet come back in our area.

When things were at their worst, folks discovered their landline phones still worked and flocked back to wireline service. Since the ATC had folded up their tents, the airplanes' radios were limited to talking to airport Flight Service Stations and local towers. We were out of touch until we got to the governor's ranch to drop Virginia off.

I had the throttle shoved to the wall and leaned slightly for best speed. It still seemed the ground was creeping by. We picked up an Omni northwest of Springfield, and I switched on the DME to get an actual ground speed. It read 198 kts; we were streaking along at 228MPH in a straight line to our destination. We should be on final at the governor's ranch in just under 15 minutes.

It was a little more than 10 minute's flight time to the Baptist Church where the director had set up a command post from the ranch. If the director was correct in his assessment that I could land in the church parking lot, we were less than a half hour from the first contact. It was the longest half hour of my life.

There were three uniformed state policemen waiting at the hangar when I taxied around. I jumped out, opened my door with the engine still running; Moshe was standing on the brakes. I slid my seat forward and helped Virginia out. The State boys were waiting behind the pilot side wing to take her hand and hustle her into a car.

I jumped back aboard and checked the fuel. I really should have gotten some, the needles were bouncing against the red, but they were bouncing. I applied power and turned for the runway. I didn't even bother with wind direction or taxiing to the end of the runway. I intercepted it midway, turned east, pulled in 15 degrees of flap and applied full power.

The engine roar filled the cabin as the crack of the prop tips breaking the sound barrier added to the distinctive sound of a Super Cat on a short field takeoff. Three hundred ponies spinning a massive three-blade prop pulled us into the air with a good 200 feet of runway unused. I love my Katmai.

I climbed to 2,000 feet. I wanted to do an engine-off flyover of the site we were going to assault so I needed some altitude to work with. Finding the target was easy; it was at a crossroads on the edge of Decatur right off of Route 36. Route 36 cuts across the prairie land of Indiana, Illinois, and Iowa as straight as an arrow. I flew southwest until I saw I-72 appear on the horizon. Route 36 runs parallel to the super slab in this area.

I turned and flew north of the highway until I saw the outskirts of Decatur appear across the nose of the plane. When we passed over the church, I glanced at the parking lot. It was more than adequate. I made a climbing left turn and circled over the church at 2,500 feet. When I came around to the south heading, I could see the ready-mix plant off to the right on the south side of Route 36.

I added 10 degrees of flap, turned the prop-nob to fully flat, rolled into a dive and shut off the mags. There was instant quiet in the cabin. The airspeed indicator was well past the never exceed speed when I rolled into the dive and headed for the concrete plant.

I glanced over at Moshe and noticed the color had left his face. His eyes were wide, and he was looking at me as if I had just grown another head.

I set up a 500-foot-per-minute descent. We crossed Route 36 at 160 knots. I had enough airspeed to make a complete circle of the concrete plant.

The ready-mix plant was a standard operation. There were three huge mounds of aggregate, a tower, and elevator to load the trucks, a maintenance shed, and an office. In front of the office, a van and a four-door sedan were parked. A line of ready-mix trucks was parked side by side in an east-west line ending perhaps a car length from the office. From our vantage point, we could see they had not moved in some time, their windshields were covered with rock dust.

We were 500 feet AGL when we re-crossed Route 36 on a north heading. I turned the prop-nob for a full bite and switched both mags back on. Instantly the "Brrrrup" of the faithful Lycoming filled the cabin. Some color came back into Moshe's face.

It was odd. He could face a dozen armed terrorists with a penknife in his hand, and it was just another day at the office, but a short flight in an unpowered glider unnerved him. I guessed he just wasn't much of a flyer.

"Let's don't do that again," he said, reinforcing my observation. He sounded quite relieved.

I leveled off at 300 feet under power and turned east a quarter mile west of the church parking lot. I pulled in full flaps, dumped the cowl flaps and pulled the power clear back to idle.

We were still a bit high, so I slipped off a couple hundred feet of altitude, straightened as we crossed the end of the parking lot and plopped the main gear down at 30 miles an hour. I stood on the brakes; the nose wheel came down, and we rolled out at the first turn off.

From Route 36 and the cement plant to the south, the church looked deserted. The director had all of his cars parked on the back side. He came out of the north door of the church followed by three men in suits and a uniformed LEO. I spun the plane around facing north on the access lane and shut it down.

***

Cement Plant – Decatur, Illinois

Elaine Martin was trussed to a chair in the center of an office. She could not determine where she was, but she knew they had driven for about a half an hour after they had taken the hood off her head. She had gotten a glance at her watch when the hood came off. Then she had been rolled into the carpet and carried from the van into the office where she was now zip-tied to a wooden chair.

She knew she could be anywhere in a 35- to 40-mile radius of the middle of Springfield.

Strangely, she was not overly frightened. The two men who had thrown her into the back of the panel van had been very solicitous toward her once she was in the truck and her hands were zip-tied behind her. They had removed the hood so she could breathe easier and had not touched her after they had her propped up against the side of the van with a section of carpet between her back and the side of the vehicle.

They were treating her as if she was a bomb that might go off if it was mishandled. She sensed the men were under orders to not harm her. They offered her water, and she accepted a drink from a freshly opened bottle. The men refused to even look in her direction. They were watching the three sides of the building carefully as if expecting company.

She had been in the office for about a half hour when she heard car tires on gravel, and a vehicle pull up and stop outside. The two men were wearing masks over their heads when they came into the room.

Instead of frightening her, it gave her a sense of relief. If they were masked, they were trying to conceal their identity from her. That meant they expected her to be around at some later date to possibly identify them.

One of the men was carrying four rifles slung around his right arm. He immediately engaged in a quietly murmured conversation with the men who had abducted her and began handing out the firearms. The man who was wearing a suit stopped at one of the desks shoved up against the outside wall and rolled out a secretary's chair. He pushed it over in front of Elaine and sat down.

"I estimate there are about five hours of daylight remaining," Elaine said before the man could say anything. "If you want to see the sunrise, I would encourage you to untie me, take these men with you, and leave."

"You're pretty cocky for someone who's tied to a chair in a room with five armed men," the man snorted. Elaine could see he had brown eyes peering out from the ski mask. He had no accent, so she placed him as an unemployed, mid-level Federal bureaucrat.

"In fact, it might be playtime," he laughed through the mask. He scooted his chair closer and fondled her left breast.

For the first time, Elaine felt a stab of fear race up her spine, but when she spoke, her voice was icy and steady.

"You have no idea the kind of shit that is about to descend on this place. You will not live to see the sunset, but if you harm me in any way, you will be begging for a quick death."

"Big talk for a captive lady," the man exclaimed, but he scooted back and took his hand away from her breast. "No one has any idea where you are."

"You dumbass," she told him bitingly. "I have a bug in my shoe." She was lying through her teeth. She didn't even know if that type of technology was still available. But she saw the reaction she had hoped for. The man straightened up as if he had been slapped.

Elaine was responding as she was trained to do. She had been through kidnapping scenarios with Moshe, at least, a dozen times. In fact, she had been handled much rougher in the training than she had so far by these turkeys. Moshe had pounded the following into her,

"Take charge. Act confident. In your mind be assured that help is standing outside the door." Deep down she knew it wasn't possible, but her training was carrying her along.

"POLICE!" one of her original captors shouted. It was if a bomb had been tossed into the room. The interrogator jumped up and ran to the window where the man who had shouted was standing. Two others joined him, and they were all peering out between the slats of the closed Venetian blinds.

The masked man who had carried the guns in came over and sat in her inquisitor's chair. He pointed the barrel of the rifle he was carrying at her face. The barrel looked as big around as a donut hole.

***

Moshe Aaron had a problem. The agent turning on him had shaken his confidence. He now could only trust the three men with him standing in the church parking lot. The deputy, his grandson, and the director of police were his only totally reliable assets.

"Did you see the car?" the director asked without preamble. Moshe nodded. "It just arrived with two men, one Caucasian, middle-aged, looked like an office type. The driver was a brown man, long nose, possibly Arab. They were both in the front seat, so the white man is a mid-manager, not a big-wig."

"How much time?" Moshe asked.

"It pulled in just moments before you flew over the church the first time. I imagine if you had been 30 seconds sooner you would have seen them go in the building."

"We need to get in there right away, Moshe," Roy Lee exclaimed. "If there is a mid-level guy in there, he is going to start to question her, and who knows what else?"

"We can't just go charging in there like the cavalry approaching with trumpets blaring," Moshe stated unequivocally. "If we do that, they will almost certainly kill her because they know they are going to die in any case."

It was generally understood there were new rules in dealing with terrorists and kidnappers in the current era. This understanding was good news and bad news.

The good news was terrorism in the heartland had almost entirely disappeared. The bad news was that when it did happen, the perpetrators were exceedingly desperate.

Moshe checked his watch.

"It's six hours until sunset, seven before it's dark enough to approach."

"I can put us almost on top of the place, behind that largest mountain of aggregate," Roy Lee told him. "If the director can give us a distraction on the highway, perhaps we can slip in the back before they even know we are there."

"What did you have in mind?" Norman asked.

"I was thinking about a civilian vehicle with four men pulled over by a marked car out on Route 36. Then a lot of activity, perhaps a second prowl car coming up; a messy arrest with some struggling and resisting — kabuki theater, you get the picture."

"We can do that," Norman said with a relieved tone, thankful to be able to do something constructive. The waiting was making him crazy. He had a 12-man SWAT team suited up and waiting just over the hill that he could have charging into the building in just under five minutes. But the governor had made it abundantly clear this was Moshe's operation.

"How do you see the assault coming down?" Moshe asked Roy Lee.

"We take one of the director's men with us. I will make a dead-stick landing behind the aggregate mound while the show is being staged out on the highway. We can slip into the maintenance shed and then come into the office area from the outbuilding."

Moshe thought about Roy Lee's plan for a moment then nodded his acceptance.

"The only thing different is," Norman interjected, "I'm going in with you."

Everyone turned to look at Moshe, but Roy Lee spoke up.

"Of course, you are, Matthew. Get your distraction going and let's move." With this, everyone scattered doing what had to be done to get the plan implemented.

The one man who could override Moshe Aaron had spoken.

***

John Palmer's Farm – Downstate Illinois

John Palmer had a massive hangover. He'd been on a four-day binge drunk. He had eaten little in that period, and had neither bathed nor shaved. He was wearing the same clothes he had been wearing when he walked out of Lyman Womack's office.

The sun was beating down on his face, and even his scrunched closed eyelids could not shield his sensitive eyes from its glaring light. He moaned and rolled over. He felt the grass on his face. When he painfully opened one eye, he could see his old pickup truck sitting askance in the driveway with the driver's door standing open.

He willed his legs to work and used his arms to push himself up into an all-fours stance. His stomach was churning, and he wondered if he would vomit. He remained there for some time willing his head to clear and the world to stop spinning.

He was finally able to force himself to his feet. He staggered to the truck and managed to get the door closed. He leaned against the door and looked down at his shirt and pants. They were covered with blood, dirt and vomit.

He tried to open his left eye and discovered it was swollen shut. He ran his tongue over his lips and found his lip was swollen. He tasted blood. Both of his hands were bloody, and his knuckles were raw. He had been in a fight, perhaps more than one.

He remembered nothing. The last thing he remembered was Ken Coward telling him he would have to deal with the sheriff before he could lay a hand on Roy Lee White.

Through the swirling nauseous mist that was his present consciousness, Palmer remembered something from the middle of the binge. He had made a decision. He had a plan.

He smiled to himself and started stripping off his shirt. He walked over to the burn barrel and started dropping his clothing one piece at a time into the blackened hole. When he was naked, he walked to the edge of the house where a 100-gallon rain barrel sat. He put his hands on both sides and plunged his head beneath the surface. He stood there soaking in the rainwater until his breath ran out.

When he stood up, he felt a lot better.

CHAPTER TWENTY

Governor's Office – Austin, Texas

"Admiral, the thing I need to know is this: How many boomers do we need to keep active to ensure I have an operational boat in the Pacific and Atlantic at all times?" J.G. Berry asked.

Julius Grover Berry's friends called him "Jay Gee." Acquaintances called him Governor Berry. This was not unusual since he was the governor of Texas. A lot of folks who knew him well still called him "General." Almost everyone sprinkled their conversations with him liberally with the title "Sir," he was just that kind of man. JG stood 6 feet 5 inches and weighed a trim 200 pounds. He still carried himself with the military bearing he had acquired at West Point.

The other 49 governors had elected him to chair the council formed after the decapitation of the Federal government. The council was meant to be a temporary expedient to handle national issues such as treaties and military affairs. It had worked so well, the temporary nature became extended, and had become a somewhat permanent situation.

A great deal of the success attributed to the council was due to the leadership skills of the governor of Texas. One of the first acts of the council had been to withdraw from the United Nations and expel the bureaucrats of that organization from the soil of New York.

The board was flying blind the first few months because they had neither real power nor any actual basis in written law. The other six governors elected to the council were an exceptional group of individuals selected for their common sense and the success they had demonstrated managing their individual states.

These six Republican governors had flown in the face of a progressive wind and had guided their individual states to prosperity and job growth when the trend nationally had been the opposite.

Perhaps it is divine intervention that provides a man like George Washington to the Republic at times of need. Washington had had Jefferson, Franklin, and Tyler. Governor Berry had one William F. Snowden. "Little Billy," as his detractors liked to call him, was an editorialist, author, and professor of military history at Yale University.

He had been writing a syndicated column published nationwide for 30 years. He had a talk radio show second only to Rush Limbaugh. The man was recognized nationally as brilliant, acerbic, and opinionated. He had been railing against abortion, euthanasia, gun control, and overweening government for a generation.

One of Little Billy's favorite themes had been that the USA was too big to be governed as a single entity. He had been advocating for a return to a constitutional government patterned after the Founding

Fathers' model. He had even drawn up a map separating the country into six regional entities.

The council was made up of a governor from each of these prospective regions.

This morning the governor was sitting at the head of a conference table in the Capitol building in Austin. He was flanked by his aide and Little Billy. The other participants in the meeting were a four-star admiral, the commandant of the Marine Corps, and two four-star generals from the Army and Air Force.

These notables had one thing in common. They were fired from their military jobs by the previous national administration. This was a trait they shared with the current sitting governor of Texas.

"Currently, we are operating three boats on each coast. So far, we have been able to keep one boat on patrol at all times. By consolidating the crews from the boats we have idled we now have three crews per operating boat. This allows us to keep the subs at sea without stressing the crews." The admiral was obviously not happy. "Governor, you know we're eating our seed corn, running those boats flat out."

"I understand, Admiral. We're doing what we can with what we have for the present time."

For more than a year, the U.S. had pulled back from the world and concentrated on rebuilding the homeland. It had pulled its ambassadors and shut down its embassies around the world. It had expelled the UN from the native soil and literally stopped talking to anyone about anything. It had sealed its borders and frozen any international travel to or from the country.

What the world knew was this: the U.S. had nuclear-armed boats patrolling the ocean depths, Minuteman III missiles loaded in silos, and B2 bombers ready to launch at a moment's notice. After Iran and Saudi Arabia, the world knew one other thing. The U.S. was not afraid to use its awesome firepower.

This caused considerable angst in countries that had been considered traditional or potential enemies of the U.S.

"I know you think we need to activate more attack boats, Admiral. But I just don't have the budget to do it. You're going to have to make do with the Seawolves and the Virginias for now."

The admiral's primary concern was keeping the boomers safe. He would have preferred to have a fast attack boat accompany each of the missile boats for their entire cruise since there was only one deployed at various times.

Along with the three Seawolves, he had been left the six Block One Virginias and the two Block Twos that had been complete when the crisis hit. All the construction on the other boats had come to a halt. So far he had been able to keep one attack submarine deployed with each missile sub, but it was stretching his people and the equipment to the limit.

"Admiral, I've had my people going over your budget. I am afraid there will be no activation of any aircraft carriers at this time. They're just too expensive. We have authorized maintenance of six of the newest carriers so they can be activated if necessary. There is money being made available to maintain and train six squadrons of Super F18s and support aircraft."

"Only six!" the admiral exclaimed in distress. "I can't even equip two carriers."

"Admiral, we have moved six more squadrons of F18s to National Guard Units and Fleet Reserve squadrons. You should be able to equip and send three carriers to sea at relatively short notice. It's the best we can do this year."

"At least, you still have a Navy," the Air Force general responded bitterly. The national Air Force had all but disappeared into Air Guard units around the country. The only national assets were 20 B2 bombers and the Minuteman Missile sites.

The governor ignored the Air Force general's remark and turned to the commandant.

"Have you been able to absorb all of the A10s, Commandant?" The Air Force had been trying to get rid of the ground support aircraft for years. They didn't have to worry about them now. The most fearsome ground support aircraft ever built was now in the hands of an organization that appreciated it.

"Yes, Sir, we have five squadrons activated, deployed and trained up to ready status." The commandant was smiling. The Marine Corps was the only branch of the services that had prospered under the new government.

The Marine division on Okinawa had been relocated to Guam. The Corps now had 10 full divisions with support battalions of tanks, artillery, and aviation assets. It was the reward for fighting the political correctness foisted on the other services during the late progressive march through the culture.

Other than a single training division at Fort Leonard Wood, and a small force of special operators stationed at Fort Bragg, the national Army no longer existed.

The Army had been broken up and reorganized into National Guard units in all the states.

"Gentlemen, your revised budgets are on the table in front of each of you. I will expect a report in 30 days from each of you on your ability to carry out the defense of the country, within the parameters of those budget numbers."

The governor stood and was joined immediately by the others in the room.

"Good day, gentlemen," the governor said, spun on his heel, and left the room.

***

Sheriff Milo Baker's Office – Downstate Illinois

"Sheriff, you're not going to believe this!" Deputy Warren said. He was standing in the door of the sheriff's office with an amazed look on his face. "Those railroad trucks that were stolen are back where they were, washed and polished."

"You have got to be kidding me," the sheriff exclaimed.

"No sir, I got a call from Effingham this morning. The trucks are right back where the railroad had parked them, cleaned up and full of fuel. It's the damnedest thing."

"Well it looks like our informant has let us down," the sheriff opined.

"I guess he figured if the trucks were returned he wasn't in any danger."

"I thought we were watching those trucks," the sheriff said sharply.

"We had people watching the road south of his place," Warren replied. "I imagine they slipped the trucks out and drove them through the country west until they crossed the railroad. Then they slipped them back in the yard by coming in on the tracks."

"Get your hat Deputy; we are going to go have a little chat with the county's largest taxpayer."

There were two burly individuals standing on the porch outside Womack's office when the sheriff's marked car pulled up. The sheriff and his deputy were carrying shotguns when they stepped out of their vehicle simultaneously. The men on the porch didn't say a word as the pair passed.

The sheriff didn't stop at the secretary's desk. He nodded in the direction of three men sitting in the waiting area, studied them for a moment, and discounted them as a threat. He and the deputy then marched down the hall, knocked on the double door with the butt of the shotgun and walked in unannounced.

Womack was behind his desk, and Victor Karman was sitting in one of the leather chairs facing the desk. His lap was full of papers.

"Good morning sheriff, what can I do for you?" Womack asked with a self-assured smile.

"Mr. Womack, I want you to be aware of a salient piece of information," the sheriff said, ignoring the presence of the comptroller. He paused for a moment to let the preamble sink in.

"I know about the trucks. I know about the plot to blow up the refinery in Carmi. I have more than enough evidence to arrest you, charge you with terrorist activity, and put you in front of a three-judge panel that will meet this afternoon. By six o'clock this evening, there is a better than even chance we would be hauling your body out to throw it in the Wabash."

The color drained from Womack's face, but he said nothing. He realized the sheriff was not going to do what he had just threatened by the way he had phrased it. Womack dreaded what was coming next.

"Luckily for everyone involved, you seem to have had a change of heart before anything worse than a felonious theft of railroad property was perpetrated."

Neither man sitting in the office replied. There was nothing to say. Any denials would be superfluous since the sheriff was quite evidently apprised of the situation. Both men waited anxiously to see what his price was going to be.

"I hope you didn't spread that fertilizer, saturated with diesel, on one of your fields. It will poison the ground." The sheriff watched Womack for a reaction. Since none was forthcoming, the sheriff guessed that had not been the case. In fact, the explosive expert had set his charges beneath five-gallon cans of No. 2 fuel oil, so the ammonium nitrate had not been polluted.

"Since you are the largest single taxpayer in the county and no one seems to have suffered a loss as a result of this little adventure, I am going to look the other way," the sheriff told the two men.

"Here is the thing, I know what happened, and now you are aware that I know. If anything even remotely linked to terrorist activity happens in this county," he paused for a moment, "you can rest assured I will be back here. When I return, I will be accompanied by a SWAT team, and you sir, will find yourself in irons standing in front of three judges of a terrorist court."

Neither of the men in the office had offered a word of denial. They knew it was fruitless and counterproductive. They were at the mercy of the sheriff. Silence was their only option.

The sheriff let the silence hang in the room for a few seconds.

"Gentlemen, thank you for your time. I will be going now." The sheriff turned and left the office, marched down the hall, and walked to his car. He waited for his deputy to reach the passenger door, open it, and lay his shotgun across the roof of the car pointed in the direction of the two men on the porch before he got in.

The deputy kept the two men on the porch covered until the sheriff started the car and put it in reverse. Deputy Warren then jumped in quickly as they reversed out of the driveway keeping a watchful eye on the men on the porch. Neither man on the porch as much as moved a muscle.

***

Cement Plant – Decatur, Illinois

The plane only had a couple of gallons of fuel so the 640 pounds the plane would normally have to lift in addition to the cabin weight was missing. I pulled the plane out into the parking lot and eased the power up. I didn't want to do a full power take off because the racket was intense. I cranked the prop over to get a full bite but kept the RPMs short of making the prop tips break the sound barrier. I lined up headed east and idled forward until we were shielded from sight by the church building, then added take-off power.

We trundled along, building up speed, and ran off the blacktop at 35 miles an hour. We were on the grass for another 30 yards until I felt the controls go heavy. I eased back, and we flew a couple feet off the ground gaining airspeed. I added climb power when I felt we were far enough away from the cement plant to avoid any suspicion.

We had climbed out to 2,500 feet before I turned back to the west. I rolled over the top of a climbing arc at 3,000 feet a half mile north of Route 36. I turned off the mags and we were a glider again. As I crossed Route 36, I saw the blue lights of the prowl car coming over the hill. I didn't see the car he was pursuing and guessed it was under the aircraft.

I made a sharp turn after we passed over the cement plant and lined up to land behind the largest pile of aggregate. I went directly into a left slip as I came out of the turn by feeding the right rudder into the turn. As the buildings dropped from sight behind the gravel pile, I straightened out of the slip, dumped in full flaps to check the descent speed. We still hit pretty hard and bounced up to the mountain of crushed stone.

We could hear the sirens of both State cars out on the highway and could even hear some of the faux argument going on. The boys seemed to be putting on quite a show.

There were about 10 yards between the gravel pile and the maintenance shed where we would be exposed to view from the office. I was debating on how to handle it when I heard gunshots from the highway. Evidently the actors on the road were going for an Oscar. We sprinted for the building.

There was a door on the south side of the maintenance shed. On our initial survey glide, Chance had spotted a padlock on this door. He came equipped with a set of bolt cutters. We popped the lock off. It was the only lock on the door. When we slipped the hasp off, the door swung open on its own. From our perspective, the garage had three truck bays where the concrete mixers could be brought in for maintenance. The doors were fiberglass with windows at the 8-foot level. The building was dim, but enough light was seeping in through the doors and the windows to let us survey the interior.

Beyond the empty maintenance area, was a desk and what appeared to be a small office. The door at the far end appeared to open into the office area where Elaine was being held.

I did a quick inventory of firepower. I was carrying my Benelli loaded with copper disks instead of buckshot. Across a room, the disks would spread to a plate size pattern that would cut a man in two. The upside was there was no stray shot to hit a bystander. The other three assaulters had short barreled ARs chambered with 6.5 MM rounds. I had my KelTek in a shoulder holster. I suspected the director and Moshe also had 9MM handguns as well. No doubt Chance was carrying a .45 or bigger.

I was trying to come up with a plan other than the four of us charging through a single door. Elaine would have little chance surviving a frontal assault.

We made our way across the maintenance area to the office. There was an open stairway with a flimsy rail that led to a storage area over the office. As the three of us walked toward the door between the buildings, Chance sprinted up the stairway. I heard him rattling around up there for a minute, then his head appeared over the office ceiling.

"Bapaw, I can get into the attic over the office. It looks like it is a suspended ceiling." I got it. He was thinking of coming down through the ceiling while we came through the door. I held up a single finger and went to the door. Moshe was already there peeking around. I didn't think we would be visible since the office was illuminated, and the shop was dark.

Moshe stepped back so I could peek.

Three of the men were obsessed with the activity on the highway. One severe looking individual was sitting on a chair in front of Elaine with a rifle trained on her head.

One of the four was thinking.

I pulled back from the door and trotted up the stairs to join my grandson. He took me over to show me the access door to the office area. A four-foot square opening gave access to the space over the office ceiling. It was dark, but as I let my eyes become accustomed to the murk, I could see little boxes of light where the fluorescent fixtures were letting illumination leak up through the pink fiberglass insulation.

"There are three dudes over there, against the far wall, all bunched together." I pointed Chance in the approximate direction. "They should be just on the other side of the third fluorescent fixture. The main threat is a dude that has a gun on Elaine. He is on the other side of that fixture." I pointed out where I thought he was sitting.

I pulled back and peeked over the edge of the office where Chance had signaled to me before. I caught the director's attention.

"Chance and I are going to come through the ceiling," I whispered. "Do you have a stopwatch function on your watch?" He nodded his head. I held up my watch and prepared the stopwatch.

"Three - two - one," I pushed the start button simultaneous with the director. "Five minutes," I told him, and he nodded.

Chance had already gone into the attic when I turned back around. I could barely make out where he was pulling up bats of insulation in front of the light fixture where I had indicated the men were standing.

The ceiling joists were on four-foot centers, which made maneuvering around silently very difficult. I had used up a good chunk of my five minutes when I finally reached my spot. I slowly and carefully pulled the insulation bat back. I could see my target through a crack between the light fixture and the tile next to it. He was sitting almost directly beneath the light fixture.

There were thick wires suspending the metal channels which in turn supported the tiles. They made up a maze I would have to work my way through to get access to a single tile. By the time I got situated, my time was almost up.

I glanced over at Chance. He was perched on the edge of a joist, eyes fixed on me, waiting for a signal. I checked my watch. Three - two - one - *go*! I jumped for the middle of one of the two-by-four tiles, caught my toe on one of the damn wires, twisted around, felt the shotgun pulled from my grasp by another wire and fell into the lap of my target, unarmed, flat on my back!

***

White Farm — Downstate Illinois

"Young lady, I'm going to have to get a new wardrobe if I stay down here much longer," the governor told Amanda. He had pushed his chair back from the breakfast table with a satisfied sigh.

"I keep telling her she needs to open a restaurant. She's a gourmet cook, and that is no lie," Delbert said surveying the spotless plate in front of him and wondering at the amount of food he had just consumed.

"I never had bass and eggs before, but I will admit, there is nothing like it."

Delbert had dragged the governor away from his satellite phone just before dark, and they had taken the four-wheeler down to the lake. They had come back with eight, good-sized large mouths for the morning skillet.

Amanda dismissed the men from the table and sent them to the front porch with steaming mugs of coffee. The governor was looking at the ribbons on the cup in his hand.

"Leroy rates these ribbons?" the governor asked.

"Yes, those are from his USMC days. He doesn't count them worth very much today. I have tried to get him to tell me the story. All he will say is there was a young lady that should have received the ribbons. He claims she got his platoon out of an impossible spot."

"That would be an interesting story."

"Perhaps more than you can imagine. According to Roy Lee, the lady was hired by the CIA and for a time was its only agent in Lebanon."

***

Langley, Virginia, 1985

"These scores are unbelievable," said the director of the CIA. He was studying the folder in front of him. The GS14 in charge of the training school was standing nervously in front of the director's desk where he had been summoned.

"Are you sure she wasn't sleeping with somebody out there?"

"No, Sir, the lady is brilliant, and I've never seen anyone that is a better instinctive shot with a pistol. She puts some of our senior agents to shame."

"Some of our senior agents *are* a shame," the director mumbled. The agency was suffering from decades of political appointees. He shook his head sadly and continued. "You're recommending we give her full agent status. We've never done that with a foreign national before."

"Sir, she loves the United States like a teenage bobbysoxer loves a rock star. I think we should accelerate her citizenship, give her a clearance, and put her to work. She will be doing us the favor, believe me."

"Okay, Charles, send her in."

When Nour Lahoud walked into the director's office, he felt his breath catch in his throat. She was a stunningly beautiful woman. There was a mug shot picture of her in the file, but it did nothing to prepare one for the lady's presence. She was wearing a black sheath skirt cut right at the knee, a white blouse with a frilly lapel, and a matching black stripe down each side. It was open. revealing a magnificent cleavage in which was nestled a silver cross. Her hair was piled on top of her head secured by a large silver clasp.

The most striking feature of her face was her full lips. He had never seen a more perfectly shaped mouth. He found himself wondering what it would be like to kiss her.

Then he saw her eyes. She had the eyes of a 100-year-old woman. When she looked at him and made eye contact, he felt a chill go down his back. "*This is a very dangerous woman*," the director thought to himself. All thought of kissing her fled to be replaced with an urge to hide under his desk.

"Please come in and have a seat," the director told her nervously. He pointed toward the love seat sofa at the far end of his office. He took an armchair across from her.

"Would you like something to drink?"

"No thank you, Sir, I just got up from lunch. I am okay."

"Since you come to us from Lebanon, let me ask you, what do you think we should do?"

The lady did not reply instantly. She seemed to study the director for a long moment as if trying to see if he actually wanted her opinion or was just making conversation.

"You should pull out of Lebanon entirely, shut down your embassy there, and advise every American citizen to leave the country."

"Really? That's a bit drastic, is it not?"

"The situation is untenable for you there. You can accomplish nothing that is in your national interest. It would be better for you just to leave." She went on for some time in intricate detail explaining the political situation with the Druze, the Shia, the Sunni, and the Iranian involvement.

It made the director's head spin. She outlined the problems within the Christian community and how power was being fought over by the half-dozen families that dominated that segment of the Lebanese culture. She talked of events during the Crusades as if it had happened last week.

Finally, the director held up his hand to shut off the flow. He was incapable of keeping up without a program.

"Welcome aboard, Miss Lahoud," the director told her.

CHAPTER TWENTY-ONE

Airborne, shortly after takeoff from the Austin airport

"How did the meeting go, General?" Sergeant Major Green asked the commandant. They were wheels up for Quantico. The two men were facing each other over a small table in the business jet they were taking back to Virginia. In the two seats behind them, the Air Force and Army generals were busy ignoring each other.

"Well Top, I'll have to say this new bunch loves them some Marine Corps."

"That's good isn't it, Commandant?"

"It will be good if they don't love us to death. They are turning over all the A10s to us."

"Oh no!" Green exclaimed. "Don't they understand our mission? We don't have runways to fly the A10s from."

"I think they have a different idea of our mission than it has been historically. This administration is defense oriented. They have no intention of sticking us on a beach half way around the world somewhere. Their entire philosophy is homeland defense."

"Maybe they shut down the wrong branch," Sergeant Major Green muttered. To the sergeant major of the Marine Corps, his branch's mission was clear. They were to land on some beach in a faraway place to break things and kill people. To sit in a pillbox or bunker and let some enemy come to you was not the Marine Corps way.

"They have shut down the Navy's carriers, so we don't have F18s for air support. They have left us a couple of helicopter carriers, but in all actuality Top, we just don't have the logistical support remaining to take the fight offshore. I guess we had better learn to love us some warthogs."

"It's a shame, Commandant."

"Perhaps," the commandant said, but then paused as if he were thinking seriously about a complex subject and remembering details. "On the other hand, I believe the military got greedy. There was never enough; not enough planes, not enough ships, not enough slots for generals and admirals. We were spending more on military than the next 10 countries combined. It was a type of insanity."

"Wasn't it a deterrent?"

"I don't know, Top," the general said, looking out the window, but seeing something from a different era. "I think the momentum overtook us and we started doing things because we could instead of because we needed to."

There was a long silence while the senior enlisted man in the corps thought about what the general was telling him. He was about to comment that those types of things were above his pay grade when the general took up where he had left off.

"You know, Top, great societies build monuments to themselves when there are inordinate surpluses. The Egyptians and Mayans built pyramids. The Brits built an empire. The ancient Sumerians built the hanging gardens of Babylon. The Romans built coliseums and bath houses." The general lapsed into silence for a few minutes, evidently pondering on the meaning of where this line of thinking was taking him.

The sergeant kept his peace, carefully studying the general while trying to follow the officer's thoughts and where they were leading.

"I think our country was rather surprised and shocked at what we accomplished during WW2. We exploded onto the world stage like a

Titan. After the war, the men came home and we started building. We built the interstate highway system and a telephone network that was the envy of the world. We built millions of houses and thousands of suburban neighborhoods. We manufactured cars and private planes. The economy was booming and we couldn't start to consume even a portion of what we were capable of making."

"You are losing me, General," the senior sergeant said after the officer lapsed once again into silence.

The general snapped his eyes back to the sergeant as if he had forgotten he was there.

"We built our own monument. It wasn't a pyramid or a coliseum. It was a military colossus like the world had never seen. We built a dozen aircraft carriers, each one of which carried an air wing larger than most countries entire air force and Top, that was just a small part the Navy. Each carrier had an entire complement of frigates, destroyers, submarines and supply ships to support the fleet."

"General, I know that's true, but weren't there actual threats?"

"Oh, there was competition, no doubt. The Russians and the Chinese would have loved to challenge us, but the Russians couldn't even build a decent flush toilet. They were never much more than a third-rate power with a first-rate nuclear force. Offshore of the Asian mainland, the Chinese were never a substantial threat to our homeland."

"I don't know Commandant; it seems there was always a war going on somewhere."

"If your only tool is a hammer, all your problems look like nails," the commandant stated in what seemed to be a *non-sequitur*, but then continued. "The men who are running the country now are patriots. They have their own idea about defense and threats to the homeland. Their idea is that our largest threat was, and is internal, a cultural rot both political and spiritual. They want to fix that first. In the meantime, they have told the world, 'You mess with us and we will nuke your ass.' So far it's working."

"I guess we start planning on how to jump on any threats that come ashore and stomp their ass into the sand. We'll let *those* sorry SOBs figure out how to get off the beach."

"That works for me Top," the general said. "It works for me."

***

Cement Plant – Decatur, Illinois

What my entrance lacked in grace, it made up for in shock and awe. One instant, Abdul Dumbass was staring down the barrel of an AK at lovely Miss Martin and the next he had a lap full of LEO. I had led with my butt, which even for me was a first. It had been crude but effective; I had managed to knock the rifle to the floor.

As I was falling through the air, I heard Chance's spectacular entrance. He had taken a rather different approach. While I was making my way to my jumping off point, he had taken his Leatherman and disconnected the fluorescent fixture directly over the group still obsessing over the show up on the road. When he saw me dive through the ceiling, he had hopped on the fixture and rode it to the floor. Since the fixture was only supported by a 16th inch of thin aluminum around its periphery it popped out square and fell cleanly to the ground.

He came down inches behind the two men who had abducted Miss Martin. Since he knew he was going to be engaging targets in an up close and personal range, he had left the rifle in the attic and had pulled his parachute act with his .45 held in both hands. *"Damn, why didn't I think of that?"*

"CRASH! BANG! BAP-BAP!" The room was suddenly filled with dust, noise, and gunfire.

I reached up and grasped my opponent in a bear hug turning my head away

"Bap-Bap!" The double tap from the door that impacted Abdul on the side of his head blew blood and gore across the side of my face. I felt his body grow limp in my grasp. A lot of things had happened in the three or four seconds I had spent falling and hugging.

The office manager type had been walking from the window back toward Elaine and his driver when the curtain went up on our little play. He had been halfway across the room. I had to hand it to him; he grasped the entire situation at a glance. He dived to the floor and spread-eagled himself in a submissive posture spinning the rifle he had in his hand across the floor.

Chance had dropped one of his opponents with a double tap from the .45, but the terrorist had fallen into the second adversary blocking Chance's second volley. He had used the falling man's momentum and shoved him into the live combatant. The dying soldier's ammunition harness entangled the second man's rifle muzzle and dragged it out of his hand. When the man stood up, Chance pistol slapped him against his temple and dropped him like a rock.

The van's driver had been about 10 feet away looking out of his window toward the front of the building and the arrest show going on. He was a little slower on the uptake. He hesitated for one second before turning and bringing his rifle to bear on Chance.

"Brrrrpt!" A short burst from Moshe's AR knocked him back and threw him to the floor.

I rolled off the corpse to my knees and looked up to see Elaine laughing at me.

"I would pay at least a $100 to watch you do that again," she guffawed in relief.

I stood up and checked my back, twisted around a couple of times, and decided nothing was broken or strained out of shape.

Chance was walking across the room toward me with his Leatherman in his hand. I nodded to him, and he walked behind Elaine and cut the zip-ties restraining her hands.

"You need to wash your face cowboy," Elaine smiled at me. "You seem to have someone else's brains all over it." I was expecting a kiss and some gratitude. I got sarcasm and smart-ass remarks. I guess some days it just doesn't pay to get out of bed.

"Bapaw, I'm going outside to check out the concrete trucks. I saw something that bothered me when we flew over the first time." What could I say? Sherlock White was on the case. I went to find a sink and some water, but I had to settle for a hose and a wash bay in the garage. I got most of the gore off and went out through the walk-through door in the maintenance shop to join my grandson. He was up on the back of one of the mixers hanging through the opening as if he was trying to get something from the inside.

It was difficult because the opening was blocked by the concrete chute. He had pulled it to one side as far as he could but it still effectively acted as a plug in a bottle. He eventually reappeared with a handful of white powder. He sniffed it, turned up his nose, and climbed down to show me what he had.

He poured some of it into my hand. I sniffed it, Ammonia and fuel oil! We were standing next to a 20-ton truck bomb!

"How did you …?"

"When we flew over, this truck had a clean windshield; none of the others did. When I came out, the tires on this one were almost flat. The others were a bit deflated from sitting here for who knows how long, but not flat."

I was beginning to think the governor was calling the wrong White. I had noticed nothing. Of course, I was piloting the plane and trying to avoid the various power and telephone lines snaking into the site from different directions. I decided to give myself a break.

***

Capitol – Austin, Texas

William F. Snowden stood in his office and looked at the map behind his desk. It was a map he had hauled around the country for years as he lectured on the premise that the U.S. was too big and too disparate to be governed as one nation.

In the end, it had not come down exactly as he had envisaged. The residents of Kentucky and West Virginia had felt a stronger affinity for the upper Midwest and had joined the Heartland. Arkansas and Louisiana had, perhaps for economic reasons, chosen to affiliate west instead of east and became part of the Lone Star Confederation.

Other than that, he had pretty well nailed it.

The confederations were not states per se. The individual states had been loath to give up power once it had been restored. Each state elected its own legislature and wrote, administered, and judged its own laws. The governors of each state then formed a governing council for the confederation. Following the example the Lone Star confederation had set, the newly elected governors would select one of their number to preside over the council.

It was all in flux at the moment and the different regions were feeling their way forward. Mr. Snowden felt confident it would eventually work out as he had envisaged. For now, the council that had been set up to administer national defense was working well. His one disappointment was that he hadn't been able to get the regions to agree on a single currency. The Heartland and Mountain West were using Lone Star dollars, but the other regions had begun printing their own specie.

He had been able to convince the governor to peg the value of the Texas dollar to a basket of metals. Instead of gold alone, the Texas dollar was also valued against silver, platinum, and palladium allowing the market to set the actual value of the dollar. So far it was working better than predicted or expected. Demand for Texas currency far outstripped supply.

He was afraid Yankeeland was slipping back into its old ways by letting its dollars float with no substantial backing. Pacifica was still involved in a nasty three-way civil war between the rural militias, La Raza activists, and the mercenary army hired by the coastal elites. There was a lot of pressure on the other states to cut California loose and let it sink into its own quagmire. Fifty years of leftist, elitist foolishness was taking some time and blood to wash out.

There had been some voices raised for intervention, but they were quickly quashed. There was a strong consensus to let each state and each region settle its own problems.

"Mr. Snowden, the governor would like to see you in his office," his aide told him from the open door to his office. Snowden nodded, picked up his iPad, and walked across his large, well-appointed room to a second door. This door led to a hallway. At the end of the corridor were two large double-hung doors leading to the governor's private aerie. One door was standing ajar.

The governor was standing behind his desk, looking out the bay window across the manicured lawn of the Capitol grounds. Snowden checked his watch; it was past 5 p.m. which explained the bourbon glass in the governor's hand.

The governor heard Snowden enter and quietly close the door behind him. Without preamble or even acknowledging the man's presence, the governor started talking. They were so used to each other and comfortable in each other's company, they were like an old married couple.

"Billy, I am beginning to think accepting the presidency of both the confederation and the national council was a mistake." Snowden didn't reply. He had advised the governor against that very thing. Anything he said would have to be construed as an "I told you so."

Since the governor lapsed into silence, Snowden filled in the gap by going to the liquor cabinet and pouring himself a Tanqueray on the rocks. He then walked over to one of the armchairs in front of the governor's desk and sat down.

"Is there a particular problem?" Snowden ventured.

"Funding . . ." the governor said and then paused as if trying to sort out details. "I have to convince the other state governors to pony up cash for the regional interests. Now I have to go hat in hand to the other regional governors to get money for defense and national needs. It seems my job has turned into begging for money."

"You are meeting with the budget committee from the house finance committee this week are you not?" Snowden understood the governor's angst now.

"Yes, those sharks are coming in here."

"No Governor! Don't do it!"

"But I have to." The governor turned from the window and looked quizzically at his No. 1 adviser.

"No, you don't. You need to turn this over to the Lieutenant Governor. Let him deal with the Legislature. You have enough on your plate with the regional and national issues." Snowden liked the lieutenant governor. He was competent and loyal to a fault. He could handle the legislators.

The governor thought about Snowden's advice for a moment then smiled. "Billy, you're right. I'll do exactly that." He then came over and sat in the other armchair beside Snowden and put his feet up on his desk. "What about the suite at Cowboy stadium?"

"You know what I think. It's not a good idea." The Cowboys owner had offered the governor a suite at Cowboy stadium gratis. It was a strong temptation for the governor because he loved football, and he loved his Cowboys. "It is just too high profile, governor. Even if he never comes looking for a favor, it just doesn't look right."

"I know," the governor agreed meekly. "It's a damn shame."

"Look, if you want the suite, pay for it. Have the Lieutenant Governor put a specific line item in the budget and pay for it. You are serving without salary. It's the least the legislators can do."

"You know, you're right," the governor brightened. He reached up and tapped a button on his earpiece. "Claire, if Henry is still in the building, I need to talk to him."

***

Mayor's Suite – Chicago

The mayor jumped involuntarily when the phone rang on the coffee table in front of him. Very few people had that particular number, and only one person he knew would be calling him. He checked the caller ID and shuddered.

"Hello, Governor," he said in a quavering voice. He listened, then nodded as if the person on the other end of the line could see his acquiescence to whatever the demand had been. The mayor got up and carried the phone into the next room and handed it to a slim dark man sitting on a sofa.

"It's the governor. He wants to talk to you," the mayor told Juan Edwardo Escobar.

"Yes, Governor," the man said. His face seemed to lose color as he listened. He then jumped up and ran to a window. What he saw out the window must have frightened him because he ran back from the window and into the rear of the apartment.

The mayor was curious. He too went to the same window and looked out. He saw nothing particularly frightening. There was a concrete ready mix truck sitting in front of the building directly under his window, but that was all. He didn't understand Escobar's reaction.

It took 48 hours and 75 million in cash to get out of Chicago. Escobar rode up to the open stairway of his G8. There were three armed guards with him plus his driver.

The SWAT team that was deployed on the tarmac beside his plane did not seem overly impressed.

They disarmed his guards and told Escobar he was free to climb the stairs. Somehow it didn't feel right but Escobar went up the stairway and entered the plane. There was neither a pilot nor a copilot in the cockpit. The flight attendant seemed to be missing as well.

There was a tall cowboy sitting in one of the leather chairs in the back. He was wearing jeans, boots, a cowboy hat, and sunglasses. When Escobar walked into the plane, the cowboy stood up and smiled.

"Hello Edwardo, you miserable son of a bitch," Roy Lee said with a malicious grin. "Welcome to my world!"

***

Hong Kong, China

No one was paying any particular attention to the two old men sitting on a concrete bench atop Victoria Peak looking down across the city of Hong Kong. One was Chinese, the other was a Gwailou. Just two old men visiting on a Sunday afternoon enjoying the view. No one gave them a second glance.

It could be considered odd since one of them was Lee Chou Fung, the premiere of the People's Republic of China, and the other was Michael Goronov, president of the Russian Federation.

"We were very lucky you know," the Russian said. "The U.S. Submarines had enough firepower to destroy both of our countries a hundred times over."

"Perhaps it would have been better than the slow death we are dying now."

"Perhaps, but who could have known?"

"There were voices in our party warning us, but we did not listen," the Chinese gentleman said sadly. "There was just too much money, too much corruption, and way too much prosperity after decades of want and deprivation. It seemed like it would go on forever."

"We called the U.S. 'enemy of the people,' for so long we started to believe our own propaganda," Goronov said disgustedly. "We cursed the people who were carrying the burdens of the world, providing protection for the helpless, feeding the starving, and buying our products. Who is there to blame now that they simply went home?"

"There are many in our country who would like to blame you."

"I know, there are forces in Mother Russian who think China is the threat to world stability as well."

"What we have is stability?"

"We are teetering on the edge of worldwide calamity. That is why we are here."

"Can it be stopped?" The Chinese premiere asked fearfully.

"There are some things that can be done to at least slow the slide. The first thing is: you will have to corral that crazy man in North Korea," Goronov told him.

"We are in the process. He will be dealt with by the end of next week. We have been negotiating with the South to come in and pick up the pieces. We should have done it years ago," Fung admitted. "But we were afraid of the USA boogie man. It was the stupid Chinese curse of 'face.' It will be the death of my people I am afraid."

"I have pulled all of our troops out of Georgia and Ukraine. It was costing us a fortune to support that ill-advised adventure," Goronov admitted in turn. "Russia is broke. Oil is $15 a barrel if one can find a buyer. The demographic bomb is catching up to us; our population is literally dying off. Alcoholism is a plague and the people just don't care."

"Our economy crashed when we had to eat all of the trillions of dollars of U.S. debt and lost our biggest market. I mean it shouldn't have taken a rocket scientist to see that coming, should it have?" The Chinese Premiere asked bitterly.

"Islam is resurgent in all the provinces on our southern periphery. The leadership after Yeltsin was so obsessed with trying to put the wheels back on the Soviet system and building their own personal wealth, they ignored the greatest threat our country faced. We should have been working with the USA to stifle the Muslims. But we didn't, and now we are facing them alone." The Russian remembered plaintively.

"What can we do?" Fung asked desperately.

"This. We do this, we sit down, and we talk, negotiate in good faith and try to work together to put Humpty-Dumpty back together again."

"What about the U.S.? Are they going to get their act together and be a player once more?" the Chinese premier asked hopefully.

"Not in our lifetime. The *people* are running things there now. Not some small elite pretending to represent the people, the actual people are in charge. As long as that is the case, you can forget the U.S. doing anything for anybody outside their own borders for at least a generation."

"It is sad."

"It is what it is. We just have to get used to it and make the best of the situation."

EPILOGUE

Elaine Martin walked out of the shower and dried herself on the huge, fluffy white towel that had been hanging on the outside of the shower door. She stepped into some black lacy panties and pulled the black teddy over her head. It barely covered her hips accenting her perfect long legs. She looked at herself in the mirror and shook her head. "*What a waste, I should have brought long PJs,*" she thought to herself.

She had not planned to sleep by herself this weekend.

The wood floor was cold, so she stepped into the black mule slippers that matched her teddy and walked over to the massive wood desk that dominated one end of the office. In the middle of the desk, an all-in-one computer was surrounded by stacks of printed paper, notepads, and books. The credenza behind the desk was cluttered with trophies and magazines. Most of the trophies were engraved with "First Place," and featured a cowboy on a horse with a rope. The magazines were back issues of American Horseman.

The cork board that ran the full length of the credenza on the wall behind it was covered in photos. A few of the 5-x-8-inch pictures were framed and mounted proportionally as if the original idea had been to feature these images alone. The original pictures were almost covered by dozens of smaller snapshots pinned to the cork in a random pattern almost covering the board.

In the middle of the board was an 8-x-11-inch framed photo. It dominated the panorama. The fading picture was a color shot of a very young Roy Lee on a horse, looking down at a girl, who was gazing back at him with one hand on the horse's bridle and the other on Roy Lee's thigh. She bore a striking resemblance to Raquel Welch. The look she was giving the rider was one of extreme affection. Elaine was struck with an immediate pang of jealousy.

Elaine glanced at the other photos, rodeo scenes that were fading now since they had been taken with a Polaroid camera. There were a lot of more recent pictures of Roy Lee and Chance, from the time Chance had been a baby right up to the present day. It was patently obvious the grandson had become the focus of Roy Lee's life. There were a few pictures of Chance with a mature but attractive dark-haired lady. Elaine surmised it must be Roy Lee's deceased spouse and Chance's grandmother.

Almost buried in grandson images were a couple of black-and-white snapshots of Roy Lee in uniform. There was one where he was featured in an armed group, standing beside a burnt out car. They were all filthy, as if they had just returned from a difficult mission. *I'll have to ask him about this one,* she thought to herself.

She stood in front of the desk and looked around at the room. Shelves on the other walls were stacked with more trophies. Some of those trophies featured a rifle instead of a horse. On one wall, a glass case containing a number of ribbons and the stripes of a staff sergeant dominated the space.

As she stood there, she began to understand why Amanda had put her in this room. This was Roy Lee's life. As she looked at the pictures, she began to realize how little she really knew about him, and how rash her diving into this relationship, actually was.

Elaine picked up what appeared to be a completed bound manuscript and walked over to sit on the bed. She looked at the clock it was barely past 10 p.m. "*Good God, these people go to sleep before the sun gets truly set!*"

Elaine seldom went to bed prior to midnight, so she certainly wasn't ready for sleep. She opened the manuscript and found it to be a collection of short, anecdotal stories of Roy Lee's life. She smiled in fascination. The first one was about growing up on the farm and visiting an uncle who was a steam engineer on the railroad, who lived in the city. It was a touching story about a farm boy being introduced to the noise, bustle, and energy of an American urban area.

It was well past 2 a.m. when she finished the last story and carefully replaced the manuscript on the desk. She had discovered her cowboy was much deeper than she ever imagined. She began to wonder if she could ever really get to know him.

She slipped out of the teddy and draped it over the arm of the sofa bed. The couch had folded out to a queen-sized bed. When she slipped between the sheets, she felt the Tempur-Pedic pad beneath the bottom sheet. It was quite comfortable. She switched off the light and lay back, but she couldn't sleep. Her mind was still filled with the images from the book of life-stories Roy Lee had written.

She was lying in the dark staring at the ceiling when she heard footfalls on the stairs.

The nightlight behind the desk revealed Roy Lee wearing a blue robe coming up the stairs into the room and walking quietly to stop beside her bed.

"I'm so weak," he whispered. "I hope you can forgive me."

Elaine flipped the sheet up and held it open in invitation.

"I'll forgive you in the morning," she murmured. "Now get in here and give me something to forgive you for."

ABOUT THE AUTHOR

One of Ted Snedeker's favorite rejoinders is: "I am just an Illinois farm boy, what do I know?" In fact, he knows quite a lot.

Ted spent six years with the US Navy working on nuclear weapons. After spending some time as an electrician's apprentice he went to work in the telephone industry and never looked back. He worked his way up from telephone equipment installer to the manager of installation for Northern Telecom. In this position, he was responsible for the entire continental U.S. Alaska and Puerto Rico.

In 1981, he started his own company. For thirty-five years the company he founded and led, designed, built and installed switching systems across the country and half the world. He worked on major projects in Guam, New Zealand, China, Venezuela, Japan, Hawaii, and Alaska, as well as smaller systems and short jobs in a dozen more countries.

Ted is a licensed pilot, motorcycle enthusiast, deep sea fisherman, and avid Bears fan.

He currently lives in a house he built on a farm in Southern Illinois with his wife of fifty-two years, two Chou dogs, and a pair of cats who allow the rest of the clan to share *their* house.

Made in the USA
Middletown, DE
20 July 2016